AUTHENTICITY

DEIRDRE MADDEN

Authenticity

ff

faber and faber

First published in 2002
by Faber and Faber Limited
3 Queen Square London WC1N 3AU

Typeset by RefineCatch Limited, Bungay, Suffolk
Printed in England by Clays Ltd, St Ives plc

A CIP record for this book is available from the British Library

ISBN 0–571–21446–0

Acknowledgements

The photographs described in Chapter Eleven were inspired by the work
of Rineke Dijkstra. The exhibition in Chapter Thirteen concerns the work
of Christian Boltanski. The book from which Dan reads in Chapter
Thirty-Two is *The Oxford Companion to Irish History*, published by Oxford
University Press.

2 4 6 8 10 9 7 5 3 1

In memory of Johnny Madden
and for Harry Clifton
with love

The practice of an art demands a man's whole self. Self-dedication is a duty for those who are genuinely in love with their art.

Eugène Delacroix

I thought, everything can be used in a lifetime, can't it, and went on walking.

Joseph Cornell

My Aunt Mary was very kind and asked me to come and stay with them in Massachusetts. Jack Kerouac said that hardly any American artist can survive without an Aunt Mary.

Charles Brady

Prologue

When she was a child, she used to wake early in the winter, when it was still dark; and she remembers that she used to lie there and make believe that she was at once both inside and outside the house. The hall light would be left on all night, but instead of quenching her imagination, which was the reason for it, it gave her something upon which to fasten by illuminating the semicircle of glass above the front door. She believed that she was a bird in a tree opposite the house. In the utter dark of night only that fragile fan of yellow light was visible, and it was the only proof that the house was there, standing against the sky like a black ship on a black ocean. She could feel the branches rise and stir under her as she waited for dawn, when the light would thicken and coagulate, and when that happened she would see that the yellow fan of light was not something floating in space, but that it was part of the solid rectangle of a house. The sky would continue to lighten and the darkness to melt away, and the big black shape of the house with the arc of light wedged in it would be standing hard against the bare sky. There might yet be the odd star; and she was the watching bird who, when the sky attained a certain degree of paleness, sang first, sang alone; and she was also the child who lay under the patched and faded quilt and heard the bird singing, heard and imagined; the child who thought of the plates and bowls sitting on the table in the dim kitchen; the child who had fallen asleep the night before to the sound of those same plates and bowls being lifted from the press and set out in preparation for breakfast; the child who drifted off to sleep again, to dream about a set table in an empty room, about a bird in a tree, about a fan of yellow light.

Chapter One

'A strange thing happened to me yesterday.'

'Mmmn.' There was no point in continuing: he was still asleep. Julia turned, her neck tight in the crook of his arm, and stared at where the morning light fell on the wall between the bookcase and the window. She thought of how, painted, it would appear as pure abstraction: the sharply defined oblong of lemon light on the pale surface, the two dark lines that bound the planes. It would be understood according to the titles one might give it: *Dawn Light: Window, Wall, Bookcase*, or simply a number.

'Mmmn? Well?' Roderic said. He was awake after all, but his voice was still slurred with sleep. 'Go on. Pleasant strange or horrible strange?'

She thought for a moment. 'Neither,' she said. 'Just strange.'

She told him that she had been walking across Stephen's Green, on her way home from having met a friend. Passing the ponds and the flowerbeds she reached into her bag for a cigarette and stopped only momentarily to light it. Her lighter was a cheap disposable thing made of transparent red plastic, and she flicked at it once, twice, three times. Nothing: not so much as a spark. Only then did she notice that she was standing level with a man who was sitting on a bench. Julia didn't even speak to him, simply held out the unlit cigarette with a quizzical smile. The man reached mechanically into his pocket and pulled out a heavy silver lighter. At the first touch it sent up a hard bright flame around which Julia cupped her hand to shield it from the breeze as she leant down and lit up. She exhaled deeply. The lighter snapped shut. 'Thanks.' She turned away, but had gone no more than three steps along the path when the man called after her.

'Excuse me?' She glanced back over her shoulder. He was looking at her with an expression of utter desolation, such as one rarely saw, an expression that literally stopped her in her tracks. 'Excuse me, please, would you do me a favour?' The voice was trembling and hesitant. 'Would you mind ... would you just sit beside me here for a few moments?'

Julia did not reply, but stared hard at the man, taking stock of him and of the situation. They would not be alone or isolated, for the Green was far from deserted. 'Please,' he said. 'You don't have to talk or anything, just sit beside me.' There would be no danger with this man, of that she now felt sure. Julia trusted her own intuition as far as men were concerned. She said nothing, just nodded and retraced her last few steps to sit down beside him. 'Thank you,' he said. 'Thank you so much.' His voice was still shaking, and so low now as to be almost inaudible.

'So we sat there,' Julia said, turning over in bed so that she could rest her head upon Roderic's chest, 'and we didn't say anything.'

It was exceptionally sunny for February and the railings of the nearby summerhouse cast dense, regular shadows upon its own ceiling, but between them flowed glittering, rippling light reflected from the surface of the pond. The quacking of the ducks made mad laughter in the distance. Julia opened her bag and took out her cigarettes, offered them to the man, who took one gratefully. He lit it with his own silver lighter, but his hands shook, and lacked the assured fluency of her own actions. He dragged desperately on the cigarette, narrowing his eyes, as though he had been parched and she had offered him cool, pure water. As they sat there smoking Julia stared straight ahead, drawing her own conclusions from what she had seen of him before she sat down. A businessman, that was clear from his suit and briefcase. He

4

was in his mid to late forties, she guessed, although she always found it difficult to judge someone's age. The impression he gave was of painstaking exactitude, with everything buttoned and fastened and polished and correct. No greater contrast could have been possible with her own wild style, her loose velvets and dangling earrings, her barely controlled mop of hair tied back with a green ribbon. Why was he there? Why was he so upset?

The world in which Julia lived was so far removed from the life of a middle-aged businessman that she didn't expect to fathom him. Her best guess was that he had been fired from his job. Given the boot. Not that it would have been put like that, of course. *Let go.* That's what they would have said to him. *I'm afraid we're going to have to let you go.* A man like this didn't do a job, he was his job. No wonder he was distraught. Later tonight he would go to a pub where he wasn't known and would drink and drink and drink, and as she thought this, she remembered Roderic. The man was crying now, very quietly and discreetly; she could hear him sniffle and gulp beside her. 'What am I going to do?' he said. 'What am I going to do?'

Having no adequate response to this, she answered his question with a question.

'Where do you live?'

'Dalkey,' he said.

'You might think to head for home.' He shook his head. 'Well you can't stay here all night,' Julia said reasonably. 'Have you a car with you?'

'I came on the DART.'

Julia thought about this for a moment. 'I'm going out in that direction. We can go together, if you like. Would that help?'

'That's very kind,' the man said. He was making a significant effort now not to cry, wiping furiously at his eyes and clearing his throat harshly. 'That's very kind,' he said again as they stood up.

They left the park and crossed the road, walked down Dawson Street together and turned right, continued on to Lincoln Place. As they passed a pub, Julia half thought he might suddenly dart into it and that would be the last she would see of him, but he didn't seem to have registered it at all. He walked with his gaze fixed on the pavement. She was struck at how there was no tension between them; thought how strange it was that this should be the case, that she should be here in the unexpected company of this anguished stranger. At Westland Row they entered the station, bought tickets and boarded the green train that was heading south. Julia settled down opposite the man, who sat bolt upright and stared blankly out of the window. She was struck again by how tense and exact he looked, how overly correct and how thoroughly miserable. People boarded the train and others left, children shouted and laughed, and none of them paid any attention to Julia and the man, were probably not even aware that they were travelling together as they did not speak to each other until the train stopped at Monkstown. Then the man said, 'You weren't coming out in this direction at all, were you? You're doing this just for me.'

Julia considered lying, but didn't think she'd be able to carry it off. So she shrugged, said lightly, 'You looked like you couldn't be trusted to go straight home on your own. When I start something, I like to see it through to the end.' She had thought he might remonstrate with her, but instead he gave a brief, weak smile, which astonished her. Up until then, he hadn't looked capable of smiling. 'You really are,' he said, 'tremendously kind.'

'Don't mention it,' Julia said, embarrassed, and now it was she who turned to stare out of the window.

They didn't speak again for the rest of the journey until they arrived in Dalkey. Even then, they walked in silence, the man now leading the way down the main street. He turned into a quiet road and pointed at an elegant house painted the colour of buttermilk, with a flight of steps leading up to the front door.

'That's it?' He nodded and held out his hand. 'Good luck,' she said. The man said nothing. She was glad he didn't thank her again, but when he took her hand he held it for slightly longer than was usual for a handshake, and so tightly that he crushed her ring into her fingers and hurt her. It was the first, the only thing about him that had made her feel ill at ease. Then he crossed the street and walked towards the pale house. She watched him go up the steps, fumbling in his pocket for his keys, but before he could find them someone inside opened up. He went in and the door closed. Julia watched for a moment longer, then turned and walked back slowly to the train station.

Roderic had been listening to all of this with great interest. 'And he gave no clue as to what the problem was?'

'None whatsoever. To tell you the truth, I didn't want to know.'

'You're tremendously kind, do you know that? Tremendously kind.'

She was taken aback that he repeated so completely the stranger's compliment: out of modesty she had omitted this detail from her account. Uncomfortable with praise for such a small act, she sought to change the subject. 'Look at the wall,' she said, 'how the light falls there.'

But while she had been talking, the sharply defined edges of the rectangle she had noted earlier had expanded, grown softer as the light became more diffuse, dissolving completely now to fill the room with the clear light of a new day.

Chapter Two

As was his habit, William sat up late that night after Liz had gone to bed. He poured himself a whiskey as he did every Friday, but a larger one than usual. Often he listened to music at this time but tonight he didn't want it, couldn't bear it. In silence he sat, and in darkness, but for the single lamp which burned beside his armchair. Through the shadows all the familiar objects glimmered: the brass fender before the ashes of the fire, the paintings and the mirror, the silver tray with its bottles and decanters. After such a day, it seemed to William miraculous that he was there, at home in his own drawing room.

Why today? What had triggered it? It was absurd but, looking back, the only way he could define it was to say that he had never properly woken up that morning. All day he had been in a strange way half asleep, in a kind of waking drowse so that everything had seemed curiously unreal, like a dream, even as he lived it. There had been more to it than a simple lack of sleep, although that was something from which he often suffered, because of his insistence on being always the first to rise in the house and the last to go to bed. Liz used to say he was the only person she knew who was both a lark and an owl, used to marvel at his energy. She didn't realise how much it took out of him. He followed this pattern because the early mornings were the pursuit of hope, the late nights a quest for consolation. Liz thought it was kind of him to bring her coffee to bed, not realising it was a way to buy time alone.

Even in a suburban garden there was a kindness, a mercy, in the freshness of the day, the purity of the light; and from the kitchen window he would watch the birds at the wooden bird table, where the children put out fat and nuts in the winter. Magpies chattered and fought, a robin came often, and a pair of thrushes, but the bird he liked best was the blackbird, with its vivid eye and orange beak, with its liquid river of song. On dark mornings he would simply watch the light seep into the sky. He knew in his heart that it was foolish to draw comfort from such things, that if such a notion as banal transcendence was possible then this was it, for the day would not ultimately be redeemed. And yet, he had come to depend to an extraordinary degree on these little islands of peace. Then he switched on the radio and started to prepare breakfast for Sophie and Gregory.

He listened to one of the commercial stations and there was comfort, too, in the fake urgency of the news reports and the traffic updates, as there was fellowship in seeing the lights come on in the houses across the street. *Yes, life is a struggle*, these things seemed to imply, *but we're all in it together*. Now he could feel the day breaking like a wave around him, could feel the tension between the pristine silence of the early morning and the increasing tide of the world that would gradually engulf it. The idling radio, the racket as the children clattered downstairs demanding cereal and juice, the rush of the shower when Liz rose, even the very thought of people all over the city rummaging for clean shirts, making tea and toast; he valued the tremendous pathos of this shared necessity.

So what had gone wrong this morning? He had failed utterly to make the transition from the night world into the day. Right from the start, everything had been grey and unclear, as though he were looking through a veil or a mist. He hadn't even felt particularly unhappy, hadn't felt anything, just a strange numbness. William remembered now that Liz had noticed something was wrong, had paused in helping Gregory on with his shoes to say, 'Are you all right? Are you not feeling well?' 'I'm just a bit tired,' he'd said, 'that's all,' although he'd known even then there was more to

9

it than that. Liz was too busy to pursue the matter. She looked in the hall mirror and slicked on her lipstick, then left the house with the children in a flurry of car keys and school bags, anoraks and lunch boxes. William heard the car doors slam and they drove off.

A short time later he picked up his briefcase, typed in the code of the house alarm and set off for the DART station. On the train into town he looked out across the great sweep of Dublin Bay. He noticed how clear Howth Head was on this fine morning at the end of the winter, the houses white and evident on the vast dark hump of the promontory. They drew into Booterstown station and he gazed at the patch of wetland on the other side of the wall, at herons and oyster-catchers. The idea that came to him now was one that had played at the edges of his consciousness for years. The first time it had entered his mind as a personal possibility rather than as an abstract concept it had frightened him. Appalled, he pushed it away, forced it down. That he had largely succeeded in doing so was because William was an expert in mental control, in will, in closing out things that were too painful, too difficult to bear. But the idea had always been there from that day on. Perhaps his control over it had been too complete, for when it broke it was like a dam exploding. This was the moment. The idea sprouted before him like a huge, dark, marvellous poisoned flower. The train moved off. Why had he resisted until now? It was the obvious solution. It would be a relief. It would be best for all concerned. He believed that nothing had been farther from his mind when he boarded the train in Dalkey, and yet, by the time he got out, together with crowds of other people at Westland Row, the idea was fully formed and resolved in his mind.

He kept exactly to his usual routine, buying a copy of *The Irish Times* in the station shop, then crossing the road into Trinity, past the herb garden outside the botany department, past the physics building, and then up between the playing fields. He turned right, as always, into New Square, past the garden with its benches and roses, and looked up at the first-floor window that he always liked to think of as his, ever since the year he had had a room there as a student. It gave him pleasure to think back to his time in Trinity; he had been happy then. As he walked past the end of the Rubrics into Front Square, he thought of how little it had changed over the years, unlike other places he had known in Dublin, and how he liked that, because it meant he could pretend that time had not passed, could pretend that at any moment he might see Liz as she had been then, with her files and her books, on her way to a French lecture. Even as William thought this he saw ahead of him, as if to deliberately point up the foolishness of such a thought, one of his own former lecturers crossing the square. He wore in his face and body every day of the twenty years and more that had passed since he taught William land law. He walked between the two small lawns with their boundary of chains to which many bicycles were fastened, into the darkness of the front arch, with its glass-fronted notice boards and its floor of wooden blocks, past the security office and out again into the brightness of the day, through Front Gate and into College Green.

The law firm for which William worked was in a side street off Dame Street, up near Dublin Castle, and as he approached it this morning he could smell hops from the brewery. When he stepped into the building Martin Kane was there, laughing uproariously at something the doorman Declan had just told him. 'It's a good one that, isn't it?' Declan was saying. 'It's a good one.'

Speechless with mirth, Martin stepped into the lift with William. 'Jesus, your man's a turn,' he said, pressing the button for their floor. 'He's lost in this place, he should be in the Gaiety.'

There was a mirror in the back of the lift, and William could not but be struck by the contrast between his own face and that of his colleague. They were like the masks for comedy and tragedy, Martin relaxed and jolly, still chuckling at whatever it was Declan had said; William tense and grim, with a frown cleft deep in his forehead.

'Few jars after work tonight, what do you say?' Martin asked as the lift stopped and the doors opened.

'I'm not sure,' William replied.

'No bother,' Martin said, heading off down the corridor to his office, 'I'll give you a shout later in the day, see how you feel.'

The fog that enveloped him still did not affect his capacity to work and William quickly settled down to dictate letters and read reports. No one else seemed to notice anything unusual about him today, and he was aware that his comportment and behaviour were exactly as always. But he felt distant from everyone: cut off. Sometimes it was as if there was a thick sheet of plate glass around him, sometimes it felt as though he was underwater, and was looking up through the refracted light at people who gazed down calmly at him. It was wretched. He was relieved to know that it would soon be over. At eleven o'clock there was a lull in his tasks, and on an impulse he picked up the phone, dialled the direct line to the office where Liz worked. 'Kelly and Begley, good morning.' Her voice was formal and crisp. He hadn't thought through what he was going to say and so he said nothing. 'Hello?' she said. A pause then 'Hello?' again, with a note of irritation now. Then the line went dead. He imagined her sitting at her desk in her stone-coloured suit and her lipstick.

He went for a late lunch to a sandwich bar which he liked because no one else from his office ever patronised it. The circular table at which he sat was cluttered with the debris of other people's food: tea stains, broken crusts, pieces of bitten apple. An elderly waitress who often served him came over and began to clear away the mess.

'Are you tired, love?' she asked.

'I am,' he said. 'I'm absolutely and completely exhausted.'

'Good that it's Friday,' the woman said. 'You'll have the weekend to rest up.'

He thought of the weekend: he saw a blank; he said nothing.

When William went back to the office he continued to work diligently and mechanically. It was important to him that everything should be left in good order. Someone brought him a cup of coffee at three o'clock, and as he drank it he took time to look around the office. How strange it was to think that after twenty years of coming in here, day after day, he would never see the place again. On his desk there was a framed picture of Liz and the children, and taped up beside the filing cabinet were some of Gregory's paintings. His colleagues genuinely admired the child's work, but William knew, too, that behind his back they laughed at the photo. The only person who dared to make any comment about it was a sly temp from the North, who had worked there for a fortnight. 'So that's what you looked like when you were a wee fella,' she said, pointing at Gregory in the photo on her last day with the firm, as though she hadn't noticed the resemblance until then. He disliked displaying the photo and paintings, recognising that they were nothing more than signifiers of a conformity against which he increasingly chafed. It was like having to play golf or talk about the Six Nations. There were certain things about which you weren't supposed, under some unspoken but iron rule, to express an interest. He remembered the insouciance with which the temp did embroidery during her tea break.

Just at that moment, Martin's bright face appeared around the door. 'Are you game for a pint later?'

'Think I'll give it a miss, if that's all right.'

'Fair enough. Another time.' William made no reply. He logged off, put his papers in his briefcase and ensured that everything in the office was in perfect order before leaving.

After the stifling atmosphere in the office the air of the street was agreeable to him, and he stood for a moment before walking down to the river. The fine weather enhanced the classic colours of the city, the grey stone of the churches and the Four Courts, the green copper dome of Adam and Eve's. He walked along the thronged quay in a daze, past the Ha'penny Bridge and down towards D'Olier Street, aware of the contrast between the absolute ordinariness of the day and the singular nature of what he was going to do. Or rather, what was about to be done, so passive did he feel by this stage. That was what he found so terrible about life – its brutal inevitability, while always there was the illusion of liberty, of free will. Still in a waking dream, he wandered through the city streets, not quite sure where he was going. Afterwards he would remember the oddly circuitous route he took to Stephen's Green, going first to Merrion Square then up to Baggot Street and eventually to the place that had become, for no particular reason, his destination.

William sat down on a bench and thought seriously about how he would proceed with the task in hand. He had no idea how long he had been there when he realised that someone was standing in front of him. He glanced up vaguely. It was a woman, and she was holding out an unlit cigarette, with a quizzical smile. Mechanically he reached into his pocket and pulled out his lighter. The woman put the cigarette in her mouth and leaned down towards the flame he offered her, cupping her hand against the breeze.

And as he looked at her, something extraordinary happened. The fog, the dreamlike state in which he had been wrapped all day, suddenly melted away. The woman's face: her fine skin, her half-closed grey eyes, startled him utterly and woke him up, like the kissed princess in his daughter's storybook. It was as though this woman was the first real person he had seen all day, the first he had seen for years. She straightened up and blew out a long column of smoke, smiled her thanks and turned away.

14

The enormity of what he had been contemplating broke over him; stunned and winded him. The thought of being alone for a second longer was terrifying. 'Excuse me.' He heard his own voice, hesitant and trembling. The woman turned round, and he heard himself tearfully asking her to sit beside him for a moment. She stood looking at him, sizing him up. Her face was inscrutable. She was young, in her early twenties: flat shoes, big coat, dangling earrings, remarkable hair. If she said no, he did not think he would be able to bear it. But she nodded, retraced her steps and sat down beside him.

Sitting now, past midnight, in the dimly lit drawing-room of his own home, his mind shrank from what had happened next. Thinking about it was like touching a wound, as if not just the unfelt pain of the early part of that day hit him, but of all his life. The young woman had actually seen him home and he'd meekly, gratefully gone with her. The whole day had fallen apart by that time, and with it, he realised, his life.

When he arrived at the house Liz opened the door before he had time to put his key in the lock. Her face showed surprise to see him home so early, that quickly modulated into concern when he said, 'I feel ill. I feel wretched.'

'You certainly look it. Do you want to go and lie down?'

He'd stumbled up the stairs to the bedroom and at once, to his own later astonishment, fell into a deep and mercifully dreamless sleep from which he awoke only at midnight, when Liz came up. And he'd gone down, in spite of her protestations, to drink and to sit in silence, to cling again to the old, familiar rituals of his life, even though he knew now that they were utterly useless. He had still barely grasped what had happened to him, but he was aware that, from here on out, things could never be the same again.

Chapter Three

'Cliona rang me this morning, said she was having a little get-together for the family Sunday week. She asked me to pass the invitation along.'

Roderic threw him the look of a hunted animal. '"A little get-together." Jesus, Dennis, those are some of the most terrifying words in the English language.'

'I take it that means no?'

Anyone seeing Dennis and Roderic sitting drinking together at the back of the pub that early February evening could easily have surmised that they were brothers. The similarities they shared were in nuance and gesture, in the way they spoke and sat and lifted their drinks from the table rather than in any physical aspect. Roderic, considerably bigger than Dennis, was a robust, big-boned giant of a man. He was wearing a thick moss-coloured jumper that had seen better days, and he managed to look both ravaged and vital, was dark-haired and striking. Fair-haired and lightly built, Dennis was neat this evening, as ever, in his herringbone tweed jacket and tie. They were in their late forties, early fifties, and life had clearly taken its toll on both of them, in its own way.

'Ah, you know how it is. Poor Cliona, she must be the last woman in Ireland with a heated hostess trolley.'

'I don't think she really expects you,' Dennis said, 'but she wanted you to know that you're invited, that you'd be more than welcome to come along.'

'I'm a heel, I know. I'll call her myself to thank her and tell her I can't make it. Maybe I'll arrange to see her in town for a coffee. I like to keep in touch with the family, but it has to be one at a time. I can't hack it in a group.'

'I think she's still annoyed with you about that time last September, when you forgot you'd been invited and didn't show,' Dennis said. To his surprise, Roderic smiled at this as though the memory gave him pleasure.

'I did, didn't I?' he said. 'I forgot. Still, I did go along for Arthur's birthday at the end of the year, do you remember?'

'I do indeed,' Dennis replied, taking a long slug of his Guinness.

Immense amidst the chintz and bric-à-brac of Cliona and Arthur's front room in Loughlinstown, Roderic had looked like a golden eagle that had landed by chance upon a suburban bird table, beside the sparrows and finches, and instead of laying waste to all around him had decided to try to fit in. He'd eaten prodigious quantities of home-made shortbread from a triple-decked cake-stand – another of Cliona's anachronistic household items – as the conversation washed around him. Property prices, the difficulty of finding parking spaces in Dublin, political scandals, golf, the new Polo Arthur had recently acquired as a second car for Cliona's use, and its merits compared with the Renault Clio that Maeve was thinking of buying; everyone painfully aware that Roderic had no particular opinions on any of these matters. But when Arthur finally cleared his throat and said, 'How's the work going, Roderic?' he'd looked, if anything, even more ill at ease and stared at the carpet. 'Grand, grand,' he said, 'the work's going grand.' Everyone was relieved, even Dennis, when he finally made his excuses and lumbered out.

'I do try,' he protested, 'and I do like them, you know that. I've always been particularly fond of Arthur, and I'm even getting on fairly well with Maeve these days. Speaking of families,' he went on, reaching for his jacket which was folded on the couch beside him, 'this arrived last week.' From an inside pocket he took an envelope with an Italian stamp and passed the colour photograph it contained to Dennis. As his brother studied it, Roderic sat behind his coffee cup with his arms folded, pleased by Dennis's admiring comments. When he handed back the photo Roderic himself looked at it for a few moments before replacing it in the envelope, and then they sat in silence for a few minutes.

'I'm going to a concert later this evening,' Dennis eventually remarked, 'and I have to eat first. I wondered if you would like to come and have a plate of pasta with me, somewhere near here.'

'Now that's an invitation I would like to take up, but I'm afraid I can't.' Dennis again drank from his Guinness, leaving a pause he hoped Roderic might fill by divulging his plans for the evening. But Roderic was up to this trick.

'What are you going to hear?' he asked, picking up his cup in turn.

'Beethoven Piano Concerto. The Fifth.'

'Great stuff. You're so well organised. Have you a season ticket again for this year?' Dennis nodded. 'We must arrange to go to something together soon. And I'm really sorry I can't eat with you tonight.'

'Another time.'

'I'm going to have another coffee, what can I get you?'

Dennis put his spread palm over the top of his glass. 'I'm fine, thanks,' he said, and he watched as his brother unfurled himself from his seat and went over to the bar. Roderic never had any trouble getting served in pubs, no matter how busy, for he towered over all around him, and it was impossible for any barman not to notice him. Not that there was any difficulty today, for it was early in the week and although a few office workers, like Dennis, had filtered in for a drink, it was a quiet evening. Contented and relaxed, he gazed down the length of the long, dim room with its marble counter, its elaborate lamps and wooden fittings, and watched the smoke from someone's cigarette twist and drift in the quiet air.

'I like this pub,' he said, as Roderic made his way back to the table, a cup and saucer clutched gingerly in his big paw. 'It's good to be able to meet you in a place like this,' he added carefully. 'You're looking ever so well these days.'

'Aren't I great?' Roderic said with no discernible irony. 'It's three years now. I never take it for granted, Dennis, not for a minute.'

'Nor do I.' They had almost said too much. They fell silent as Roderic emptied two packets of sugar into his coffee. 'Work's going well too. Sold a painting last week, a big one. What about yourself, how's it going in the bank?'

'Much as ever; it's fine.'

'What about the hill walking, are you getting out at all these days?'

'I'd be lost without it. I was up in Glencree on Sunday. Walk for miles then stand, just listen to the silence. Magical.'

Roderic had changed his position slightly when he sat down again, leaving Dennis a clear view of the length of the room. As they talked about his day in Wicklow, the front door of the pub opened and a young woman came in: scruffy, and wild haired. He casually watched her progress. Although there were plenty of empty places at the front and middle, she was moving down towards the corner beside the back door, where Dennis and Roderic were sitting. By the time the penny dropped, and Dennis realised what was happening, she had come up right behind Roderic who, sitting with his back to her, was oblivious to her presence until the moment she put her hand on his shoulder.

'Julia!'

'I came early. I didn't expect you to be here for an hour yet, so I thought I would sit and read my book for a while. You don't mind if I join you?'

'Not at all, not at all,' Roderic said. Flustered, he moved his jacket from beside Dennis to make room for her, replacing in the pocket, Dennis noticed, the letter from Italy which had remained on the table until then.

'This is Dennis, my brother – Dennis – Julia.'

19

'Roderic has told me lots about you,' she said, a politeness Dennis couldn't in honesty return. They shook hands and he gave her the tight little smile that was, in the circumstances, all he could manage. Julia took out her purse and dumped her velvet shoulder bag on the couch. 'Can I get either of you a drink?' she asked as she moved towards the bar. Roderic had barely touched his coffee, and Dennis again demurred. He was relieved when he heard her ask for a glass of Smithwicks, which was quickly served, for he didn't know how he and Roderic could have easily filled the awkward minutes it would have taken the barman to pour a Guinness.

'We were just talking about Wicklow,' Roderic said when she sat down.

'Oh really? That's where I'm from,' she added, addressing Dennis. 'What were you saying about it?' They tried to flog the conversation back into life, but without success. Subjects were raised – hill walking – concerts – Julia's forthcoming exhibition – but they rapidly foundered on the brothers' lack of ease. Only Julia remained calm, evidently bemused at the effect of her arrival. Eventually Dennis looked at his watch, drained his glass and said he would have to be off.

'So that's the famous Dennis,' she said when they were alone. 'He's attractive, but I don't think he knows it himself,' a comment Roderic found remarkably shrewd. His brother's habitually stern manner usually masked his looks, something people generally failed to see through until they knew him well. 'Why was he so uptight? What was all that about?'

'Oh Dennis is Dennis, you know. It's a long story.'

Julia turned over in her mind this not particularly illuminating response and decided not to pursue the matter for now. They relaxed into Dennis's absence and talked about all that had happened to them in the days since they had last seen each other, Roderic's big booming laugh occasionally causing people to turn and look at them.

After a time Julia opened her bag and took out a few sheets of paper. 'This is the text for the catalogue,' she said. 'Have a look through it and tell me what you think. I hate things like this,' she added as he smoothed out the pages on the table.

'Everyone hates this side of it,' Roderic replied, 'except vain, silly people, and perhaps even some of them find it a chore.'

He picked up Julia's curriculum vitae. He ran his eye over the list of qualifications and exhibitions. A page easily held all she had done so far.

'Every time I look at it I think how false it is,' she said. 'I look between the gaps and see all the things left out: all the projects that didn't come through, the failed exams, the rows, the relationships that didn't work, the whole bloody lot.'

He glanced at her over the top of the page, thinking of his own CV: the long list of hard-won achievements; and its shadow side, the unspoken horrors between the lines. Julia didn't know what it was to have broken hearts and wrecked lives, including one's own. Poor Dennis. No wonder he was so easily spooked by anything to do with Roderic by this stage.

'That looks fine.' He turned his attention to the essay entitled 'Julia Fitzpatrick: Found Objects for a New Millennium', and started to read. He had almost finished it when he noticed that someone had come up and was standing beside them.

'Roderic.'

'Brendan.'

Brendan stood staring down at Roderic. He bit his lower lip, frowning slightly and nodding. 'So how are things? Tell me everything you've been up to. What's new?'

'Things are fine,' Roderic said evenly. Brendan didn't respond, but continued to bite and stare and nod and frown, hoping that Roderic would be made to feel uneasy, and blurt further information into the protracted silence. Instead, he sipped his coffee and stared insolently back at Brendan.

21

'Good,' Brendan said eventually. 'Good.'

'Julia, do you know Brendan? Brendan Halpin, the art critic? Julia Fitzpatrick.'

Until Roderic spoke to her, Brendan had paid no attention whatsoever to Julia. He looked at her now with unfriendly curiosity, and he didn't respond to her greeting – 'Hello, Brendan' – but turned back to Roderic and gave him a sly smile.

'Julia's in a group exhibition that opens in March,' Roderic said. 'Go and see it,' and he named the gallery.

Brendan considered this information, still nodding and frowning. 'So everything's fine?' he said eventually.

'Everything's fine.'

'Good. Good. Well, see you around, Roderic.' Julia was not included in this farewell, by either word or gesture. They watched him as he made his way through the pub to the front door, weaving his way between the tables.

'I always regard meeting Brendan as a spiritual exercise,' Roderic said, 'and I'd advise you to do the same. He's got a good sharp mind, but no heart. Don't fret about his ignoring you. It's only in the past year or so, since my star has been somewhat in the ascendant, that he'll give me the time of day. The good thing about having been at the bottom of the heap is that you have no illusions left when you start to move up.'

He finished reading the essay and made a few suggestions, including a change of title; she thanked him for his help.

'Do you know anything about the other artists in the show?'

'One is a photographer, whose work I must confess I don't like at all. She demythologises women too completely, I think.'

'So you'd like them to be just a little bit mythologised?' he teased her, and she smiled.

'I'm not explaining it well. I mean, if you reduce every-thing to the purely physical, you're missing the point. At least, that's my view. You'll see what I'm getting at when you see the photos themselves. And as for the other artist, I don't know her work. She isn't a painter, she makes constructions. I've been told that she's good; we'll see in due course. What are you doing for the rest of the evening?'

'I'm heading back to the studio myself for a few hours now,' he said, 'I got very little done when I was over there this morning. What about you?'

'I think I'll sit here and read my book a while, as I didn't get to read it earlier.'

He took her hand. 'I'm sorry about Dennis,' he said.

'Put it out of your mind. There's nothing to be sorry about.'

'Oh but there is, Julia,' he said, 'that's the problem. There's lots and lots to be sorry about.'

As he walked towards the front door of the pub he shrugged on his jacket, almost knocking a pint glass from a table as he passed. William caught it just in time and looked up, annoyed. The person who had unwittingly almost spilt the drink was such a giant, however, with the face of a hardened drinker that he decided to let discretion be the better part of valour, and to let it pass. Martin, whose drink it actually was, hadn't even noticed, as he yammered away. It was William who had suggested to Martin that they go for the drink that they hadn't had on the Friday. It put off the time when he would have to go home, something which was becoming an increasing strain. He had managed to get through the weekend somehow, after that shocking Friday. Mainly, he'd stayed in bed, pleading illness, but Liz knew by Saturday that there was more to it than that. It was only a matter of time before he stopped functioning completely. She knew he was in trouble, had urged him this morning to take the day off work. 'Why?' he'd asked, interested to see what she would say. Perhaps she might be able to throw some light on it, but she had folded her arms and looked at him shrewdly. 'Why don't you tell me?' she said. He wondered listlessly how much longer he would be able to struggle on before it all fell comprehensively apart. Today was Tuesday. He knew he wouldn't make it to the end of the week.

Martin, a man who noticed nothing, was tremendously relaxing company. He chattered away brightly beside William about everything and nothing: it was like sitting dozing under a songbird's cage. No more than the occasional nod or the odd murmur of consent was necessary to maintain the illusion that a conversation was taking place. Martin fascinated William, even as he bored him: his gift for happiness, the way he plunged and sparkled through every facet of his own life like an otter in a mountain stream was a source of wonder. What was so strange was that his life was so eerily like William's own in everything except this contentment. His wife Elaine was Liz's best friend; they also had a boy and a girl, although their children were older than Gregory and Sophie; their home in Clonskeagh was fashionably austere, while William's own was more traditional in both architecture and furnishings. They worked in the same office, had both gone to Trinity, he was also the son of a lawyer . . . and yet, and yet . . . Many people considered that Martin was William's best friend. In his darkest hours even William would allow himself to go along with this ridiculous notion in his own mind, but in general he realised that this was nothing more than perfect evidence of the false nature of the life he had made for himself. In the deepest, most fundamental points they had, he thought, little in common. There were even times when he despised Martin, particularly when he talked about women as he was doing now.

He had focused on a woman who was sitting up at the counter, out of earshot, in a pale blue suit and drinking gin and tonic.

'I could buy her a drink, what do you think, do you think she'd join us? I think she's drinking on her own, just waiting for somebody to take pity on her, wouldn't you say? I'd say she's desperate for a bit of company.'

This talk was typical of Martin, and that was all it ever amounted to: talk. William couldn't bear it, and used to marvel that someone of Martin's age – on the short road to fifty, like himself, and with twenty years of marriage behind him – could gain any satisfaction from it. He would have called it adolescent were it not for the fact that even adolescents nowadays would have gained no thrill, and expected more action.

'There now,' he said, as a young man in a sharp suit swept into the bar, kissed the woman. 'There's my chance gone.' He sounded delighted. The woman said something to her companion and nodded towards Martin, who abruptly turned away.

All gong and no dinner, as William had heard one of the women in the office describe him. It was William himself who had almost wrecked his own marriage with a stupid fling that had caused misery all round, and left a crack in his life with Liz that he now realised would be with them for ever. It was Martin who had seen what was happening, who had tried to stop him. It had been a reckless affair; he intended it to be destructive. Martin had hauled him off for drinks, had told him he was mad, that it wasn't worth it, to stop now before any more harm was done. After Liz found out and wanted to leave him Martin had asked his own wife to talk to her, to coax her to stay. Elaine had told William in no uncertain terms that she was only doing it because she thought it was in Liz's best interests, and to this day when she was in William's company made no effort to conceal that she thought him beneath contempt. Martin, to his credit William thought, had never made any further allusion to the matter.

'I'll tell you this, though,' he said now, nudging William, 'you're in with a chance down there.' He nodded towards the back of the bar. 'She's pretending to read a book but she's been giving you the eye this past ten minutes and more.' William glanced wearily in the direction indicated and was utterly thrown to see the woman whom he had met on Stephen's Green a few days earlier. He felt his face grow hot, and to his mortification Martin noticed it. 'Fancy her, do you?

25

She's young, but I've seen better. I wouldn't have thought she was your type. Fierce head of hair.' William was so embarrassed he couldn't speak, picked his glass up and almost dropped it. Martin looked at him narrowly. 'Do you know her?'

'Does she look like the sort of person I would know?' William said: an inspired remark in the circumstances, for it was enough to put Martin off the trail.

'Not likely,' he said. Getting bored with the subject of women now, he unfolded the evening paper he had bought earlier. 'More scandals,' he said, pointing at the headline. 'Will it never end?' and he was off again on another rambling line of conversation.

William was still consumed by the thought of the woman at the far end of the room. Should he go over and thank her? If he did, he would have to wait until Martin was gone, and that might be hard to arrange without looking suspicious. Worst of all, what if she came over to him, when he had more or less denied knowing her to Martin? His mind played over increasingly labyrinthine possibilities and complications.

Martin jumped to his feet. 'I'd better fly,' he said, putting his paper in his briefcase. 'You take your time, finish your drink.' He nodded again towards the back of the bar and winked. 'And behave yourself. Good luck.'

Left alone, William gazed at the table, almost frightened, imagining that the woman's gaze was boring into him. But when he did finally look up and saw that she was gone, that she had slipped out the back door, he was far more disappointed and confused than he would have expected.

Chapter Four

This is why Julia thinks she became an artist: because of a game she used to play with her father when she was a child. He devised it himself to occupy her on winter evenings. He would show her a picture, usually from an old greetings card or an outdated calendar, for a short, fixed period of time, and then she would have to describe it to him in as much detail as she could recall. She was good at this game. Her mind became quick and sharp; it was difficult for her father to find images complex enough to challenge her. She remembers one in particular, an old Christmas card, with a scene of men and women in old-fashioned clothes, skating on a frozen river, and wonders now at her father's patience, sitting peering at it as she reeled off as much as she could recall. From time to time he would ask her leading questions to nudge her along. 'The man you mentioned on the left, skating between the two women: can you describe how they're dressed?' How vexed she was when she said that both the women were in scarlet dresses and her father said no, it was the man who was wearing a red coat.

When she was too familiar with the image to have any further use for it in the game, still she liked looking at it. The painting had a peculiar atmosphere, frozen, golden, wistful, that drew her into the world of the picture in the way a photograph could never have done. She used to stare and stare at it, and imagine that if she looked at the picture long enough and hard enough, she would be able to break its spell. Then she would be able to see into that lost world, and the diminutive skaters would begin to move across the ice. Some of them would slip and fall, and those who were shown as having tumbled over in the painting would pick themselves up, and wobble away on their bladed feet, and the vanes of the icy windmill would turn, and the tiny crow would fly from the tree.

Her father noticed that she got enormous pleasure from the picture, and what he did next was a stroke of pure genius: from a barrow of second-hand books in a street market he brought home a large book full of colour reproductions of old-master paintings. They used it for the memory game, and even she felt that she had met her match in Bruegel's proverb painting: the running egg! The roof slated with fruit tarts! But afterwards, she was quite happy to sit on her own and leaf through the book, looking at the pictures and entering those other worlds, as she saw them, where things were similar to the world she knew, but different too, in a way she found impossible to define but which she knew to be real. In this frame of mind, it was not the most detailed pictures that interested her, but the still life paintings. A wooden platter of curled, frail wafers and a bottle of wine sheathed in wicker. Lobsters and oysters, a cut lemon, its pared peel hanging off the edge of the table. A streaked tulip, translucent grapes and a songbird's nest. She stared and stared at these things, wondering how it was that they seemed more exact, more true, than the apples that grew in their orchard, than the cakes and biscuits her father provided for them. Her beloved father! He acted from the purest of motives; did not wish her to 'get on' in life, was not covertly trying to educate her. He had handed her the book with the words, 'You'll enjoy that.'

But even this was not enough. He led her on, further and further, like a blind man leading his companion to the very gates of a palace that he himself cannot see. 'What do you like so much about these pictures?' he asked her one day, glancing over her shoulder. 'The things in them are realer than real things,' she replied, which she knew her father would not challenge or ridicule, even though she didn't expect him to understand. He nodded gravely and continued to stare at the page for a few moments before pointing to one particular picture and saying, 'Just imagine someone sitting down and painting that.'

It was a casual observation but she took it as an instruction. For days afterwards, she studied intently the painting he had been looking at when he had spoken. Two chased silver vessels, two drinking glasses, one long, ribbed, upright and full; the other elaborate, fluted and empty, lying tilted on the tabletop; and two plates, one of which bore an elaborate fruit pie and the spoon which had broken it up to serve it. The other plate held the portion that had been served, and stood at the edge of the table, so precariously positioned that it looked as if it might at any time fall forward, spilling the pastry and fruit on the floor. (Because there was a floor, there had to be a floor, didn't there, even if she couldn't see it.) What else? A few scattered hazelnuts and walnuts, a few shattered nutshells and a knife with a bone handle; the whole bathed in a rich buttery golden light that made much of the curves of the tilted fluted glass, and the soft lights hidden in the silver vessels.

The artist had set all these things out on the table, spent a considerable period of time arranging them to pleasing effect, and then begun to paint. She thought of the concentration it must have required, of how he would have stared at the things to get to their essence, but how he then managed to translate that to the canvas in paint was beyond her understanding. She could imagine, though, his thrill of satisfaction when the work was complete, in that short interval when the two existed together: the arrangement of objects on the table and, a few feet away, the painting that would preserve them for ever, perfected. And then the painter would have broken that link between the objects and their image, by leaning over and lifting up the tall ribbed glass, and the plate that contained the portion of pie. She imagined that he topped up the glass of wine, and perhaps served himself a more generous portion of the dessert. Maybe he took the silver spoon with which to eat.

She knows that he went out into the garden of his house, for by now she has entered so fully into his world that she can feel how stiff his fingers are, and his eyes are strained. For all that, he has the deep satisfaction of work well done, done as best he possibly could. She can feel the sun on his neck and shoulders, taste the short pastry and the sharpness of the apples and blackberries that the pie contained. She imagines him chewing, drinking, wiping the back of his hand across his mouth and lifting his face to the sun, its power and heat.

So deep was her pleasure in the scene she had conjured up that she decided to share something of it with her father. 'I like to think,' she said to him, 'about how, when the painter had finished this picture, he ate the pie.'

His response knocked her flat. 'Maybe there never was a pie,' he said. 'Maybe the painter made it all up.'

For a moment she literally couldn't speak, so extraordinary was the idea. 'What do you mean?' she said at last. 'How could there not have been a pie?'

'Maybe he just imagined one from all the pies he had seen and eaten in his life. He might have painted it from a sort of picture he had in his head, rather than from a real thing. If he was as good a painter as all that he probably just made up what he painted, having in his mind all the pies – and glasses and knives and tables and silver cups – that he had ever seen in his life. Don't you think that's possible?'

She didn't know. The idea had never occurred to her. She only knew that what he said destroyed at a stroke the pleasing image she had cultivated in her own mind, of the man with paint on his hands and crumbs on his lips, sitting in the sunshine, as delighted with himself and his work as she had been. But the man she was left with now, taking his ease having finished making a pie out of nothing but paint and imagination: that someone could do that seemed more extraordinary still. That night she couldn't get to sleep for thinking about it, and she raised the subject again with her father the following morning.

30

'You remember this picture?' and she pointed it out again in the book. 'Are you sure it's as you say?'

'I never said I was sure of anything,' he replied. 'And what does it matter? There's a pie there now made of paint and canvas, what more do you want? What do you mean by real, anyway?' He leafed through the book. 'I don't know why you like those ones so much,' he said. 'They're too ordinary. I never see the sense when people go on about something being lifelike in a painting. Where's the point in that? This is the sort of picture I love,' he said. He was pointing at a picture of a bearded man suspended in midair, and she could see what her father meant when he said he wondered if the angels who were clinging to him, his legs gripped firmly in their arms, were trying to carry him off into the sky, or if he had wished to ascend to the heavens before his time was due and the angels had been dispatched to haul him back down to earth where he belonged.

'You're not going to tell me that's real,' he said, 'that it all happened in front of the person who painted the picture.'

'How do you know?' The idea of just such a scene delighted her, and seemed to her mind no less likely than the painter of the still life having no objects before him to copy. She loved the thought of the painter working at his easel with the group of figures floating before him, beams of light coming through the ceiling to illuminate the scene, a light breeze keeping their vivid draperies in an exact, billowing arrangement.

'So what happened then when the painter stopped painting?' her father challenged her.

'They floated down to the floor of the room and rested themselves. And then all of them – the saint, the angels and the painter – sat down together and ate a fruit pie that didn't exist.'

Chapter Five

The cacophony of the tuning-up died away. Silence, then applause as the conductor came to the podium, followed moments later by the soloist. And in that instant, something strange happened to Dennis: it always did at this point. He fancied that he was the pianist in evening dress walking on to the stage. The illusion was brief but complete. He looked out into the blackness of the auditorium beyond the footlights, and bowed to acknowledge the applause; was aware of the musicians behind him. Dennis liked to think of himself as utterly unimaginative. It was one of the flaws in his self-knowledge. Other people saw him as dull and unfanciful and he, oddly, colluded in this, even to himself. He was seemingly unconscious of his rich inner life, something that he could at times barely keep under control. He had a remarkable memory, and an astonishing imagination. The conductor tapped his baton and Dennis was back in his seat, beside a woman whose pearls gleamed in the dimness. Then the music started, pure, complex, sublime; and Dennis vanished into it.

The interval came and he shuffled out of the auditorium with everyone else, collected the small bottle of Chardonnay he had booked and paid for before the concert started, and stood alone drinking it in the crowded foyer under the majestic crystal chandelier. He felt his solitude keenly tonight; noticed that, apart from himself, everyone appeared to be part of a couple. Usually this was not something that troubled him, for Dennis did not believe in the concept of the Perfect Stranger, the person to whom one could become closer than to the siblings with whom one had grown up. 'The thing about Beethoven,' a man standing near him was saying loudly, 'in fact, the thing about all Romantic music . . .' His female companion threw in the odd murmur of assent but was otherwise silent as the man droned on. It was Roderic who had first drawn his attention to these one-sided supposed conversations. He thought that one of the reasons women were so fond of Roderic was that he never held forth in this way: he was a good conversationalist, but more than that, he was a good listener.

He regretted now that he had been unable to hide his shock and dismay on meeting Julia. She had noticed it, he felt sure, although it had been impossible to read what she made of him.

Dennis had guessed not long before Christmas that Roderic was involved with a woman again. Nothing was said, but Dennis knew his brother too well to think otherwise. He and Roderic understood each other in an almost animal fashion. They were like dolphins clicking and chittering at each other in the deep, or like bats sending out high frequency signals through the silence of the night. Their understanding of each other was uncanny, at times it even unnerved them. So Dennis knew that the air of contentment and relaxation Roderic suddenly manifested could have only one meaning, and that worried him. Women had never been the root cause of Roderic's troubles, but they had always been so deeply implicated that Dennis could not, in his mind, disassociate them from disaster. And yet Roderic loved women, seemed to need to always be involved with some-one. He had been on his own for three years now, something of a record in his adult life.

The crisis that had finally come to a head three years ago had clearly taken its toll on Roderic – it had almost destroyed him – but it had exacted a heavy price from his brother too. A doctor had pointed this out to Dennis, had advised that as far as he possibly could he cultivate psychological detachment from Roderic. Roderic acknowledged this, and had promised in a fumbling and contrite fashion never again to burden

33

Dennis with his problems. At the time Dennis had been glad, and would never have believed that the day would come when he would miss the deep involvement he had had in his brother's life; that he would even resent being spared Roderic's woes.

He'd known something was up from around the time of the Paris trip at the end of last October. In the months leading up to it, Roderic had been cheerful and fairly relaxed, better than Dennis had seen him for a long time. He'd put it down to the Italian trip in June having been a success, even though Roderic admitted it had been far from easy. Still, he'd been happy during the summer, but then in September something definitely went wrong. Roderic became tense and despondent, right up until the time he went to France; yet on his return he was transformed. A mere holiday wasn't enough to explain his elation. There was a woman at the back of it, there had to be.

'Were you in Paris by yourself?' The question came out one day over the Christmas holidays before Dennis could help it, but Roderic seemed grateful for the opening. 'I was alone there, yes,' he said, 'but as a matter of fact I have been seeing someone over the past while. All very low key, you know, no heavy duty stuff. She's a fine woman though, Julia, completely authentic. Solid. Yes, it's good, Dennis, it's going well.'

Solid. From this one adjective and from what he thought Roderic needed, Dennis tried in spite of himself to construct an image of this Julia. A mature woman, he thought, that was the first thing. She would be at least Roderic's age, perhaps even older. A widow, or someone who was separated from her husband: in any case, someone who had been through her own dark marital experience, who had no illusions left, and for whom a part-time, take-it-or-leave-it, like-it-or-lump-it relationship was ideal. She wasn't bitter. Kind hearted but tough, she lived alone in a big townhouse, where Roderic went to stay for a few days every couple of weeks. *All very*

34

low key, you know. She would cook him dinner, big feeds of chops and spuds, and the puddings and sweets he had become addicted to since he stopped drinking, and then she would take him up to her bed for companionable, unthreatening sex. *No heavy duty stuff*. No, he was glad for Roderic, he thought, really glad.

And then tonight Julia – the real Julia – had marched into the pub and sat down beside them. He had barely been able to conceal his shock and dismay. She was too young, he thought, far, far too young. Why, she could almost be his daughter. Did she know about Roderic's past life? As Roderic had attempted to keep some semblance of conversation going, Dennis had stared appalled at this slim woman, with her wild hair, her wispy scarf and her easy manner. He thought back with some bitterness to the darkest, most wretched days that he and Roderic had been through together. Did she imagine for a moment she could have coped with all that? And as for the fond domestic images he had conjured up, it was laughable. She looked like she existed on a diet of tea, toast and cigarettes, this Julia. With uncanny prescience he imagined her kitchen: the sink clogged with teabags, the rancid butter, the cans of tuna and packets of orange lentils, the cartons of sour milk. He would be cooking for her, more like. What on earth, he thought, could this girl give to Roderic? In his head, clear as an auditory hallucination, he heard Roderic's voice. *Intellectual companionship. Good humour. Compassion. Complete sexual fulfilment. Need I continue?* Dennis had left the pub as soon as he decently could.

A shrill bell rang, announcing that the second half of the concert was about to begin. He drained his glass and returned to his seat.

The tall, redbrick house in a leafy road near Seapoint to which Dennis returned after the concert had been bought many years earlier, shortly after he started working in the bank. It had stretched his finances at the time but his

35

father had strongly advised him to do it, saying it would be a good investment, and had even helped out with a discreet but considerable loan. Property prices had of late risen to such a degree that it was now worth more than his father could ever have possibly imagined. It was a much bigger house than Dennis needed, and apart from the few years when Roderic had occupied the attic he had lived alone there. The house was warm when he went into it: he had the heating system on a timer. He paid a man to come and cut the grass, he paid a woman to come and do the housework. In the past few years, sometimes he felt as if the house was living a life of its own. He tapped in the code for the alarm and a deep silence fell, calling forth the same unusual loneliness that had cut into him in the concert hall. It was better that Roderic and he lived apart now: they both knew that, but that didn't stop him from regretting it at times.

A smell of bleach and furniture polish reminded him that Mrs Hughes, his housekeeper, had been there today. When he went through to the kitchen there was further evidence of her labours in the form of seven crisp white shirts hanging from the backs of chairs and doors. Momentarily their still presence startled him, so strange did they look. It reminded him of a work of art he had seen at a group show in which Roderic had participated, where empty cotton dresses were suspended from the ceiling of a darkened room and lit eerily by lamps. Because he didn't know anything about contemporary art he couldn't understand why he had found it so disturbing, but Roderic said that was the whole point.

Dennis felt restless tonight. He went into the drawing room where his piano was, his fiftieth birthday present to himself, but couldn't settle to play and so he went back to the kitchen. A cautious drinker, he reckoned that the Chardonnay and Guinness he had had earlier in the evening were enough for one day, so he eschewed the half bottle of Chianti that was sitting on the counter and opened the fridge for some

cranberry juice. The lit interior was full of chilled meals –
lasagne, ratatouille, salmon in a lemon butter sauce – and
bags of salad leaves, for Mrs Hughes also did his shopping
for him. He stood at the sink as he poured and drank his
juice; saw his own face reflected back in the black mirror that
night made of his kitchen window.

Glass in hand, he wandered aimlessly through the house,
looking at his paintings. Over the years, almost by default, he
had amassed a considerable collection of his brother's work.
The earliest, a small, fluent watercolour of the house itself
that Roderic had painted and framed as a housewarming
gift when he was an art student, was, perhaps, Dennis's
favourite, although Roderic dismissed it as a trifle, and
would even be faintly annoyed if its merits were too
much insisted upon. The drawing room was dominated by
a huge canvas, and that too had been a gift, given to him
by his brother shortly after he left hospital. Roderic was
an abstract painter. His mature style, which had evolved in
the years after his return to Ireland and for which he had
recently achieved much acclaim, consisted of stripes
executed in pastel colours; his canvases likened memorably
by one critic to 'the pale flags of imaginary countries'.
'Intelligent', 'haunting' and 'luminous' were words
frequently used to describe his work. Dennis thought the critics were at a loss to know what to say about paintings with
no subject.

For the truth was, and Dennis would admit this to no
one, didn't even like to admit it to himself, he didn't
particularly like abstract art. Even though he had actually
bought some of the paintings he owned, he had done so only
out of kindness, only to help Roderic out of the occasional
financial black hole. He wouldn't have given them house
room had they been painted by anyone else, and yet his
attachment to them was considerable, although emotional
rather than aesthetic. He couldn't imagine now living
without his paintings.

Even so, he hadn't wanted the big painting in the drawing room, in truth he hadn't. Looking at it as he sipped his cranberry juice, at the bands of pink oils melding into cream, into soft blue, he remembered the day Roderic had summoned him to the studio, pointed at the canvas and said simply, 'It's for you.' Dennis hoped that his immediate reaction – 'God no, Roderic, I can't, I can't possibly accept such a gift' – had sounded like consternation at his brother's generosity rather than simple alarm. But he'd insisted; wouldn't take no for an answer. 'It's for you, Dennis. I want you to have it. If you like, I'll come to your house and help you hang it, advise you how to show it to best effect.' It had taken the three years that had passed since then for Dennis to understand what Roderic had been doing in giving him the painting. It was, as he said at the time, a thank you gift for everything he had done for him down the years, 'Not that anything could ever adequately repay you.' But it was also, Dennis gradually realised, a farewell present. Roderic was withdrawing from him in a particular and final way, becoming distinctly separate from him for perhaps the first time in their adult lives. And although he had always thought that this would be a good thing, that it was something he actively wanted, now that it was actually happening he wasn't quite so sure, no, not sure at all.

In all of this the actual painting was somehow incidental to Dennis: a symbol rather than a thing in itself. He didn't understand what it meant until Roderic borrowed it back, together with a couple of his other canvases, for the retrospective of his work that had taken place a year ago. It had been a remarkable critical success and had definitively confirmed his reputation as a painter. Dennis was the only member of the Kennedy family to attend the opening of the exhibition and in this there was nothing new. His sisters had always shown scant interest in Roderic's work. Watercolours framed and given to Cliona and Maeve for Christmas many years earlier had been coolly received and never displayed. Dennis suspected they might even have destroyed them; and his sisters' indifference annoyed him more than it troubled Roderic. That they didn't understand the paintings, simply hadn't a clue what their brother meant by his daubs and were amazed that anyone else saw merit in his work was, as far as Dennis was concerned, no excuse, because he didn't understand the work either. 'Forget about understanding,' Roderic used to implore him. 'There is nothing *to* understand. Just look at the damn thing and enjoy it.' It was no reason not to be supportive. If Roderic believed in what he was doing, that was enough for Dennis. It was an act of faith, like believing in some particular religious teaching to do with, say, the fate of the dead and life to come, that ran in complete opposition to common sense and logic but which was irresistible. At least, Dennis found it so.

At the opening of the retrospective he stood with a glass of white wine in his hand watching Roderic from a distance as he moved through the room accepting kisses and praise, shaking hands with people, smiling and laughing, loathing every minute of it. Only Dennis knew this, Dennis who adored such occasions, with their odd mix of people – some wilder than Roderic, some squarer still than Dennis. He loved the glamour of it all. ('Glamour!' Roderic exclaimed. 'Sweet Jesus, are you serious?')

'Hello, I don't know you,' said a voice at his elbow. The man who had addressed him was one of the most correctly dressed people in the room. Normally a shy man, Dennis was happy to chat to people tonight, his pride giving him courage. The man introduced himself. His name meant nothing to Dennis, but the man gave the impression that it ought to.

'I'm Roderic's brother.'

'Are you indeed?' They fell to talking of the works in the exhibition, to which people were generally paying scant attention. How moved Dennis was to see his own painting in this context. The fact that it was being ignored served only, Dennis thought, to enhance qualities that he had never appreciated until today, most particularly its remarkable presence. The painting created its own well of calm in the hubbub of the room. If people were indifferent to it, well, it was indifferent to them. Its cool, magisterial stillness astounded him, and when he told the man it belonged to him, his response, 'I hope you have it insured for plenty,' struck him as tawdry. 'Don't you think,' Dennis said, 'that's a rather vulgar line to take?'

His wanderings through the house tonight had brought him, still holding his glass of cranberry juice, to the attic. It was cold: he only put the heat on there occasionally now. This had been Roderic's room at the period when he lived with Dennis. It was still 'his' room in a certain sense, for he still stored there many things for which there was room neither in his studio nor in the small rented house in the Liberties, where he now lived. Tea-chests with the names of Indian plantations stencilled on their sides; stacked canvases, old sketch books, a folding easel; there were even, Dennis knew, some clothes still hanging in the wardrobe, a cord jacket and a blue shirt. Over in the corner was a pair of boots: absurdly big, they looked. Roderic's 'stuff'. Every so often when visiting he would ask if he might go up to look for something, would come back downstairs twenty minutes later shamefaced. 'I simply must do something about all that junk, truly I must. It's ridiculous after so many years. Half of it could go straight into the bin, you know. As soon as I have a free afternoon I'll come over and sort it out.' But he never would, Dennis knew. If he ever did, he didn't think he could stand it. Books everywhere: art books, poetry, thrillers. He picked up a volume on French Gothic and leafed through it, looking at the grainy black and white pictures of dizzyingly high cathedral naves and gently smiling angels; at the coloured plates of stained glass.

It was only when he was at the bottom of the stairs that he realised he had left his drink up there. It didn't matter: he would fetch it later.

Going into the drawing room Dennis sat down at the piano. Carefully he opened the lid, paused for a few moments. And then he began to play.

Chapter Six

He had been practising chromatic scales for twenty minutes when the door of the drawing room opened.

'Do you have to, Dennis? Do you absolutely have to?'

'Of course I do, Mum. There are only two weeks left until the exam.'

'How much longer will you be?'

'I thought I'd keep going until lunch time.'

'It'll be a good hour before the meat's ready.'

'I know,' he said. His mother gave him a pained, long-suffering look. She withdrew from the room and Dennis resumed his scales.

Almost everything about his home and family irritated him these days, not least the drawing room in which he was practising, with its botanical prints of daffodils and narcissi, its red velvet curtains and slightly dank smell. The room was separated from his father's surgery by a thin wall and they each habitually complained about the noise the other made. He could hear now the sound of his father's deep voice but not what he was saying, and then there was an explosion of laughter. Frank Kennedy was something of a legend amongst GPs in south Dublin. A complex and compassionate man with a volatile streak, he aroused strong feelings in his patients. Many loved him and were fiercely loyal; others found him simply terrifying. His rough charm and large personality were complemented by his physique, for he was a handsome, imposing man, well proportioned and exceptionally tall. Once, a patient had actually fled when Frank's back was turned. Dennis had happened to be standing at the window of the drawing-room at the time and had seen the man stagger away at speed down the garden path with his left sleeve still rolled up above his elbow. The sight of all six foot four of Frank bearing down on him with a hypodermic needle had obviously been more than he could endure. The miracle, Dennis thought, as he bent down to take a music book from the leather case at his feet and leafed through it for the piece he required, was that it had happened only once. Through the wall he could hear a woman's voice, and then more loud laughter. He flexed his fingers and prepared to play.

He was six bars into the Field nocturne when the door opened again. He swore as he stopped playing and turned around in annoyance. A big gentle child with thick dark hair was peering round the door, and when Dennis saw who it was his face softened.

'Oh hello, Roderic.'

'Sorry to disturb you. I just wanted to ask do you know where my football is? I've looked everywhere.'

'I haven't seen it. You can borrow mine if you want, until such time as you find your own. It's in my room, in the usual place.'

'Thanks, Dennis. That was a nice piece of music you were playing on the piano when I came in,' and he approached where his elder brother was sitting.

'Did you like it? Do you want to stay while I play the whole thing through?'

'I can't. I promised I'd set the table for lunch.'

'Didn't you set it just the other day? Isn't it Maeve's turn?'

'Dunno. I thought it was too but she says it isn't.'

The piano was old and quaint, with an inlaid design of flowers worked in marquetry, and on either side candelabra on brackets that could be folded out. Roderic now reached out and did just that. Had his mother or sisters interrupted him and fidgeted with the piano in this way, Dennis would have complained bitterly, but because it was Roderic, he didn't mind. The brothers unconsciously evoked the Renoir print that hung near by of two sisters: the fair-haired one seated at the piano, the dark sibling leaning attentively against it.

'You could put candles in these, blue candles,' Roderic said, 'and then put out all the lights and play. That would be magic. It's a nice piano.'

'No it's not, it's a lousy piano,' Dennis replied. 'I wish Daddy would buy me a new one.'

Roderic ran his finger across the painted gold words in Gothic script just above the keyboard. 'Leipzig,' he said. 'What does that mean?'

'It's a city in Germany, where the piano was made. Bach lived there. I'm going to visit it.'

'Are you? Does Mum know? When are you going?'

'Oh, some day. Not for years yet. When I'm my own man.'

Even to Roderic, Dennis didn't want to talk about all Bach meant to him; all that Leipzig stood for. Against the dreary round of his own life as a suburban schoolboy, he carried with him always a perfected image of the German city. It was as if his heart was a camera obscura, the tilted mirrors of which could capture the past, offering up to him the image of a specific morning more than two centuries ago. The narrow streets and tall houses with their red tiled roofs, grey spires against the pristine blue of an icy winter sky; Kantor Bach, anonymous and unremarked as he makes his way through the city to the Nikolaikirche, and over it all the music, the music, sacred in every way. No, he didn't want to share this, not even with Roderic. Not that he would have understood: he was too small, a mere ten to Dennis's more grown-up fifteen. In years to come this difference would mean less, but for now it was crucial.

Dennis could remember his younger brother from before Roderic's birth. Their mother, Sinéad, in an enlightened fashion for the time, told Cliona and Dennis well in advance that they were going to have a new brother or sister to play with. 'A brother,' Dennis said at once. 'Maybe not. A girl would be nice,' said his mother, frankly partisan. 'Don't you think so, Cliona?' But it would be a boy; it *was* a boy. Dennis just knew. She let them put their hands each in turn on her belly, so that they could feel their new sibling within. Dennis was five, and he remembered it as well as if it had happened yesterday. The excitement to think of his brother in there! He imagined a small boy sitting cross-legged inside their mother, with a full complement of conkers and marbles, reading a comic until such time as he could join them.

He was therefore not in the least surprised when Frank turned up to collect him after school one day and announced somewhat lugubriously that they had a new brother. The surprise – the shock, even – came when he was taken up to the Coombe to meet the new arrival. His mother was sitting propped up in bed, a study in pink: pink night dress, pink quilted bed jacket, pink even the carnations on her bedside locker and the shawl in which the baby was wrapped. The baby! He'd been promised a brother: no one had said anything about a baby. And here now was this helpless thing, no bigger than one of Cliona's dolls, and seemingly more fragile, certainly more self-willed, yowling and yowling in his mother's arms. But at least it was a boy.

'Would you like to hold him?' Sinéad asked. 'Be careful, now. Will you look after him always?'

Dennis took the bundle in his arms. Unlike a doll it was pliant, warm, and its cries abated. He gazed down at his brother, whose dark unfocused eyes met his, then they closed, and he slept.

'Yes,' said Dennis. 'I will. I'll look after him.'

'I suppose I'd better go and set the table,' Roderic said. 'Thanks for the football. I'll put it back when I've finished with it.'

Saturday lunch was sacrosanct in the Kennedy household. No excuses were accepted for absence from the table although afterwards they could, and did, flee to their own friends and amusements. Roderic returned to his football, his crayons, his endless strings of chums; the girls went shopping with their mother. In summer and on fine winter days Frank went hill walking in Wicklow. When the weather was bad, he tussled with Dennis over occupancy of the drawing room, usually getting the upper hand and closing himself away there to listen to opera music at full volume. Saturday was the one day in the week when they ate in formal splendour. Their father turfed out his last patient of the day at half past twelve, and at one on the dot would sweep into the dining room, bringing with him a faint smell of antiseptic and a latent sense of threat. It was already clear to see that his younger son would inherit his height and his dark good looks. Dennis and Cliona were fair and fine-boned, like their mother. Her beauty faded but not completely gone, Sinéad carried through life the weary air of someone attending a disappointing party, where she was not the shining triumph she had expected to be.

'Grand looking bit of lamb, that, Sinéad.'

'Thank you, dear.'

The menu was always planned around a large piece of meat, a pork roast or a joint of beef, with gravy or a sauce to complement it. There would be potatoes, roast and mashed; two kinds of vegetable, one of which was always cauliflower. That it was a difficult vegetable to get right and that she did not have the necessary knack did not seem to put Sinéad off preparing it. There was a family myth that she was a marvellous cook. In response to praise she would modestly say, 'I'm just a good plain cook,' but it wasn't true, she wasn't even that. She was a very average cook indeed: no proud boast. Her broccoli was invariably overcooked, and her cauliflower, her sprouts waterlogged. There was always a pudding: apple sponge or plum crumble with cream or custard in winter, in summer a trifle or ice cream. The unchanging nature of this meal, its details and attendant rituals, had recently begun to annoy Dennis.

46

'Can't Mum carve?' he asked today, as his father sliced the leg of lamb. 'She cooked it, so why can't she carve it?'

'Don't give me any lip when I've got this thing in my hand,' his father said, waving a huge carving knife in his direction. 'Pass me up those plates. Where's the mint sauce? Maeve, go and fetch it, will you?'

'You go, Roderic, you're nearer,' she said. Roderic obediently slipped off his chair and went into the kitchen.

He had done a thorough job of setting the table. A dextrous child, he had taught himself how to fold napkins in three different ways by following the diagrams in a book of Sinéad's about home entertaining and on each of their plates today was a perfect water lily. The white tablecloth embroidered with a sprinkling of violets had been worked by their mother before she was married. Unfortunately, there was a wine stain on it, in a place where it could not be concealed by a judiciously placed pot-stand or table-mat. The cloth was too good for everyday use, but because of the stain, which repeated soakings and launderings had failed to eradicate, it was not considered fitting for company and so it graced their private family table.

'This looks delicious, Mum,' Cliona said.

'Thank you, dear. I hope you all enjoy it.'

Every single week Cliona said exactly the same thing, and their mother responded with the same words. It irritated Dennis beyond belief, he found himself clutching at the table. It was like waiting for the other shoe to fall. 'We need a new piano, Daddy,' he said as they started to eat.

'What's wrong with the one we have?'

'It's crap. It's out of tune and two of the keys stick.'

'Don't use language like that at the table, Dennis, I'm tired telling you,' his mother interjected.

'Well, you'll just have to make do with it, we can't afford a new one. I'm not made of bloody money. I've told you before not to practise when I'm in the surgery. It upsets the patients, makes them nervous. You spend far too much time hammering on that damn thing anyway. Find a girl, be more your line.' Cliona and Maeve looked at each other and sniggered. To his horror, Dennis felt his face go red. He was livid with his father, but couldn't think of a quick, smart response.

'I have a crow to pluck with you, Roderic.' He stared at his mother, appalled. He had never heard this figure of speech before and thought she was literally going to produce a dead bird and make him pull its feathers out; but instead she narrowed her eyes and said, 'Doilies. Does that mean anything to you?'

He blushed, bit his lip and looked down at his dinner. 'Sorry. I meant to replace them, but I forgot.'

'You'll do it this afternoon and you'll buy me two packets, what's more.'

'What the hell were you doing with doilies?' Frank demanded of his younger son. 'Giving a coffee morning, were you?'

'You can . . . you can do a drawing on the white bit in the middle,' he whispered, 'and then the picture's got a nice lacy frame.' This amused his father, who gave a bark of laughter. He became more relaxed and expansive as the meal went on, relishing the prospect of a day and a half's freedom from the surgery. 'Looks like rain,' he said briskly. 'Still, forecast's good for tomorrow. I'm going to try to make an early start for the mountains in the morning, be away by eight if I can manage it. I'll make a few ham sandwiches for myself tonight. When you're out this afternoon, you couldn't think to get me a couple of bars of chocolate to take with me?'

'You haven't forgotten, have you,' Sinéad said – she knew perfectly well that he had – 'that we're having the Bourkes tomorrow?'

Frank's cutlery clattered into his plate. 'Ah, sweet Jesus Christ no, not the bloody Bourkes.'

'Language, Frank. This has been arranged for weeks. Don't you remember we went to their house, just after Easter?'

'So what if we did? Does that mean they have to come round here and break our hearts? If it were an Olympic sport, Eammon Bourke could bore for Ireland.'

'Evelyn Bourke is my friend.'

'Bully for you. See Evelyn Bourke then, have her round to dinner, go shopping, go to her place, do whatever you fancy, but why in Christ's name do you have to drag me into it?'

'It's nice, don't you think, that we socialise as a family from time to time? Anyway,' she said, 'it's not a sit down dinner; I'm preparing a finger buffet. Pinwheel sandwiches and baby quiches, that kind of thing, you know.' At the words 'finger buffet' Frank slumped back in his chair, his face ashen.

Suddenly something crossed Dennis's mind. 'What do you mean, "socialise as a family"? You're not expecting me to be there? And they're not bringing Mick with them, are they?'

'He's invited, of course,' their mother replied, 'and Evelyn didn't say that he wouldn't be along.'

'That means he will. Mick Bourke is a pain in the arse,' Dennis said.

'He must take after his father then,' Frank said, before his wife could complain about her son's language.

'Well, this is very nice I must say,' she exclaimed bitterly. 'This is all the gratitude I get for the effort I make, for slaving after you all.'

'Slaving?' Frank said. 'Gratitude? Don't start me! Answer me this: does anybody like going to the doctor? No. They don't. Nobody likes going to the doctor. I am the doctor. I work like a horse to keep us all in comfort, and I don't think I ask a lot in return. I want to go hill walking. I want to listen to my opera records. All I want is a bit of peace and quiet. Is that too much to ask? Is it? Well, is it?' They all knew better than to reply to this rhetorical question, and he answered it himself. 'I wouldn't have thought so, but seemingly I was wrong. I can't even have my lunch in peace without being pestered to buy pianos and told that I'm going to have to spend Sunday eating pinwheel sandwiches with Eammon Bourke. Sweet Jesus Christ, all I want,' and his voice broke with emotion as he said it, 'all I want is to be left alone.'

Chapter Seven

It was past eleven when he got to Francis Street and found the place. Looking up, he saw a single lit window. The ground floor was all in darkness. As with many of the buildings on the street it was occupied by an antique shop with a metal grille fastened over the window, through which he peered at the heavy furniture of another time. Amongst the mahogany sideboards and dusty decanters there was a mirror that reflected back to him his own pale, hunted-looking face. There was nothing else for it. He pressed the button on the doorjamb and expected to hear the bell ring far in the distance, but did not. Perhaps it wasn't working. He pressed again, then held it down. What he heard now was the clatter of feet on the stairs and a woman's voice calling, 'All right, all right, keep your hair on, I'm coming.' But her voice was full of merriment and she was laughing as she opened the door, until she saw who was standing there. Her face, smiling and expectant, closed immediately. He'd known she'd be surprised to see him but was taken aback at how shocked, even frightened, she looked. She didn't speak.

'I was just passing.' A ridiculous remark, he knew, so absurd that he even hoped she might laugh, but her face remained shut and cold. 'I wondered if I might . . . could I come in for a minute?'

'It's very late.'

'I've brought you something,' he said, fumbling open his briefcase. She looked like she wanted nothing from him, until he pulled out the book she had been reading in the pub some nights earlier and handed it to her.

'Oh great! I thought I'd lost this for ever.' It changed the atmosphere totally. They both laughed and smiled.

'It's very kind.' At that moment, a few drops of rain started to fall. 'Why don't you . . . come up for a moment if you wish.'

The hall contained nothing but a narrow flight of stairs. At the top he stepped into a living room, lit low. On a small table before the fire was a teapot, two mugs and a plate containing the ruins of a chocolate cake, its red box and yellow ribbon abandoned on the floor beside it. An overflowing ashtray completed the scene of casual domesticity, and now he understood that someone had been with her until moments earlier. When he rang the bell she thought that person had forgotten something and come back. Understandably, it must have been a shock to see William. 'Please sit down,' she said, pointing to a chair. He preferred the look of the sofa, so he settled there instead. She flung some pieces of turf on the fire, then went out and he heard the sound of a kettle being filled, the whoosh of a gas burner. There was a large orange cat sitting in front of the fire, that had woken up when they came into the room. It stared balefully into the flames that the fresh turf sent up. William called to it self-consciously, 'Puss, puss, puss,' and the cat turned to him with a look of stony contempt, blinked its eyes and looked away again.

'Max suits himself.' She was back in the room now. 'He's a bit aloof until you get to know him.' She picked up a packet of cigarettes from the table and offered them to him. 'I have my own, thanks.' He took out his silver lighter too, but she had already picked up a lighter of her own, a cheap green plastic one, similar to the one which had failed her when they met. They made no reference to it, but for the first time since they came up to the flat, she gave a faint smile. 'I'm delighted to have this,' she said, picking up the book. 'I went back the next day to the pub where I left it, but they didn't know anything about it, so I thought it had gone the way of all good things. It's not an easy book to get hold of.'

'It looks interesting,' he said.

She looked at him shrewdly, not believing him, wondering why he was trying to curry favour in this way.

'Yes,' she said. 'It is.'

He was genuinely interested in the book – a collection of essays on aesthetics, with a picture of a Chinese vase on the cover – but the strange circumstances by which he had come upon it gave it a particular significance. The blue spine was whitened with use, and while nothing in it was underlined, the corners of two pages had been folded down. He had carried it around with him in the days since he had noticed it in the pub, on the couch where she had been sitting. He had taken it out at home and at work in moments when he knew he would not be interrupted. It was like a thing from another world, and he had felt uneasy with the hold it had over him. He liked that it had been used, there was an intimacy about it. It had been like having one of her shoes, he thought, and looking at the scuffed toes, the worn heel; or a wispy scarf, similar to the one she had been wearing in the pub that night.

'The thing is,' she said, 'it's not my book. I had borrowed it from a friend. He'll be glad to have it back. I told him I'd lost it, and he was very good about it.' He felt cheated now; felt foolish, thinking of the times he had spent turning the book over in his hands, slightly furtively. It had lost all its allure, now that he knew she didn't own it.

Suddenly she looked up. 'How did you know where to find me, anyway? How did you know I lived here?'

'There's a card,' he said. 'In the book, it's . . . I suppose you were using it as a bookmark.' She picked the volume up again and leafed through it, found no card. He opened his briefcase and pretended to look in it, took the card out and gave it to her. She studied it briefly: looked at the picture, turned it over and glanced at the written side, looked across the room at him. He had been trying to hold on to the card and she knew it. He had studied it with even more fetishistic attention than the book.

The picture on the postcard was of a fifteenth-century painting, showing a woman with a demure pale face, wedged into a cleft mountain of crystal. She wore a dress with a belt that pulled the waist in tightly, and a clean white collar. On her head was a type of wimple. A clear stream ran from the crystal mountain, and before her were two lions with faces like angry teddy bears, bearing shields of burnished gold. In the landscape behind the mountain was a small walled city, all turrets and pointed red roofs. The whole scene, which the woman dominated from her lofty situation, was painted in soft tones of olive and ochre. 'Hans Memling. *Allégorie de la Pureté,*' was printed on the back, and there was a colourful French stamp. The right-hand side gave Julia's name and the address of the house in Francis Street. William knew the message off by heart by now:

30th October

Dearest Julia,

It's raining here and Paris is grey, but grey like a pearl, all the hipped roofs slicked with rain, the river and the sky full of soft light. The galleries full of marvels: we'll come here together someday, that's a promise.

Miss you. XXXX

P.S. I know <u>exactly</u> what you'll think of Madame in her crystal!

William, however, had no idea at all of what Julia would think of the woman, and dearly wanted to know. He couldn't, however, think of how to ask her without drawing attention to the fact that he had read her card, even though she knew he had. But the message was too private to make any comment that wouldn't be rude or intrusive. He hoped she might remark upon it herself, for she didn't replace the card in the book, but propped it up against a bottle on the fireplace, and stood for a moment looking at the picture. With a hysterical whistle, the kettle in the kitchen came to the boil. 'Coffee or tea?' she asked.

While she was out in the kitchen, William had his first opportunity to look around with frank curiosity at the place in which he was sitting. It was a dim room, softly lit. Not since he was a student had he been in a room like this, perhaps not even then. It half appealed to him and half alarmed him: it was a shock to think people lived like this, for Julia wasn't a student, he would have guessed. He had been married and had bought the house he was living in now before he was thirty, and although they had done a considerable amount to it since then, and bought many pieces of furniture, even at the beginning it had been infinitely more prosperous than this set-up. The sofa, for example, on which he was sitting was covered with a woollen blanket in heathery colours of purple and green, but it slipped away slightly at the arm to reveal that the original upholstery was torn and stained. Looking around, he could see that much else was like this, improvised and shabby: cloths not quite covering boxes that served as tables, a bookshelf constructed from planks and bricks, flowers in a cut-down plastic water bottle that served as a vase. Strangest of all, at the far end of the room were a few good pieces of antique furniture, including a hunting table and a wooden trunk: overstock from the shop downstairs, he correctly guessed. And yet for all this, William couldn't remember when he had last been in a room that appealed to him so much. It was warm, not just because of the fire in the hearth, but because of the soft lighting and the general relaxed air. The sofa was comfortable. You could have burned a hole in the rug with a cigarette or knocked over a glass of red wine and it wouldn't have been the calamity it would have been in his own house, for it was evidently something that had already happened here. He envied the cat, slumped now in front of the fire, and the cat knew it.

Max looked at him smugly, stretched, gave a quick and dramatic yawn, showing a ferocious collection of teeth, and then slept again. He envied the cat who was in for the night. It was raining hard now and a wind had picked up. William would take a cab home; would ask the driver, as always, to take him out along by the sea. He thought of the rain, the roads falling away: it depressed him to consider the journey ahead.

Julia came back into the room with a teapot and mugs, as unceremonious with him as she had evidently been with her last visitor. 'You can have some of that if you want,' she said, pointing to the cake on the table. 'Or I think I might have biscuits.' She went back into the kitchen and returned holding a packet of shortbread and a carton of milk. 'I'm a bit low on milk, but I think there'll be enough. Max would drink me out of house and home. Good thing cats don't eat biscuits or there'd be no hope.' The cat opened its eyes, and Julia laughed. 'You know I'm talking about you, don't you, you divil?' she said, bending down and tickling it under the chin. 'Do you like cats?'

'Not particularly,' William said. He actually loathed them.

She poured two mugs of tea and as she leaned over to hand one to him she was closer to him physically than she had been since the first moment they met, when he lit her cigarette. Oddly, this proximity made her seem more separate and distant, bringing home the fact that she was, indeed, a stranger to him.

'Thank you, Julia,' he said as he took the mug. It was the first time he had addressed her using her name. 'I'm William, by the way, William Armstrong.' They were both conscious of how odd it was that they should have got to this point without having exchanged names.

'Help yourself to whatever you want,' she said, indicating the sugar and milk, the cake and the shortbread. This lack of finesse was, like the cluttered, shabby comfort of her home, a novelty to him.

'I like your flat.'

'Yes, it's magnificent, isn't it? It's to be the main feature of *House Beautiful* magazine next month. Be sure not to miss it.'

'Really?' It was out before he realised she was joking.

'It's a simple place, I know, and small, but it suits me. This part of town has become much more chic since I moved in, but then where hasn't in Dublin? I keep thinking Hester's suddenly going to triple the rent and sling me out.'

'Hester?'

'The woman who owns the shop downstairs. I work for her part time.'

'What do you have here?'

'Well, this room, and the room directly above, which I use as a studio.'

'Studio?'

'I'm an artist.'

'Really? Why, you should have said!' He was genuinely astonished and pleased to hear this, but she looked suspicious at his enthusiasm. 'I love art.'

'Do you?' She thought he was trying to flatter her, as she had when he said he thought the book looked interesting.

'Could we go up and see your work?'

He knew he was being pushy, knew that she would refuse, but he hoped she would give him some kind of opening, that she might even say, 'Maybe the next time.' Instead she said nothing at all, just sat stroking the cat's head. Her silences were eloquent and tactful; she knew how to say a great deal by saying nothing.

'There's a little bathroom beside the studio,' she went on a moment later, as if he hadn't spoken, 'and that's directly above the kitchen, which is equally small. And that's the lot.'

She hadn't mentioned a bedroom. Maybe in the circumstances, the peculiar intimacy of sitting drinking tea with this stranger late at night, she didn't want to mention it, and William himself was too embarrassed to ask.

'I know what you're thinking,' she said, 'and the answer is, no, there's no bedroom.'

He could scarcely believe this.

'So where do you sleep, then?'

'You're sitting on the bed.' Then she laughed. 'I wish you could see your face,' she said. 'It's a study.'

William laughed along with her, with some effort.

'You sleep on the sofa? Really?'

'It folds out,' she said.

She really didn't have a bedroom: didn't even have a bed. He scarcely knew what to say to this. 'Where do you keep your bedding?'

She pointed to a big dark wardrobe at the back of the room. 'In there. It's not as bad as you might think. It's a bit of a nuisance some nights when you come in late and you're exhausted and you have to set the whole thing up, move the table and everything, but you get used to it. And it's nice to fall asleep in front of the fire.'

'What do your family think of what you do?'

It struck her as an odd question, but she answered it anyway. 'I only have my father and he doesn't mind. He's quite indulgent towards me. That's him there.' She nodded towards a black and white photograph on the mantelpiece, and he noticed that even as she pointed to it her face relaxed. The photograph showed a small, jolly looking man in a dark coat, with a hat pushed back on his head at a rakish angle. A cigarette dangled from his lip and he was tugging on a piece of string, his cheerful glance skywards implying a kite on the other end of it. She smiled over as though acknowledging the presence of an actual person rather than a photograph.

'Does he have any interest in art himself?'

'None whatsoever. Can't understand it at all.'

'And doesn't that bother you?'

'No, why should it? If I'd studied to be a physicist and brought him into the lab to show him what I did, he wouldn't understand that either. It's just not his thing, you know? He has his own life, and he accepts that I have mine. He's always trusted me to know what my own best interests are and left me to make the big decisions for myself.'

'And do you always know best?'

'No; but I take full responsibility for my own mistakes when they do arise. What about you? Have you a family; children?'

'Yes. Two.' He took his wallet from the inside of his jacket pocket, flipped it open and passed it to her. There was a picture of Liz and the children on the inside flap, behind a rectangle of clear plastic. Julia took it and moved closer to the lamp to study it. He had noticed already how closely she looked at things: the cover of the book, the postcard and now the photographs. It was far from the cursory glance that most people gave. 'They look like they're the same age,' she said. 'Are they twins?'

He nodded.

'What are they called?'

'Sophie and Gregory.'

'Good Irish names,' she teased, but he was stung by this.

'What should we have called them?' he said. 'Brigid and Patrick?'

'You could have,' she said. 'It would have been unusual in their circle, I imagine.'

He wouldn't have expected this sly blow from her, but she was right. Liz had wanted to call the girl Kathleen after her own mother, the child to be known as Kitty, but William wouldn't hear tell of it. So bog-Irish a name, he said, it just wasn't possible. He wanted something more unusual and they eventually settled on Sophie; but it turned out that there were three others so called in her class at school.

'Sophie's a good name for a girl,' she said. 'Sophia. Holy Wisdom. The female aspect of the Holy Spirit.' Julia could see

59

to look at him now that he hadn't known this. 'How old are they?'

'Seven. That was taken a while ago, they're bigger now.'

'The boy looks a lot like you. And this is your wife?'

'Yes. That's Liz.'

'Thank you for showing it to me.' She handed the wallet back to him.

While she was looking at the photograph he realised that he wanted to tell her everything: that he too had wanted to be a painter, and how it was the failure of that – the realisation that his life was passing and he hadn't done it – that had in essence brought him here tonight. It had all been so gradual, his capitulation. He had read law to please his father, telling himself that once he had finished he would do as he wished. Then his results when he graduated had been so excellent that he bowed to pressure to follow through, to become fully qualified. Then there had been Liz, and marriage, and then gradually the life he had imagined for himself got pushed aside and another life took over. He became tired. Everyone became tired. Necessity wore people down, until just to keep their heads above water was as much as they could manage. Then a few years ago he had realised that the life he thought of as his real life was all an illusion, all a thing in his head, and that he had built around himself an impregnable reality, which was not compatible with the fantasy.

'Do you know why I came here?' he asked.

Julia studied him for a moment. 'Yes,' she said, 'I do. You came to bring the book back to me. And I'm very grateful.' There was nothing in her face to reveal what she was really thinking. 'I'll call a taxi for you, if you wish,' she said.

He didn't want to go, but it was clear that she didn't want him to stay. He wouldn't have minded leaving if there had been some opening, if she had given some signal that he might see her again. But then, he thought, why should she? His actual life had nothing in common with hers, his imagined life everything. All she could see was a man in a business suit, a man whose world was alien to her own.

She had found a number for a taxi company and was speaking softly into the phone, giving her address and phone number, asking for a car to Dalkey. Already he saw himself sitting in the back of the cab, moving through the city at night. She put the receiver down. 'It'll be here in five minutes.'

'I was planning to kill myself the day I met you.'

'Were you indeed?'

'Yes.'

'Then your children would have had no father. Did you think about that?' As she spoke she took up her cigarettes and lit one. She didn't offer them to him, but threw the packet and lighter back down on the table.

'I didn't, no.' If he was looking for sympathy, he had come to the wrong place.

'Sophie, Gregory,' she said. 'Maybe you should think about them. Maybe you should stop being selfish and think about other people for a change. From what I can gather, your life isn't a bad one. You've lots of things other people haven't got and won't ever have.'

'Such as?'

'Do you really need a stranger to tell you? Your wife. Your children. You have a job, I suppose, and enough money to live on; you have a fine home.'

'It's a brick box. It amounts to nothing. I hate my life and I hate myself.'

The vehemence with which he said this startled her, and at that there was the sound of a car horn from the street below. 'That's your cab.' He gathered up his affairs – she made sure that he had forgotten absolutely nothing – and she saw him down to the front door. There was a tremendous awkwardness to their parting. They both felt they had said the wrong things and now could not bring themselves to say anything more, not even goodbye. The cab driver gave them a sly smile, as though their tense and clumsy reticence on the doorstep was for his benefit but didn't fool him for a minute: he knew exactly what had been going on when a buttoned-up middle-aged businessman was leaving a young woman's house at near midnight.

'Dalkey, is it?'

'Dalkey,' William said. 'Drive out along by the edge of the sea.'

Chapter Eight

'Let me get this straight,' Roderic said. 'You're going to go and see some woman you've never met before to tell her that you think her husband, whom you met on a park bench, is having some kind of nervous breakdown?'

'I wouldn't have put it like that, but in essence I suppose, yes, that is what it amounts to,' Julia said.

'And you'll tell her as well that he came to see you at your home late at night?'

'Of course not. That would only worry and upset her.'

'I bet it would. Well, seeing as how you've told me all this, I can only presume you're asking me for advice and here it is: leave well alone. Don't get involved.'

They were sitting in the kitchen of Julia's house, having breakfast, and she had just told him everything about William. Although Roderic didn't say so, she suspected he wasn't particularly pleased about her having invited William into her flat late at night. 'If you tell her the whole story it'll do more harm than good; if you tell her only part of it – about meeting him on the Green – you'll get caught in all sorts of half truths and evasions. She'll only become suspicious and then where will you be?'

'I hoped you wouldn't take this attitude,' she said. 'I only want to help.'

'More trouble starts by people wanting to help than in any other way.'

In the days since William's visit to her house, the thought of his unhappiness had troubled her greatly. The resolution to do something about it had crystallised the preceding afternoon, in a supermarket, of all places. Standing in the queue, she watched idly as the woman in front of her set her shopping on the moving belt. Julia was aware how much she could extrapolate about the woman's life simply by looking at her purchases: gin, dog biscuits, a cake in the shape of a football, a bag of carrots already washed and chopped. The man behind the till rang the items up quickly and the woman hurried to put them in bags. To look at her confirmed what Julia had surmised: mid thirties, sober suit and briefcase, wedding ring and a cluster of diamonds. This will never be me, Julia thought; and at that, she suddenly perceived the other woman's life in all its strangeness and complexity, as though it were some remarkable, extravagant construct. A dream palace, absurdly ornate, all turrets and domes: that was what she was building. Julia saw her painstakingly painting her nails. She saw her paying a telephone bill; saw her collect her son from a football match. All of these actions, no matter how small or banal, contributed to maintaining the strange, elaborate artifice that would someday vanish, as though it had never been. And although the woman's life was alien to Julia – in many ways she was out of sympathy with the values that underpinned it – there was no denying its immense pathos.

The man behind the till rang up the total, and the woman took out a tan leather purse. She flicked it open and revealed a neat row of credit and cheque cards on one side, one of which she pulled out and handed to the man. On the other side of the wallet was the inevitable window, with the inevitable photographs, this time of a man and two children. And in that moment, Julia knew what she had to do.

'So you're going to ring her up,' Roderic said. 'What will you say to her in the first instance?'

'I'll tell her I want to talk to her about her husband.'

'She'll love that. Married women love it when a woman they don't know rings up to say that they want to talk to them about their husbands. I can just imagine how mine would have reacted.'

'I'll tell her I barely know him, that I'm almost a stranger.'

'And she, not unnaturally, will want to know who you are.'

'Roderic, you're not making this any easier.'

'I'm trying to make it as difficult as possible so that you'll drop the notion.'

'Well, my mind is made up. I'm going to do it.'

'All right then,' he said, 'do it. Do it now. Look her up in the phone book; ring her and arrange to meet.'

'I will,' she said. 'I'll do just that.' She stood up and moved to the door.

'Oh, and Julia?' he called after her.

'Yes?'

'Good luck.'

The cat hopped up into the chair she had vacated and Roderic sat listening. Through the closed doors he could hear her voice in the sitting room, but not her exact words, and his heart went out to her. She was well intentioned; he hoped her kindness wouldn't backfire. As she came back into the kitchen Roderic and the cat turned to look at her, as though both were anxious to hear how she had got on. The effect was comical, but Julia was in no mood to be amused.

'What on earth,' she said, 'am I getting into here?'

Standing in the hall of her home in Dalkey beside the longcase clock, Liz thought the ground had opened in front of her. Her hand was shaking so that she could barely replace the receiver. *You don't know me, but I need to talk to you. It's about your husband.* She had thought never to hear those words again. She went into the drawing-room and crossed to the window. The garden was in its own way as restrained as the room in which she stood: with its formal lines and cropped grass, it bore William's stamp. Liz would have preferred it to be wilder, for she liked trailing, straggling plants, sweet pea or honeysuckle. But he would have none of it, had objected even to the laburnum tree, because it grew at an angle. He was more overbearing than he knew, she often thought; in the house too, he subtly insisted on certain things: the sombre clock, the old dark furniture, the modern paintings she disliked. On the lawn a blackbird tugged at a tenacious worm. The idea that it could be the old problem back again was almost more than she could bear. She thought of all that had happened in recent weeks and tried to fit it like a template over her memory of that time.

When it started, all those years ago, she hadn't been able to put her finger on it, couldn't define even to herself what was happening. It wasn't, at first, anything William was doing but rather something he was. He'd been in a dream: she'd gradually realised that he was living in some kind of haze, as though he were sleepwalking through his days. And then when she realised she'd been wrong – he *was* doing something, the doing and being were linked – she'd chosen not to waken him, she'd chosen to join him in the haze. She'd been like a small child that thinks it cannot be seen because it has its eyes closed. She knew in time that William wanted to be woken up, but she determined not to do it. He wanted to be challenged and caught: that was part of the cruelty.

And so William would come back late at night.

'Where have you been until now?'

'Where do you think?' a question she didn't deign to answer. In time when he arrived back at midnight she would say nothing.

'Aren't you going to ask where I've been?'

'No.'

She suspected the woman worked with William, a suspicion confirmed on meeting Martin. The concerned way in which he'd taken her hand and held it, the way he said, 'Ah Liz, how are you at all?' told her everything she didn't want to know. ('Fine,' she'd replied, 'never better.') If he knew then Elaine knew. She brought up his name deliberately next time they met ('William's always so thoughtful') and the cold hostility of her reply ('Is he? Is he, indeed?') was final proof.

He'd become more audacious, had rung the woman from home. *Hannah? Is that you? Are you free to talk?* One night amongst the contents of his emptied pockets, left on a flat china dish he kept in the bedroom for that express purpose, she found a receipt from a restaurant, Quo Vadis. The name was a nice touch, she almost wished she could have remarked to him on the elegant irony of it. She scanned the listed dishes, despised herself for being able to know which were William's choices: melon and ham, cannelloni. It became ridiculous, the nadir possibly being the morning when she got into the car, and there was a golden earring, in the shape of a crescent moon.

It was left then to the other woman, Hannah, to act, and she must have been pretty desperate by that point. What had gone on between her and William before she had taken the final step of ringing Liz and forcing things into the open? *You don't know me but I need to talk to you. It's about your husband.*

And given that Liz had known so much at that point, she'd been taken aback by her own surprised rage, for in spite of everything it really was as if, until that moment, she hadn't known. Her sudden fury had shocked William too, who had at least the grace not to say 'But I thought you knew.' He arrived home from work that night to be attacked by Liz as soon as he opened the door. She tore at his hair, scratched his face, 'You pig, you pig,' and he'd tried to resist her without harming her, but then she was gone, out into the car, a scorching of tyres and over to Elaine and Martin's house. More tears there: 'I knew, I knew, I wanted to tell you but I didn't want you to be hurt.' But it was Elaine who in the long run had persuaded her to give her marriage another chance; and she took some persuading, again surprising herself at how reluctant she was to forgive William. She finally agreed to stay solely on condition that they would start a family, something he had long resisted. In time, Liz even felt sorry for the woman involved, who had

had the misfortune to get tangled up in William's mysterious pain. It had been so clear that he was acting out something that troubled him deeply, but that he barely understood, and Liz pitied her for having thought that anything could ever come of it. But was the same thing now happening again? In all honesty, she thought not. His present distress seemed of a different order, although she couldn't understand what was at the back of it.

Later that day, as Liz led Julia through the hall, past the longcase clock, the mirror and into the dining room, Julia though momentarily of her own flat, and how extraordinarily tatty it must have looked to someone who was used to all this. But she was too preoccupied with how the meeting was to go to take in more than a general sense of comfort and wealth, a dimness of rugs and silver.

'Do please sit down.'

On the chair facing her now was a small pale woman, about whom there was something soft and hesitant: not at all what Julia had expected, for Liz had been quite sharp when they'd spoken on the phone.

'You're quite sure we won't be disturbed?'

'Certain. William's out at the moment, he won't be back until much later.'

'Well, then, the first thing I had better say is that I hardly know your husband. To be honest, he's all but a stranger to me. But I met him recently and he was in a bad way, so much so that I thought it best that those close to him be told about it. Just, you know, in case anything happened.'

She paused, not knowing quite what to say next.

'Do please continue.'

And so, as circumspectly as she could, Julia described meeting William recently on Stephen's Green. She said he had been upset, and she had kept him company for a little while; they'd smoked a cigarette together and then he'd gone home. She omitted to say that she'd gone with him.

'Did he tell you anything about himself?'

'A little.'

'What did he say?'

'Oh we talked a bit about our families, our lives,' she said vaguely. 'Nothing of any great consequence.'

Liz stared hard at her. 'Was this Friday two weeks ago?' She nodded, and then Liz asked her exactly the same question Julia had asked William: 'How did you know where to find me?'

'Your husband told me his name and mentioned where he lived. I looked it up in the phone book. He was very upset; please believe me, that's why I came here today. Truly, he's a stranger to me still.'

In all of this, Liz felt there was something that didn't quite add up, but she didn't know what it was. She certainly didn't know what to make of this odd young woman.

'Friday, two weeks ago?' she said again.

'Yes.'

'And the following Thursday – late at night – can you shed any light on that? I think it was the last day of February.' At that, the phone rang in the hall. 'Excuse me, I'll be as quick as I can.'

Julia was immensely relieved by the interruption, saving her as it did from lies and evasion, for Thursday was the night William had visited her. Left alone now, she had her first chance to look around at the room in which she was sitting. Everything in it, burnished and glowing, bespoke money. The walls were painted a dark red that set off the gilt of the picture frames, and there was a vase containing a kind of flower Julia had never seen before, each stem bearing a tiny pointed cone of white blossom. Traditional in its overall style, with many antiques, the few modern pieces in the room were carefully chosen and perfectly integrated. On the table beside Liz's chair was a lamp made of sea urchins, next to it, a row of antique paperweights. They had the air of limpid, luminous creatures dredged up from the bottom of the ocean as the sea urchins, oddly, did not. There was a heavy scent of tuberose: some kind of room perfume, Julia guessed. Although she liked individual elements – the fine rugs, the delicate tables – the overall effect was stifling and oppressive; and suddenly she felt as though the strange dream palace she had imagined recently as a figure for another woman's life was a real place, and here she was in it.

She could still hear Liz talking in the hall. Turning her attention to the bookcase beside where she sat she found to her surprise that it contained a remarkably eclectic and interesting library of art books. There were catalogues, monographs, biographies and collections of criticism, covering all periods of art history but with a marked bias to the twentieth century and to contemporary work. So he hadn't been simply trying to flatter when he said he was interested in art, she thought, as she lifted down a volume on Joseph Cornell and leafed through it. She was not a covetous person – there was nothing else in the room she wanted – but for a moment she did envy William his fine cache of books. Replacing the volume, she stood up to look now at the pictures, which reflected the interests suggested in the bookcase and complemented the traditional nature of the room more harmoniously than she might have expected. There was a large fine nude in red chalk and a small abstract triptych of considerable power. Over by the window was a landscape painted in an expressionistic style, giving an idea of greenness, of vegetation and the heat of a summer's day rather than an accurate representation of trees and fields. It was slightly slapdash, but not at all bad. It wasn't an artist whose work she knew, and the signature was just a squiggle. She turned to walk back to where she had been sitting, and was utterly astounded by what she saw. There was no mistaking it: hanging on the wall behind the chair on which she had been sitting was one of Roderic's paintings.

She could tell it was not a recent work, both from the colours – blues and greens, much more intense than the pale tones in which he now worked – and from the style, which was looser, less rigorous than it had become of late. It was a fine painting for all that, full of energy and confidence, and she was still standing there, gazing at the fields of colour, when Liz came back into the room.

'I was just admiring your painting.'

'That thing? Do you like it?'

'I do, actually,' Julia said, offended on Roderic's behalf by Liz's tone.

'It's William's pride and joy. He bought it years ago, wouldn't part with it for anything. It means a lot to him for some odd reason.'

'And the other picture?' she asked, pointing at the landscape over by the window.

'He did that himself.'

'William? William paints?'

'He used to,' Liz said. 'He doesn't have time now.' She indicated that Julia might sit down again. 'I think you've been straight with me, so I'm going to be straight with you. William had a kind of . . . collapse, I suppose you could call it, earlier this week. It has been in the offing for some time now – and yes, I had noticed. He's taken time off work; he's been to see doctors. He's getting good care, and I know he'll be fine in the long run.'

'Good,' Julia said, and she meant it. 'Good.' She stood up, and suddenly Liz knew exactly what it was that she reminded her of. It was a wild animal: not in the sense of her being dangerous or violent, for she was if anything rather a gentle person. But she had about her that otherness of a small creature that one might see in a forest, going about its life without feeling in any way linked to people. There was about her a kind of completeness that didn't need to explain itself.

'Goodbye,' Julia said. 'I'm glad I came. I'm sure now that your husband won't come to any harm.' And this remark, which was meant to comfort, had exactly the opposite effect, finally getting through to Liz the message she had come to bring. Only now did she see the danger that William was in, that had been apparent to this stranger, but not to his own wife.

Chapter Nine

Even after they had all grown up, and Dennis and Roderic no longer lived at home, they were still expected to return every Saturday for family lunch. Apart from their now partaking of a bottle of Côtes du Rhône during the meal (it didn't go far amongst six) and Frank occasionally inviting his sons (but not his daughters) to join him in a glass of whiskey afterwards, the proceedings bore, Dennis thought, an eerie similarity to what they had been when they were all children. It didn't bring out the best in them.

'Open the wine, will you, Maeve?' Frank said. She removed the foil from the neck of the bottle, then handed it silently with the corkscrew to Roderic, who without comment opened it. Frank was busy carving.

Sinéad, setting a dish of carrots on the table, chided her younger son gently for his scuffed shoes and the paint on his leather jacket. 'You should wear nice clothes. Don't you have any nice clothes?'

'I didn't have time to change, I was working.'

'But you don't teach on a Saturday.'

'I mean, I was in the studio.'

'Oh. Well, you could at least take your jacket off while you're at table.'

As he did so and went to hang it over the back of his chair, a book fell out of the pocket. Cliona bent down and picked it up, remarking as she handed it to him, '*Art as Art*. What a silly title. What does it mean?'

'I'll tell you when I've read it,' he said, taking it from her and replacing it in his jacket pocket. 'I wanted to ask you Mum, would you mind if I only came to lunch every other Saturday?' He could see by her face that she would: that she'd mind very much. 'It's just that I have so little time for my own work, and it breaks up one of only two free days . . . Oh well, it was just a thought.'

'This looks delicious, Mum,' Cliona said.

'Thank you, dear. I hope you all enjoy it.'

'You look done in, Roderic,' Frank said, sending plates of beef up the table. 'What have you been up to?'

'I'm just very busy these days, what with the job and then my own work, that's all.'

'What time did you get to bed last night?' his mother asked.

'I really don't remember,' he replied looking rather irritated, as well he might, Dennis thought, being asked such questions at the age of twenty-two.

'What was her name?' Maeve said slyly.

Roderic thought about this for a moment and decided to stir the pot. 'To tell you the truth, I can't quite remember. I think she said it was Beth, but I couldn't swear to it.'

'Roderic!' Sinéad exclaimed, genuinely shocked. 'Frank, don't laugh. What sort of talk is this at all?'

'Well, seeing as how you're all so fascinated with my life,' he said, uncharacteristically ratty, 'let me fill you in. I don't remember what time I got to bed last night, but do know I was in the studio and painting by half eight this morning. I'm here now. This afternoon I'm going to help Tony and Jim to clean the flat. I'm going to go to the launderette and then I'm going to buy in a load of groceries for the week. After that, I'm going to correct twenty-seven essays by twenty-seven teenagers on the difference between Impressionism and post-Impressionism, in not one of which, I can tell you now, will there be a single original thought. After all that, if he will be so good as to join me, I'm going to drag myself down to the pub and have a few pints with Dennis. Tomorrow I'll spend in the studio, and Monday I'll be back in the classroom. Have you all got that? Any questions? May I now get on with eating my lunch?'

Dennis had seen his brother by chance in town one day during the week. He was stopped at the traffic lights in Merrion Square when he noticed Roderic ahead of him, at the gates of the National Gallery ushering a class of uniformed schoolgirls back on to a coach. Dennis had tooted the car horn in recognition before he thought better of it; thought Roderic might be embarrassed by this show of sibling affection when he was in the presence of his pupils. Not a bit of it. Clearly delighted, he lifted his hand to Dennis, then got on to the coach and evidently said to the girls, 'That's my brother in the blue car, give him a wave,' for as the traffic lights changed, and Dennis drove past the coach, every window was a forest of frantic, waving hands. Some of the girls blew him teasing kisses. The effect was hilarious and made Dennis, shy, staid Dennis, feel famous and loved, and he laughed out loud alone in the car for sheer pleasure.

He told Roderic in the pub on Saturday night how much this little encounter had entertained him. 'I love the kids,' he said in reply, 'I absolutely love them. Until you've sat in a darkened room with a class of fourteen-year-old girls, showing them slides of the Sistine Chapel, you haven't lived.'

'I'm glad to hear things are going well,' Dennis said. 'I sort of got a different impression over lunch.'

'Yes and no. It's hard to say.'

After he graduated from art college, Roderic took a teaching qualification and then applied for a job in the school in south Dublin where both Cliona and Maeve had been pupils. He had secured a year's contract and this was how he planned to earn his living, devoting his free time to his painting. In theory it had sounded fine. In practice he was frustrated by having much less space and energy for his painting than he had expected would be the case. On top of that, he now told Dennis, he was beginning to realise that he had made a serious mistake at the start of the academic year

75

by letting it be known – or rather, by not actively concealing the fact – that there *was* other work, that he was privately dedicated to painting. It surprised then unnerved and irritated him as the months passed, to notice the subtle and insidious way this was held against him. He was well organised, he knew, hardworking and punctual, but on the rare occasions when he did overlook or forget something, little jokes would be made about 'our dreamy artist, with his head in the clouds' that had amused him until he came to realise the criticism implicit in them. The headmistress would go out of her way to suggest that exceptions were being made for him, while Roderic thought the exact opposite was true: that it was incumbent upon him to reach higher standards than were expected of the other teachers, simply to counter the unspoken implication that he didn't pull his weight and wasn't fully committed to the job. He felt, too, that his considerable popularity with the pupils was also resented and silently held against him. All of this was wearing him down, he said to Dennis.

'It's the whole ethos,' he added. 'It's lots of little things. And it's the staffroom, not the classroom. Let me give you an example: Rory Wilson, one of the maths teachers. Nice man, not the worst in there, not by a long way. I was busy at break time the other day so I took a mug of tea back up the art department, as I didn't have time to drink it in the staffroom. Two days later Rory comes to me and says, "Roderic, I think you have my mug. It's got a rabbit on it. Do you think you could bring it back down here some time?"' Roderic put his head in his hands. 'This is a grown man, Dennis, a man of thirty-five. He has an honours degree from Trinity in maths, and he's fretting about his rabbit mug. I mean, can you believe it? I lay awake that night thinking, if I stay in this job, will that be me when I'm his age?'

'So are you thinking then that you might not apply for the permanent post when it comes up, as you'd been planning to do?'

'God, yes, I'll be putting in for that all right, Dennis. I mean, this is my job now. It's only the first year, after all. Things will settle down, it's bound to get better.'

Dennis nodded his head, but looked doubtful. They each took a sip of their pints and fell silent.

Just at that moment Roderic happened to glance up as a young woman turned away from the bar counter with two glasses in her hand.

'Why hello, Aideen.'

'Mr Kennedy! Oh shit!'

He ignored this odd, rude greeting and smiled at her. She was wearing a short pale blue woollen dress, trimmed with marabou at the neck. Her eyes were sooty with mascara, her lips painted a dramatic film-star red. All of this made her look absurdly young, although clearly she had intended it to have exactly the opposite effect. 'Fancy meeting you here,' Roderic said. 'You're not on your own?' And he indicated the two glasses.

'I'm with Colette. She's sitting over there,' she said, pointing across the bar.

'Why don't you join us? Go over and fetch her; I'll mind your drink. Two of my pupils,' he explained to Dennis after she had gone. 'I think they're a bit embarrassed at bumping into one of their teachers in the pub.'

'How old are they?' Dennis asked as he watched them cross the room towards where the brothers were sitting.

'Fourteen, fifteen, at the most. Hello, Colette. What a surprise. This is my brother, Dennis, sit in there beside him, have you room?' They settled in at the table together.

Colette, like Aideen, was conspicuously dressed up and made up; she looked even younger than her friend. They fluttered and giggled. Together they looked like small coloured birds from a tropical rainforest, and Roderic admired their finery. 'I like your dress; the feathers are great. Don't they tickle, though?' he asked. 'Are you going dancing afterwards? Where?' They chatted to him and gradually

77

relaxed, but were shy of Dennis, who was shy of them. He tried to imagine standing before twenty-five such girls, teaching them art – teaching them anything – and felt weak even at the thought of such an ordeal. He could see how attractive and engaging they found Roderic, as they stared at him with a somewhat hypnotised fascination.

'Can I ask you something, Mr Kennedy? Somebody told me that you were a real painter, not just a teacher, that you have a studio and everything. Is that true?'

'It is, but I don't get to do as much of my own work as I'd like to. I'm too busy teaching you lot.'

'I'd love to see that, I mean a real artist's studio,' said Colette, who was slightly more forward than Aideen. 'Do you think you might take us and show us some day?'

'Probably not,' he said frankly, 'but you've just given me a good idea. I have some friends who are part of an artists' co-operative in town. About six of them have studios in the one building, and they're having an open day in about a month's time. Maybe I could arrange to take your class along; you'd get to see all sorts of different work, get to talk to the painters. Would you like that?' They nodded their consent. He asked them if they had enjoyed the gallery the other day, and which of the paintings they had particularly liked.

'This is very pleasant,' he said eventually. 'Wasn't it lucky that it was me you met, rather than one of the other teachers?'

'God, yes,' Aideen said. 'Mr O'Hara,' and they both giggled.

'Or Miss Davis,' Colette suggested and they exploded into laughter.

Roderic bit his lip and frowned. 'I can't imagine Miss Davis is a great woman for the pub,' he said, 'although then again, you never know. After all,' he added reasonably, 'I certainly never expected to see *you* here.'

They chatted for a short while more, then he looked at his watch and said, 'I think you should maybe be on your way. It's your round next and Dennis usually moves on to shorts at this stage in the evening, so it could cost you dear.' They parted in good spirits, and Dennis was surprised when Roderic almost immediately fell into a gloom, a brown study.

'You handled that very well.'

'No I didn't. I should have taken their beer off them and set them on the street as soon as I saw them.'

'They'd only have said, "Sod you," and gone straight off to the pub up the road.'

'That argument would never stand up in a disciplinary hearing,' Roderic said, 'which doesn't mean to say that you're not absolutely right. And what if some other member of staff had walked in and seen me, apparently sitting drinking with a couple of fourteen-year-old pupils? That would have looked nice.'

'I never thought of that,' Dennis confessed.

'Well, I did. I was thinking of nothing else the whole time that I was talking to them. And yet you can see, they're not a bit streetwise, that pair. I made a snap decision that the best, the safest place for them was to sit here with us. I'm a hopeless disciplinarian. Absolutely hopeless.' They sat in silence for a few more minutes. 'They're sweet kids, though, aren't they?' he said. 'You couldn't not like them.' He covered his face with his hands and started to laugh. 'God, I almost let the side down when they mentioned Miss Davis. I was in kinks, Dennis, absolute kinks, I didn't think I was going to be able to hold it in. You'd have to know the woman. I'd say the last time Vivian Davis was in a pub the Book of Kells had just come out in hardback.

'By the way,' he went on, 'there's a call I must make. Do you know where the phone is in this pub?' Dennis said that it was in the lobby between the door of the lounge and the front door of the building. 'Won't be a minute.' As Roderic went out he collided with one of two women who were coming into the pub together. Both Roderic and the woman were moving at speed, and they made full impact, head on, from shoulder to knee. 'Oh, excuse me!' Roderic said as they extricated themselves from each other. 'I do beg your pardon.' But he had clearly enjoyed the accident and gave the woman a look and a lingering smile that told her so before continuing on out to the phone.

The two women stood there for a moment, then collapsed into giggles. They were standing right beside Dennis, who had observed all of this. 'Oh, I liked *that*,' said the woman with whom Roderic had collided. 'I've had sex that wasn't anywhere near as good as that. I wonder who he is?' and she peered at the frosted glass of the door behind which he had disappeared. Still laughing, the two women proceeded through the lounge and into the public bar.

He felt that Roderic would be flattered and amused to hear what had happened, but when he came back Dennis was too shy and embarrassed to tell him. Roderic himself made no reference to the women, although Dennis noticed how his eyes scanned the room looking for them.

'To get back to what we were talking about earlier: I have to actually do an interview for this job, and I wondered if you could lend me a tie?'

'You mean to say you don't have one?'

'I do. I have at least two, but I can't find one of them, and the other one isn't up to much.' Dennis could imagine the sorry shred of fabric behind this euphemism.

'Absolutely no problem,' he said. 'I can certainly lend you a tie.'

He could have gone to a shop, Roderic thought, and not had as good a choice. There were ties of every imaginable colour and texture. Watched by Dennis, who was sitting on the end of his own bed, he selected one in plain dark green silk and moved to the mirror to experiment in tying it.

'Is anyone else in line for this job?'

'I think three others have been called for interview. They couldn't just give it to me, the permanent contract, they have to advertise it, go through the formalities, you know.'

Dennis paused before risking the next question. 'And what if you don't get it?' He was dismayed to see that this possibility hadn't even crossed Roderic's mind.

'What are you on about? It's my job.'

'Yes, but they don't *have* to give it to you, do they?'

'They have no reason not to.' He was clearly baffled by Dennis's line of questioning. 'I've put in a good year, worked like a horse. Everyone says how much the girls' work has picked up, that I've transformed the department. Even the other art teachers would credit me with that.'

'But in principle, they would be within their rights to give the contract to someone else.'

'In principle, yes,' he conceded, with great reluctance, 'but I mean, God, do you really think . . . ?'

When he arrived at his parents' house the following Saturday, Roderic was already there, sitting alone in the drawing-room. From his inside jacket pocket he took a letter, and handed it to Dennis.

Dear Mr Kennedy,

I regret to inform you that it has been decided not to offer you a permanent contract. May I take this opportunity to thank you for your efforts in the course of the past year, and to wish you every success in your future career.

Yours truly,

B. Nolan

'Efforts,' Roderic said, as Dennis handed the letter back to him. '*Efforts!*'

At that, Cliona glanced into the room. 'Oh hello Dennis, I don't think Mum knows you're here. I'll tell her she can serve up.'

'This,' Roderic said when they were alone again, and he held up the letter, 'was in my pigeon-hole in the staffroom. The headmistress didn't even have the courage to tell me to my face. So I went straight to her office and asked why it had "been decided" not to offer me the post. She said they felt that for various reasons – I liked that, various reasons – it was felt that I wasn't fully committed to my teaching work. I told her she knew that wasn't true. So then she said, "You're pushing me to this: you have a bad attitude to the pupils. You over-identify with them, you're too keen to be liked." I said, "You know that isn't true either. I don't see the need to be disliked by them to bring out the best of which they're capable; and that's another thing entirely from wanting to be liked." She told me to stop contradicting her. I asked her what I was going to live on. She said she had no idea, and that it wasn't her concern. Then she had the nerve to say that she thought I would be glad, because it would give me time for other things in which I was interested. And then she said she was busy and would I go, and so I did.'

'And what has the reaction been generally in the school?'

'The girls are up in arms. My two drinking companions came to me in floods of tears, they thought it might have something to do with them. Quite a few of the other teachers have come to me privately to say they think that it's outrageous, and I've been treated disgracefully and the head and the governors should be ashamed, and so on and so forth. For of course none of it will make a blind bit of difference. No one will speak up for me in public or do anything to have me reinstated, because they're afraid for their own skins. Fear and power, that's what so much of what goes on in the workplace comes down to, Dennis. I've learned that in the past year, if nothing else. And here comes the cherry on the cake: Tony announced yesterday that he's going to buy a house. Jim is moving in with Moira, so that's that happy home blown to the four winds. I don't even know where I'm going to live come the autumn.' Down the hall, they could hear the voices of their sisters and mother. 'Jesus, Dennis, I've lost my job!' and he spoke as if he was only now realising the enormity of what had happened. 'I've lost my job; what am I going to do?'

The response was out before Dennis had even thought about it.

'Well, you could always come and live with me.'

Chapter Ten

There was no sign of life from the little house. No smoke from the chimney, the blue door shut, and all the curtains drawn as though it were a house of mourning, which, coincidentally, it was. This aspect of the windows gave the façade a blank, shut look; but for all that it looked perfected in the preternaturally sharp light of morning, pristine, rinsed. Henry stood for some moments staring at it, and wondering what he should do. He could simply put the letters through the door and continue on his round. Lifting the black painted metal flap he slipped in a phone bill and a white envelope, heard them fall on to the floor within. He listened in expectation for the sound of footsteps as someone came to pick up the letters, but there was only silence now. All around the house there were hedges of wild fuchsia, vivid, dripping red blossoms after the night's rain. There was no wind. The orchard was utterly still, the twisted trees, to Henry's eyes, weird and strange, pregnant with small fruit. Birdsong.

He lifted the black knocker, let it fall once, waited, listened and was about to knock once more when suddenly the door opened. Standing in the hall beside the two envelopes, one buff, one white, was a frowsy child. She was five, maybe six, wild-haired and sleepy-eyed; shoeless but otherwise fully dressed.

'Morning, Princess. Are you long up? You don't look it.'

'Hello, Henry.'

'Is your da in?'

Yawning, the child nodded, held the door open wide for him, and he followed her through to the kitchen. The curtains here were also closed, but as his eyes became accustomed to the half light, Henry could see that there was a man sleeping on the sofa. He was covered with a quilted eiderdown, part of which, at his side, was bunched to form a kind of nest, a hollow, like the warm empty depression a small sleeping animal might have left pressed into long grass by the side of the road. There was a sinkful of unwashed dishes, and an unwrapped loaf on the bare board of the kitchen table. A bag of sugar sat sodden and split in a puddle of spilt tea. Before the sleeping man was an overflowing ashtray, a glass and an empty whiskey bottle. Henry stood in silence looking at these things, reading their meaning as fluently and profoundly as a scholar might have read the symbolism in a vanitas painting. He moved to speak, but the child theatrically held an index finger against her shut lips, and indicated the sleeping man. Henry hunkered down in front of her.

'Look at that for a face,' he whispered. 'You'd scare a goat off its tether. Away upstairs and give yourself a wash.' Without another word and with seeming obedience she trotted out of the kitchen, but took care not to close the door properly behind her. Half-way up the stairs she stopped and sat down to listen.

There was the brisk, whishing sound of curtain rings against a curtain rail, then a low groan. 'Dan? Dan? It's me, Henry.' *Whish*: the second set of curtains. 'C'mon now, wakey wakey. Shake a leg.' Another groan, a request to know what time it was, and then, noticing that the child was missing, an urgent, almost panicked demand to know where she was, and Henry's voice, calm, reassuring, saying that she had gone upstairs. The sound of the tap, of water running, of the kettle being filled and set on the hob. 'Are you out of smokes? Here, catch.' The sound of a match being dragged across the rough side of the matchbox, the small explosion of it igniting, then, momentarily, silence.

'Right now, Dan, listen to me. This isn't going to do. Look at the state of the place.'

'I'm doing my best.'

85

'Aye, well, that's as may be, but you're still going to have to do better.'

A pause, then her father's voice. 'It's only six months,' and Henry's response, surprisingly brutal:

'How long do you want? How long is it going to take?'

'I'll never get over it.'

'Aye, well,' Henry said again, 'that's the point, you're going to have to.' A pause, and then: 'The thing is this: if you don't get yourself sorted out, you might lose her in the long run, the child. They might take her off you.' Vehement protests at this, anger mixed with fear, into which Henry cut dismissively almost at once. 'Oh you can say that, Dan, you can say that. Talk's cheap. Say it wasn't me showed up at your door this morning, your old friend Henry. Say it was a social worker. What then?'

'It's not that bad.'

'Child sleeping fully dressed all night on a sofa with you – with you, mind – empty whiskey bottle on the floor. Not that bad – social worker sees worse every day in the week, but it doesn't look too good either, does it? And my point is this: what'll it be like in another six months? A year? Six years?' He spoke quietly now. 'The teachers are noticing, Dan. Everybody's noticing. My Felim's in Julia's class. Said she came in the other day in two odd socks and her jumper on back to front, the label sticking up to her chin. Two days later, she fell asleep at her desk: sound asleep. They had to put her in the bookstore with a rug over her for the rest of the afternoon, and she only woke up when it was time to go home. Now if you was Lord Muck and had a pot of money you might just get away with it; they'd give you the benefit of the doubt. But you, you, working man, on your own, bringing up a child: if you can't manage it, don't expect sympathy, 'cos you won't get any. They'll take Julia away from you, and do you know what you'll be able to do to stop them? Sweet fuck all. Have you got that, Dan? Have you got that?'

Dan mended his ways. He got his drinking under control and instigated a stricter regimen in the house under which Julia, a traditionalist and arch-conservative like all children, flourished and thrived. In his grief he had been indulgent to her, and she hadn't liked it; had been cool about the dolls and bears and chocolates with which he showered her, as a cheated wife takes no pleasure in the flowers and jewellery her husband buys to placate his own guilt. She was six. He fixed regular bed-times and meal-times, established a routine, but left latitude within the order, so that when he went once to buy a sliced loaf in the local shop and saw a mango, he bought that too, because he had never seen one before. When a family of hedgehogs wandered up to the house late on a pale summer night, he woke her out of a sound sleep to come and see them, to give them milk.

For all that, he never became a paragon of domestic management. The local women who found occasion to drop in noticed his slightly slapdash housekeeping. Dan noticed them notice, and Julia in turn took all of this in, closed her heart against women, for whom her father would never quite come up to the mark.

When school ended for the day, she would walk the short distance to the garage where her father worked as a motor mechanic, to wait there until such time as his day was also over and they could go home together. Usually she sat in the stuffy glass box that was the office, where Edward, warmed by a gas fire, presided over a high clacking typewriter and a black Bakelite phone. She read a book or a comic, did her homework, or drew pictures with the paper and pens with which Edward furnished her. When bored with this, she would go out and dawdle around the garage, watching the men as they worked. What she liked best was to see things being welded. The radiant white light dripped and blazed; threw high, flickering shadows up to the vaulted roof of the garage, making of the place a sudden temple. The man with the welding torch, in his curious long metal mask, was the high priest of some archaic rite, the fitters his acolytes. And amongst all this Julia wandered, little vestal, isolated from her own sex but conscious already that from her loss came a certain power over men, from whom she expected nothing but kindness.

'See you tomorrow, Dan. Bye, Julia.'

'Cheerio, lads.'

Dan's fear that she might be taken from him atrophied, but in its place grew a more potent terror: that *he* might be taken from *her*. This was not an irrational thought, which made it all the worse. Last spring he had sat at the kitchen window and watched Julia and her mother together in the orchard, wading through the thick cow parsley beneath a canopy of apple blossom. Now he sat and watched Julia alone. What if something was to happen to him? What then? How would she cope? He fretted silently about this, and could not bring himself to talk about it with anyone, not even with Henry or Edward, his closest friends. She was a good child, mature and companionable, not weepy or clingy, and he could only pray that she would stay that way. He would teach her, he resolved, to be capable. He would teach her to cycle and to swim. He would show her how to run a bank account and to make tax returns. As soon as she was old enough he would buy her a tool box, spanners, her own drill. They would do simple car mechanics, move on to basic plumbing. She would learn to drive. He would ensure she had a good education. In his heart Dan knew that, useful as these skills would be, they were not enough to protect her from what it was that he feared for her, as his own competence had not saved him.

The night before it happened, he had gone outside to look at the stars. He often did this. 'Don't get lost in space,' she'd called after him, teasing. How delicate the sky looked, how fragile its beauty! Far, far above the trees of the orchard, he picked out the constellations he knew: Orion's Belt, the Plough, Cassiopeia. Standing there at the gable of the house, he knew who he was and where he was and what he was. He was fixed and rooted in his place in time: Dan Fitzpatrick, living out his years with his wife and daughter in Ireland, in Wicklow, as the twentieth century ended. The ancient sky was charged for him with the memory of the countless men and women who had also looked at the stars down the years, down the centuries. Now they were so completely forgotten that to think of them, as he did, was not true remembrance but an act of imagination. That this would be his fate too did not disturb him, but consoled him rather. He felt close to these men who worshipped strange gods, to these women who spoke dead languages.

But after what happened to her, everything changed. He couldn't bear to look at the night sky. It became to him a thing of horror. Looking at the stars, he felt atomised and helpless, adrift in time itself. There was only him, only Julia, they were two specks of dust in the immensity of the universe. Her teasing warning had come true: he *was* lost in space. No longer could he feel the silent presence of the ancient people; and the loneliness was overwhelming. Stunned, winded, he beat a retreat.

Dan spoke of this to no one. He knew that others would assess his grief against another measure, but that until he could look again at the night sky, he would not know peace. It seemed to him impossible that the pain would ever diminish. It did happen, but not until many years later.

By then, he understood that he was already living in eternity.

Chapter Eleven

The place was open; the thick metal grille he remembered from his nocturnal visit folded back. Then he had peered through the bars, this time he could see all too clearly. And there was Julia herself sitting in the shop. He had hoped that this would be so, had come over to this part of the city with the express wish of seeing her again, even though he was reluctant to admit as much, even to himself. But now that he was so close to his goal, he felt a mild sense of panic and confusion. For a moment he considered simply walking on; but surely she would have noticed him by now, lurking on the pavement. She might think his behaviour odd or even slightly sinister if he didn't follow through, and so he forced himself to go in.

Not only had she not seen him on the street, she failed to notice him immediately when he walked into the shop. Julia, who to William's considerable disappointment was not alone, was seated on a particularly tall wooden chair with arms and a short back, like a barstool from a rather grand pub. The chair lifted her high above her companion, a middle-aged man who was sunk down in a low wing-backed armchair, upholstered in faded floral stuff. Their chairs were at some distance from each other, and on his knees the man was holding a wooden solitaire board, with coloured stones instead of the usual glass marbles. As William closed the door behind him, a longcase clock struck the hour, and in the light of its presence the whole shop appeared to him suddenly as a strange subverted version of his own home. There were the same rugs and sconces, the same blue and white china, the same delicate tables and solid chairs, even the same kind of fireplace, with coloured tiles and long brass fire irons lying on the fender. In his own front room all these objects were arranged with care and restraint, but here they were packed together higgledy-piggledy, any old way, with this rather strange couple lolling in the middle of it all. The effect was, he thought, highly disconcerting.

Julia, who was smiling over at the other man, slowly broke her gaze and turned to look at the newcomer. 'It's you!' she exclaimed. William wanted to flee but she waved him in. He had imagined a dozen times meeting her again, but not in this scenario, and not in this mood, for there was an odd atmosphere in the shop, something he couldn't quite define. 'This is Roderic Kennedy,' she said. 'Roderic, William Armstrong.' The man in the chair gave a brief nod in William's direction. Roderic Kennedy the painter: it had to be him, William remembered photographs he had seen from catalogues in the past. He wondered momentarily if he should mention how much he liked his work, but Roderic looked as though he would be indifferent to anything William might have to say.

'Feel free to look around. Hester had to go out for a moment,' Julia said, as though she thought William had come to buy antiques. 'We're minding the place.'

'No, we're not,' Roderic said, 'we're just innocent bystanders. Max is in charge.'

For the first time William noticed that the cat was also there, sitting bolt upright beside the empty grate. 'You might not believe it but that cat,' Roderic said solemnly, 'is an expert – that cat is a *world authority* – on Georgian silver.' Julia laughed, out of all proportion, William thought, given the silliness of the joke. It was the middle of the afternoon, and William wondered if perhaps she had been drinking. He remembered reading an article about Roderic in the paper once that alluded to his having a drink problem; he certainly had a toper's face. 'It's true,' Roderic said, 'He's an expert, aren't you, Max? Wouldn't you know it to look at him?' At that moment, the cat put its head on one side and closed its eyes. The effect was comical, as though the animal was pleased but embarrassed to have its erudition spoken of so publicly, and both Roderic and Julia exploded with laughter. There was something about their mirth that made William feel he couldn't join in; that he wasn't supposed to.

'I'm going to test you now,' Roderic said to Julia, 'see how well you know your semiprecious stones.' From the solitaire board on his lap, he took up a translucent purple sphere.

'Amethyst.'

He replaced it, held up another one, this time of an opaque, dense, radiant blue.

'Lapis.'

They continued in this fashion as though William wasn't there, Roderic slowly holding up the coloured stones in silence and Julia naming them. 'Rose quartz . . . Alabaster . . . Chalcedony.' They hadn't been drinking. They had been in bed, William realised as he watched. The cluttered shop was full of the sense of them together, and the physical distance between them only heightened the strangely erotic nature of the little game they were playing with the stones. 'Agate . . . Moonstone . . . Obsidian.' Roderic looked at her quizzically. 'Jet?' she said. 'It could be jet. You don't know either, do you?' He shook his head and they both laughed, again in that closed, complicit way. William might have been able to settle the question for them, but he wasn't asked.

Julia stretched out and reached into a basin of pot-pourri on a dresser beside her chair. She stirred it idly with her hand, releasing into the air a warm scent of cloves, orange peel, resin and cones, enhancing, whether unwittingly or not, the charged atmosphere. It reminded William of just such an episode in his own life, many years earlier; of being in a hotel room in Seville with Liz. Something there had that same faint scent of citrus and spice: perhaps the soap provided in the bathroom, perhaps the perfume Liz was wearing. It was a hot afternoon, the powerful light seeping in even through the closed shutters. Everything in the dim room was white: the walls, the curtains, the marble tiles, and the sheets of the bed on which he was making love with Liz. He remembered the feeling of being deep within her, the exquisite tension of the moment just before he came.

He was shaken at the memory; so sudden was it, so vivid and intense, that when Julia turned to him now and said, 'And you, William, how have you been since last I saw you?' the question confused him. For a moment he could not speak.

'Fine,' he said at last, but he could hear his own voice become unsteady. There was no reason for this, he told himself. He could take protection from the fact that Roderic was here, saving him from a kind of confidence that he wanted with Julia, but that also made him feel uneasy. 'Well, not bad,' he qualified his earlier remark. 'I'm very tired. I've taken some time off work at the moment. That helps. I'll be all right. I'm going to London soon for the weekend.'

'With your wife?'

'With Liz, yes.'

There was a pause. 'You're the painter, aren't you?' William blurted out.

He was keen by now to deflect attention from himself but his appeal to the other man's vanity failed, as Roderic merely glanced at him, then looked away again and said quietly, 'I'm a painter, yes.'

'William has –' Julia started, but at that a most bizarre thing happened. She stopped speaking abruptly, almost violently, as though an invisible hand had gagged her from behind. The two men stared at her, mystified.

'Well?' Roderic asked after a moment, as she did not continue. 'What were you going to say? William has what?'

'I don't know. I can't remember. It's gone.'

'It must have been a lie,' Roderic said coolly.

'I'm very interested in contemporary painting,' William said.

'That's what I was going to say,' Julia claimed, adding, 'you told me so the last time I saw you.'

Neither man believed her. William was about to add that he owned one of Roderic's paintings, and then he thought again of the strange aborted sentence Julia had uttered. A curious idea formed in his mind. There was a certain logic to it, but she didn't know about the picture. How could she? He definitely hadn't mentioned it to her. In one way it made perfect sense, but she didn't, couldn't know. He stared at her, puzzled, and she bit her lip, blushed, looked away. 'Yes,' he said, 'art is my main interest in life.'

'If that's the case,' Roderic said, 'you should go and see Julia's work. She's in a group exhibition that opened last week,' and he named the gallery. 'It runs until the end of April.'

'I shall most certainly do that,' William said, addressing Julia. 'I'd very much like to see what you do.'

Roderic had already lost interest in William and turned away, lifted the solitaire board off his lap and picked up a flat leather case that was sitting nearby. 'Aren't these fine?' he said, snapping it open, and holding it up to show her the enamelled antique buttons it contained. 'When my ship comes in I'll buy you these. You can sew them on to your jumper; won't they look stylish?'

Julia laughed. 'How much longer is this woman going to be?' she said, turning to look at the moon-crowned face of the tall clock. 'Would you like to come up for a cup of coffee with us when she does come back?'

Roderic snapped shut the case. 'Maybe that wouldn't be such a good idea,' he said in a voice so low as to be almost inaudible, but William did hear: he was meant to hear. He could imagine the state of the room upstairs, the dishevelled, abandoned bed that wasn't even a bed.

'On second thoughts, maybe not,' she said. 'There's . . . um . . . there's no milk.'

'No milk! There's never any milk, is there, Julia? Or else there is, but there isn't enough. Or there's plenty, but it's all sour. I tell you what, as well as the buttons I'll buy you a cow, then there'll always be milk. We can tether it on the stairs. What do you say?'

And then Roderic did something that shocked William. He stood up. Unfurling himself out of the depths of the low chair, he revealed himself to be impossibly tall, impossibly robust, massive to a degree William would never have guessed at when he saw him seated. It was like watching a river god step out from a carving on the side of a bridge; like watching Poseidon or Triton emerge living from amongst the statues of a baroque fountain.

The cat walked over and sat at his feet. 'Max, Max, Max,' he said, 'come here to me, you great old patriarch.' He bent down and scooped up the cat, which had looked dignified and magisterial when sitting on its own, but now looked tiny and kittenish in Roderic's great hand. He allowed Max to run nimbly up one arm, across the back of his neck and down the other, catching the cat dextrously as it reached his open left hand. He carefully placed the animal in the chair he had just vacated and as he straightened up again, he turned and looked at William. His brief, direct stare was full of intelligence but devoid of warmth. This glacial assessment – this hostility – was the last thing William expected after the horseplay with the cat. Which was why Roderic was doing it, he realised: he was warning William off. And Julia didn't even appear to notice that anything had happened.

'I must be going,' William said. As he left the shop the longcase clock chimed again.

Roderic and Julia watched him through the window as he walked away. 'So that's your mercy mission,' he said. 'So that's William Armstrong.'

'Why didn't you like him?'

Roderic didn't deny the implication of this. 'He made me feel uneasy.'

'I suspect you had the same effect on him.'

'I may well have done,' he conceded. 'There was something sinister about him, I don't know how to express it.'

95

'You think he's just a dabbler, do you?'

'I doubt if he's even that. But yes, he's a classic example of a certain type of man: the moonlighting accountant.'

'He told me he was a lawyer.'

'Whatever. You know what I mean. The kind of person who dislikes the situation in which he finds himself, and wants to do something creative; who wants to get in touch with another life, which he likes to think of as his real life. But the secret agenda is that never, not for a moment, will he do anything that might threaten his real, *real* life; that is, his money and his position in society.'

'You're in a very cynical mood all of a sudden.'

'I'm just being realistic.' Julia was about to challenge this when Hester returned. The woman had a rare gift, Roderic thought, for appearing at exactly the moment when she wasn't wanted. She'd done it twice now today. By the time he and Julia were alone again the thread of their conversation had effectively been broken and they forgot about William; they spoke of other things.

William's subsequent visit to the gallery was an odd second take on his visit to the shop. Then all was clutter, now all was bare and stark. Again, he saw Julia through the glass door from the street before she saw him. He had brought the children with him for protective colouring, just in case she happened to be there.

The warmth of Julia's greeting when she saw them all was evidently genuine. 'You must be Sophie and Gregory,' she said, recognising the children from the photograph she had seen. The girl smiled trustingly, showing a gap-toothed mouth; the boy's face remained closed. It had amused Julia when she saw their photos in William's wallet to see how much the boy resembled his father, but in real life the effect was not so appealing. It shocked her to see in so small a child the same tightly buttoned air, the same cleft forehead, the same air of controlled anger.

Sophie was staring hard at her. 'You have really funny hair,' she said to Julia. 'Can I touch it?'

Her father started to remonstrate, but Julia ignored him. 'Of course you can,' she said, crouching down. The child patted her gently on the head. 'You too, if you want,' she said to Gregory. The child leaned over and gently stroked her hair, as though she were a cat or a rabbit. He smiled for the first time since entering the gallery, and Julia, struck by how funny the whole thing was, laughed aloud. The little girl giggled and touched Julia's hair again, and now all three of them were laughing, especially Gregory.

'I think you can leave it at that now, children,' William said, and they drew back. Julia, still laughing, stood up.

The gallery was a series of interconnected rooms. 'My work is in there, and there are photographs in the other room.' On the wall immediately beside where they stood was a thing made of dark red velvet, fold upon fold receding to a bright bead stitched in the centre. 'I like that,' Sophie said, pointing to it, 'it's like a spider's web.'

'It is a bit, isn't it?' Julia said, biting her lip and trying not to laugh at William's discomfiture. 'You look around,' she said to him, 'and I'll show the children these other pieces. You're going to have to take your shoes off,' she said to them. 'Do you need help with the laces, Gregory?'

Julia's work consisted of a series of long wooden boxes, each sealed in front with a pane of glass. Over the glass hung a veil of white ribbons that fluttered and twirled in the draught made by a freestanding fan. This meant that the contents of the boxes could be glimpsed rather than plainly seen, like things partially concealed by the branches of trees. One box contained rolls of fur, of thick wool, of pleated muslin, heaped together and piled up against the surface of the glass. They made one long to touch them, which was of course impossible. In another box were displayed on shelves a series of china cups and saucers, each one perched precariously, as though they might fall at any moment. The third held shells and stones. There was a lump of pink quartz, uncut and unpolished, reminding William momentarily of the scene he had witnessed in the shop, and there was a small cairn of plain black stones, dull and uniform in size. There were shells such as one might find on almost any beach in Ireland: winkles and cockles, modest bivalves, ridged or smooth, arranged in pale heaps. They were complemented by a few larger, more exotic shells, one spiked, opening into a glassy void pink as flesh; one a long fragile cone stippled with colour, one a solid whirl of pure iridescence, as though made of some kind of fabulous glass.

The final box contained a series of documents: faded newsprint, torn letters, faint and blurred snapshots. This William found the most frustrating, even more so than the box with the fur and the wool, because his inclination was to attempt to read the fragments of text it contained but the constantly fluttering ribbons prevented him from doing so. There was about all of them, he thought, a mysterious, elegiac atmosphere, each presenting a small, sealed, rather beautiful but utterly inaccessible world.

He turned away into the next room, and was shocked by what he found there.

On each of the three walls was a photograph, larger than life-size, showing a naked woman holding a naked baby to her breast. The women were young, perhaps all teenagers, unsmiling and with a shell-shocked, sullen look. The babies were tiny, wet, ugly, and all looked as if they had barely been ready to be born. How long was it since these women had given birth? Less than a day he would have thought, on the strength of the photos. Although they were young and attractive, there was not the slightest shred of eroticism or sexual appeal in them. They looked like people who had been through a violent and exhausting ordeal, which of course they had. A trickle of blood ran down the inside of one of the women's legs. His mind habitually shrank from the memory of how Liz had suffered when the twins were born: the violence of it, the screaming and the blood. But the following day when he had gone to see her she was sitting up in bed smiling, with the babies in her arms. 'I feel,' she said, 'as though I'm at the centre of a crystal made of pure light.' And what of these young women: had they also experienced this intense joy that drove Liz to express herself in such a mystical way? There was no evidence of it in the photographs of their stunned, blank faces.

From behind him he could hear the chuckles and laughter of his own two children.

'Me now, me now, I want to go again,' Gregory was shouting.

'Off you go,' said Julia.

William turned around to where they were. He saw the sides of the canvas tunnel undulate as his son moved through it, like a small struggling animal passing through the gullet of a boa constrictor. It reminded him of taking them to a funfair, the same flushed faces, the excitement, *I want to go again, again*, as Gregory tumbled chuckling out of the end of the tunnel, into the gallery.

'You do it, Daddy,' Sophie said.

He looked at Julia.

'Why not? It is intended for adults rather than children,' she said, with monumental understatement and an admirably straight face. 'But you must take your shoes off first.'

He felt foolish standing in his loud argyle socks, and was glad to disappear into the first tunnel, the inside of which was lined with soft white feathers, so that in walking through it he felt that he was moving through a cloud. Some kind of illumination had been arranged, a series of tiny lights, so that he could see the whiteness that surrounded him. The tunnel was a collapsed tube that closed in on itself as he progressed through it, so that he had to gently push his way forward. Neither did he know when he would emerge: he could literally see no light at the end of the tunnel. He was

99

disconcerted, therefore, when he suddenly popped out into the room again. Julia was sitting on the floor with her arm around Sophie. Gregory immediately grabbed William's hand and hauled him across the room, 'The next one too, Daddy, the next one too.'

The inside of the second tunnel was darker, although like the first it was illuminated by tiny lights. There were no feathers: this tunnel was lined with dark red velvet, the same material from which the object on the wall was made. Again, he had to gingerly press his way through, again the tunnel closed behind him. The velvet brushed against his face, his whole body, and he could hear the laughter, the voices of the children. Suddenly he wished that he hadn't brought them here, that he had come alone. He was swept with a feeling of confusion, and just at that moment he fell into the brightness of the room again.

'Powerful piece of work, isn't it?' she said.

'Put your shoes on,' he said curtly to the children as he sat down and fumbled his way into his own brogues. Sophie, who was still sitting beside Julia, stood up and slipped her feet into her simple pumps. As she waited for William, who was helping Gregory on with his shoes now, she wandered over towards the entrance of the room where the photographs were displayed.

'Sophie! Come here, don't go into that room, do you hear me?' and Sophie backed away, frightened by the force of his anger. The children could not understand why the atmosphere, so happy before, had suddenly gone sour. Gregory was angry too, truculent and struggling as his father attempted to tie the child's laces. It was impossible to know what Julia was thinking. She was standing now, leaning against a wall, with her arms folded, looking at the floor. Her face was inscrutable, as it had been the night he had shown up unannounced at her house. William finished tying Gregory's shoes and stood up. He started to thank her with cold formality, but she rolled her eyes and turned away. She said goodbye to the children, and held the door open as they passed into the street.

All the way home William fretted about what to do next. If he told the children not to mention the visit at home, it would, coupled with the strange atmosphere in which it had all ended, compound their suspicion about the whole business. Then they might – or at least Gregory might – tell Liz just to cause trouble for William. Although his son was still so small, William already saw him as an adversary. If, however, he didn't warn them off, they would probably tell Liz, and he was anxious that she should know nothing about it. He finally decided to simply hope for the best.

And after it happened, he would wonder how he had ever been so foolish as to think he would get away with it, and that nothing would be said. In the end it was Sophie, not Gregory, who piped up as they were sitting over their evening meal, the children with their chicken nuggets, their parents with their tortellini.

'We met ever such a nice lady in town today, somebody Daddy knows. She was in this place full of odd things. There were big tunnels we could go down, only you had to take your shoes off first. Daddy did it too.'

Liz paused with her fork in mid-air and looked brightly from father to daughter and from daughter to father. 'Did you? Did you indeed? That must have been fun. Tell me more.'

'It was brilliant,' Gregory said. 'It was like being swallowed up by a big red animal. I loved it.'

'And what about Daddy?' Liz said. 'Did he love being swallowed up too?'

William gave a small, forced laugh, which he knew sounded utterly unconvincing. 'It was an art exhibition,' he said, 'some conceptual pieces, an installation, whatever you want to call it. There was a woman there, an artist, I don't know her,' he said, denying Sophie's claim, 'she's all but a stranger to me,' a remark which for some odd reason seemed to thicken Liz's suspicion rather than allay it. 'That's all there is to say. Gregory, sit up straight, how many times have I told you not to slump down in your seat like that?' Gregory's face, which had been bright and animated as he described the afternoon, closed into its habitual sullen tension. They went on eating in silence for a few moments.

'Anyway, I saw what was in the room,' Gregory eventually said in a sulky voice, 'the room you wouldn't let Sophie go into.' He shoved a piece of chicken into a puddle of ketchup on the side of his plate. 'I peeped into it when you were in the tunnel thing.'

'What was in the room?' Liz said.

Gregory held up the gobbet of chicken on his fork. 'Ask Daddy,' he said, then he crammed the food into his mouth and began to chew slowly.

'What did you see? What was it?' Liz asked again, her voice beginning to take on a hysterical edge.

Neither father nor son spoke. William thought of the trickle of blood running down the woman's leg, of the spidery angry looking infants, of the women's hostile, shocking faces. There was nothing he could say that would console Liz. He stared helplessly at Gregory.

'What was in the room?' Liz insisted.

The little boy swallowed his food with a loud gulp and threw his father a look of dismissive adult contempt. 'Just photographs,' he said. 'Big photographs of three women with their babies. I don't know why Daddy wouldn't let Sophie see them. It was nothing bad. It was just photographs.'

Chapter Twelve

'You must be mad,' Maeve said, when she heard what he was proposing. 'Absolutely mad. How could anyone live with Roderic?'

Reasonably, Dennis pointed out that they had all lived with him from his birth until his second year in art college, when he had moved to a shared flat. Frank, eager to boot his offspring out of the nest, had been happy to bankroll this until such time as Roderic graduated.

'He's changed a lot over the years,' she insisted, fixing her cold blue eyes on him. 'Roderic has become very odd.' She stretched this last word out as she uttered it to give a sense of horrid transformation, as though Roderic had grown an extra eye in the middle of his forehead or developed a forked tongue, instead of merely cultivating a modest and rather flattering beard. 'I shouldn't be surprised if his friends were strange too. Oh, I wouldn't live with him if I were you.'

There had always been a certain amount of mutual dislike between Roderic and Maeve, and Dennis therefore took a sceptical view of this unsolicited advice. Frank's opinion on the situation was more pertinent. 'I believe Roderic's giving up his job and moving in with you.'

This wasn't quite accurate but Dennis confirmed the statement none the less.

Frank stared at him hard. 'What are his plans, do you know?'

'He's found some part-time work, teaching evening classes in drawing; and he's keeping on his studio. I don't really think he has any game plan, he's just going to work it out as he goes along: get by, you know.'

Frank absorbed this information without comment.

'I'm only asking him for a nominal rent. I'm sure he'll be all right financially; he's not someone who wants or needs many material things.'

'That's true; he's always seemed to manage to get along on half nothing.'

One thing that gave a rather bizarre slant to all of this was that Roderic had grown up to look exactly like his father, giving Dennis the sensation that he was conducting this rather guarded conversation about his future with Roderic himself. Although temperamentally they were, Dennis thought, utterly dissimilar, both men had the same unnerving intelligence and intense physical presence. Often, neither of them was aware of the effect these qualities had on those around them. Frank was still staring hard at his elder son. It didn't seem possible that he hadn't guessed the truth of Roderic's situation.

When Dennis's own dreams of a career as a concert pianist came to an end because of stage fright, he had found in Frank a surprising ally. It was the things he hadn't said – 'You'll get over it, and in any case, I'm sure you'll be just as happy teaching music' – for which Dennis had been most grateful. He didn't complain about the wasted fees when his son said he wanted to change course one year into a degree in music; but he had been concerned about whether or not Dennis would ultimately be satisfied with the business and economics he said he wanted to read instead. Frank urged him to take his time in making a decision and to follow his heart.

Immersed in his own disappointment, Dennis did not fully appreciate the remarkable delicacy of feeling that Frank displayed at the time, but he remembered it now, seeing much the same thing manifested as they discussed Roderic's career problems. He suspected that Frank wanted to ask why Roderic lost his job, but he refrained from doing so, saying instead, 'I'm glad he'll be living with you. You can keep me posted on how things develop.'

'I'm sure it will all work out well.'

Frank stared at him thoughtfully for a few minutes more, considering this. 'You're probably right,' he said at last. 'Roderic has always seemed to know what he's about. Mind you,' he added as caveat, 'I'm buggered if anyone else does.'

Roderic moved into the house over a weekend in late August and was thrilled with the attic room. A veteran of shared houses, he asked Dennis if he wanted to draw up a cleaning rota or to establish a milk kitty. Dennis, who had only ever lived alone or with the family, had no idea what he was on about. 'There are no rules and regulations,' he said. 'The only thing I would ask you to do,' and he pointed at a pine wine rack as he spoke, 'is not to drink my claret.'

He expected a painter's life to be somewhat haphazard, its patterns of work dictated by inspiration and mood, and was surprised by the iron routine into which his brother quickly settled. He realised that he didn't know Roderic as well as he had imagined. There was, for example, his remarkable popularity with women, something of which Dennis had been vaguely aware but to which he had given no particular thought. Three days after Roderic moved in, Dennis innocently pressed the button on his own answering machine. *Thank you for calling,* he heard his own brisk voice say. *If you have a message for either Dennis or Roderic, please speak after the tone, and we'll get back to you as soon as possible. Thank you.* An ear-shattering bleep, and then a woman's hesitant voice. *Roderic, um hi, this is Cathy. Sorry I missed you. I'll try again later, or maybe you could, um, give me a call?* Another bleep, another woman's voice, this time confident and firm. *Roderic, this is Janet, just to say thanks for helping me move the sculptures the other day. You really got me out of a jam there, and if there's ever anything I can do for you, don't hesitate to ask.* Another bleep. *Roderic, this is you know who. So you're out and about. I wonder what you're up to. I can just imagine. Hope you've recovered from the other night. Call me soon.* The words were

105

innocuous enough, but the tone in which they were uttered made Dennis's reflected face go pink in his own hall mirror. Another bleep. *Roderic, this is Bernie. We're having a party on Saturday night and I hope you can make it* . . . It went on and on and on, and Dennis stood listening, astounded.

Some weeks further into the autumn, Frank discreetly took Dennis aside just before Saturday lunch to ask how things were working out. 'Roderic himself tells me it's fine and that the teaching's going well, that they've given him some extra hours.'

Dennis concurred with this, and reported well their situation. But he was struck too at how much he couldn't tell Frank. The many girlfriends were the least of it, and wouldn't have fazed him in the slightest. Frank was probably more concerned by Dennis's apparent complete lack of interest in women than by Roderic's fondness for them. Dennis had thought that temperamentally Roderic in no way resembled his father, but he had been wrong. Both men were capable of a remarkable degree of intellectual detachment, and as this was not a particularly endearing characteristic, Dennis thought it best not to comment upon it. Physically present but mentally remote, it was as though they were leading double (but not clandestine) lives. In fairness, Roderic had a cheerful disposition and little of Frank's irascibility. He was tremendously sociable, but it was precisely this combination of emotional warmth and icy withdrawal that Dennis found so disconcerting in him.

He continued to think about this at lunch as he watched Roderic making small talk with Sinéad, as he watched him help to clear the table. This part of his life that he shared with his family and that was visible to them was only the tip of the iceberg. No one asked about, nor did Roderic allude to, the concealed massive bulk of his other, his real life. He thought about it again the following afternoon when the rain poured down and they stayed at home reading. Dennis drank tea and leafed idly through the Sunday papers, their magazines and supplements, while Roderic sat silent and immobile for three solid hours immersed in a book called *The Dynamics of Modernism*. He thought about it again as he ate his breakfast alone on Monday morning, his brother having already left for the studio, and again that night, when Roderic emerged from two hours closeted in the kitchen with his former flatmate Tony, 'Just talking about painting,' he said. This in itself impressed Dennis, who rarely managed to jemmy more from the taciturn Tony than 'Hello', except for one memorable occasion when they were left together for a few moments and Tony volunteered without any prompting, 'Your brother's a fucking brilliant painter so he is. Fucking brilliant,' before lapsing back into impregnable silence.

He rather liked the effect that Roderic had upon his friends and colleagues at the sedate supper parties he occasionally gave. Towards the end of the meal he would hear the sound of a key in the door. 'That's my brother now. He'll come in for a couple of minutes to say hello.' He knew that his guests were expecting to meet someone similar to Dennis himself, which only made the effect of Roderic's sudden presence all the more electrifying. Handsome, ebullient, larger than life, he was a great stone crashing into the still pool of their evening, and the effect remained, like ripples, long after he had swept out of the room again.

In general, Maeve's warning about his friends was ill founded. With few exceptions Dennis enjoyed their company. The stream of short-term girlfriends who came and went throughout the autumn ended abruptly just before Christmas, when Roderic started going out with a photographer called Laura. It was a good time in both the brothers' lives. They had settled down comfortably into their domestic arrangement. Dennis was doing well in his job, with promotion and a rise in salary. Although Roderic's situation was precarious, and was to remain so for many years, he was satisfied with the time and freedom it afforded him. Dennis came to know Laura well in the months she was with Roderic, and was fond of her for her monumental calmness, her dry wit. The relationship lasted until the summer, after which time they parted amicably. Dennis regretted it and although the couple remained on friendly terms, Roderic occasionally meeting her and passing on her greetings to Dennis, she no longer came to the house.

It was a pattern to be repeated in the years that followed. The arrangement they had undertaken lasted much longer than either of them had expected or intended. They reviewed the situation in June and decided to continue at least for the time being living as they did. Roderic took a job for the summer in London, living in the flat of a friend of a friend while its owner took over his studio in Dublin. Dennis went off to the Salzburg Music Festival for his holidays. In the autumn Roderic resumed his teaching, and towards the end of the year he took part in an important group exhibition. Dennis barely saw him in the weeks leading up to it as he put in longer hours at the studio than ever before. Roderic's energy, his application, had always impressed him. Dennis changed his car and upgraded his private pension plan. He took up hill walking, and although they never went out together, it brought him closer to Frank, who shared with him his favourite routes and paths. And so the years went on.

People who knew both brothers marvelled that they could live such different lives in close proximity with no apparent friction. This was due in part to the strong emotional bond between them. There was no resentment because each understood the price the other was paying for the life he led and the things he had. When they chafed against their own situations, they didn't have far to look to see in full detail and with all its implications a wholly other life, which never failed to reconcile them quickly to their own fate. Dennis's house was their common territory, and neither of them felt wholly comfortable when he strayed into the other's world. Roderic rarely called to Dennis's stuffy, overheated office with its grey filing cabinets and tidy desk. How did he bear it, month after month, he silently wondered, not knowing that Dennis had been similarly appalled when he called to the studio and found him working with no heating in the depths of winter, his breath misting white before him when he spoke. The studio was too big and too high to heat: quite simply, he couldn't afford it. But more than the tedium or the discomfort, each shied away from the atmosphere of the other's life. Living like Dennis, Roderic thought, he would feel that his life was already as good as over. Living like Roderic, Dennis considered, would be ultimately too hard on the nerves.

During these years there were periods of time when Roderic was completely absent from the house. He went to stay for a few months with a friend who had gone off to live in a remote part of Scotland; he went to Amsterdam on a residency for a month. In Kerry, he taught painting at a residential summer school. He started going out with a woman from Galway, and when she moved back to the west he went down to stay with her for increasingly lengthy visits. Just at the point when Dennis thought he would probably leave Dublin definitively and move to Galway, the relationship came to an end. Although he enjoyed his brother's company in the house – there was something energising in just being around him – Dennis neither resented nor relished these absences. When, shortly before his twenty-seventh birthday, Roderic was awarded a six-month stay in a centre for artists in Italy, no one was more delighted for him than Dennis.

Chapter Thirteen

When they were in London in April Liz insisted, much to his annoyance, on going with William to an exhibition on the Saturday morning.

'You won't enjoy it.'

'What sort of art is it? Is it old stuff?'

For a moment he hesitated, tempted to lie before admitting, 'No, it's contemporary work. It's a one-man show I very much want to see.'

Liz freely admitted that she had no real interest in or knowledge of art. There were about three painters in the whole of the western canon whose work she could easily recognise and that she liked: Van Gogh, Monet and Renoir. Her lack of an 'eye' for a picture – she couldn't see the difference between works of the Flemish school and those of the Italian Renaissance – was something William simply failed to understand. 'All old paintings look the same,' she said. 'A crucifixion is a crucifixion is a crucifixion.' Her dislike of religious art ('If I see another angel, I'll scream') was as nothing compared to her pathological dislike of mythological and classical subjects. 'Battles, bums, lardy white women sitting around in fields having picnics with goats: how could anyone like this stuff? *Landscape with Aeneas at Delos*. Who was Aeneas? Where was Delos? And did anyone really care?' It was all, Liz said, boring, boring, boring. And as for the twentieth century: green-faced women with three eyes? Daubs and blobs of paint? No thank you.

In spite of this she had, when newly married, tried to take an interest in William's passion and tagged along when he went to galleries and exhibitions. This irritated him enormously and the novelty soon wore off for Liz. She had hoped he would be able to show her what it was that she was supposed to see, but her antipathy to painting was only confirmed and reinforced. An afternoon spent at a Poussin exhibition was one of the low points of their life together. But in trawling the galleries, they did make an odd discovery: Liz was quite receptive to contemporary art, although she didn't like everything she saw and didn't hesitate to say so.

Gallery going remained William's 'thing': he had never known her to go by herself to see an exhibition but when she accompanied him he was always struck by how open minded she was, how willing to take the work on its own terms. She entered freezers and tents and tiny wooden cabins. In darkened rooms she watched videos of people singing, screaming, slapping themselves around the face, setting fire to their hair, giving birth, sleeping or simply gazing immobile into the eye of the camera. She looked at works made of ice, chocolate, flowers, toenails, rotting meat, briars, sand, old clothes, dead animals, beams of light. William had seen her enthuse over the beauty of cones of coloured pigment, turmeric, crimson and blue. He had seen her shocked by photos of tattooed pigs and baffled by rows of empty wire cages. In a dim room full of old and worn soft toys he had seen her moved to tears.

But today he wanted to be alone, and deeply resented her company. In the underground on the way to the exhibition he chose not to sit beside her to make the point clear. It would be an embarrassment to be seen with her in the gallery. How suburban she looked, how conventional, with her twin-set and her quilted handbag. 'She'll put silk flowers in the bathroom if you're not careful,' his own mother had warned him when he decided to marry Liz. 'She'll fill the house with Waterford glass and bits of Royal Doulton.' Spiteful, yes, but true, he thought. She'd never fully settled into the money marriage had brought her, had never become completely at ease in his world. She caught his eye and smiled across the carriage at him. He stared back, stern and unbending.

The first room they entered on reaching the gallery was large and high, not brightly lit, and covered from eye level to ceiling with hundreds, perhaps thousands of photographs. They were all the same size and showed black and white portraits of people: old men and babies, soldiers, toddlers, grannies, young girls, middle-aged women, young men. The quality of the images varied. Some had evidently been taken from newsprint and enlarged, and the blurred, somewhat blank effect this created, particularly in the eyes of the subjects, only served to heighten their remarkable pathos. Some of the clothes they wore suggested they had lived many years earlier, most probably during the period of the Second World War, so that the babies would, if still alive, be old men by now, and the old men dead. There were no names given or nationality or ages, nothing to say who these people were; and now no one would ever know. William noticed that when visitors to the room spoke to each other, they did so in hushed and reverential tones, as they might have done in a church. Some people merely glanced up at the immense walls, taking in the general sepulchral effect before moving on. Others, including Liz, lingered for a long time, studying in turn as many of these anonymous faces as they could take in, as though paying silent tribute to the individuality of each person. 'Isn't it extraordinary?' she whispered to William.

The effect of the photographs neutralised the annoyance he had felt towards her earlier. Together they went into the next room, and he watched her discreetly as she studied the work there: a series of small beds, high-sided like cots, each lit with its own harsh light-bulb. Although they contained pillows and blankets, they radiated a sense of emptiness. Not to have children was the greatest tragedy that could have befallen her, he thought. Without them she would have been in the same depressed fog in which he now found himself, the same dumb misery. As she moved to read a text on the wall relating to the exhibit, he noticed a woman, cool, young, who was looking Liz over. She whispered something to her companion, and his eyes also flickered in Liz's direction. He whispered something back to his friend and she laughed. The man looked again at Liz, smiled sardonically and turned away. William was hurt and angry on her behalf even though Liz hadn't noticed a thing; even though on the way to the gallery he himself had sneered at her in exactly the same way.

They had lunch in a restaurant of William's choosing. He liked eating out, enjoyed the opportunities it gave for small displays of dominance and control. He chose a bottle from the wine list; discreet and deferential, the waiter served it.

'What will you do this afternoon?'

'I'd like to go shopping. I'll buy presents for the children.'

As they ate he watched her, thinking of their shared life.

'Do you remember Spain? Seville, that little hotel?'

'I don't think so,' she said. 'Was it the place with the coloured tiles all the way up the stairs?'

'No, that was in Granada.'

She shook her head. 'Then I don't remember it. What was the hotel in Seville like?'

'It doesn't matter.'

'Then why did you ask?'

'Liz, I said it doesn't matter.'

They finished their main course in silence. William could feel a familiar mental darkness begin to close in around him. His attempt to establish a point of contact with her had only served to drive them further apart. The waiter came and removed their plates.

'Did you enjoy the exhibition?' she asked.

'I don't think "enjoy" is quite the word.'

'I liked it. I thought it was sad. All those people, all so completely forgotten now.'

'As we shall be.'

'That's why I liked it,' she said.

William, surprised, didn't know how to respond.

'William, what is it you need? What do you want?'

'I want a studio.'

He didn't know how she'd hesitated before asking that simple question, for fear that he'd slipped so far out of her reach that he might ask for anything, that he might reply, 'I want to leave you.'

'A studio,' she said. 'I'm sure that can be arranged. There must be places in town you could rent. I don't know how you'd go about it, but we can ask around, look into it.'

'I want it at home.'

'But there's no space in the house.'

'There's the spare bedroom.' He could see her dismay. For the past year the spare bedroom had been her pet project. She'd spent an inordinate amount of time and money on it, and only two months ago had she completed it to her satisfaction. The effect she sought was countrified, all cream and pink, with muslin curtains and a narrow brass bed. William didn't know why she'd put such effort into the making of this room: he'd never asked her. Every summer when she was a child she'd gone to stay with her grandmother on a farm in County Roscommon. She remembered it as a luminous place full of hooting birds. Corncrakes at dusk, the smell of the hen house, the stiff white wing with which her grandmother brushed flour from the griddle, the printed roses of the cheap wallpaper: all of this lost world she could re-enter by sitting quietly alone in the room she'd created. 'When I was little, like you,' she told the children, 'I slept in a bed such as this.'

'You asked me what I needed. I'm not asking for much. A plain bare whitewashed room, that's all I want.'

'Whitewash the walls?'

'Yes.'

'And the bed?'

'We can sell it. Give it away.'

She wouldn't rise to the bait, wouldn't get angry. He knew how much he was asking of her, the magnitude of the sacrifice, even if he didn't know why. If he'd acknowledged the effort she'd made, asked her would she mind, she'd have seen it differently. The room was something in her gift, and she'd have gladly given it if she thought it would make him happy. But he'd asked her, she thought, in such a way as to deliberately hurt her, to disregard her feelings.

'Do as you wish,' she said evenly. 'It's a pity, of course. I had thought I might move in there myself before long, make that my bedroom.' He hadn't been expecting that, nor was it true. He made to speak, but she brushed him aside. 'Do as you wish,' she said again. 'Shall we go now?'

William moved to take his credit card from his pocket, but before he could do so Liz had pulled several banknotes from her handbag. She gestured, smiling, at the man who had served them and handed him the money. The waiter returned with a silver dish bearing coins, a receipt, and placed it beside Liz. 'Thank you, madam.'

Alone in the city, the lassitude and darkness closed in around him again. He walked the streets, ended up in the National Gallery in the late afternoon, ended up in tears. No one saw his distress, or if they did, they pretended not to. Perhaps they felt there was nothing they could do. Perhaps they were embarrassed by his emotion, or perhaps they were silently agreeing that his response was wholly natural. Who would not weep before *The Agony in the Garden*, Mantegna's arid study of affliction: the bare rocks, the sleeping indifference of Christ's companions, the unsettling perspective, the shut, walled city, and the crowd of soldiers approaching in the distance? Tomorrow was Sunday. They would not go to church, although Liz always took the children to Mass when they were at home. The galleries would be crowded. Art had taken the place of revealed religion for so many people nowadays; loss of faith was taken for granted. But what of the death of Imagination? Who recognised that in themselves? Who mourned it? William didn't even bother to wipe his eyes.

A small boy sitting on the bench beside him looked ostentatiously at his watch. 'We've been in this place now,' he said, 'for exactly two hours seventeen minutes and thirty seconds.' If Gregory were here, he wouldn't be counting the minutes. He would be absorbed in the paintings, in the worksheet that the little boy held crumpled in his hand, his mother negotiating with him now, bribing him, cajoling, buying herself more time. Lots of children liked to paint: it was Gregory's delight in pictures that was strange. In recent months he had shown more interest in his father's books than his own. William had been astonished on coming into the drawing room one day to see him with a heavy volume about Kandinsky open upon his knee. The child had looked up, his eyes full of fear. 'Is it all right?' he asked. 'I washed my hands before I started.' William nodded, tried to smile. The child turned his attention again to the book, and William noticed his unnerving concentration, how he spent a considerable period of time studying each picture in turn, before slowly turning the page and moving on to the next one. Already he had learned how to look at things, something some adults never mastered. Most middle-class parents would have spent a fortune in the hope of interesting their child in art to this degree, but William had not encouraged Gregory. On the contrary, art had always been for him a private passion that he did not want to share. It afforded him an escape from family life, and he realised now with a start that for his son it had exactly the same function. Their home life was something from which, even at the age of seven, he needed a refuge. The child was a fetch, a tiny ghost made in his own image to walk beside him in life and to torment him.

The previous week Gregory had been playing in the garden when he suddenly exploded into the house, bawling, to the room where William was sitting. 'What is it, Gregory, what happened?' But even as he reached out to comfort his son, the boy pushed him violently away and continued on into the kitchen, to his mother. William sat listening, as Liz shushed and comforted him. He could feel the spot on his chest where the child had placed his hands to thrust himself out of his father's enclosing embrace, as if Gregory's hands had been burning and had scorched him. The shrieks dwindled to sobs. He rose from his chair and went into the kitchen. Two faces looked up at him.

'It's nothing serious,' Liz said. 'He nipped his finger on the swing, he got a fright, that's all.'

'Well, if it's nothing serious,' William said, 'is there really any need for all this racket?'

He flushed with shame to remember it. In the gallery shop he would buy something special for Gregory, a book or a kit. He stood up and attempted to shake himself out of his grief, walked from room to room and tried to focus on the works displayed. It struck him, not for the first time, that what was singular about the pictures was not the skill that had gone into their making, nor even the vision, but the energy they contained, contained and radiated. To look around the room without focusing on any one work was to be aware of how each picture demanded attention, seemed aware of its own weight and significance. What must it have been like for the artists to have felt that energy flowing through them, to have been a controlling channel for it? The power of the work contrasted sharply with William's own weariness.

He could barely drag himself around the gallery, and he soon sat down again, this time near Holbein's *Portrait of a Lady with a Squirrel*. The painted lady, with her tethered, bright-eyed pet snuggled to her breast, was being studied by a young woman. Would he have noticed her had she stopped in front of any other picture? Perhaps no other would have afforded a more striking contrast. He examined them both closely. The young woman's hair was cropped shorter than William's own, and she had three stars tattooed on her foot, just above the ankle bone. He could see her nipples through the tight white T-shirt that was cropped to reveal a flat tanned midriff. It took only a slight mental effort for him to see her as naked as one of the vast goddesses in the paintings which were displayed in adjacent rooms. The woman in the painting was also dressed in black and white, but in clothes that concealed everything, from her angular bonnet of white fur to the white folded stole draped across her shoulders. The young woman standing before him was not the final word on the fate of women. It was hard to believe that she might look, some hundreds of years from now if her image was preserved, as quaint as the woman in the painting. *I know* *exactly* *what you'll think of Madame in her crystal!* There was something hard and cynical about the young woman's face. He had often noticed this in young people recently, particularly in girls. It was the look of someone who had no illusions about society: what it offered, what it amounted to. Liz was always fretting about the children, especially Sophie, and what her life would be when she grew up. 'Everything's changing so quickly now. How can I prepare her properly for the future when I have no idea what sort of world she'll be living in?'

He was so lost in thought that he forgot the woman wasn't a painting but a real person until she turned to him and gave him a taste of his own behaviour, until she looked him over coldly, long and hard, every inch of him. 'Seen enough, granddad?' Determined not to lose face, he did his best to stare back insolently. 'Piss off. You give me any hassle and I'll call the security guards, d'you hear?' She had raised her voice, and people turned to stare at them both. Suddenly William lost his nerve. He stood up and walked quickly away, forcing himself not to break into a run.

In the gallery shop he chose a book about Giverny for Gregory, and a postcard of the squirrel painting, then went to the café and bought himself a cup of tea. The girl at the till reminded him of Hannah: she had the same unusual and attractive combination of blonde hair and dark brown, almost black eyes. He almost never thought of Hannah these days. There had been other women since then. Not many: the opportunity didn't present itself often and he had to be careful. Liz had said she would leave him if it happened again and he believed her. He didn't know why he had been so indiscreet about Hannah, didn't understand what had possessed him at the time. At least now, he thought, he had the sense when he sought release elsewhere not to let emotions come into it, his own or anyone else's.

The postcard was for Julia. He would write it now and post it before meeting Liz at the time they had arranged. She had nothing to fear in Julia, no reason to be jealous, but she wouldn't necessarily understand that so it was best she didn't know. He drank his tea and wondered what he should write. He was embarrassed about how things had ended when he went to see her exhibition. It was strange and fortuitous his meeting her at just this moment in his life, and he was keen not to break the connection. On the back of an envelope he took from his pocket he drafted out what he might say to her, anxious to strike exactly the right tone. When he was satisfied, he took out the card. He glanced momentarily at the image again, at the woman's odd bonnet and decorous clothes, at the lithe, bright squirrel.

And then he started to write.

Chapter Fourteen

Dear Dennis,

*Well, I got here, just about. What a journey! First off, a huge
THANK YOU for taking me out to the airport and helping me
with the luggage and everything. I must confess I had a sinking
feeling in the pit of my stomach when I arrived in Fiumicino and
stood by the baggage conveyor looking at all the cases coming out,
waiting for mine. It came eventually, although all my bags seemed
to have mysteriously doubled in size and weight somewhere
between Dublin and Rome. I stood in the boiling heat sweating
like stuck pig, hearing people all around me talking, and I wasn't
able, quite naturally, to understand a single word that was being
said. So I realised at that moment that from here on out I really
am going to have to rely on the comfort of strangers, and look out
for myself, and stand on my own two feet and all that jazz. If I
have a problem now there's no point in thinking 'I can ask Dennis
and he'll help me, he'll know what to do.' I will just have to deal
with it myself. And about time too, I can hear you say. All this is
a very garbled and inarticulate way of thanking you not just for
seeing me off yesterday morning, but for everything you've done
for me over the past years.*

*So the trip from Rome up to Siena was my baptism of fire in Italy.
It was all fairly frantic from the moment I arrived. I had arranged
with Enzo, the man in charge here, before I left Ireland that he
would meet me off a particular train and bring me out to the Villa
Rosalba. I was worried that if I missed the connection I didn't
know how I would make contact with him, or how I would get
here. Every stage took longer than I thought and it was all cut
very fine. I almost got on the wrong train, and then got the right
one just at the last gasp; the doors of the carriage literally clipped*

*my heels as I got in. I did manage to relax during the journey and
admire the landscape which is so marvellous: the hills, the little
towns, the remarkable colours, the light. I know I'm just going to
love it here. I began to worry a bit as we approached Siena, that I
might not be able to find Enzo, worried more when I actually saw
the hordes of people in the station, but there in the middle of it all
was a man with a huge placard saying 'R. Kenedy'.*

*I've only been here for twenty-four hours and I'm still
overwhelmed by it all. For anyone to be here would be a pleasure –
you for example would just love it, I feel sure of that – but for a
painter it's something more again. I know I'm going to do good
work. I'm still getting the studio set up, but I hope to start
tomorrow. It is, as you know, the only thing that really interests
me. I need to be painting and what with preparing to come out
here I haven't done anything much in the past week, so I feel
restless and mad keen to get started again.*

*The Foundation is well organised. We each have a studio and a
bed-sitting room, with a little kitchen corner: fridge, hot plate,
press for food and crockery. We cater for ourselves at breakfast and
lunch, which is good because it means you can put your own
shape on the day, rise early or late as you wish, and work straight
through what should be lunch time if you feel so inclined. Then
we all come together in the evening to share a meal cooked by
Marguerite who, together with Enzo, runs the place. We ate out
on a terrace, with a view of the valley below, and the olive trees
and the cypress trees, and night fell and bats came out in the dusk.
We ate pasta with an aubergine sauce, then roast chicken with
spinach, then fruit and cheese.*

*As regards the company of the damned, there are six artists in
residence at any one time, three Italians and three foreigners. We
all stay for six months, but the arrivals are staggered, so that there
are only ever two new inmates wandering around like lost souls at
any one time. The other person who arrived yesterday is an
American called Ray, who's from Maine, and seems decent; in fact*

they all seem quite nice. There's one man I haven't met yet, Karl from Heidelberg, who is off in Rome for a few days. There's Elsa, from Turin. She's a lovely woman and speaks fluent English, which is a help to me. Gina is a sculptor from Catania (doesn't speak a word of English) and Mauro is a painter from Milan. From my point of view this is no bad thing, as it means I have enough people to talk to easily, but also a good incentive to learn the language. I'm determined to learn as much Italian as I can while I'm here and I listened to my cassette for an hour this afternoon. I haven't seen any work by any of the others yet, although I'm curious to do so. I feel there's a bit of needle between Elsa and Mauro, but that's only a hunch. I don't think I should have too many problems fitting in. As I say, they seem like a decent bunch, and I like having a bit of company in the evenings when I've been working all day.

I'll finish up here. I'll write again at the end of the week when I'm more settled. I'll be sending cards to the family soon, but in the meantime give them all my love. These are just first impressions in a note to let you know that I've arrived. It is important for me to be here Dennis – good for me too. And again, I really can't thank you enough for everything you've done not just over the past mad week, but over the years. I really am grateful.

Best love,

R.

Dear Dennis,

I'm glad you were pleased with the little cakes from Siena. I know you could live on marzipan so as soon as I saw them I thought, 'Dennis would kill for these.' I bought a box of them for you on the spot. Let me know if you can think of anything else that you'd particularly like from here. I'm always on the lookout for things that might please you. A wine buff like yourself would be in heaven: I'm developing a great taste for it myself. I wish I could see my way to sending you a few bottles but I don't know how it might be done. You'll just have to come out here and drink it on the spot. I'm still trying to think of what I might send Dad. Speaking of gifts, I sent three silk scarves for Mum and the girls, do you know did they ever arrive? I posted them at the same time I posted the marzipan to you, but I thought they would have arrived long before now. Mind you, I haven't had a cheep from anyone in the family since I've been here, apart from you. Thank you for all the letters. There's a table in the common room where Enzo sets out our post for us to collect, and I love to walk in and see one of your blue envelopes with the familiar handwriting sitting there waiting for me. It's good of you to write so often, as I know that after a long day at the office sitting down at night to write a letter must take considerable effort. I love to hear your news. The stuff about the builders made me laugh, although in all seriousness you must have been damn glad to see the back of them. The new windows will make the house more comfortable for you, especially that big front room that was always hard to heat.

I get on well with everyone here except Mauro. As Elsa remarked the other day in her grammatically perfect but heavily accented English, 'I think we are all developing a Mauro complex.' Late that night she had a tremendous row with him. I'm not sure what it was about, but I can make an educated guess. She wouldn't tell me but I notice that she hasn't had a good word to say about him since then. He's well off: his father, she says, is a wealthy industrialist who has funded Mauro on this particular little flight of fancy for the past couple of years. When the novelty wears off, she says, his father will set him up in something else, and he'll hold artists in contempt for the rest of his life. I think the end can't be too long in coming: terminal boredom has already set in. I told Elsa I don't think he'll last the whole of his six-month stay. He isn't doing a stroke and there really is nothing else to do here all day except work, as we're out in the middle of the fields. He makes no secret of the fact that he thinks us all dull dogs because we spend our days closed away in our studios.

Anyway, enough about him. Elsa is a tremendously fine artist. I've learned ever such a lot from talking to her. She works on lithographs, something I never enjoyed when I did it at college, but she has let me spend some time at the stone with her and has taught me a lot about the technique. There's a great generosity of spirit in the people here. We've all been into each other's studios at this stage, and have all (again, with the exception of Mauro) done enough work to give each other a sense of what it is we're about.

Gina is the exact opposite of Mauro, if anything a bit fanatical. She has the studio beside mine, and when I wake in the mornings (and I wake early, because of the light) more likely than not I hear the sound of her chisel on stone. I often fall asleep at night to the same sound, because she frequently goes back to her studio after dinner and works again. The rest of us, I must confess, either walk down to the little bar in the village for a beer, or else we sit around on the terrace or in the common room drinking red wine and talking until all hours. I can't really communicate with her because of the language barrier, but she doesn't talk much to anyone really, she's just not a verbal person. The only thing she can say in English is 'I love stone', and she knows the words granite, marble and so on. She showed me a portfolio of photographs of sculptures, and they were remarkable. She can make stone liquid, can make it flow down the side of a table, she can make it appear soft as a fleece. As Ray said with some humility after he'd seen her work, 'If I could do what Gina can do, I think I'd spend all my time closed away too, I wouldn't ever want to do anything except work.'

Because the sad fact is that Ray isn't a very good artist. He's a great guy, and we get on like a house on fire, but I can't let my feelings sway my judgement as far as work goes. I'm even cold enough to say it interests me to see how bad an artist he is. I was so disappointed the first time I went to his studio. He works in *collage, but it really has nothing going for it: no energy, no ideas, even his sense of design is weak. When you look at it you're aware that it's just bits of paper stuck together. That is of course technically what collage is, I know, but the end result should be so much more than that, just as painting is something more than paint and canvas. What he does is all too tightly controlled and too small. He's trying to work on a bigger scale but doesn't feel comfortable with it. He knows the work isn't good enough, he keeps saying that he needs to relax more into it, and he's exactly right, but he doesn't seem to be able to do it. Every artist wants to do better work: you're always pushing against your own limits, and I know myself from bad times what it's like when you know it's not good enough – not good at all – and there seems to be no way through. Yet you do also know when you're on the right track. He has, he says, good ideas, but he can never seem to push them through to any satisfactory degree. And yet the odd thing is, he's a tremendously dedicated artist. I mean, he's a real artist, even if he is a bad one. I think if someone forced Ray to stop working he wouldn't be able to go on living, he needs to be doing it.*

I've been thinking about this whole question a lot since I met him. One always tends to assume that someone who is an artist, a real, driven, anointed artist, is also a good artist, but that may not always be the case. There are people of great technical ability but no vision: they're not really artists, but they pass as such. Poor Ray. I have a horrible feeling that no matter how hard he tries he's never going to get any better. Perhaps I'm wrong. I hope I am, and maybe after years of effort he'll break through and do something utterly original and beautiful.

Why am I telling you all this? I know it can't interest you. I'm just thinking out loud. I don't want to talk to anyone here about it in case it seems underhand or uncharitable to Ray, but it has been on my mind a lot lately.

Enclosed are a couple of photographs – you might think to show them to the family, although whether or not they'll be interested is anyone's guess. Karl took them yesterday and got them developed when he was in town today. The first one was taken in my studio. Left to right, Gina, Elsa, the dreaded Mauro, yours truly, Enzo and Ray. Looking at this picture, you will not be surprised to learn that my nickname here is Gulliver (as he was perceived on his Lilliputian travels rather than in his Brobdingnagian phase). The second photo was taken on the terrace where we have dinner. You'll recognise who's who from the first picture, apart from the two people sitting under the tree who were just there for the evening. The man is an old friend of Elsa's from Turin, whose name I must say I've forgotten already. He's an expert in fresco restoration and is overseeing a project in a church near here. The woman beside him is Marta, a colleague of his. She speaks good English and I enjoyed her company. It was nice to have some new faces around the table. We arranged that Elsa and I would go out to the church tomorrow to see them, and I'm pleased and excited about that. I've never seen a fresco being restored before. They both made a good contribution to the evening, which went on until all hours.

I feel tremendously at home here, and so contented; I think I could stay for ever. You wouldn't ever think of coming over to live here? I really believe at the moment that the only thing I would miss if I never went back to Ireland would be the odd pint and your good self.

Best love,

Your brother,

Roderic.

Dear Dennis,

A quick postcard, to congratulate you. I know how much this promotion means for you and I am DELIGHTED it came through. Ray was in the common room reading his post when I received your letter. I said to him, 'I think I'm going to cry. I've got everything I want and I don't think I'll ever be so happy again in my whole life.' (To which Ray replied, 'That's what Scott Fitzgerald said, and look what happened to him.') Anyway, I am thrilled for you. Congratulations again, and I'll write a real letter soon.

Best love,

R.

Dear Dennis,

I'm afraid this isn't going to be particularly cheerful, so please bear with me. I've been a bit pulled down during this past week and I had a letter from Cliona this morning that didn't help. I strongly suspect that it was written under slight duress; that is, that you had told her to drop me a line, for shame's sake, so that she would have written to me here at least once before my time is up. For all it amounted to, she needn't have bothered. It was full of grudging jokes along the lines of, 'Isn't it well for some, off gadding about leading the life of Riley in Italy while the rest of us have to work for a living.' It's no more than I would expect from her, indeed from any of the family, except you, and it would probably just have irritated me slightly at any other time. But it caught me at a bad moment and tipped me into a deep gloom that I haven't been able to shake off since then. The first point is that I have been working here harder than I've ever perhaps worked in my life. I've been amazed at the quantity of work I've managed to do in just over five months, and the quality is good too: I've made a quantum leap. It has been a period of extraordinary intensity and development for me. But what Cliona can't see is that it has been just that: an _exceptional_ period in my life, not the norm.

We each make our own choices in life and then try to be true to them. I know the family (and I of course exclude you from this) have always thought of me as a dreamer, a drifter, a loser, when they have thought of me at all, for their abiding attitude with regard to me is one of absolute indifference. Well, let me tell you

127

this, I would far rather die by fire than by ice. They see the best
side of my life at the moment. What they fail to recognise or
acknowledge is that this exceptionally good part of it is about to
end. Take my life and Cliona's all in all and ask Cliona to choose.
Yes, you can have six months in Italy, your time your own to do
as you wish, and a small bursary to help you do it, but the
condition is that you have to take the whole life. That means Italy,
yes, but also the bits and scraps of teaching, the not having a
regular salary, the knowing you won't be able to have a house or a
car or anything much in material terms for a long time, if ever,
the comments of people who regard you as simultaneously having
beaten the system and living a life of idleness and luxury, while
also being a failure. And then there are your own feelings of
failure, the days, maybe weeks when you're not happy with
anything you do, when you have no luck, when you think it is all
self-delusion, that you have no gift, no ability, that it's all vanity,
a joke. But you've burnt your boats too, because there's no going
back now. When you jump ship from the expected thing you cease
to be Our Kind Of Person, so you might never get a conventional
job again. Imagine if you offered all of that, the whole package, to
Cliona: what would she say? No thank you, that's what. She'd
run shrieking back to the life she has chosen, the life that's
mapped out for her. She'd stay with the job she has and that
nice man Arthur who's probably going to marry her in a year
or so.

I realise that years from now I may bitterly regret how I have
chosen to live my life, but it's a risk I'm prepared to take. The
thing is, Dennis, if I don't keep faith with the life I'm leading now
I can definitely see myself at fifty or so, probably even sooner,
feeling angry and bitter, feeling that I haven't had a life at all and
being too deeply entrenched in some other reality – having
damaged my consciousness to such an extent that it would be too
late. And that's what it comes down to, Dennis, consciousness. I
just couldn't live that other life. You know that. It doesn't of
course mean that it's a bad life, or wrong in itself, just not right

for me. And to try to deny that would be to do great harm. I would be doing no favours to anyone.

As you know, my time here is almost up, and I've been thinking about what happens next. My heart sinks, frankly, at the thought of going home. I've already been in touch with the college: I can probably get a few classes in the autumn again, but nothing definite has been arranged yet. My studio will be available; I'll write soon to the person subletting it to confirm when I'll be back. But that's about all there is for me to return to, I feel. Not a lot, is it? Above all, I'll have to find a place to live. I know you have always said that the room is there for me, and I'll always be grateful to you for that, but I don't want to go back to being dependent on you. You have helped me so much already, and I feel that any more would be an abuse of your kindness. So I've written to a few friends to ask them to keep an ear to the ground and let me know if they hear of a suitable (dead cheap) flat. Failing that, I will probably rent a room in a house to start me off, until such time as I get something sorted out.

But the biggest problem of all is that I don't want to go back. I don't yet feel that I've exhausted the experience of being here. I've sold some work and a gallery has offered me an exhibition for later in the year. I'm just at the point where my contacts are developing – I can even speak reasonably good Italian at this stage – and it seems such a waste to simply walk away from everything. Ray is staying on: he's found a job down in Florence, teaching painting and art history to students over on study trips from the States. I've looked for something similar, but although there are a few openings, the colleges only want to employ Americans. I'll keep looking, but I think my chances of finding something like that are pretty slim.

The final and most important element in all of this is, of course, Marta. I'm sure you realise how close we are now, and the idea of saying thank you and goodbye, of just walking away, seems like unbelievable rudeness, as well as folly of the first order. I suppose *we could try to keep things going at a distance – were she in England or even France we'd try that – but Italy is so far. And I just couldn't ask her to come to Ireland. God knows, there's little enough there for me, so what would there be for her? There would be absolutely no work for a specialist in her field of art restoration. She has a good job, her own car and apartment. She's close to her family – she's an only child – and she loves her life here. It breaks my heart to say it, but I feel that I have absolutely nothing to offer her. If we went to Ireland, the circumstances would undermine the relationship in no time at all. So I don't know what to do and I don't know what will happen. I lie awake at night trying to think of a way to square the circle. This is the idyll Cliona envies me. If you have any ideas on how I might crack this particular problem do let me know. I'll write to you again soon, and I promise it won't be such a dismal letter. Sorry to moan, and thank you for listening to me,*

Best love,

Roderic.

Chapter Fifteen

'*Pronto?*'

Silence at the other end of the line, and then a female voice, but not Allegra's as he had expected. Roderic always spoke to his daughters at this time on a Wednesday evening ever since renewing contact with them.

'Um, Mr Kennedy? Have I got a wrong number?' His response had clearly thrown the caller and he apologised, explaining that he was due to receive a call from abroad at any moment.

'I'll try to be brief then,' she said. 'My name's Julia Fitzpatrick. I think Maria mentioned me to you, Maria Hill.'

Maria had had a studio in the same building as Roderic, just after the latter's return to Ireland, and they had remained good friends after she moved to a new space. Earlier that week, he had met her by chance in a bookshop. 'Speak of the devil,' Maria said. 'I was talking about you only the other day to a former student of mine. She might be going to Italy on a fellowship next year, and I thought it would be interesting for her to talk to you about it.'

'By all means,' Roderic said. 'Tell her to give me a ring,'

And yet, after he had chatted to Maria for some time and then said goodbye to her, he wondered what he could sensibly say to her protégée. In the ensuing days when he had thought of this woman at all it was to hope that she wouldn't get in touch, but now that she had he felt it would be rude to refuse to see her. It was Maria to whom he had said yes, and after all she had done for him, he could never let her down.

They arranged to meet the following Friday afternoon in a city-centre café.

'You'll know me,' she said, 'because I have strange hair.'
No sooner had he put the receiver down than the phone rang
again.

'*Ciao Babbo.*'

'*Carissima ciao . . .*' And for the next half-hour he forgot all
about Julia Fitzpatrick.

She had very strange hair indeed. He had thought her
description of herself on the phone was self-deprecating; as
soon as he saw her he realised that it was merely accurate.
She walked into the café and he raised his arm, waved her
over to the table where he sat. She approached him smiling,
introduced herself and shook hands. Months later, at
Christmas, they would discuss that moment. He would tell
her how struck he had been by the easy way she dumped her
bag on the floor and offered to buy him a coffee, how he
watched her as she went to the counter and took a tray,
narrowing her eyes to look at the choice of cakes scrawled
faintly on a small slate. He would be able to describe to
her the long green skirt and white blouse she had been
wearing on that hot July afternoon long after she herself had
forgotten. She would ask him frankly if he had found her
attractive right from the start, and he would answer with
equal candour no, not particularly; that in the first instance
he hadn't been looking at her in that light at all. Nor,
unusually, had he thought of his daughters, as he habitually
now did when in the company of young women. It had been
himself he thought of when she finally sat down opposite
him and said, 'I've brought you here on a fool's errand, I'm
afraid. I'm not going to Italy after all.'

She had received the letter that morning saying that her
application for the residency had been unsuccessful. 'I feel
embarrassed now, I shouldn't have contacted you at all until
I was sure.' She had phoned him at once to cancel the
appointment but he wasn't there, had already left the house
for his studio.

'You must be bitterly disappointed.'

'Gutted.'

He thought of himself, of how delighted he had been when he opened the envelope and received the news all those years ago. 'Where in Italy is the place you hoped to go?'

'In Tuscany,' she said. 'A foundation called the Villa Rosalba. It's a long-established place, I believe. Perhaps you've heard of it?'

'Indeed,' he said. 'I have indeed.'

'Gutted,' she said again. 'I'm trying to be philosophic. When one door closes, another one shuts, or whatever the saying is. I've got that wrong, haven't I? Well, that's what it feels like.'

'Have you ever been to Italy before?'

'Yes, that's the problem. I went there briefly when I was a student and I've always wanted to go back for a longer spell. Were you there for a long time? Maria didn't say.'

'I went for six months in the first instance,' Roderic replied, 'about twenty years ago. I stayed on for eleven years before coming back to Ireland.'

'I suppose you return to Italy from time to time?'

'As a matter of fact I was there recently, just a few weeks ago, in June,' he remarked. He didn't tell her then that it had been his first visit since leaving eight years earlier, and that he was still somewhat emotionally shell-shocked as a result.

'It was foolish of me,' she said 'to think that everything was going to work out the way I wanted.'

'Tell me about yourself. Are you a painter?'

'No, I work in mixed media. I like your work very much,' she went on quickly, and he would tell her when he knew her better that he hadn't believed her. He thought it merely a tactic to direct attention away from herself, until she spoke of the one-man show he had had in Dublin the year before. The degree to which she remembered individual works, and homed in on the best, surprised and slightly unnerved him.

133

'I liked the big cream and grey grid on the right of the door when you went in.'

'And what about the blue and white painting at the bottom of the room?' he said, deliberately singling out what he considered to be the weakest picture. 'Do you remember that?'

'Mmn.'

'And what did you think of it?'

Julia looked at the floor. 'It didn't please me anything like as much,' she said, 'as the painting in cream and grey.'

This ethical refusal to flatter reminded him of her mentor. 'So Maria used to teach you?'

'Yes. She wrote me a reference for this place in Italy.'

'Maria's an old friend of mine. When I came back to Ireland we both had studios in the same building. It was a difficult time in my life and she was exceptionally kind to me.' He sat in silence for a moment, thinking of the reality behind this and then, 'She was,' he said again, 'exceptionally kind.'

'So how do you manage?' he asked Julia.

'You mean what do I live on? Well, I live very simply, for one thing, and I have a part-time job in an antique shop. I get by on that, just about.'

'It's good to have a bit of security,' he said.

'Security,' and she ground out her cigarette. '*Security!*' The scorn in her voice startled him.

'Well, stability, then,' he said, and she considered this.

'Stability's different,' she said. 'Stability, yes, I'll grant you that, but there's no such thing as security. It doesn't exist.'

'What makes you so sure?' he asked

She looked him straight in the eye. 'Experience,' she said. 'What else?'

He hadn't allowed her to buy him a coffee when she arrived, but in the course of their conversation he had drained the mug in front of him. He went up to the counter ('I couldn't get over how tall you were when you stood up, I almost laughed out loud,') and now it was Julia's turn to look at him and draw her own conclusions. Even after they knew each other well, he had to wheedle and coax to find out what she had thought. 'I'd never seen a man,' she finally admitted 'who looked so lonely and forlorn. And yet I thought you were good company. I came close to saying, "Why don't we go and have a walk after this, then maybe have something to eat, go to see a film or something?"'

'Just think,' he said, 'of all the time we might have saved if you had.'

'I was trying to remember what was on in the cinema, but then you came back to the table with your tray, and suddenly I felt intimidated. I remembered that you were established and eminent, a real big cheese, and I was just a tiddler straight out of art college. I wasn't feeling very confident that day, as you can imagine. And so I said nothing.'

Roderic did notice that a sudden shyness had fallen over her when he returned to the table, but failed to guess the reason for it. When they left the café together she thanked him for meeting her. He brushed aside her renewed apologies for having wasted his time and said goodbye. They were going in opposite directions now and he moved to cross the road against a red pedestrian light. Immediately he felt someone tightly gripping his upper arm, pulling him back, and he turned around, astonished and even slightly irritated. 'The light's red,' Julia said. 'Wait until it turns green.' She hadn't struck him as overly cautious. He resisted, pulled against her and turned back to the road. At that moment, a motorbike he hadn't seen shot past, missing him by inches. Julia gave him a look in which there was just the faintest hint of *I told you so*. The traffic stopped and the light turned green; she released his arm from her grip. 'Goodbye,' she said again. 'Look after yourself.'

Roderic saw her again within the week, in an incident so brief, so strange and full of otherness that even when he came to know her well he never asked her about it, not least because he sometimes wondered if it was something he had imagined.

He had been in the middle of the city, again waiting to cross at a busy junction, when he saw her in the crowd on the far side of the road. He would have noticed her anywhere: with such extraordinary hair she was easily visible from a distance. She was standing still and looking up at the sky. The lights did not change and as he watched her he became aware that something out of the ordinary was happening. It was as if she were in a trance or having some kind of vision: rapt, silent, utterly cut off from the crowds who moved around her. He wondered how long she had been there like that, and if she was safe. He jabbed at the button on the panel fixed near by and it became illuminated, blue and white, *Wait*, as though chiding him for his impatience. He considered darting across the road against the lights in spite of her former warning, but the traffic was too heavy. Just as the walking green man lit up, he saw her move. He was swept across the road with the people who surrounded him to where she stood, but she was walking away now from where she had been. He considered calling to her but felt it would have been foolish: she could not have heard him in any case, above the noise of the city. The crowd thickened around her as he approached, someone stopped and blocked his way, distracting him momentarily, and when he looked up again she had disappeared.

He had reason to call Maria again a few days after that.

'Are you ringing about Julia?' she asked. 'I may as well tell you, I was livid about her not getting that fellowship. There's no justice in the world.'

'Are you only finding that out now?'

'I wouldn't have suggested you meet her, only I was convinced she was on to a sure thing. Perhaps they thought she was too young; she's only a year out of art college. I'm sorry for wasting your time.'

'Don't be silly, it was a pleasure. She's nice; seems very bright.'

136

'She is, believe me. Did you see any of her work? Well you ought to, you must. Give her a ring. Here's her number.'

She was flustered when he called, thrown, in a way he hadn't expected. 'Visit my studio? Well you could, yes, I suppose. Why not? Maybe it's awkward for you,' and she seemed less than enthused when, on hearing that she lived in Francis Street, he said he was just around the corner. They made an arrangement for late in the afternoon two days later.

When she opened the door to Roderic she struck him as more severe than he remembered, more unsmiling. They went up to the sitting room where she made a great fuss of looking for her cigarettes and lighter, but didn't seem particularly pleased when they were eventually found under a cushion.

'The studio's upstairs,' she said rather shortly, and they were on the third step when he realised what he was doing.

'We could,' he said, 'wait until another time.'

Julia stopped and turned to him. 'Well, you've come all this way,' she said, but he could sense her relief that he was offering her a way out.

'I'm five minutes from home, if that.'

'That's twice now I've brought you on a fool's errand,' she said.

He told her he was capable of being extremely foolish on his own account, with help from no one, and she laughed. She was looking now for a final and gracious way out.

'I could make tea,' she said. 'We could just talk for a while.'

They went into the kitchen and she made tea in the absent-minded, hit-or-miss fashion with which he was to become so familiar. He noted for the first time the details of her imperfect housekeeping: the broken biscuits, the milk that was just on the point of going sour. She introduced him to the ironic tomcat – 'Say hello to Max' – who surveyed the scene, perched, fastidious, on the top of the fridge, and subsequently disconcerted Roderic as he drank his tea by moving around the room at eye level, from the fridge to

137

the top of a press, to a shelf cluttered with tins of food. It was an enormous cat, with a huge thick neck and feet like pot scrubbers.

'So how did Max come into your life?' Roderic asked.

'My father gave him to me,' Julia said. 'I was home in Wicklow one weekend, and I happened to say I would love a kitten. And the next time I went back, there was Max, waiting for me. My father spoils me rotten,' she added. She said it without shame or qualification, stated it as a bald fact.

'What do you do about Max when you go away?' Roderic asked, and she pointed to a cat basket with a wire mesh door in the corner of the room.

'Doesn't he mind?'

'Watch this,' she said. She picked up the basket and the cat immediately shot behind the fridge. 'QED. It's all right Max, only kidding. We're not going anywhere; you can come out now. There's a souvenir of our last trip home,' and she held her hand out for Roderic's inspection, displaying a long red scratch mark. 'He loves it when he gets there, climbs trees in the orchard and chases birds, but the hour of our departure is not for the faint hearted.' The cat had still not emerged from its hiding place.

If she'd gone to Italy, Julia said, her father would have looked after Max while she was away, and Roderic asked her then if she'd got over her recent disappointment.

'Oh, sure,' she said. 'There's no point in brooding on things, is there? Who knows, maybe something even better's going to happen to me soon.' Almost immediately she qualified this, to Roderic's mind, almost perverse optimism by adding wistfully, 'Don't know what it could be, though. Italy would have been great. It was the smaller cities I particularly hoped to visit. Ferrara. Urbino. Also, I'm trying to change direction in my work at the moment and I thought it might help to go away for a while.'

'Change in what way?'

'When you're ready we can go up to the studio and I'll show you.' He demurred but she insisted. 'It's all right. I'm asking you now.'

In the studio she showed him a series of boxes on which she was working, full of coloured feathers and glass beads, old photographs and torn letters. On some of them she had been experimenting with tinted glass that subtly altered one's perception of the boxes' contents. He complimented her sincerely on the work, remarking upon its beauty.

'I'm glad you said that. I know it's old-fashioned, but it's important to me that the work should be beautiful. There's enough ugliness in the world without me adding to it. I'm always struck by the – pleasure, for want of a better word, although it's something much more than that – to be had by simply looking at a beautiful object.'

'Beauty is in the eye of the beholder.'

'That's where I want to go next,' she said. 'It's why I want to move away from making objects, because it's not just the thing, it's the person who's looking at it. You know this idea that everyone can be an artist? I don't believe that. But I do think that many people are artists without knowing it. It has nothing to do with craft, you know, the ability to paint or draw.'

'I'm not sure I'd agree with you there,' he said, 'but that may be because I'm more than twenty years older than you.'

He couldn't help feeling slightly piqued when she didn't contradict this, but nodded and said, 'Yes, that's probably true, but let me explain. Take my father. I was out for a walk with him a while back and he pointed out to me a little tree that was growing in a clump of wild yellow irises. There was something about the relationship between the two – the fragility of the tree, the sense of multitude the flowers gave, yellow, green, and the whole thing moving in the wind, it was alive. I can't explain. But it was for just that moment, that *particular* moment when my father noticed it, because

I passed the same spot a week later and it looked quite nondescript. It was just, you know, a tree.'

'And that makes him an artist?'

'In my book, yes.'

Propped against one of the walls beside where she was standing was a cork pin-board to which were fastened several papers including a telephone bill, an invoice from a shop selling art materials and a postcard reproduction of a still life. While they were talking his attention had been caught by the image on the postcard, and he gazed at it now: at the silver and the glass, the nutshells and the broken pastry, the luminous yellow light in which the whole was bathed, and suddenly it astounded him. 'To think,' he said 'that people once painted like that. That was how they saw the world. And now we can't trust our own eyes, can't believe that what we see before us is what it is: a table, a bottle, a dish. Why is it, do you think, that people like still life paintings so much nowadays? Is it for the quality of attention that is in them?'

Together they looked at the postcard for a few more minutes.

'No,' Julia said. 'A still life is full of repose. That, above all, is so hard to find in the world as it is now. That's what people respond to, that's what they seek.'

'So where,' he asked, 'do you see your work going?' and she laughed.

'That's another story altogether. I'm experimenting at the moment, but I'm going on with the boxes in the meantime. It'll be a long time before I have the confidence to show the new work. I'm playing with ideas for the moment. Perhaps you could help me?'

He said he was willing and she gave him a paper and pen, asked him to write down all the most evocative smells he could think of. It took him quite a while, for he paused to think for a long time, then wrote something, then paused again. At last he handed her the paper and as she read it, she started to laugh. 'I should have told you,' she said, 'to be more specific. I was thinking of things like coffee, you know, or bread, things like that.

This was what he had written on the page:

Smell of the hall in the house where I used to live in Italy
Candlewax and incense (old church?)
Antiseptic (sort of: as in a doctor's surgery)
Perfume
The inside of a piano

'What was the name of the perfume?' she said.

He told her that he didn't remember, and he knew by the way she looked at him that she didn't believe it. 'I hope you're not going to ask me,' he said, 'what they mean to me?'

'Not these things, no. But the project would be developed around that, about finding scents and offering them to any number of people, and then asking what they summon up to them. I have this theory,' she said, 'that it'll all come down to either sex or childhood.'

'I think,' he said, 'you may be on to something there.'

Chapter Sixteen

London, 15th April

Dear Julia,

My only luck at this difficult period of my life has been to meet you. Your kindness and understanding means more to me than I can easily say. My behaviour when I called to the gallery must have appeared at best strange, at worst rude, and for that I offer sincere apologies. I should always regret anything that were to lower me in your esteem.

With affection,

William.

P.S. I wonder what you'll make of this particular woman?

The draught Julia made as she left the room had wafted the postcard right to his feet. Roderic glanced down at the image; knew it at once for a Holbein, and picked it up. Unthinkingly, he turned it over. The handwriting was as neat and legible as print, and before he knew it, his eyes had scanned the message. He disliked the general tone of it, and the last line hit him like a hammer blow. He turned the card over again. The woman, in her oddly shaped fur bonnet, stared off inscrutably into the middle distance, as though pointedly ignoring him. The squirrel crammed a nut into its mouth and looked, Roderic thought, as though it was trying hard not to laugh. He turned the card over again and re-read the message, this time with conscious intent, for he needed to be sure that there was no mistake, that it wasn't some wild fantasy of his own.

In his mind's eye, as vividly as though he were watching a film, Roderic saw himself sitting at a café table in Paris. His recall of the scene that day at the end of last October was perfect: the small, thick white coffee cup, the sugar cubes wrapped in paper, one torn open, one intact, the glass and carafe for water, the scatter of silver coins, and the bill, crumpled and torn by the waiter, the fake marble of the table itself. And in amongst all of that was the paraphernalia of pens, stamps and the postcards he had bought in the galleries. He saw himself writing the cards, checking them off in his mind: one each to his daughters, choosing which would suit them best, one for Dennis. He had had Julia in mind when he bought her particular card and the teasing note he would add as a postscript.

But how did this other man, this William, know about it? How did *he* know?

He could hear Julia clumping back upstairs now from the shop. Hastily he replaced the card on the mantelpiece from which it had fallen, and just as he sat down again she came into the room. She had only been gone for moments, but the impact of her presence was considerable. Roderic gave her a look that he hoped would come across as merely enquiring. 'Hester said someone bought the wardrobe today, so there'll be room in the shop for the table,' and she nodded towards the item as she mentioned it. 'Someone will come to help move it down tomorrow morning. I can't say I'll be sorry to see the back of it.'

'What about the trunk?'

'Oh, I'm hoping she's forgotten about the trunk,' Julia said. 'It's been there for so long I sort of consider it mine now.'

She went on talking about how much she had learned about antiques since she started to work for Hester; that the table was a hunting table, that the wood it was made of was actually . . . Roderic's attention drifted away from her, and he became again wholly absorbed in his own thoughts.

143

He hadn't known that William had called to the gallery in March. Julia hadn't mentioned it: why not? And what had happened there? He wondered if he should bring up the subject of the postcard, but didn't know how to broach it. The matter of his having read it made the issue a delicate one, as did the weird coincidence of the final message. Perhaps she would be angry, would think he had been deliberately prying in her private correspondence. He had always known his visual memory was good, but never, until now, had he thought of himself as having a particular aptitude for remembering language. And yet every last line of the text, every prissy phrase and stiff conjunction was burned on his mind . . . *understanding means more to me than I can easily say . . . for that I offer sincere apologies . . . With affection.*

'Roderic? I said, don't you think so?'

He stared at her dumbly.

'You haven't heard a single word, have you? You haven't been listening.'

He couldn't even begin to hazard a guess at what she had asked him, and had to admit as much.

'Oh, it was nothing too important,' she said, and his absentmindedness appeared to amuse rather than annoy her. How irritated Marta used to get when this happened, and it had been a common occurrence. She would begin some long discourse about getting the shutters painted or buying new bed linen or planning a dinner to which her family were to be invited: domestic details that bored him so immensely his mind would simply close down and move on to a more absorbing subject.

'I see you're admiring my postcard,' Julia said unexpectedly. Without realising it, his eyes had kept straying back to the picture of the woman with the squirrel. 'William sent it to me from London recently. You remember him – William Armstrong? He's got nice handwriting, hasn't he?' She lifted the card down and handed it to him.

Duplicitously, Roderic pretended to read the message. 'The last line,' he said. 'What's that all about?'

'I thought that was a bit cheeky myself. Your card was in the book I lost that he brought back to me. Obviously he read it and remembered.'

'I didn't know he came to the gallery.'

'Surely I told you about that? No? I could have sworn I did . . . oh, he came all right, it was a weird session. It really spooked him; he's quite prim and proper.'

'Oh, I can believe it,' Roderic said quickly. 'Awfully tight arsed and buttoned up, I'd have thought, just on the strength of that one meeting.'

'He's not that bad,' Julia protested. 'A bit stiff in his manner, but good hearted, I think. The photographs, you remember? The women and the babies? They really shocked him, and as for the installations . . . I shouldn't laugh, for he really was mortified, but it was terribly funny.'

'I'd have thought taking off his shoes and crawling up a fake vagina was just what he needed,' Roderic said.

'Why do you dislike him so much?' Julia said. 'What is it you have against him?'

'If he's as great an art lover, a collector, even, as he claims to be, he should be more at ease with contemporary art, I'd have thought.'

'In fairness, he had his children with him, and I think he was bothered about the effect it might have on them.'

'And what did the kids make of it?'

'They had a ball. Of course they hadn't a clue what it was about. As far as they were concerned it was just some kind of funfair.'

'Children are pure hearted,' he said, 'and unless a thing is in and of itself corrupting, it won't harm them.'

'They liked the gallery,' Julia said, 'the boy, I think, in particular, but the way their father reacted made them uneasy.'

'Speaking of the exhibition,' Roderic said carefully, 'I wonder if you've seen this.' Reaching down to a bag at his feet he took out a magazine and handed it to her folded open. 'Brace yourself: it's pretty grim. Begin with the last paragraph.'

In contrast to these squalid and explicit images, Julia Fitzpatrick offers us an art of concealment, which also fails utterly to engage. Closed and cryptic, her work is derivative. The pieces on show here focus upon objects and images (shells, stones, pieces of fabric) which evidently hold some private and talismanic significance for her, but the meaning of which she fails to share with us, and wilfully so. Fluttering curtains of white ribbon serve to exclude the viewer from Fitzpatrick's work. Hers is ultimately a self-absorbed vision, and the viewer who struggles to make sense of her world finds himself deliberately and definitively shut out. One is left, however, with the conviction of being excluded from something that is of neither interest nor importance.

Brendan Halpin.

'Jesus,' Julia said.

She tried to smile at Roderic, but she couldn't quite manage it, and he noticed that the hand that held the magazine was shaking. He wished he could tell her that the first time was the worst, that in the future something like this would fail to bother her, but he knew it wasn't necessarily true. Instead he said, 'If it's any consolation, he hated the photographs and the vaginal thing even more. I mean, what can you say about a man who finds pictures of women with their babies squalid? Put it out of your mind. You've met Brendan: I rest my case.'

They had, at least, stopped talking about William, but Roderic knew that wouldn't be the end of it. When they met again three days later, she said that he had called to the shop that morning.

'And how is he?'

'Slightly better form, I thought. He's converting a bedroom in his house into a studio.'

'I hope he doesn't think that's going to solve all his woes.'

'Who's to say? He seemed pleased about it. If I had his money I wouldn't settle for a bedroom. I'd set myself up in a first-class studio with loads of space, but I got the impression it's important to him that it be in the house. I think it's some kind of declaration of intent. Good luck to him. Anyway, he didn't just call for a chat. He told me he'd liked my work very much and he's interested in buying a piece.'

And Roderic was genuinely pleased to hear this.

For well over an hour now they had been in the studio, choosing things that she might offer for sale. The ones they settled on were all smaller than those she had shown in the exhibition. The smallest of all was a kaleidoscope containing not fragments of coloured glass but a series of tiny photographic transparencies that appeared and disappeared, multiplied and were reduced in number as the viewer turned the ring. The largest was a peepshow: a long wooden box with the side farthest from the viewing aperture covered in parchment. The box contained leaves, hundreds of pressed leaves arranged with a series of mirrors and magnifying glasses so that the viewer saw them doubled exactly, saw green ribs and veins, saw the leaves receding away to the back of the box. It gave the effect of being absorbed into the still and silent heart of a forest irradiated with light.

Roderic straightened up and stood back, glanced over at Julia. She was staring hard at one of the other pieces and was chewing her thumb, as she always did when she was anxious. It was as if he had never known her, as if their relationship counted for nothing when faced with the work and the knowledge of that distant, inviolable part of herself from which it came. He was so fond of her he sometimes forgot how good an artist she was, and he chided himself silently for it now. Was he already beginning to take her for granted?

147

Julia noticed that he was looking not at the work but at her. 'Well?' she said. 'What do you reckon?'

He pointed to each of the pieces in turn and named a price.

'God, as much as that?'

'You do good work,' he replied. 'You should never sell yourself short.'

'Still and all, I don't want to price myself so high as to put him off. I don't want him to think that I'm pushing my luck.'

'He said he wanted to buy. You're not doing him a favour, nor he you.' But he knew himself that he *was* pushing it, and that the figures he advised were at the limit for a young and unknown artist. He took out a paper and pen, and wrote down each price in turn, saying it aloud and revising downwards from his earlier suggestions. 'Go no lower than that,' he said as he handed her the page. 'Above all, don't give an inch on the one with the leaves.'

Still she looked doubtful.

'People like William Armstrong are not like us,' he said simply.

'We need them, though.'

'They need us too. The difference is, they don't realise it. Remember that he's doing this for himself. He wants a bargain, and he'll be getting one.'

She smiled. 'Thanks for helping me with this. For the moral support, as much as anything. I can't tell you how glad I'll be when this is over, however it goes.'

'Don't let him try to haggle. Be businesslike with him,' Roderic urged. 'Be distant, and be firm.'

Julia nodded, and he risked adding, 'Be wary of him.' She looked at him curiously.

'What makes you say that?'

'He's a bit of a lame duck. The depression and so forth, you know. People like that can be more dangerous than they realise.'

148

'Dangerous.' She repeated the word in a tone that implied he needed to explain further.

'Someone as devitalised and miserable as that needs energy. He'll take yours, if you give him half a chance. He'll suck you dry.'

'You make him sound like a vampire,' Julia said, laughing. 'He's due to call tomorrow afternoon. I'll let you know how I get on.' And the moment did not seem right for Roderic to press the matter further.

He dreamt that night that he was in a railway station made all of white marble. From high windows, shafts of light came down to where he was standing under the clock, waiting for someone. When that person arrived they would take a train together, and it was vital – a matter of literal life and death – that they did not miss it, although he did not know why that should be, nor even the identity of the person for whom he was waiting. All he knew was that his expected companion had not arrived and that the train was due to leave in five minutes, five minutes that took an hour to pass. Someone in the endless crowd that streamed past, jostling and pushing him constantly, murmured without looking directly at him, 'Why are you here? You were to meet at the ticket office, not under the clock.' Was this true? What if he left his post and the person he was waiting for arrived? What if they were indeed waiting for him at the ticket office? Should he move or stay where he was? There was no luggage at his feet. He had had a suitcase – hadn't he? A shrill train whistle blew, and then he woke up.

'Guess which one he bought.'

'The one with the feathers? No? The one with the leaves?'

She nodded, and Roderic was genuinely surprised. He had been silently sure that William would balk at the price, and his delight for her was sincere. She told him she had felt anxious and that William when he arrived appeared to be completely on top of the situation, which had only made her feel worse. He had considered what was on offer and the prices; had talked about her work and then spoken more generally. Just when she was sure that he was about to say he would think about it and be in touch – a polite way of saying no – he made her an offer for the box with the leaves.

'Lower than the price you asked?'

'Lower, yes, but not by as much as I'd feared. I told him it wasn't negotiable, and suggested the feathers again. But he wanted the leaves.'

'Of course he did. It's the best piece.'

'So he thought about it for a few minutes more, and then he said yes.'

Roderic congratulated her again. Later, he would think he should have been more explicit at that point, should have warned her off. 'Let that be an end to it. If he rings you or makes contact again, refuse to see him. Tell him you're busy.' It wasn't that he didn't think of it at the time, those very words of warning formed in his mind, but he had thought too: 'Who am I to tell her this? What right have I to lay down the law?' In any case, Julia would never stand for being told what to do. He had made his unease concerning William plain enough, to say more at this stage would be to keep the issue open, just at the point when it seemed to be quietly drawing to a close.

Chapter Seventeen

'Did you get one of these too?' Maeve asked. Dennis nodded dumbly. She propped the card up on the mantelpiece and they both stared at it for a moment. 'It'll be a very grand affair if the invitation's anything to go by,' she said. 'Look even at the envelope,' and she thrust it under Dennis's nose so that he could inspect the calligraphy and the thick, heavy paper lined with tissue.

'I told you, I got one myself.'

The invitation was engraved, silver on white; the flowing letters looked as if they had been iced on to the card by a master baker. There were no images at all, no silver bells or golden rings, no silhouettes of bride and groom, no fake stained-glass windows and no candles. It was under-stated, elegant and in perfect taste, and as such, Dennis thought, wholly inappropriate as an invitation to Roderic's wedding.

That Roderic would someday either marry or set up home with someone was a thought that had crossed Dennis's mind from time to time over the years. It had come close to happening once or twice, with his girlfriend in the west, and with another woman, Annie. It had never bothered Dennis then as an idea, and, given that it bothered him so much now that it was becoming a reality, he asked himself why this should be. It was when Roderic had decided to extend his time in Italy and moved in with Marta that Dennis had started to feel uneasy. That he was now marrying her meant that he would probably never live in Ireland again. He stared at the invitation on Maeve's mantelpiece with something close to anguish, as he had sat looking at his own in the house that morning. It was all wrong.

Now that it wasn't going to happen, he could imagine the wedding Roderic might have had with one of the women he'd known when he lived with Dennis. He could see the invitation: a big jazzy card the size of a paving stone, WEDDING! written across it in thick paint, and surrounded by an ironic slather of ribbons and sequins and spangles, cheerfully over the top. Better that than this icy, mass-produced thing that had arrived. Or perhaps there wouldn't have been an invitation at all. He imagined his brother sitting beside the telephone, working his way through his address book. *Jim? Jim, it's me. I have a bit of news for you. We're getting married. Yeah, cheers. We're having a big bash that night, Friday fortnight. Will you and Moira be there? Great stuff.* He saw Roderic with a gardenia pinned to his jumper, the bride in some mad muslin confection of her own making, barelegged and with a crown of wild flowers on her head. He saw the riotous party that was their wedding reception, with no speeches and no receiving line, no clear soup and no white cake: nothing that was conventional.

'Chiesa di San Stefano,' Maeve's voice said, cutting into his thoughts. 'Does that mean it's to be in a church?'

'Yes.'

'Well I suppose that's something, anyway. And she's an arty type too, I gather?'

'Who's "she"?'

'Why, this woman,' Maeve said, 'that Roderic's marrying.'

'Your future sister-in-law's name is Marta, and she's an expert in art restoration. Whether or not that makes her an "arty type" I couldn't possibly say.'

His irritation irritated Maeve, but she decided to let it pass.

'Her father's a judge,' she said. This was news to Dennis.

'How do you know that?'

'Mum asked Roderic when he rang to tell her he was getting married. I suppose you'll go over to the wedding?'

'Of course. What about you?' She shook her head.

'Mum won't be going either but Cliona's thinking about it, and Daddy definitely wants to be there. Maybe you'll take out presents from us to give to him?'

Dennis nodded. He couldn't speak now. Maeve peered at him curiously. He looked as if he was going to cry and she couldn't for the life of her think why this should be.

As the invitation sat uneasily with any idea of a wedding to which Roderic might be a party, the gifts, too, when they started to filter in, added to the sense of dislocation. Dennis saw that the embroidered linen Cliona bought, Maeve's crystal and the silver cutlery his parents offered were suitable wedding presents in so far as they were typical. But as gifts for Roderic they seemed mystifyingly inappropriate, unless since moving to Italy he had undergone some tremendous sea change, some transmogrification of personality and lifestyle of which there was no evidence in the cheery letters he continued to send to his brother; nor in the enclosed photographs of him standing with his arm around Marta, or lifting his glass to the camera. Dennis himself was at a loss to know what he ought to buy. It was a particular source of anxiety because Roderic himself had, Dennis thought, a kind of genius for selecting presents, remarking once, 'When you choose the right thing, it's a way of saying to someone, "I know who you are."' For all that, he found himself falling in with the general ethos, found himself wandering glumly around displays of china and crystal in department stores. On one of these excursions, he saw a couple standing with a clipboard-wielding sales assistant before the dinner services.

'Well, which *do* you prefer?' the woman asked the man crossly. 'The one with the ivy or the one with the gold line?'

'I really don't mind,' the man replied. 'They're both nice. You decide.'

The woman glowered at him. 'You're not being helpful Joe, not helpful at all.'

It was, Dennis thought, like a vision of hell. Did they have wedding lists in Italy? At this precise moment was Roderic trailing around some china shop in Siena undergoing a similar ordeal?

A week before he left, a woman phoned him late one night. 'You probably won't remember me,' she said, and Dennis didn't recall the name she gave. 'I'm an old friend of Roderic's. He invited me to his wedding and I have a present for him. I wondered if you'd be so kind as to take it out to Italy for me?' They arranged that she would call to his office the following day.

'Do you remember me now?' she asked when they met.

'I do indeed,' Dennis said. The image of her that came to his mind was of seeing her sitting at his breakfast table wearing nothing but an old shirt of Roderic's that came to her shins. They had been a couple for a few months in the early days, and had remained friends thereafter.

'It's kind of you to do this for me,' she said. 'I'd have posted it out but it wasn't ready until yesterday.' She was holding a bundle of coarse buff calico tied up with a silky green ribbon. 'I wrapped it like this for the customs. I'd better show you what it is, in case you get asked,' and she pulled the ribbon. The bundle contained a blanket made of thick, soft wool in colours of mosses and turf, shot through with blue. 'I had a woman I know, a weaver, make it specially,' she said. Dennis stared at her, unable to speak. 'Tell him I'm sorry I can't be there. Tell him I said good luck.' And as Dennis watched, he saw a crown of wild flowers descend, and settle gently on her brow.

He arrived in Italy several days before the wedding to be met at the airport by Roderic and Marta, and to be swept up, all at once, into his brother's new life. To begin with, Dennis was glad he had given Roderic no indication of his misgivings, for he felt now that he had been completely wrong. He had never been to Italy before. In spite of all Roderic had told him in letters, in spite of the photographs he had sent, in spite, even, of his own preternaturally vivid imagination, nothing had prepared him. He was enchanted, completely won over. Marta, whom he had dreaded meeting, visualising in the watches of the night her chill initial greeting: 'So you must be Dennis,' introduced herself by throwing her arms around him. 'My dear brother,' she said and she kissed him. 'My dear, dear brother.' At dinner on that first night, his brain fuddled by tiredness and the buzz around him of a language he could not understand, by too much wine drunk with the huge plates of food, pasta and chicken and salad that Marta's mother had pressed upon him, he happened to glance up at Roderic. He was sitting with his chin propped in his hand, staring across the table at Marta who was staring back at him in the same wholly absorbed way. They were besotted with each other, Dennis thought, completely besotted.

They had been living together for about six months when they decided to get married, at which point they moved from Marta's small apartment into the house which had been her grandparents' home. They were well established there by the time of the wedding. The morning after his arrival Roderic showed Dennis around the cool interior, with its long rooms and high ceilings; and the walled garden with its tomatoes and courgettes, its extravagant roses. 'That's my studio,' Roderic said, pointing at a long outhouse on the left. 'Come and I'll show you.' They went up three wooden steps and into a white room flooded with light.

Although he was in no way territorial or secretive, Roderic had always been selective about who he did or didn't let into his studio. To force the matter, to show up uninvited, to insist on being allowed in, was to risk disturbing the deep-seated irritable streak he got from Frank and that one engaged at one's peril. 'Letting someone into your studio is like letting someone into your head, so they can see how you think,' he once said. 'You have to be careful.' Dennis had been one of the few who was always welcome, but even he would never have called unexpectedly to the studio in Dublin without good reason. He sat down now in a blue armchair and looked around. It was all, he thought, reassuringly familiar. It wasn't just that Roderic had obviously set the place up along exactly the same lines as his old studio in Ireland – the comfortable chair beside the door, the trestle table pushed hard against the back wall and laden with painting materials, the bookcase, the easel, the lot. It was more than that: it was an atmosphere, a climate. His windows in Dublin had given on to a faded Georgian townhouse, his windows here the lush garden, but somehow it didn't matter. Both spaces had the same brightness and cheer, with the sense of something serious, even sombre, at the back of it all. It was indeed, Dennis surmised, as close as one could get to being inside Roderic's head.

'I've done good work while I've been here. I've moved on to another level; it's been great.' As he spoke, he turned around some of the many canvases that were leaning against the wall, so that Dennis could see them. The patches of colour in which he worked had become more muted, and finer, more regular. That was the only difference Dennis could see, and he didn't know what it amounted to, but Roderic seemed pleased. 'It's been a real breakthrough,' he went on. 'Funnily enough, I don't think it has anything to do with being in Italy. I used to think it was the change of scene that had opened things up, but now I feel that it would have happened anyway. Something had to give. It's like banging your head against a brick wall for ages and then you look round, and there's an open door behind you. The relief! You can't imagine, you just can't imagine.'

Dennis nodded, still staring at the paintings. 'It's good that Marta's in the same line of work as yourself.'

'She is and she isn't,' Roderic said, beginning to turn the canvases round to face the wall again. 'There's a considerable difference between what we do.'

'Surely there's some common ground?'

'Yes, of course. I mean, we both love art. She's got a good eye, Marta, extraordinarily good. But it's a completely different approach, you know what I mean?'

Dennis didn't really, but he nodded and let it pass.

They went back out into the hot garden. 'That's a passion flower,' Roderic said, nodding at a vine that was twined around a trellis at the back door. 'Hard to believe, isn't it, me living in a house with a passion flower growing outside it. Sometimes even yet it all seems unreal. I think it's a dream and I'm going to wake up back in your house, listening to the rain battering on the slates.'

Oh, you should be so lucky, Dennis thought bitterly. You should be so lucky.

That night, Dennis found it impossible to sleep. Marriage! How could *anyone* do it? It had always held for him a peculiar horror. He usually tried not to think too much about this side of his own life, but in the small hours of the morning he had no defence against it. People thought they had the measure of him, but they didn't. They assumed in him an indifference to women which wasn't the case at all, just as they usually failed to see that his gruff, rather forbidding manner hid a desperate shyness. Roderic probably thought that he had never had a girl in his whole life, but he would have been wrong.

When Dennis was in his first year at university, he had been befriended by a young woman called Edith. Like him, she was studying music, with the violin as her specialisation. It was a time of such emotional turmoil and uncertainty for Dennis that looking back he wondered how he had come through it at all. He had to face up to the fact that he wasn't going to make the grade as a concert pianist, and the rest of his life loomed before him, empty. Edith succoured him in his woe. She talked through his options with him, and gave him precious moral support when he had to summon up the courage to tell Frank he wanted to change to another course of studies. Together they went to concerts of baroque music and to the cinema, often going for a drink or a simple meal afterwards. Edith lived in a cosy, tiny bed-sit in Ranelagh. With its clutter of books and music, its candles and posters and potted plants, it became a haven for Dennis, who was still living at home, and it was there one Friday night in front of the gas fire that, to his immense relief, she finally seduced him.

She was only slightly less timid and marginally more experienced than he, so it was a somewhat fumbling and awkward encounter, but it didn't matter. He loved being with her, and thought that her going to bed with him on a regular basis, as she did in the weeks that followed, was an act of great kindness. Their sedate, discreet affair continued and evolved until one day, just before a composition lecture, a mutual friend remarked, 'I hear yourself and Edith are an item.'

A cold, sickish feeling swept over Dennis. 'Well, you heard wrong,' he said shortly.

He didn't take in a single word the lecturer said that day, didn't write down so much as a note. His mind raced. What was he to do? He didn't want to lose her, but he didn't want to be trapped. *Trapped*. That was what he had always feared, getting sucked into something from which he would never be able to extricate himself; and their relationship becoming public knowledge somehow seemed to make it more likely that this would happen, although he didn't understand why. He felt anxious and confused. Much as he liked Edith, what if it all turned out to be the thin end of the wedge, with the thick end a life like Frank's?

He told her he didn't want to go to the film she suggested that Saturday night, and didn't know if he would be free for the concert on Wednesday; if he was, he would ring her. In backing off, Dennis didn't mean to freeze her out, but he did. He didn't want to lose her friendship. He didn't want to lose the physical relationship either, but he didn't want what these things, combined, seemed to imply. 'I think you haven't got a clue what you want,' she said, with bitter accuracy. She couldn't understand why he dropped her so abruptly, and was terribly hurt. It all fell apart, with not just Edith but also her friends staring icily through Dennis when their paths happened to cross. Edith. To this day he was grateful to her; to this day there was nothing he found so deeply arousing as the smell of a gas fire.

He was subsequently tempted – on occasion sorely tempted – by the usual paths open to men seeking release without emotional involvement, but it was too sordid and depressing, he could never have gone through with it. It would have surprised Roderic to know when they were living together that it was his casual girlfriends he envied him, rather than his more stable relationships.

And yet when he suggested to him that he handled his affairs with great skill, Roderic would have none of it. 'That side of my life is a mess. Great fun, much of it, but a complete shambles.' Dennis could see what he meant, but didn't agree. He was particularly impressed by his brother's ability to end relationships without bitterness or acrimony, how he could make them modulate into friendship, or simply fade out amicably.

The secret of his success was sometimes most clearly seen on nights such as the one when Dennis awoke to hear a woman's tearful voice on the stairs.

'I'm sorry, but I can't go through with this, I just can't.'

'You don't have to do anything you don't want.' Roderic's voice was soft and reassuring. 'Nothing has to happen. You can just sleep beside me; I'll hold your hand if you like. Please don't cry. Would you prefer to sleep on the sofa downstairs?'

Again the woman's voice, weepy and inaudible now.

'Don't apologise; there's no need. You do as you wish. Look, go back down to the sitting room and I'll fetch you a pillow and quilt.'

There followed a prolonged sequence of footsteps up and down the stairs, snivelling, whispers, doors opening and

159

closing and then a sudden and profound silence. Whoever she was, she had disappeared by morning: Dennis came down to find Roderic alone in the kitchen, making breakfast.

'I hope I didn't disturb you last night, coming in.'

'No, not at all. Were you late?'

'Late enough.'

'Did you have a good evening?'

'It was all right.' He was completely inscrutable, Dennis thought, and with that he found himself wondering where in fact the woman *had* ended up spending the night: in Roderic's room or on the sofa. The gentle approach he had taken might well have made the woman yield, and brought her to his bed; and for all his kindness was there not a wily streak in him that had known this? Watching him as he rummaged through the cupboard looking for the marmalade, Dennis couldn't be sure.

And yet he had his bad times too. Women ditched him, quarrelled with him, fled when he pursued them, clung to him tenaciously when he had long since lost interest. Dennis watched him hanging around the house, glum and disappointed when things were not going as he wished; or flapping his hands in anxious denial as Dennis answered the phone, mouthing to him silently, *Tell her I'm out!* Had it not been for moments such as these, their living such disparate lives in close proximity might have been a source of tension and frustration. But for Dennis to see the whole gamut at close quarters was highly instructive. He thought things through, and he drew his own conclusions. Roderic might let himself make the same mistake as Frank, but *he* wouldn't. It was as simple as that.

Dennis liked Marta a great deal and felt guilty about his growing conviction that she and Roderic were not suited to each other. He found it hard to say exactly what the problem was. Perhaps it was that she was Italian. Marriage was difficult enough in any case, but to add cultural differ-ence to the mix was only asking for trouble. This theory also collapsed the following afternoon, when their friend Elsa arrived from Turin from the wedding. 'So, Gulliver, you're going to walk the plank, eh? This I had to see.' Was it only because she *wasn't* marrying Roderic that Dennis felt he wouldn't have minded if she had? No: it was simpler than that, he decided, as he covertly watched the two women side by side, drinking an aperitif in the garden and talking to each other. Elsa would have been a more suitable companion in life for Roderic than Marta, and the fact that she was Italian would have been a thing of no consequence.

The small detail of Roderic never having given the slightest indication that there was anything other than friendship between them, and that Elsa herself had recently set up home with a man from Mantua, was, Dennis thought, neither here nor there. He struggled to find words, but could find only attributes and indicators. She was sharper than Marta, and less elegant too, less evidently preoccupied with the concept of *bella figura* (the meaning of which Roderic had solemnly explained to Dennis and an understanding of which was seemingly essential in relation to the forthcoming wedding).

It was the *bomboniera* that came closest to embodying for Dennis what was wrong. When they sat down to dinner at the wedding reception, Roderic told him, each guest would find at their place a small white porcelain dish, 'yours to take home and treasure as a souvenir of the happy occasion,' as he drily expressed it. Each dish would be full of sugared almonds, swathed in net and tied with ribbon that matched the bridesmaids' dresses. The colour was a secret that had not yet been divulged, even to Roderic. It had cost, he admitted, a 'terrifying sum' and of all the aspects of the wedding, it was the one that had preoccupied Marta the most; she had literally lost sleep over it. Would Elsa have wasted two minutes of her time on this nonsense? Dennis wondered. No, and Roderic ought not to be marrying any woman who would. But it was too late now to point this out.

'This is such a busy time,' Marta said to Dennis the following morning. 'You must come back to visit us again soon, when all the fuss of the wedding is over, so that we can get to know each other. I really do believe that you don't just marry another person, you marry a whole family, so it's important that we become friends.'

Dennis noticed Roderic register this remark, but he made no comment. Although nothing had been said, Dennis had sensed in Marta's mother a suggestion of disappointment, a feeling that her daughter could have done better – much better – than this rather odd foreigner. 'Roderic seems to be marrying into a nice, respectable family,' Sinéad had said, just before Dennis left Ireland. 'You mean rich,' Frank said bluntly. 'You mean he's fallen on his feet.'

Frank turned out to be the Kennedy family's unexpected trump card. Imposing and distinguished, his temper sweetened by the prospect of going to see *Aïda* in Verona, his arrival made a remarkable impact. Family and friends were arriving in number now, as the wedding approached. Cliona was with Frank, Ray came up from Florence, and many of Roderic's old friends made the journey from Ireland, including Tony, Jim, Moira, and others whom Dennis recognised and knew. It was odd for him to see these people not just out of the context in which he usually met them, but to see them in a different configuration: to see sitting together the presidential Frank and the silent Tony, who had never met before now. How much stranger must it be, he thought, for Roderic.

During that week Dennis stayed in Marta and Roderic's house, but the day before the wedding the brothers moved to a hotel, where they shared a room. Dennis slept fitfully that night, listening at first with feelings of pathos, and then with growing irritation as Roderic snored peacefully in his twin bed. Sometime towards dawn he must have fallen into a fitful doze, for when he awoke Roderic was already up, standing at the open window with the shutters folded back, looking down into the street. 'What was it Elsa said: walk the plank? Well she was right. That's what it feels like.'

Had he not said this, Dennis would never have guessed that Roderic was anything other than the life and soul of his own wedding. He looked handsome, but translated and unfamiliar in his elegant formal clothes. As on his first day in Italy, Dennis found himself being at first caught up in the spirit of everything around him. The wedding took place in a tiny fifteenth-century chapel, beneath an altarpiece of the coronation of the Virgin. Marta had told Dennis with some pride that she had worked on its restoration some years earlier, and later, when he thought back to that day, as though taking his cue from the painting, he would remember it as a series of static, radiant images. Marta, exquisite, with her ivory silk, her roses. The chapel, lit, gilded, like the interior of a reliquary, a shrine. The blazing torches in the scented garden of Marta's parents' house, where dinner was held that evening. The moon, pitted and absurdly huge, like a costly lantern of beaten silver that the family had suspended above the garden for the pleasure of their guests. Her father placing Marta's hand in Roderic's and proclaiming to applause and laughter, '*Qui incipit vita nuova.*'

At the end of the meal, one of Marta's uncles plied Dennis with grappa, more than he could take. Ray acted as interpreter and negotiator for them. 'He says it's good for you, that it's from the mountains.' Dennis put his outspread palm across the top of his glass. 'He says it'll make you feel happy.' Ray then said a few words in Italian. 'I told him you're happy already,' he said. The uncle, not to be fooled, shook his head and made again to fill Dennis's glass.

When Dennis finally got back to the hotel, he sat and stared across at where Roderic had slept the night before. The chamber-maid had made up the bed, the sheets and blankets were tightly stretched and tucked in. The sense of emptiness it gave troubled him. He looked, too, at the things he had brought back to the room with him: the crumpled flower

163

from his lapel; the white porcelain dishes that had been pressed upon him to be taken back to Ireland for his mother and sister; the bottle of grappa that Marta's uncle had finally stuffed in his jacket pocket as they rose at last from the table.

And then Dennis did something he had never done before, and about which he would never tell anyone for the rest of his life. He took a glass from the bathroom, opened the grappa, settled down and started to drink. He drank slowly, industriously until the air seemed to thicken and become heavy around him, and the quality of silence in the room changed in a way he couldn't define. He kept drinking until he couldn't trust himself to stand up, until his body no longer seemed to be under his command. When he awoke the following morning he was in bed, half undressed, although he couldn't remember anything of how his night had finally ended. He realised that he might have killed himself, quite literally, had been vaguely aware of that fact even as he drank. Never in his life had he felt so sick, so wretched.

It was an act he never regretted.

Chapter Eighteen

When Roderic was at art school he had been close to a painter who was much older than he, a man in his seventies. It had been an important friendship, with the same freedom, the same lack of pressure that he valued in his relations with Julia. As he got to know her better over the course of that summer when they first met it helped that she was not his peer, that they were not constantly and discreetly measuring their own lives against each other. This was something he found impossible to resist with people of his own generation, even his best and oldest friends, and it was a painful exercise, for he was always aware of how much ground he had lost through the vicissitudes of his life. If he did make comparisons with Julia, it was with himself at the same age, and the result was favourable. Cheerful, sociable, she reminded him of himself at one of the happiest times of his life. He was in her house one day when the phone rang three times in quick succession. The first call was from someone inviting her to a party, the other two from friends just wanting to chat and whom she promised to ring back later that evening.

'Perhaps I should leave it off the hook, or we'll never get any peace.'

'At least you don't know what it is to be lonely,' he said.

'No,' she admitted, 'I don't.' At the same age he could have said the same thing: it was only when he got married that he had found out what loneliness was.

When he passed the shop in the mornings he would see her inside. Usually she was engaged in one of the minor tasks of maintenance or restoration that her job entailed, waxing tables or polishing silver, but he noticed that she also used her time at work to catch up with her social life. Glancing through the window as he passed by, he would see her chatting with some young man or woman who clearly wasn't a customer, and he even came to recognise the regulars, her best friends. One day at the end of July he called in himself to find her in the company of a slight, fair-haired man whom he hadn't noticed from the street.

'If late Thursday afternoon doesn't suit, we could make it Friday,' he was saying to Julia.

'Next Thursday's definitely out,' she replied. 'I'm not free then. Oh, hello, Roderic.'

The young man, whom she introduced as Stephen, clearly regarded him as the fifth wheel on a cart. He refused to let himself be drawn into conversation and left the shop in something of a huff five minutes later, his appointment with Julia still unresolved. She made no particular comment about him after he had gone, nor did Roderic expect her to.

'So what are you up to these days?' she asked and he told her he was going to Edinburgh for a long weekend. 'Are you indeed? Lucky for some.' They talked about his plans for his time there and then she said, 'We must get together when you're back, so you can tell me about it.'

'When would suit?'

'What about Thursday?' she said, with only a ghost of a smile. 'Next Thursday, late afternoon, I'm not doing anything special.'

This little instance of duplicity amused him, but he was not so vain as to think of it as flattering him, saw it rather as a case of Stephen being given the brush-off. He had a clear distinction in his own mind between himself and these other friends of hers, to whom she was close or who wanted to be close to her. Their own relationship was warm but somewhat impersonal. He found her reserved and incurious, which suited him perfectly as his tribulations had made him more private and cautious than he would have been in the past.

166

He didn't want to talk about all he had been through, and she didn't seem to be interested in knowing.

The central facts of their lives – his years in Italy, her family situation – were established through oblique or passing references. When, for example, they were talking one day about art restoration and she commented that he seemed to be exceptionally well informed on the subject, he explained why. Every ten days or fortnight they would arrange to meet, sometimes at her house, more usually at a café. They loaned each other books and music, suggested films and plays each thought the other might like. Occasionally they went together to exhibitions. Roderic mentioned that he was interested in the impact of new technology on art but that he didn't know a great deal about it, and so Julia arranged for him to meet a friend of hers who worked in this field.

Each unwittingly said things at times that surprised or intrigued the other, that gave a glimpse of the unspoken hinterlands of their lives. Once they were talking about Joseph Beuys, and Julia said she had read somewhere that the story of his being wrapped in felt and fat by nomads in the Caucasus when they saved him from his crashed plane simply wasn't true. And Roderic immediately said, 'Oh I believe it. I believe it's true. If you've ever been distressed, at an absolutely critical moment in your life, and someone puts a blanket round you, you never forget it, *never*, because you know that the worst is over. Now you're going to get help, you're going to be saved.' The depth of feeling with which he spoke startled her and she didn't know what to say, and then he in turn was embarrassed, as if he'd said too much. 'Like, you know, if you were drowning and they pulled you from the water, and then in the lifeboat they put a blanket around you. That sort of thing. Drowning, yes.'

Another time it was his turn to be surprised, when he said something about the zeitgeist, and she said, 'The what? Oh *that*. I'm not interested in that.'

'Why not? What are you interested in, then?'

'Things that go beyond time, that sort of manage to get behind it or deny it in some way. Like Joseph Cornell falling in love with the dancer. It didn't matter that he lived in New York in the nineteen forties and she'd been dead for a hundred years, he loved her so much that one day he saw her, in a building across the street.'

In the shop she would occasionally show him particular pieces that caught her imagination. 'Hester says that vase was made to hold celery, not flowers. People ate raw celery at the end of formal dinners in the nineteenth century.' More often she was taken by objects that folded intricately into themselves, concealing their function with complex artifice: a gold locket that became a lorgnette, a walking stick that was also a telescope. Although he became used to seeing her in the shop there was something about it that never quite added up. It wasn't, he thought, watching her as she unfolded an ivory fan, that she was a quintessentially contemporary person surrounded by outmoded things. He didn't know what it was.

'Would you like to have lived in the past?' he asked, in an attempt at elucidation.

'It depends. I wouldn't like to have been the owner of this,' and she slowly closed the fan again. 'At least, I don't think so. I hate the thought of the whole world it suggests – overstuffed, tightly buttoned – where women were supposed to be completely passive. And yet, who's to say? Maybe the woman who owned this fan had a highly developed consciousness. It's what's going on in your head that matters. Maybe in herself she was completely free. I'd like to think that was the case.'

Aware that he occasionally visited her but that she never visited him, Roderic gave her his address and urged her to call in whenever she wished. She took him at his word and arrived one Wednesday evening at the end of August shortly after seven, to be quickly ushered in. 'I'm on the phone, long distance. It may take some time.' He made to bring her into the sitting room, but when she saw that the telephone was there, Julia drew back.

'I'll stay in the hall.'

'There's no need, truly. You'll be cold here,' but she insisted and Roderic, anxious to get back to his call, had no option but to let her have her way.

Settling down on the stairs, Julia immediately understood that her scruples on this point had been misplaced. Roderic's house was tiny and the door between the two rooms didn't close properly, so that she could hear him as distinctly as if she had indeed been sitting right beside him. More to the point, because he was speaking in Italian, she couldn't understand a single word that was being said. Having no choice but to listen, she was struck by how fluent he was, how perfect his accent. From the inflection of his voice, she knew when he was asking a question, when reasoning, when explaining something. Whoever was at the other end of the line had evidently said something funny, for he laughed, asked something in tones of incredulity, listened to the response and laughed even more. He said goodbye, there was a pause, then he extravagantly greeted a new person on the line, and she noticed that his whole tone altered now, subtly but distinctly.

Julia could follow all of this, but still had no idea of what he was specifically talking about. Nothing could have brought home to her more completely the reality of this other life he had had and about which she knew so little, this life in another country with the wife and daughters of whom he seldom spoke. Nothing could have better served to reinforce the idea of all that was closed to her and inaccessible in him than this wall of incomprehensible language. So powerful was the effect, so disconcerting and so distancing, that when he finished his call and reappeared, she was faintly surprised to see that it was indeed Roderic she had overheard some moments earlier, and not a complete stranger.

He for his part was aware of the distance that had been created and sought to diminish it. 'That was my daughters. I've been trying to mend my fences with them of late. We were estranged for a number of years. As you've probably gathered by now I had a major drink problem in the past and it pretty well blew my family life to smithereens. So ever since I stopped drinking a couple of years ago I've been trying to get things back on a better footing.'

Julia nodded. For a moment she wondered if she ought to move the conversation back on to neutral ground then decided to follow through on the area he had opened up. 'My father also drank heavily at one stage,' she said, 'but I think I understood why, even though I was quite small at the time. And it didn't last too long, six months or so, if that.'

'Are you saying it didn't bother you?'

'Oh, it bothered me hugely. I hated it. I was glad when he stopped. It was a short-term, intense thing, dreadful for both of us. It was a dreadful time.'

'And he stopped completely?'

'He got it under control, yes.' She smiled ruefully. 'After that, once, twice a year at most he used to go on a real bender. Maybe he still does. I don't think he knows I know about this. He made a big effort to keep it from me, so I did the decent thing and pretended not to know.'

He dropped in when passing the shop about ten days later, in mid September, surprised to find her there so late in the day as she usually worked mornings.

'Hester asked me to switch with her, she had to go somewhere this afternoon. Tell me, what do you think of this?' and she showed him a brooch made of three peacock feathers, cut short and sheathed in gold. She held it up against the jumper she wore, and the feathers shimmered. It didn't suit her at all but would have been the perfect gift for Marta.

'Not your style, I'd have thought.'

'I know. Even if it was, I could never wear it,' she replied, putting it back in the box. 'My father has a hundred odd superstitions, things I've never heard from anyone else, and one of them is that peacock feathers are unlucky. He won't have them in the house under any circumstances.'

'You could wear it, still,' Roderic said. 'Your father doesn't have to know about everything you do, does he?'

She raised her head and smiled at him. 'Oh he doesn't know the half of it,' she said. 'Not the half of it. And he's not going to, either.'

This amused Roderic for an instant, until he thought of his own daughters, particularly of Serena.

'But here's the rub,' she said, 'what if I wore this, or something like it, and my luck turned. What if bad things started to happen to me, what then?'

'So you're saying that you're superstitious too?'

'Sounds like it, doesn't it, although I like to think I'm not.'

'What's he like, your father?' he asked suddenly.

Julia thought about this for a moment, then said, 'Oh, he's unique,' still studying the feathers of the brooch.

'Isn't everybody?'

'No. They ought to be, but the world tries to make people conform, makes them want to stamp out everything in themselves that's individual. Stupid world. Stupid people. They don't even realise what's happening to them. And that's the tragedy of life.'

'One of the tragedies,' Roderic said.

'One of them, yes.'

'What about your parents?' she asked him then. 'Are they both still alive?'

'My father died a few years after I went to Italy, my mother about a year after I came back. His death made a big impact, hers much less so. I wasn't close to her, and at that time I was pretty much overwhelmed by other difficulties, all of them, it has to be said, of my own making.'

'I can't imagine the loss of a parent not being a trauma,' she remarked.

He considered this for a moment. He felt that by now he knew her well enough to ask the next question. 'How old were you when you lost your mother?'

'Six.'

Her reply shocked him, for somewhere along the line he had got the impression that she was in her teens when it happened. 'Do you remember her?'

She looked at him with immense sadness. 'No,' she said. 'Isn't that wretched? I can't remember her at all.'

'Nothing?' he said and she covered her face with her hands as though the better to concentrate, to see what she could dredge up out of the depths of her mind.

'Oh, so little,' she said eventually. 'Strange things, nothing direct, nothing significant. I remember lying in bed when I was a child, late at night and hearing someone setting the table for breakfast. It must have been her. My father's often told me he did no housework, none at all, when my mother was alive, and when there were just the two of us left, setting the table was my job. I did it in the morning, while he made the breakfast. The sound of cups and saucers. It isn't much, is it? That's what I remember.'

'And nothing else?'

'Yes, but like that, little things, fragments, scents, sounds, you know. I can't see her, that's the problem, I have no clear image in my mind,' and her voice had a note now of frustration, even anger, 'I can't *see* her.'

Roderic was just about to tell her of his own experience with Oriana when the door of the shop opened and Hester came in, all fuss and business, shattering the privacy of the moment, much to his annoyance. Not that Hester noticed.

'Julia, hello. Oh hello, pleased to meet you. Did the man ring about the mirror, the man in Naas? I knew he'd let me down, I just knew it. And Mrs Hall, has she made her mind up about the cabinet? Well that's something, I suppose.

You can go along now, thanks for doing the afternoon for me.'

'Come upstairs, Roderic,' Julia said as he made for the door. 'I have books belonging to you I want to return.'

They did not resume the conversation Hester had interrupted. Julia put on some new music she had recently bought, and as they sat talking, in a general, desultory way now, the room grew dark as the evening drew in. She switched on the light and asked him if he would like to stay for dinner. 'It'll be nothing special, believe me.' Even as Roderic thanked her and said yes, something in the back of his mind told him he ought to refuse. She pulled her hair back with a tortoiseshell comb and washed the dishes. They continued to chat as she scraped carrots, spuds thundered into the sink and Julia rubbed the soil from them with a stiff brush. Why did he feel so uneasy? It was absurd that he should be so self-punishing. She was good company, intelligent and cheerful, so why this gnawing guilt? Two pork chops hissed and spat under the grill. Max, who had wandered off earlier, came back into the room and mewed to be fed. Roderic's feeling that he should not be there persisted, no matter that he tried to damp it down. 'The cutlery is in that drawer over there,' she said, as she jabbed at the meat. 'Could you set the table?'

The meal was as enjoyable as it was basic, and it was as basic as could be imagined. Over coffee afterwards, she brushed away his thanks. 'You might as well have been here, you'd probably just have been sitting at home on your own otherwise.'

No he wouldn't. Cliona. He covered his face with his hands and sat in silence for a few moments, then looked at a bemused Julia through spread fingers.

'May I use your phone?'

'I am going to skin you, Roderic. Skin you alive; and do you know something else? I'm going to enjoy it.'

'Cliona, I can't begin to apologise. . .'

'You're telling me. We waited for ages. You should have seen the salmon by the time we sat down to it.'

'I can't tell you how sorry I am. I knew there was *something*, all evening it was at the back of my mind, that I shouldn't be where I was, that I ought to be elsewhere.'

'I rang your house. Twice.'

'I'm terribly sorry, truly I am.' He continued to apologise profusely, but was aware that nothing he said now would neutralise his sister's annoyance.

When the call was over he remained sitting in Julia's living room for a few moments. How familiar it all seemed: the dusty bookcase, the odd mix of make-do furniture and fine antiques, the shabby rugs. Familiar, too, the scene that had been called up to him as he spoke to Cliona: the diminutive paper napkins handed round with the drinks, the jug of orange squash ostentatious beside his place at table, the pastry-forks, the doilies, the numbing chit-chat, the wretched salmon itself; how glad he was to have missed it all. He returned to the kitchen. 'Did you hear that?'

Julia nodded.

'Did I sound convincing?'

She shook her head. 'Not in the least,' she said. 'Not in the *least*!'

And then two nights later he came home from the studio to see the green light flashing on his answering machine. He flopped down in a chair and pressed the button to hear the message without bothering to turn on the light: there was still just about brightness enough to see what he was doing.

'Roderic, hello, this is Julia. That book you mentioned about land art. Could I borrow it before this weekend? Give me a call tonight or tomorrow. Look after yourself. Bye.'

She had left messages on his machine before every bit as banal as this, and he had listened to them, called her, wiped them and forgotten about it. So he didn't understand why tonight he pressed the button again. 'Roderic, hello, this is Julia.' Her voice was hesitant but clear, her words to the point

174

as always. When the message had finished for the second time he put the receiver on the table beside the phone, pressed some more buttons, and now her tones filled the room. He sat back in his chair, listening to her accent, the exact timbre of her voice that he had heard so often but had, perhaps, never before truly listened to for its own qualities. The machine was set now so that the message was repeated endlessly, 'Roderic, hello, this is Julia,' and he sat there in the gathering dusk listening, at peace, deeply happy in a complete and sudden way, such as he hadn't known for years.

Chapter Nineteen

She'd said it late one night, shortly before the end. They were sitting in the kitchen, at odds with each other but not quarrelling. Marta was slumped at the table, exhausted and resigned with her head in her hands, while Roderic drunkenly attempted to justify his ways.

'There have been no other women,' he said portentously. 'I want you to know that, Marta. Whatever else, I've always been faithful to you.'

Slowly she had lifted her head and stared at him, incredulous. 'But who would have you, Roderic?' she said and she actually laughed. 'What woman in her right mind would want anything to do with you as you are now?'

He was too shocked to reply. In those last weeks and months they each said deliberately hurtful things to each other; probably she would have been surprised to know that none of it cut him so deep or stayed in his mind so long as that single remark.

The marriage collapsed shortly after their tenth anniversary and Roderic fled to Ireland. For the first month he stayed with Dennis, who was appalled by the situation, much more than he had expected him to be, and who made futile attempts to bring about a reconciliation. Roderic then moved into a place of his own, a small dingy flat in Rathmines. He hated it from the moment he saw it but took it as a stopgap, never thinking that, lacking the will or the energy to move elsewhere, he would be there for the next seven years. The life that he embarked upon now was a distorted version of the one he had lived before going to Italy. Although he still had friends from the old days, his whole social circle had subtly but profoundly changed: people had settled down, moved on, moved away. Nowhere was the difference more apparent than in his relations with women. *But who would have you, Roderic?* Well, now he was finding out. Like him, the women who gravitated towards him at this point in his life had something to expiate, something to prove. In the past he had had encounters as short-lived and casual as he now did: one-night stands, affairs that had burnt themselves out in the course of a few nights, the occasional fling after a party. Even when they had been botched or disappointing they had never been depressing, but invariably now he felt hollow and desperate afterwards, his loneliness more acute. It was a revelation to him that sex could be such a sordid, even squalid, thing. And then he met Jeannie.

Like most of the women with whom he associated at this time, he met her in a pub. He noticed her one night near closing time, sitting alone in a corner crying. 'Tell me what's wrong. It can't be that bad.'

'I've lost my children.'

There was nothing she could have said better calculated to engage his sympathy. The barman rang the bell and put towels over the taps, started to turn out the lights and stack chairs on tables in the hope of driving home the last patrons.

'Come with me,' Roderic said. 'I'll look after you.'

She went with him, as meek as a lamb, something he was to remember with astonishment later when he was acquainted with the full force of her rage. They went back to his flat and although she attempted to tell him something of her life, it was some weeks before he could piece together exactly what had happened.

Her story was not an unfamiliar one. Roderic had read variations of it in a couple of novels from the nineteenth century, but had never expected to come across so classic and painful a version of it so close to home. Early in life Jeannie had married a man much older than she. Within three years they had a son and a daughter, but the marriage was a cold, quarrelsome affair. Although she was unhappy she resigned

177

herself to her fate, accepting that her children were to be her sole consolation in life. She denied it vehemently to Roderic, but he suspected that it was during these years that she started to drink. And then when the boy was nine and the girl eight, something completely unforeseen happened: Jeannie fell in love. She admitted that in leaving her family to be with the other man, as she did within a few weeks of meeting him, she hadn't fully understood what she was setting in motion. 'I was only trying to be honest,' she said. 'We could have kept the whole thing hidden and met secretly, but I believed that would have been wrong.' She had thought that in her new situation she would be able to work out something in relation to the children when the dust settled, but within three months, everything had fallen apart. Her lover's wife said she would take him back on condition that he broke off all relations with Jeannie and, for the sake of his daughter, he went. She found herself alone, locked in a bitter battle with her own husband over custody of their children. Much was made of her drinking, her desertion, and she lost the case, was granted only the most limited access. Her grief, her fury over her fate, knew no bounds, and Roderic was to bear the brunt of it.

He settled into a relationship with her that, like the tenancy of his flat, dragged on pointlessly for years because he lacked the necessary resolution to bring it to an end. Such affection and companionship as existed between them was continually undermined by their mutual unhappiness. What he felt for her was at best a kind of pity, and it was the pity that sustained him throughout those years. Her sorrow for her life took the form of anger and, while Roderic had an irascible streak, he was not a violent man, which served her ends perfectly. Their main reason for being together he now saw had been to punish each other, an unspoken contract they had fulfilled with absolute dedication. He could still feel his scalp tighten when he thought of her pulling his hair, could still feel on occasion the tracks of her nails down his cheek. If his life in those years had been hell, Jeannie had provided the company of the damned. It was she who finally brought things to an end, telling him she never wanted to see him again.

A few weeks after they parted he stopped drinking, and the numb misery of being constantly drunk was replaced by the searing pain of being constantly sober and obliged to face up to the harm he had done. But if his past behaviour towards Dennis, Jeannie and his friends was a scar on his life, the thought of Marta and the children was a wound, a living open wound, and he suffered on their account as he suffered for no one else. He had nightmares about Marta at that time which were peculiar because they were not in themselves unpleasant. He dreamt about her with unnerving clarity as she had been when they first met; saw her at work, perched on the scaffolding high above the nave of a church, waving down at him and smiling, far lovelier than the blank-faced saint whose image she was restoring. She gestured towards the ladder. *Do you want to come up and join me? Do you want to come up?* They were sitting in the garden at dusk, beneath a trellis covered in white roses. He had his arm around her and could feel the weight and the warmth of her body leaning against him. Silently he marvelled that he should have the luck to be loved by her.

And then he would awake, and his conscious mind supplied the memories that transformed the dreams to nightmares. Furious rows about the amount of time he spent closed away in the studio; about his having been rude to her mother, about his not wanting to go on holiday with her parents; about his not wanting to go on holiday at all; about his indifference to decisions concerning the house and garden; about his drinking, his drinking, his drinking. Marta late at night, crying and trying to stifle her sobs so as not to wake the children. *I married you in good faith, Roderic, and I've done my best, but I can't take any more, and I can't go on. I can't go on.* At two o'clock in the morning he paced the floor

179

remembering all of this, chain smoking, wishing to Christ he could have a drink and knowing that if he did so it would only be to bring his whole life unravelling around him again.

Concomitant with all this emotional tribulation when he stopped drinking had been a great number of practical problems to be sorted out. In the first instance, he needed a place to live. He couldn't face going back to the flat in Rathmines, and moving in with Dennis again was out of the question. Through a friend of a friend he heard of a house that was available to rent, an artisan's cottage in the Liberties. He went to see it and walked from room to empty room. The last tenant had painted it white throughout to maximise the light. The effect this gave was of a series of tiny interlinked cells, as in a monastery rather than a prison. Standing at an upstairs window he listened to the bells of Christchurch. It was the morning, and a patch of light fell on the wall in a soft rectangle. Surrounded by this quiet austerity he remembered the night of his wedding, and how in the middle of all the lavish celebrations, Marta's father had taken her hand and placed it in his: *Qui incipit vita nuova*. He went downstairs and told the landlord who was waiting there that he would take the house.

Although he had continued to paint, and painted remarkably well during all the years that he was drinking, what he referred to as 'the business side of things' – galleries, dealers, exhibitions – had been neglected and required serious attention. He was keen to be on better terms again with Cliona and Maeve, from whom he had drifted away and whose kindness to him when he was in hospital drying out had filled him with gratitude. Above all, he wanted to restore relations with his family in Italy and, as he expected, this proved to be the most complex and delicate of the many problems now confronting him. Given all of this, to think that there was no possibility of any imminent emotional entanglement was no hardship at all. There was as much likelihood, he told himself, of him embarking on a new relationship as there was of him setting out to walk across Antarctica.

Although in his new sobriety he was often anxious and depressed his principal problem, he came to realise during that time, was a massive lack of confidence. With the doing of his work excepted, it permeated every aspect of his life and was what people were unconsciously referring to when they said how much he had changed; that he was quieter now, less sociable and ebullient than in the past. Roderic himself was occasionally taken aback at how it manifested itself, as on the day when he saw his friend Jim on Grafton Street. Instead of calling out to him and going over to say hello he instinctively shrank into a doorway, hoping he hadn't been seen, and for the rest of that day he asked himself why. They had known each other since art college. Jim knew what Roderic had been through in recent months and they had even met and talked a few times since he came out of hospital, but today he simply couldn't face him. His emotional resources were so depleted that he had nothing left over to give to another person and couldn't believe he wouldn't be found severely wanting, even by Jim, that most sympathetic of men.

As time passed and things slowly resolved themselves this situation began to change, and if his great lack of confidence had ambushed him unexpectedly, so too did the beginnings of its resolution. Shortly after his first, abortive attempt to see his family again after he stopped drinking, he went one day to collect a jacket from the dry cleaners. There was some minor confusion over the docket and as it was being sorted out he made a little joke that genuinely amused the young woman behind the counter. Roderic laughed too, and he then smiled at her. The effect was startling, creating that sudden aura of connectedness that he had, in the past, deliberately drawn women into at will. This skill had been in abeyance during his years of tribulation, and to find it reasserting itself now so completely and so effortlessly astonished him more than it did the woman, who was experiencing it for the first time. He hardly knew how he found himself back out on the street again, with the jacket on its wire hanger and swathed in polythene. In the weeks that followed he cautiously tested his powers again and was reassured by the results. To begin with, these fleeting relations with strangers were enough. Later, when he occasionally chanced to meet someone particularly attractive or engaging he would wonder for a moment if his life might not be different, if he should perhaps take things a stage further. But with that an immense weariness would sweep over him as he remembered Jeannie's drunken fury, her temper and her rages, remembered Marta's face blotched with crying, her eyes swollen and red. *But who would have you, Roderic?*

It was actually the prospect of seeing Marta again that precipitated his taking action, although he only realised this after the event. His starting to plan for his June trip to Italy – and this time he was determined to go through with it – coincided with a couple of short affairs that he embarked upon in a spirit of experimentation. If they didn't lead to anything or weren't particularly satisfactory it didn't much matter, he told himself (which was just as well, because they didn't and weren't). He was glad, though, that they'd happened, doubly so because of Gianni, Marta's new lover. He met Julia for the first time shortly after returning from Italy, but as he was preoccupied with consolidating his new relationship with his daughters and busy with his work he didn't think of her in that light even as their friendship developed. The whole issue of women slipped quietly back down the agenda.

And then in mid September Julia left the message on his answering machine.

The following morning he took the book for which she had asked and went straight round to the shop. To his annoyance she was already with a customer, some early bird who had nothing better to do on a Friday morning than dither over firescreens, and so he sat down to wait until she was free. Watching her, Roderic measured up the reality against the image he had had in his mind and didn't find it wanting, found it surpassed. Did this indecisive fool – 'The one with the grapes is nice but I like the colours of the other one; it's so hard for me to make up my mind' – did he know the luck he had had to call in this morning and meet Julia? He gave no sign of it. Why wouldn't he just go away and leave them alone? 'I'm also interested in candlesticks,' he announced now. Was there no mercy? The door of the shop opened and a woman came in, wanting to buy a wardrobe. There was no mercy. Roderic set the book on a table and indicated to Julia that he had to go on. She smiled her thanks and regret, promised to call him soon. In fairness to Mr Firescreen, he thought as he continued on his way, he too had failed to fully appreciate Julia when he first met her. What was it he had said to Maria Hill? *She's a nice young woman. Seems very bright.* Something absurd like that. Why on that first day hadn't he suggested that they spend the rest of the evening together, to cheer her up after her disappointment about the fellowship? They could have gone for a meal or to the cinema and then, in the great euphemism of his youth, 'seen how things developed from there'. Part of the problem now was that he knew her too well. He had always found it hard to fathom the need many women seemed to have for getting to know someone extremely well before going to bed with them. To him it was illogical; it made far more sense for sex to come into the picture early on – as soon as possible – and then to take things from there. The problem with going about it the other way and trying to get the emotional side sorted out first was that it raised the stakes too high. There was more potential for misunderstanding and embarrassment, more likelihood of people getting hurt. And this, by default, was the position in which he now found himself.

He loved her and wanted her, of that there was not the slightest doubt in his mind. He could spend four hours in her company talking and not see the time pass. When he was apart from her, he thought of her obsessively: of her wit, her thoughtful silences, the exactitude of her pronouncements on certain things, her insistence on accuracy; of the texture of her skin, her clear grey eyes, her breasts, her lips, her wrists. He wanted her so much that when he saw her again it was impossible that she wouldn't know, that nothing would happen.

She called round to his house that night. 'So how have things been with you since last I saw you?' she asked, lighting a cigarette and shaking the match to extinction.

I've thought of nothing and no one but you. You've been the last thought in my mind before I go to sleep at night, and my first thought in the morning. I want to take you to bed and stay there for about a week.

'Well?' she said again, puzzled that he hadn't answered her. 'How have things been?'

'Fine,' he said. 'Things have been fine. Well, all right. Not bad. I mean good.'

'Do you think,' she said, 'you could be a bit more specific?'

She was wearing jeans and a blue and white check shirt. There was a sticking plaster on her left hand. 'Did the cat scratch you?'

'No, I burnt myself on a pot.'

She looked different, more – there was no other way to put it – more *real*, as if she were someone he had known only through photographs and was meeting for the first time. He stared at her and gave monosyllabic answers to her questions. She told him that she was going home for the weekend, to see her father.

He had been wrong, he reflected after she'd gone. The main problem wasn't that he knew her too well but that his confidence had once again completely deserted him. He sat imagining his younger self watching him with amazement and incredulity. In his youth he had never been gauche in this way and had been puzzled by men who were.

If the relations between men and women were a language, it was one he spoke and understood fluently, down to the most complex rule of grammar, the most subtle nuance of idiom. But he had lost his nerve, lost the knack. It was like being thrown into a lake and discovering that it was indeed possible to forget how to swim.

He was still brooding on it the following day, when he went to Dennis's house for lunch. Roderic sat at the kitchen table while his brother moved around the room preparing the meal. Sometimes the perfection of Dennis's life depressed Roderic: there seemed to be not a single aspect of it that he had bungled. Although it was never spoken of, Roderic knew that all Dennis's affairs were in perfect order, that his life was hung around with financial securities, like a Viking long-ship hung with shields: life insurance and house insurance; health insurance and pensions; savings plans and financial investments.

'Have you made your will?'

Dennis, who had just set a glass of apple-juice in front of Roderic and was helping himself to some white Burgundy, looked surprised. 'Of course I have,' he said shortly. 'Haven't you?'

'I'm thinking of getting round to it very soon.'

Dennis shook his head slowly in disbelief. 'You must be mad,' he said. 'Stark raving mad, not to have seen to it before now. Your pictures alone – the contents of your studio. If anything were to happen. . .'

'I know, I know, I know,' Roderic said, sorry that he had spoken. 'I told you, I'm going to do it any day now.'

'I'm glad to hear it,' Dennis said. 'Cheers.' He sipped his wine and started to rub the papery pink skins off some garlic cloves.

His job, too, Roderic considered, as he watched him: he'd risen steadily as the years passed, promotions and salary increases following on from each other with the regularity of the seasons. He'd made sensible home improvements that increased the value of the house, installing a sophisticated central heating system and having the garden landscaped, front and back; and then the economy had obligingly taken property prices to astronomical levels, making Dennis's home worth a mind-boggling sum. Roderic drank his juice and looked around the kitchen with its electric juicer, its ceramic hob. It was the attention to detail that staggered him. On the wall there was a little slate on which Dennis wrote the names of things as he needed them. *Olive oil*, the slate read. *Muesli. Cling film.* He always had a pen beside the phone and kept a pair of scissors strictly for kitchen use. There was always a supply of spare light bulbs, and candles in case of a power cut.

The peeled garlic looked like huge, strange teeth extracted from the jaw of some monster. Roderic imagined his father briskly whipping them out with a pair of pliers; imagined the monster whimpering and Frank telling it to belt up. Dennis placed one of them under the wide blade of a knife and brought his fist crashing down upon it hard, to smash and crush the clove.

'Penny for your thoughts, Roderic.'

'Oh, just the usual.'

Dennis sprinkled salt from a salt pig on to the garlic and crushed it again.

'Meaning?'

'I was just thinking for the billionth time about how you've made such a good fist of your life, and I've made such a pig's arse of mine. That's all.'

Dennis stared at him neutrally for a few moments, then took a drink of wine. 'If you're referring to this place the housekeeper does pretty well everything, not me. Nothing else in particular bothering you?'

God, he was a shrewd old coot too, Roderic thought. In general, he understood and fully accepted the difference between his brother's life and his own. Dennis knew this, knew that it troubled him only when he was flagellating himself over some other problem in his life, as he was now over Julia.

'What could I possibly have to bother me?' Roderic replied rhetorically.

'You tell me. Anything special on your mind?'

'Nope.'

'Delighted to hear it,' Dennis said, clearly not believing him for a minute.

Once, years ago, not long after they started living in the same house, Roderic had tried to fix Dennis up with a woman. One Friday night at a party he'd met the sister of a friend of his. Irene: he could still remember her name after all these years. She was a reserved and soft-spoken woman, who worked in a building society and loved going to the theatre. As Roderic sat on the floor beside her chatting, a plot hatched in his mind. It evolved as the evening wore on and matured overnight, so that by the time he burst into the kitchen the following morning he was positively bubbling with enthusiasm for his scheme. 'I've got great news for you, Dennis. *Great* news!'

Dennis, hunched owlishly behind his *Irish Times* with a pot of tea and a rack of toast, glanced up briefly at his brother, not quite catching what Roderic said and not particularly interested either. 'The kettle's full. Bring it back up to the boil if you want to make coffee.'

'No, no, listen to me. I met a woman last night . . .'

'Now, there's a novelty.'

'I know you'll really like her. You've got ever such a lot in common.'

Dennis stared at him now as he rattled on, at first genuinely not getting the point, but as the meaning became clear embarrassment and annoyance showed on his face.

'Knock it off, Roderic,' he said, 'I'm not remotely interested.' Frowning, he pointedly turned back to his newspaper.

'Her name's Irene, she's just your type . . .'

'Drop it.'

'When you meet her you'll see what I mean, you . . .'

'Roderic, did you hear me? Did you hear what I said? I SAID NO!'

It wasn't so much the vehemence of this reply that surprised him – although that in itself was striking, for Dennis rarely raised his voice – as the distinct note of fear that he could detect. Remembering it now he cringed with embarrassment. He wished he could apologise, but guessed rightly that Dennis would not be best pleased to have the subject brought up again after all these years. In spite of their closeness, Dennis had remained for a long time an enigma to Roderic in terms of his emotional life. The seeming complete absence of women in his life had made him briefly wonder if his brother might be gay, but a complete absence of men seemed to give the lie to that too. Such friendships as he had tended to be work related, and struck Roderic as affectionate but detached. Against this, of course, had to be set his volcanic relationship with his father and, most particularly, his overheated and somewhat febrile attachment to Roderic himself. The rather solitary life he led clearly suited him. Roderic admired Dennis, and wondered if he had ever told him this explicitly. Now did not seem to be the moment.

'Confidence,' he said now. 'My confidence has taken a battering over the past years, and I feel it keenly these days.'

'Don't try to force anything,' Dennis said. 'Let things take their course.'

'Do you ever wonder is there a finite number of errors one can make in life? I mean serious, life-changing errors? You know, like a cat being supposed to have nine lives; only you don't know how many there are, so you just go blundering on. Or at least, I go blundering on.'

'You're doing well these days,' Dennis urged. 'Don't force things, don't put yourself under unnecessary pressure.'

He didn't have the heart to ask him about necessary pressure.

He enjoyed the rest of the day with his brother. It provided some distraction from his obsession with Julia, although he fell to thinking about it again as soon as he was back in his own house. The stakes, he told himself the following day, were too high. Much as he valued her friendship, he wanted more now, but was afraid that if he forced the issue he would spoil everything. He spent all of Sunday trying to wean himself off her by the rather unpleasant exercise of focusing on her bad points and weaknesses, starting with her physical shortcomings. Her incisors were too pointed, and made her, when she smiled, look uncannily like the dreaded Max. Her hair, when she didn't have it pinned up or pulled back, could look distinctly odd, like Shockheaded Peter in the children's book, and she had a strange way of walking, ungainly and slightly hen toed. Having quickly run out of ideas, he turned to her faults in a moral sphere. She was spoilt, she admitted it. An only child brought up by her father, she was used to being the doting focus of male attention, and expected it, took it for granted even. She was a man's woman, and he was just one of many men. He remembered Stephen, poor Stephen, as he now thought of him, and how ruthlessly she'd dispatched him from the shop. If she knew the turmoil he was in she'd laugh at him for being so foolish as to think she would ever consider him in that light. He was just someone she happened to know. If there was an atmosphere, if there was some impulse or signal coming from her, she was just amusing herself, teasing him, practising so that she would be ready when she met someone whom she really did want. She was coldly . . . no. Not cold. Never cold. Whatever else, she was never that.

He succeeded in holding a reasonably unflattering image of her in his mind for all of Sunday until the evening, when Julia appeared unexpectedly at his door, having just arrived back in Dublin, with Max sullen in his cage. That strange, unique mane of hair, that sensual feline smile, that walk – in less than a minute he was back to square one. She stayed only

189

long enough to ask a few unwittingly pertinent questions –
'So how was your weekend? What did you do today?' for
which he had no adequate answers. 'Look at him now,' she
said to Max when she stood up to leave. 'He's going to sit and
sulk for the rest of the evening, the fool. I can tell it just by
looking at him.' Roderic was about to defend himself against
this remarkable slur when he realised, just in time, that she
had actually been speaking to him about the cat and not to
the cat about him.

Having failed to find adequate fault in her, he turned to the
simpler task of finding fault in himself. Why would she want
him? What could she possibly see in him, with his drinker's
face and his wrecked marriage? He was more than twenty
years older than she and he looked it: it would be embarrass-
ing for her to be seen with him. She was too intelligent to be
won over simply by the eminence he had achieved as a
painter, and that notwithstanding, he had made a complete
bags of everything else in his life. She might not have got
that fellowship in Italy, but it was only a matter of time:
something would come through and then both her life and
her career would take off. He imagined her disappearing into
the future as though it were a radiant forest, where the fruit
on the trees were glittering prizes that showered down on
her, and other men were waiting. No doubt some Good
Samaritan had already shared with her tales of some of his
more humiliating adventures, things he hated to remember,
and forced himself to think of now. When she stared at him
with her clear grey eyes and her mind appeared to be
elsewhere, that was the kind of thing she was thinking of, not
that she wanted him as a lover. The night he had thrown up
in Maria Hill's studio, for example, but he suspected Maria
had kept that one to herself. More public humiliations then:
almost anything involving Jeannie, such as the night she
picked a fight with him in the pub, and they were both turfed
out on to the street. Or what about the night he went round
to her house and she wouldn't let him in, and he had

bellowed up at her window until the neighbours, quite reasonably, called the guards, and he'd been hauled off to the barracks, and Dennis had to come and get him. For no matter how pissed he'd been, he'd always been able to remember Dennis's address and phone number, hadn't he?

In late September he set himself a deadline. At the end of October he was to go to Paris for a short holiday: the situation would be resolved before he left. To make this decision helped him; to know that he was working within a specific timeframe brought everything into sharper focus. When they were together now he was conscious of the tension there was in the absolute absence of physical contact, so that the spaces between them, across a table, across a hearth rug, were charged with a strange energy, like the spaces in an oriental painting. He moved into a hypnotic state, in which he thought of what he needed to do – reach out and touch her hand, stroke her cheek with his finger, lean over and kiss her – but he didn't, still couldn't do it. He remembered being in the chapel with Marta: the cool darkness, the sound of the coins falling and the flood of sudden light, the intense wave of desire.

The month melted away until only a week was left. He was to go to Paris on the morning of the last Friday in October, and on the Monday he returned to his house from the studio to find the green light blinking on his answering machine. Even before he pressed the button, something told him it would be bad news. 'Roderic, hello, this is Julia. My father rang to say he's not well, so I'm taking time off work and going down to look after him. I probably won't be back up in Dublin before you leave, so have a good time, and look after yourself. I'll see you when you get back.' A loud shrill bleep discreetly drowned out the torrent of effing and blinding with which Roderic greeted this information.

The black mood into which this plunged him did not disperse in the following days, and was not helped by cold, rainy weather that showed no sign of breaking. He was taken aback at how keenly he felt his loneliness that week, with Julia away and no possibility of communicating with her; hoped the same mood wouldn't dog him when he was in Paris. Thursday was ghastly. Dennis had called on Wednesday to say he was off work with flu, but refused Roderic's offer to come and look after him. 'Aren't you going to France soon? I'm sure you're busy. Don't worry about me, I'll be all right.' In spite of this, he decided to drive over to Dennis's place shortly before twelve the following day. He stopped off on the way to buy some things, and let himself in using a key that had been entrusted to him for emergencies such as this. The house was absolutely silent and still, eerily so. He picked up some letters that were scattered on the hall floor and carried them through to the kitchen, passing by his own paintings. Coming back, he spoke his brother's name once, hesitantly, but there was no reply and then, trying to make as little noise as possible, he crept upstairs. The door of the main bedroom was ajar and standing on the threshold Roderic looked into the room.

Dennis, tucked up under his duvet in his blue pyjamas, was fast asleep. On the bed beside him was a large box of tissues, on the bedside table a glass and a plastic bottle of water, together with a blister pack of aspirin, the foil punched through in several places. The air in the room was heavy and stale. Sleeping, he looked vulnerable, almost childlike, wholly unlike the fully taxed and insured, garlic-crushing Dennis who had recently entertained him. It broke Roderic's heart to see him like this. The last time he had been in this room had been one of the worst days of his life; and if it upset him so much to see his brother brought low by a mere flu, how must Dennis have felt watching Roderic in his darkest hour. A detail that he'd forgotten came back to him now, of how he'd struggled to get his shoes off and hadn't been able to manage it until Dennis offered to help him, had actually knelt down at his feet and untied his stinking trainers for him. Vividly he could see again the fragile crown of Dennis's

fair head bowed before him and the guilt and shame that
he'd been too far gone to register at the time swept over him
in a hot wave. As he remembered this his brother suddenly
opened his eyes very wide and stared at Roderic with something close to terror, as though he too were thinking of that
dreadful day and could hardly bear it. Then he closed them
again.

'Jesus, you frightened the life out of me. I didn't hear you
come in. I thought you were a burglar.'

'I'm sorry. I was worried about you being sick here on your
own. I brought you some things: apples, orange juice, a
newspaper. If there's anything else you need or want I'll go
and get it.'

Dennis opened his eyes again. 'Aren't you very kind?
Aren't I lucky to have such a thoughtful brother?'

The weather was still bad when he left the house. He got
stuck in traffic, arrived back at his studio much later than he
had expected, and was running behind schedule for the rest
of the day as he struggled to get things tidied and finished
up. Back home he packed his bags and it was well after nine
o'clock before he had his evening meal, a dismal affair
cobbled together out of the dregs of the fridge: an old piece of
chicken, a hard boiled egg, and some lettuce on the point of
no return. He was clearing up afterwards when the phone
rang. It was Julia, back in Dublin sooner than either of them
had expected.

He left the house immediately and went straight round.
'I've been thinking of you all week,' she said as she led him
up the stairs to the flat. 'I was really disappointed to think
that I wouldn't see you before you left.' There was a fire
burning in the grate and she knelt before it to stoke it up. She
looked, Roderic thought, drawn and tired and when he asked
her how her visit home had been she said frankly, 'Difficult.
Extremely difficult.' She told him that her father was a bad
patient, that because of having to look after her and be strong
in the past he had developed an intense dislike of being

weak, of being himself looked after. She sat back for a moment on her heels and looked into the flames. 'And yet it's exactly because of that, because of all he's done for me that I want to help him. Do you understand?' she added, turning to him.

'Oh I do.' He told her that Dennis had also been ill and of the guilt he had experienced on visiting him, and she listened carefully without comment as he spoke more frankly than he had ever done before about all he had put his brother through.

'It's not good to always be the one who takes,' she remarked when he had finished, 'but trying to break out of that pattern isn't easy, as I well know.'

She had settled down on the sofa with the cat beside her, and as they sat talking and the night wore on he remarked in her that hyper-real quality that he had noticed before but that struck him now with greater force than ever. She was completely *there*, solidly, physically present in a way that was oddly reassuring. Taking a hallucination as one aspect of perception, Julia as she was this evening with her grey skirt, her glass beads, was its exact opposite. Although he was enjoying talking to her it eased his heart also simply to look at her. Their conversation became desultory, with long pauses in which there was no tension or awkwardness. When he arrived she hadn't put on a cassette as she usually did but the silences filled the room as though they were music.

'Are you ready for Paris?'

He told her that he had his bags packed, pulled his passport and tickets from his inside pocket.

'Wish I was going,' she said.

'So do I.'

He looked at his watch. It was almost midnight, and still the weather had not eased. The rain was blowing against the window and he wished he didn't have to go out into it. She had kept the blaze in the hearth going; it crackled and flamed.

194

'It must be comforting to fall asleep at night looking at the fire,' he said.

'It is,' Julia agreed, and then she added, 'you'll see for yourself shortly just how good it can be.' The silence in the room was immense now. Julia said nothing more, but she smiled at him and stretched out, touched his foot gently with hers.

What happened next was, Roderic thought, bizarre. She stood up and unfolded the sofa. 'I can tell you now,' she said, 'you'll be too tall for this. Your feet will stick out over the end. Will you give me a hand with the bedding?' The strange ordinariness of it, that was what he would remember, as she pulled a duvet from the press at the end of the room, and took clean, rough dried sheets from a blue plastic laundry bag. They made up the sofa bed with great care: 'Pull the sheet down a bit more on your side, will you? You'll need more than that to tuck in at the bottom.' Anything more unlike the heat of passion would have been hard to imagine, he thought, as she threw him a pillow and a pink pillowcase printed with tiny cream flowers. It clashed with the blue and white striped one she was now hauling over a pillow, and he even began to wonder had he misheard or misinterpreted what she said: had she simply asked him to help her make up the bed before he left? Given her dislike of housework there was a certain logic to it, reinforced by the homely effect of the finished bed, with its candy-striped sheets and mismatched linen. Had he imagined the whole thing?

And then it dawned on him: Julia in recent weeks had had fixed in her mind exactly the same deadline as he.

Chapter Twenty

The brothers arrived at the funeral home moments after the rest of their family, who were getting out of their cars as Dennis drove up. His mother offered Roderic a dry cheek to kiss, as did Cliona and Maeve; Arthur offered him his hand, his sympathies, half embracing Roderic whom he had always liked. 'This is a bad business, a bad business,' he said as they went into the building and sat down in the waiting room beside each other on steel and moulded-plastic chairs. 'It's a sad homecoming for you.'

'Yes,' Roderic replied, grateful for his concern. The room, cold and discreet with a vague nod to religious sensibilities unnerved him.

'Bloody awful places these, aren't they?' Arthur said. 'Bed but no breakfast.'

Roderic, taking in the garish stained glass, the stiff carnations thrust in a vase, could not but agree. As always, he felt scruffy beside Arthur. No matter how well he polished his shoes or brushed his jacket, he could never bring himself up to the sartorial heights his brother-in-law seemed to achieve effortlessly with his gold signet ring and his lime after-shave, his brogues like black glass and his well-cut overcoat. 'I feel bad that I didn't get here in time,' Roderic added, but Arthur narrowed his eyes and shook his head.

'Would have made no odds,' he whispered, 'no odds, so don't think about it, don't fret. Once the stroke hit, that was that. Believe me, I was there. Those extra two days in hospital . . . well, it was a mercy it was only the two days. No, Roderic, put it from your mind. You're here now, that's what counts.'

'I came as soon as I could.'

'Of course you did.'

It was Maeve who had rung Roderic to tell him that their father was in hospital. It was the call he had dreaded receiving ever since he went to live abroad and had imagined many times; but in the event it baffled him.

'How is he? Is it serious?'

'Well, he's not marvellous,' Maeve said slowly after some thought, which told Roderic precisely nothing.

'Should I come home?'

'You can if you want,' she replied calmly.

'But what do you think?'

'It's not up to me. You must decide for yourself.'

'Yes Maeve, I know that, but I think you're missing the point. It's impossible for me to know unless you tell me how critical the situation is. I need the information to make the right decision. You can appreciate that I don't want to leave Marta at the moment unless it's absolutely vital.'

'Hmm, I was forgetting about Marta. When is she due?'

'Yesterday.'

Maeve gave a pettish sigh, sounding exactly like their mother. 'This is all very inconvenient, I must say, but it is down to you. Mum said that someone should probably ring Roderic and tell him what has happened so I've rung you. What more can I do?'

At that Roderic gave up. He said good night and went back into the sitting room, where Marta was draped out full length on the sofa, which she completely filled, before a huge fire. Smiling, she held out her hands to him and he went over, kissed her, then perched behind her head.

'What news from Ireland?'

'Only bad news, I'm afraid. It's Dad. He's had a stroke.'

'Poor Frank! Why, that's terrible,' Marta said.

Some months after their wedding the preceding year they had made a short trip to Ireland so that Marta could meet his family and friends there. Frank had hit it off surprisingly well with his daughter-in-law at their first meeting and when she was in Dublin their mutual fondness for each other had been renewed and strengthened.

'Will you go home to see him?'

'That's what I don't know,' he said. 'I don't want to leave you, now above all.'

'Yes, but if it can't be helped . . .' At that the phone rang again.

Dennis was annoyed at how Maeve had handled the call and was as direct as she had been oblique. 'You must come home,' he said, 'unless Marta is absolutely opposed to it. Under the circumstances I'd understand if she needed you there. I'll square it for you with the rest of the family, if needs be.'

'I'll come as soon as I can get a flight,' Roderic said, and with Marta's blessing he left for Ireland early the following morning, only to be met by his brother, red-eyed, at Dublin airport.

He knew what had happened even before Dennis said: 'It's all over.'

'This was bad timing for you,' Arthur remarked, and Maeve, overhearing, interjected,

'It's a bad time for all of us, actually, not just for Roderic, what with it being so close to Christmas and everything.'

'But it's particularly bad for him,' Arthur gently insisted, 'what with Marta, you know.'

'I see, yes,' Maeve said, 'I keep forgetting about that,' and she shrugged, turned back to speak to her mother.

'I suppose then you'll be heading off as soon as possible after the funeral?'

'I will,' Roderic said. 'I'll be in Rome by late tomorrow night, and I'll get a train north the following morning.'

'I know you'd like to be there, but I'll tell you this for nothing: when the time comes, she'll have that baby whether you're there or not,' Arthur said, in a blunt attempt to console him.

While they had been talking the room had slowly filled with other, more distant family members, with colleagues and friends come to pay their respects. The undertaker appeared and in a low voice ushered them into the room where the coffin was.

Frank made a terrifying corpse. His face, grim in death, made him look more formidable than ever he had done in life, a thing Roderic would not have thought possible. He also bore an uncanny resemblance to Dennis, something that had not been evident heretofore. They made awkward conversation about the coffin and the shroud Frank wore, about how it had been a mercy that he hadn't lingered. In one of the lacunae of these exchanges, Roderic suddenly burst into violent, passionate sobs. At first no one said anything. Even Dennis and Arthur were too mortified to make any move to comfort him.

'Roderic, please,' his mother then murmured, frowning.

'I'm sorry, excuse me, I'm sorry . . .'

He fumbled his way out and stood in the hall, trying to get a grip on himself. From the room he had just left he heard Maeve's voice: 'Oh, Roderic always was so *emotional*.' He went out of the building so that he could hear no more.

When Dennis came out to look for his brother a few moments later he found him sitting on a low wall smoking a cigarette. He looked like a truant schoolboy, Dennis thought. Roderic had an odd knack of being able to look utterly child-like, something his brother had noticed in him many times before. In spite of the height? In spite of the beard? In spite of the odd grey hair? Dennis asked himself, incredulous, every time he noticed it, and the answer was always yes. For years he had tried to work out what was at the root of this discon-certing trait; as Roderic now fumbled a cigarette packet out of his pocket and offered it to his brother, Dennis realised what it was. Even as an adult, Roderic was still capable of that absolute open-heartedness that is the essence of children. He wasn't even aware of it himself, Dennis thought, didn't see how vulnerable it made him, like a walled city with its gates left unlocked and unguarded at night. Without speaking he accepted a cigarette and lit it from Roderic's; sat down beside him on the wall.

'I realise it's important that none of us show any emotion over the next few days,' Roderic said. 'I don't understand why that should be the case, why it should be such a crime to shed a few tears, but I promise I'll do my best to keep the lid on as required.'

'It's not a question of not expressing emotions,' Dennis replied, 'it's a question of there not being any feelings to show.'

Roderic considered the implications of this, and gave him the wounded look of a six-year-old.

'I'll do what I can,' he said.

But it was Dennis who cracked next, and in dramatic fashion. They returned later that day for refreshments in the family home where Maeve and their mother still lived. The curtains in the drawing-room had been closed in keeping with tradition. Maeve brought in a large plate from the kitchen. 'Egg and onion on brown bread,' she said, removing the cloth that covered the serried ranks of triangular sand-wiches. 'Ham and mustard on white. Roderic, will you ever pass them around? There are plates and napkins on the sideboard.' She slipped wearily into an armchair with an air of almost professional languor. 'Dennis . . .'

'Yes, yes, I'll serve the sherry,' he said, making no effort to hide his annoyance.

'I was going to ask you if you'd ever put the kettle on, actually,' Maeve replied calmly.

'I'll do it,' Cliona said. 'Go ahead, Dennis, the decanter's over there.'

Cliona had returned to serve the tea and Dennis was going round the room for the second time to top up glasses when, over the buzz of conversation, he heard heavy familiar foot-steps descending the stairs. He glanced over at the open door of the drawing-room and there, standing in the hall, was his father.

Frank was dressed in his hill walking clothes: the close-fitting woollen hat, the top-class anorak, the practical but bizarre-looking combination of knee-length trousers, knee-high socks and heavy boots, about which he had always been utterly unselfconscious. The knapsack he was holding in his hands gaped open, and just before he closed over the flap Dennis could see the thermos and sandwiches it contained; they looked as solid and convincing as the crystal decanter Dennis held in his hands. He looked cheerful and relaxed as he always had done when setting out for the Wicklow mountains, and for a few moments he stood looking into the room. No one but Dennis seemed to be aware of his presence. Frank took it all in: the sherry glasses, the chintz, the small talk. 'Sweet Jesus Christ,' he exclaimed, 'what a way to pass the afternoon. I'd rather be dead.'

He turned away. Dennis could hear the sound of his boots clumping down the hall, the front door of the house closing behind him. And then Dennis started to laugh. Everyone in the room, including Roderic, stopped what they were doing and stared at him. 'Please forgive me,' he said, as he struggled to get the outburst under control. 'I must apologise,' but at that another yelp of laughter escaped him.

'Roderic,' Cliona said, 'why don't you ... why don't you ... take Dennis out for a walk?'

'Excellent idea,' Roderic said, putting his tray down and taking the decanter from Dennis's hands. 'A bit of fresh air would do us both good.

A couple of pints would be even better,' he added in qualification moments later, as they stood on the front step of the house. 'The usual place be all right?'

Dennis nodded.

'I don't know what came over you back there,' Roderic said as he carried two pints of Guinness over to their table from the bar, 'but at least it got us out of the house. Ghastly business: I couldn't help thinking of Dad and how much he would have loathed it. It's a good thing people don't have to attend their own funerals.'

It startled Dennis that Roderic could unwittingly be so close to the mark about what had happened. He said nothing as his brother moved in beside him on to the curved banquette of buttoned red dralon. The pub was pretty well deserted at this hour and they sat in silence, staring at their drinks for some moments. Such was the state of Dennis's nerves by this stage that he was hardly surprised when he noticed that a third perfectly manicured pint had appeared on the table, behind which, sitting between the two brothers, was Frank.

'Well, cheers, then,' Roderic said.

'Cheers,' Dennis replied, lifting his glass.

'To Dad,' Roderic added, and Frank smiled indulgently as his two sons drank to him.

He looked well, as he had when Dennis saw him in the house, fit and relaxed, youthful, even.

'Poor man,' Roderic said as he put his glass down. 'I've been thinking about him all the time, ever since I got the call in Italy; about his life, and what it amounted to.'

Dennis, alarmed by the idea of post-mortem eaves-dropping, moved to interrupt, but Frank raised his right index finger to his pursed lips, then smiled.

'Well?' Roderic asked. 'You were going to say?'

'Nothing,' Dennis replied.

Frank sat back in the banquette and folded his arms.

'We were talking about you the last time I was home,' Roderic said, 'about how good a life you had made for yourself; the job, you know, and your house. He admired you more than you might realise, and he said then, "Dennis is like me: an absolute loner." It was only afterwards I realised what a tragedy it was, that someone who defined himself in that way should have ended up in the thick of family life. I don't think he even knew that that was what he was telling me: he had buried the regret too deep.'

'Oh, he knew all right,' Dennis said and he stared hard at Frank, but Frank would have none of it, and kept his eyes fixed on his pint. 'He knew exactly the degree to which his life hadn't worked out.'

'Why do you think he did it?'

'Did what? Got married? Oh, because he was a passionate man, impulsive too, and you know what a beauty Mum was when she was twenty.'

'True. He always got on much better with women than with men,' Roderic said, 'and there was something about him that women loved. Even with Marta, when she met him, he charmed her totally. But of course there's a world of difference between that and getting married.'

At this Frank lifted his head and gave Dennis a shrewd sideways glance, for again Roderic had come eerily close to the mark, closer than he ever could know.

'So Roderic's going to jump the stick,' Frank had said to Dennis when the wedding was announced. 'Now there's a turn-up for the books. Never thought Roderic would go and do a thing like that.'

'Didn't you?' Dennis said, surprised. 'Why not? He's always had plenty of girlfriends.'

'Oh, come off it. Getting on famously with women is one thing,' Frank had replied, 'getting married is quite another,' somewhat exasperated that this nice distinction was not self-evident to his elder son.

Roderic took a long pull at his Guinness, then said to his brother with real concern, 'Dennis, *are* you all right? Do you feel well?'

'What? No. I mean yes. Why do you ask?'

'You seem a bit distracted, that's all. You're not looking at me when you're talking. You keep looking away. You keep staring at something here,' and Roderic pointed at Frank, who grinned wolfishly at Dennis.

'No I don't,' Dennis said, and he fixed his gaze on Roderic's face, made a considerable effort to keep it there. 'I'm fine, really. Go on, go on.'

'And that the medical thing didn't work out was a great blow, although he so rarely spoke of it. He'd have made a fine surgeon.'

'Yes. I always thought he'd have found people easier to deal with if they were under a general anaesthetic and with their body cavity cut open,' Dennis said, still not daring to look at Frank.

'But if he hadn't decided to get married so young I suppose we wouldn't be sitting here today. And yet it was the wrong thing to do. The wrong thing.' Roderic paused for a moment. 'It's tragic,' he said, 'to make an error early in your life, and then to have to live with the consequences for ever after, to have to try and limit the damage to other people who happen to be caught up in your stupid mistakes. He did try, Dennis, to live honourably, to behave with as good a grace as possible, given the circumstances.'

'But did he succeed?' Dennis said pitilessly.

Again Roderic paused for some time before he answered.

'When I was a child,' he said, 'I was terrified of him. I thought him choleric and cold. I was afraid of the lash of his tongue, those sardonic remarks that could cut you to the core. When I grew older, I began to understand him more although I know he thought my life odd, painting, you know, and not seeming to get anywhere much with it. But I know he loved me passionately, as I loved him. I grew to realise over the years how alike we are – were,' he said, correcting himself. 'If he was cold, well, so too am I, only his coldness was a mask, whereas with me it's the absolute centre of myself.'

To look at Frank had suddenly become for Dennis the more bearable option, but his father did not return his gaze. He was staring fixedly at his younger son and listening intently to all he said, his face full of sorrow and compassion. He had aged completely since the start of the conversation, looked tired and elderly now, as he had done in the weeks before his death.

'I hope we have a daughter,' Roderic said. 'I don't know what I'll do if it's a boy, truly I don't.'

'Don't you know already? Aren't there tests nowadays?'

'Yes, but Marta absolutely refused to be told in advance. I know I'd be a bad father to a son. I'd make a better go of things with a girl, I feel sure of it. I wish these days were over. I dread tomorrow, I don't know how I'm going to get through the funeral, and I keep thinking of how much Dad himself would have loathed it all.'

Dennis looked from Frank back to his brother.

'We should have had him cremated,' Roderic said, 'and scattered his ashes over the Wicklow mountains. That was the one place on earth where I think he was happy, where he felt free.'

'I'll always feel close to him there, no matter what,' Dennis replied. That had been his gift to Dennis, the love he shared for the hills in winter, for the rowans, the tumbling boggy rivers and the high bare skies.

'If you could speak to him now, is there anything you would like to tell him?' Dennis asked.

'I hope he knew that I loved him, in spite of everything. I could never have told him that, any more than he could have told me. But I hope he knew. I hope he knew.'

But when Dennis looked back, Frank had disappeared. Nothing remained but an empty glass where he had been sitting, its sides laced with traces of froth, like the foam left by the waves on a deserted beach in winter.

Chapter Twenty-One

He rang her from the airport. 'I had an idea in the taxi: why don't you come to Paris with me? I'll buy you a ticket now for a flight going out later today, and you can collect it here. I'll meet you when you arrive. Please, Julia.'

'I wish I could but I can't. My passport expired six months ago and I haven't renewed it. By the time I get it sorted out you'll be back. In any case, Hester would go mad if I asked for more time off.'

'Then I won't go,' he said, but she dismissed this at once.

'I'll be here when you return, you can tell me all about it. Someday we'll make a trip together. There's no rush now, we have all the time in the world.'

He told her he loved her and said goodbye. As he walked away from the phone, past people trailing luggage, past straggling queues at the check-in desks, under the black destination board with its red lights, it occurred to him how strange it was to experience such happiness – no, elation, it was, pure *joy* – here, of all places. For years now, Dublin airport had been a particularly bitter and painful station in his way through life. How far back did he have to go to find a good memory? Perhaps not since he left for Italy for the first time all those years ago had he had a truly carefree trip. There had been visits home with Marta in the early days when he had fretted on her account, when the warmth of Frank's welcome and interest in her did not quite cancel out the effect of his mother and sister's cool indifference. Later came trips with Serena and then Allegra to rented houses in the west where the Irish weather conspired against them. The unseasonal wind and rain astounded Marta – that July could be so cold! – and sent them all back to Italy sneezing and coughing. Because it was Roderic's country he felt that it was all somehow his fault. Eventually the expense and effort of travelling such a long distance and trailing through departure lounges with small children and their aristocratic quantities of necessary goods – pushchairs and teddy bears and bottles and bibs – made them give up in despair. They took family holidays in Positano which bored Roderic intensely, and he came back to Dublin on his own from time to time to see his family. He remembered hurrying back when his father was seriously ill and Dennis meeting him here in the airport, telling him it was too late, that Frank was dead.

The screw tightened as the years went on, and his life in Italy soured. Apart from Dennis he had no strong bonds to Dublin now, and both departure and arrival left him miserable, torn between two realities neither of which was right. Drinking solved nothing, yet still he drank. His marriage fell apart and he compounded the error of having settled in Italy with Marta by returning eventually to Ireland. He remembered arriving back in Dublin airport knowing that he was doing the wrong thing, but he was too fuddled with alcohol and misery to know what he should do. A disastrous trip back to see Marta some months later, then nothing for years until the botched visit a year after he stopped drinking, and at last the final nervous departure in June when he went to be reconciled with his daughters. That was his experience of being in the airport.

And now this. Now this.

This sense of sudden transformation continued when he arrived in Paris. The weather there as in Dublin was bad, and yet still he found the city radiant under a wet silver sky, and strong winds were bringing down the leaves in the curiously formal gardens. He sat under the awning of a café and watched the life of the streets, thinking that if things had not gone well between him and Julia the city would have looked utterly different. Without the lustre given to it by love it would have seemed claustrophobic and grim, just as he could objectively see that many of the women who passed him in the streets were more beautiful than Julia and yet still he thought her lovelier. He couldn't believe what had happened to him, couldn't believe his luck. That Julia loved him. That he himself was alive and sober with a roof over his head, that he was working well, that he was reconciled to his daughters; the cumulative grace of these things almost overwhelmed him. Rain dripped from the awning and the people in the streets huddled under coloured umbrellas. What would they think of him, these strangers, if they knew the truth of his life? No doubt they would consider him a failure on so many levels. They would not be able to grasp how astonishing an achievement it was for him to be there at the still centre of an ordinary life, ordinary happiness, something that had eluded him until now.

In the Louvre he saw a painting that he thought perfectly expressed this sense of beatitude: an angel, painted on a tiny gilded oblong of wood. He stared at it for a long time, at the branch of moist olives it held in one hand, the other calm upon its flat breast, its shock of hair, not dissimilar to Julia's, its perfect fingernails and mild, androgynous face, its atmosphere of peaceful benevolence. Near by hung another much larger painting by the same artist. In the centre were the Madonna and the Christ Child, and at their feet, one on either side on a richly patterned carpet, knelt the donor and his wife. Behind them were the serried ranks of their children: seventeen in all, the girls behind their mother, the sons behind their father. Had anyone believed even then, all those years ago, that the painting had been commissioned out of religious faith, out of anything other than the sheer pride of parenthood, so that the stiff-faced citizen could show off his children? His sons, so magnificent, and his daughters, his brown-eyed, snub-nosed, clear-skinned girls, in their veils and linen bonnets? *I have three daughters.*

Apart from a guard slumped in a chair at the far end of the room there was no one else around. The next painting Roderic noticed was a crucifixion which he judged to be from the fifteenth century, given its style and content. At the foot of the cross on a landscape of broken stone were four female figures, two on each side and disproportionately small, who stared out sternly at the viewer. They wore pleated gowns of jewel-deep colours: emerald, sapphire, garnet and topaz; and on their heads were stiff linen wimples. Female martyrs who bore the emblems of their suffering: Saint Barbara with a model of the tower in which she had been imprisoned by her father; Saint Lucy, whose eyes had been gouged out and which she now displayed on the silver tray she held in her hands; Saint Agatha, whose breasts had been cut off and which she also offered on a platter for the viewer's delectation. Roderic, familiar with the iconography, could identify these, but the last figure baffled him. Standing on the extreme right of the painting, she was also carrying a silver tray and on it were an array of flasks and flagons together with a drinking glass. He racked his brains but had no idea who this last saint could be, even though there was something about her face that was vaguely familiar. *The Master of the Unfortunate Decision*, he read on the label pinned near by. *Italian School, early 15th C. Crucifixion with Four Female Martyrs, SS. Barbara, Lucy, Agatha and Marta*. Marta? But she wasn't a martyr! Even as he thought this a little voice said, 'Are you sure about that?' Wildly, Roderic looked back again at the painting and he saw now that the four tiny figures were alive, were living, breathing women and yes, the one on the right was Marta. Her stern features had now taken on an air of personal affront and without further ado she heaved forward the tray she was carrying, threw it straight out of the picture and into the room. It landed at Roderic's feet with a tremendous clatter out of all proportion to its size, for it was like nothing so much as a doll's tea set. The glass smashed on impact, wine and spirits poured from the broken flagons.

Marta wiped the palms of her hands against each other in a brisk gesture of dismissal and finality, while her diminutive companions, clearly appalled, struggled to maintain their sangfroid. Then she turned on her heel, marched towards the frame of the painting and simply disappeared like an actress going off into the wings. Simultaneously with all of this an alarm had gone off in the gallery, a shrill, urgent bell, and the slumped guard leapt out of his chair. 'That's him,' he shouted, pointing at Roderic as more guards poured in from adjacent rooms and bore down on him. 'He's to blame. It's all his fault.' As Roderic tried to protest his innocence – feeling in his heart that this was not strictly true, that he had caused the mayhem although how he wasn't exactly sure – a guard even bigger and stronger than he, a monster of a man, wrestled him to the ground and put him in an armlock . . .

He awoke, and knew at once that he wasn't at home in his own bed. The weather he could hear, the wind and heavy rain, was the same as on the night he had been with Julia and he thought then for the briefest fraction of time that he was still there, that she was asleep beside him. He reached out his hand to touch her but the wide bed was empty and he remembered with an overwhelming sense of disappointment where he was: alone in a hotel room in a foreign city. Then far below, down in the narrow street, he could hear the familiar sound of a drunken man shouting and roaring. Most probably he was speaking in French but the rain and the wind made it impossible to hear properly. All at once Roderic had a weird out-of-body experience as though his self were split, as though he were both the man lying warm in bed listening and the lost creature down below howling his woes against the elements. Was it possible that his past self was not integrated into the man he now was, but was capable of detaching itself and walking abroad, haunting him like a ghost?

To distract himself from this disturbing idea he tried to imagine those he loved as they were at this precise moment.

He thought of his daughters off in Italy, in the same rooms into which he had crept at night when they were small children to watch them sleeping and to warm his soul. Julia, back in Ireland, would be curled up amidst her mismatched linen on the sofa. But a memory then arose unbidden in his mind of being with Marta some twenty years earlier, during his time at the Foundation. They were in bed together in her apartment late on a summer evening, talking about how his time in Italy was about to run out and what he might do to prolong his stay. It was then she had made her offer: 'You could always come and live with me.' Many times since then he had asked himself if he had engineered this moment. Had he put her in the position where she couldn't but suggest they live together? Even in his darkest hour he had acquitted himself. He'd been genuinely surprised at what she said, but in accepting her offer he was sealing both their fates by opening the way to his own suggestion, a year later, that they should get married. Why had he done it? Because all his life he had been the recipient of others' generosity and had reached the stage when he needed to be the giver rather than the recipient. But he had nothing to give except himself. And Marta, alas, said yes.

Having slept only fitfully, he was tired and overwrought the following day and the elation he had felt on his arrival in the city was beginning to ebb away. Not that there was any harm in that, he thought over breakfast, if it were to be replaced by a deeper understanding of the state he had come to. He was even glad now that Julia was not here with him: what he was facing he needed to face alone. How urgently his past pressed in upon him these days, as though insisting that it be integrated into his present life. It was something he hadn't expected in Paris, as he had no strong personal links with the city and in itself he found it a neutral and detached place. And yet, as in the gallery, everything conspired to remind him of things that had happened in the past. As he sat in the glass-fronted café tearing apart a brioche, he saw out on the street a little incident played out in dumb-show that did exactly this.

It reminded him of quarrelling with Jeannie; about what, he could no longer recall. They'd been standing on a corner in South Great George's Street, and for once Jeannie was listening as he harangued her, or at least she seemed to be, as she stared away thoughtfully into the distance. Roderic suspected she was only preparing the more ferociously to tear into him when the time came but all of a sudden she walked away, just ten paces or so. 'Hello, you. I'm Jeannie,' she said, crouching down in front of a small boy who was howling and wailing. 'What's your name? You've lost your Mammy, haven't you? Will we go and look for her?' The little boy, who said that he was called Donal, stopped crying as though a switch had been thrown and cheerfully took Jeannie's hand. 'He wandered out of the arcade,' she said to Roderic, nodding up the street. 'I was watching him the whole time you were doing your nut.' The three of them set off together. Not only had the child brightened up no end, giving them a long garbled monologue in which the story of his life and the events of that day were confusingly mixed, but Jeannie had also undergone an astonishing metamorphosis, not just of mood but of personality since meeting Donal. Playful, jolly, expansive – Roderic had never seen her like this, but then he had never before seen her in the company of children. He was familiar with her in the aftermath of access visits to her own son and daughter and would bolster her through the black depressions into which she then fell. 'I bet your Mum's in here,' she said to the child as they turned into the arcade. 'I bet you anything you like.'

A woman with a baby in a pushchair and a girl of about three who looked exactly like Donal were at the far end of the arcade. 'Where did you get to?' she said severely. 'How many times have I told you not to wander off like that?' The child released Jeannie's hand without a word and took hold of the handles of the pushchair. In doing so, he was completely reabsorbed into his own family; it was as if he had moved into another dimension and could no longer even see Jeannie. His mother, however, looked her over coldly, taking in her dishevelled clothes, her hair in need of a wash, and turned away without speaking. And Jeannie was desolate, as desolate as Roderic had ever yet seen her. He put his arm around her shoulders and for once she didn't push him away impatiently but slumped against him as though depending on him now to keep her vertical.

'Come on,' he said, 'let's get you a drink.'

Where did such moments go, he wondered? He would have liked to believe that there was some kind of place, some repository where incidents of such exquisite suffering were recorded and preserved. That they simply vanished and no meaning could be taken from them was, he thought, too cruel, as he watched the incident out on the Parisian pavement draw to a more cordial conclusion, the mother shaking hands with the woman who had restored her child to her, the stranger ruffling the curls on the little boy's head before walking away.

But it was Marta not Jeannie he thought of as soon as he stepped into Notre Dame later that morning. The cathedral was thronged with tourists, many of them lighting candles at the stands to the right of the entrance, beneath a great dark crucifix. There was something eerily alike about all these people. He studied their faces as, with intense concentration, they touched the wicks of the small flat lights to the flames of the candles already in place. What was it that drew these people here? To look at them was to feel that their cast of mind was utterly contemporary. With their expensive casual wear they had literally bought into the prevailing values of society. Were their actions today driven by mere sentimentality, or did it speak of a wish for something more, a wish that they would be embarrassed about, a faith that would have exhausted itself before the candles had burnt themselves out? The lofty greyness of the cathedral was pierced by the millefiori discs of the great rose windows. He perched himself on a small chair with a seat of woven straw and inhaled deeply that strangely musky odour of candlewax and stale incense that was so characteristic of Catholic churches and was for Roderic so evocative.

The day after he'd gone with Elsa to see her friend at work, high on the scaffolding, he rang Marta at the number she'd given him. She told him there was another project she'd worked on, an altarpiece in a church near where she lived, that she particularly wanted to show him. Would he be free that Friday? As soon as he saw her waiting beside her blue car parked at a discreet distance from the Foundation on Friday midmorning, he knew that they would have made love before the day was out. The subtle manner in which she greeted him left him in no doubt that Marta knew this too. The shared sense of anticipation was so strong that it was as if they had already been together and were moving in the memory of each other's touch, of their mouths, their bodies.

'Well then,' he said, 'where's this famous painting?'

'We'll get to it in due course,' she replied. 'What's the rush?'

But in truth, for all of the rest of that day he felt as though she were showing him a picture. It was as if her life was a series of great hinged wooden panels that she was continually opening up and folding back to reveal a series of bright scenes, ever more intricate and beautiful. They went to a market in the town where she lived, bought wine, bread and ham, peaches and cheese, then drove out into the country to visit a farm belonging to people she knew. There they were shown a wooden press for olives, were given a bottle of its fruits that Roderic held up to the light so that he could admire the deep jewel green of the heavy oil. The neck was sealed with a thick drip of red wax. In years to come he would take Dennis to some of these same places to entertain him during holiday visits. The traders who knew and greeted Marta today would come to know him too and in due course his children, would ask after Serena and Allegra if he went to the market alone. They made a picnic of the food they'd bought, ate it by the banks of a river. It was late afternoon by the time they returned to town. She parked outside the church. 'My apartment's up there,' she said, pointing at the first-floor windows of a tall shuttered house, 'so we don't have far to go afterwards.'

They stepped from the heat of the street into the coolness of the empty church. It was silent and sombre and dim, with that fusty smell of incense and candles that he was never to forget. 'We need change,' Marta murmured as she led him to the front of the nave. From her bag she took a handful of coins, sorted through them and fed a few into a small coffer beside the altar rails. All at once the painting, which hung behind the main altar, was flooded with light. The effect was startling: such a wealth of colour, such gold. The painting showed the coronation of the Virgin and was densely packed with sternly worshipping saints. Surrounding them were crowds of angels with long wings, and bright, urgent faces like the heads on coins new minted. Christ, enthroned, placed upon His mother's head a crown whose delicate filigree was suggested again in the white stone of the canopy, bristling with little spires, beneath which they sat. In a low voice Marta explained to Roderic the work that had needed to be done to bring the panel back, after years of neglect, to such stunning glory. The time-switch expired, plunging them into abrupt darkness that seemed deeper than it had been before now that their eyes were used to the light. Marta put more coins in the machine and the painting was illuminated again.

'I was christened in this church,' she said. 'My parents were married here.' While they were down by the river she had told him of the great pride she took in her job, and she spoke of it again now, of the central place it had in her life. It was a joy, she said, to help save a work such as this from what she called 'the harms of time', so that it might be preserved

215

for people in the years to come. That this particular painting and the church in which it was displayed had for her a close personal significance made the satisfaction, the sense of privilege, she said, all the greater. With that the light went out again, but Marta had no more coins. Roderic took a handful of loose change from his pocket and felt her fingertips on his palm as she sorted through it, selecting what she needed. Once more they heard the preternaturally loud clinks the coins made as they dropped them into the coffer.

And then, standing before the lit picture for the third time, something strange happened. It was as though their future life together had already been lived and the essence of all that was good in it was encapsulated in those few moments. Only now, with hindsight, more than twenty years later could he begin to understand what had happened as they stood there in the dim and dusty chapel before that radiant image, breathing in the scent of incense. It was as though they had moved into a condition where the ordinary rules of time did not apply. Neither he nor Marta spoke. He barely knew her, but never in his life had he felt so close to anyone. It wasn't that he was imagining things that might happen in the years to come – in truth, he had thought no further than of the night ahead – but the spirit of their future fell over them as completely as the light did. Sitting in the garden on a summer evening with Serena when she was a toddler, helpless with laughter at the funny things she said. *Why has a tiger got stripes, Serena? So that it'll look like a tiger.* Going out to the Aran Islands with Marta and her delight when a seal popped up near the boat and swam along beside them, with its sleek fur, the soft pools of its eyes. The night in winter when they stayed in Rome and awoke to find snow falling on the ancient city. The wholeness and perfection of moments such as these were figured forth years before ever they happened, as they stood together in the silent chapel.

And then with a loud click the light expired, plunging them into darkness.

Chapter Twenty-Two

There was no question of her not going to Wicklow to be with Dan on her birthday. It was in early June and fell on a Friday that year. 'I'll work as usual and then drive down in the evening,' she told Roderic, who was not bothered by these plans. He realised that her family circumstances had given rise to certain fixed habits and customs, and one of these was that she always went home for her birthday. To break with the tradition would upset her father unduly. 'But I'm not just doing it for him,' she insisted. 'I want to go.' She did, however, spend all of Thursday evening with Roderic and stayed with him that night.

On returning to her own house the following morning she found a scattering of birthday cards on the doormat, found Max sullen at having been left alone. She fed him and took him into the shop, let him sit on her knee and stroked him as she opened her post. Placated, the cat slept. She was pleased to find that Dan had enclosed a letter with his card. Ever since she arrived in Dublin to attend art college, her father had written to her once a week. Sometimes he asked if there was any point in his continuing to do so as they also frequently spoke on the phone, but she urged him not to stop. Julia was always grateful to receive his letters. She needed their pure-hearted simplicity to set against the petty slights, against the vanities and small-mindedness she encountered and herself fell prey to as she tried to find her way as an artist, and establish herself in the city. Reading Dan's letters was like receiving a blow from the stick of a Zen master, waking her back into reality.

I found a bird's nest in the orchard yesterday. It was lying in the grass. I will keep it to show to you when you come home. It is made out of moss and feathers. The last time I found a nest it was broken but this one is all right. The sky was very clear this morning when I went out, with only a few high clouds. I hope the weather holds until the weekend. On Monday night I was in the pub with Henry. He says Felim is home from Manchester for a holiday and that he was asking after you. He likes England. I don't suppose he will come back to live here again. We had a good night. I am reading a book about the First World War.

Her day turned out to be busier than she had expected, and she was later in leaving for Wicklow than she had hoped. Julia had her own car; without it she would doubtless have gone home much less often. Dan had bought it cheap for her from an ad in a newspaper and retuned it in his spare time. He regarded a car as a necessity rather than a luxury, and Julia found it useful for transporting work and materials. This evening she was bringing one of her boxes back to Wicklow to store it. Max, perhaps in a spirit of vengeance for having been neglected, was particularly uncooperative when the time came for him to be put in his cage. She had hoped her delayed departure would mean that she missed the worst of the rush hour, but almost immediately found herself stuck in jams and tailbacks. This didn't bother her too much; like her father she was an excellent driver and a patient one. She found she could concentrate on the road and also think about things, allow her mind to wander constructively. Often it was like this that she found solutions to problems that had defeated her when she gave them more serious and considered thought.

Her work absorbed her in two ways: as ideas for new pieces and in the practical problems that their execution required. How to make triangular holes in a series of mirrors. How to suspend feathers in a box so that they looked as if they were floating there. How to break a glass cleanly into two equal halves without smashing the whole thing to pieces. Sometimes good ideas foundered because she could not find a way to implement them and lately she had been worried that the project to do with smells might come to nothing for this very reason. She had let the idea lie fallow for some months but had taken it up again recently, making a list of scents with which to work. Friends had been given a new loaf to sniff, or a freshly laundered sheet, had been asked for a written account of what it evoked. The responses so far showed the whole scheme had potential but how was she to present it? More to the point, how was she to replicate the fragrances in a gallery so that visitors could experience them for themselves? And if she couldn't, would the whole idea fail? She recalled some of the things that people had already told her.

Looking out of the window she had an idea for something else she might do. Visitors to a gallery would be taken into a room, alone, where there was no light whatsoever. Perhaps they might have to be guided in so as not to stumble and fall. There would be a soft place for them to sit; there would be music. The air would be scented with – what? Roses? Sandalwood? Mint? Something pleasant and soothing. The whole idea would be to create an environment that was completely sublime, with this one condition: that it would remain in pitch darkness. There would be nothing to see. And in every other way it would be a completely exhilarating experience. She turned it over in her mind and decided it couldn't be done, because people were too unalike. What to one person would be soothing or pleasurable in terms of music, sounds or smells would be to another neutral or even unpleasant. Each experience would have to be geared to each person. It was too particular; no, it couldn't be done.

From time to time she looked down at her lapel to admire the new brooch that was Roderic's birthday present to her. It was a striking and unusual combination of materials – slate, copper, mother-of-pearl – that worked together particularly well. The iridescence of the fragment of shell, its rainbow colours like oil on water, was enhanced by the slate, blue-grey and dull, like a winter sky. The box that held it had been under her pillow when she awoke that morning, and she again wondered how Roderic had managed to put it there without waking her, for she was a light sleeper. Although her past relationships with men had been good, the experience she had been living with Roderic in recent months was the best, the deepest, the most complete. Tapping her fingers on the steering wheel she thought about being with him the night before, smiled with pleasure at the memory. She liked the sexual side of their life together, the complicity of it; liked living this secret, intense ecstatic reality.

Gradually the traffic became lighter. She was glad to get out beyond the city, to see ahead of her the Dublin mountains, then the Great Sugarloaf and the Little Sugarloaf. Ever since she was a small child, to see them from this angle had been to know that she was headed for home.

As she drove up the lane and parked outside the little house she blew the horn to let her father know that she had arrived. He appeared at the window, came out to greet her.

Julia lifted the cage from the back seat of the car and opened the door, whereupon Max shot out as though he had been spring-loaded and ran over to the nearest tree. Like a pianist striking chords on a new piano to test it, he ran his claws briskly against the bark several times to make a sharp ripping sound, and then in a single bound sprang up into the branches and disappeared. 'Happy now?' Julia called after him laughing, as she went into the house with her father. As she took her jacket off to hang it up, she noticed Dan looking at her lapel.

'Roderic gave me that for my birthday.'

'It looks like it's made of slate,' he said, peering at it.

'It is slate.'

'Oh.' She could see that he didn't like it. Dan was of the old school, thought that jewellery should be made of gold and precious stones, the best you could afford, but he had long since come to realise that Julia and her friends had tastes and ideas that he could not fathom. 'That was kind of him,' he said diplomatically. She had been drip-feeding him selected information about Roderic in recent months. The complex of emotions that made Dan slightly possessive with regard to Julia also made him completely indulgent and sometimes these two attributes cancelled each other out.

'You go on with what you're doing; I have something to bring in from the car.' She fetched the box and carried it up to the room in which Dan permitted her to store her work and the materials she was hoarding until such time as she found a use for them. For a few moments she stood looking around, at the piles of old sheet music, maps, at the skeins of ribbon and rope, and thought of how often people who were closely connected to the arts and professed an interest, even a love of them, were unhelpful and unsupportive towards people like herself. More often than not it was Dan, or someone like him who afforded her the practical assistance and support that made possible the work he admitted he found baffling.

She went back down to the kitchen where he was in the middle of preparing the roast chicken that was his standard dish for special occasions. Completely self-taught, he was inordinately proud of his own cooking and liked to be praised for it. Celebration was vital to Dan. It was precisely because of the great sorrow at the centre of his life that he insisted on marking Christmas, Easter, birthdays and the like with as much ceremony as he could muster. 'Life will give you plenty of kicks in the teeth and there'll be nothing you can do about it,' he used to say, 'so why turn your back on the good times?' Glad to be here with him, Julia watched as he scraped carrots, as he lit the gas under the potatoes. The beauty and complexity of his personality was unfolding itself to her as the years passed, and she understood now that at the centre of him was something quite free of time and society. Later that night he would probably go outside to admire the stars. Julia could imagine him in another life that was wholly different in externals but in essence the same. She could picture him in Japan of the distant past, could see him standing with his friends on a wooden balcony, giving the order for cranes to be released across the face of the full moon when the moment was appropriate.

'Go and look at the nest,' he said. 'It's on the fireplace in the other room.' In its artful perfection it humbled her, this tiny ball of moss, redolent of wildness, and she thought of the bird that had built it. Sitting near by was Dan's book. The cover bore a drawing of poppies, their elegiac beauty part of the myth of its subject, part of the lie. Julia fell to leafing through it, became absorbed in the text and then sat reading until he called her to say that dinner was ready.

It was precisely because Dan rarely asked for proof of anything that she was sometimes keen to justify her life to him, and so when he said to her over dinner, 'How's the work going?' it was not a question she took lightly.

'It's going fine. Do you remember some months back I was gathering leaves? Well, I made a box with them and I sold it to a man recently.'

His delight at this pleased her. 'That's tremendous altogether. And what will he do with it? Is he going to give it to a museum or something?'

'No, he's a private collector. I expect he'll put it in his house.'

'And did he pay you well for it?'

'I got what I asked for.'

She could see he was amazed by this remarkable world where people paid good money for the things she made, but he was glad that this odd state of affairs was working to her advantage.

'That's something else now for us to celebrate.'

At the end of the meal he said 'Have you guessed yet what I'm giving you for your birthday?'

'No idea.'

'It's something special.'

From his pocket he took a small package, clumsily wrapped in flowered paper, and handed it to her. Inside was a slim flat leather case, slightly worn. She pressed the brass dimple on the side to release the catch and open it. On the faded cream silk lining was a watch, a gold wristwatch with a lozenge-shaped face. The supple bracelet was made of overlapping gold scales, as though it had been fashioned from the skin of some fabulous mythical fish. Julia stared at it.

'I gave it to her,' Dan said, 'for her twenty-fifth birthday. I've been keeping it safe all these years to give to you on yours.'

She didn't, couldn't speak.

'Put it on, why don't you?' he said, and she removed her own watch, took her mother's from its box and Dan leaned over her wrist to help her fasten the catch. 'It's a good one. I only ever bought the best, even when I couldn't afford it.' He didn't seem to mind that she still hadn't spoken: he could see that she was completely overcome, and then he guessed why. 'Have you seen it before?' he asked hesitantly. 'I mean, do you remember it?'

'Yes,' she said eventually. 'I do.'

Dan realised that she had remembered it as soon as she saw it. She had comprehensively forgotten it for all the years that it had lain upstairs, hidden away in his room, and if during that time anyone had asked her to describe her mother's watch she wouldn't have been able to do it.

But what he didn't guess, and what she couldn't yet tell him, was that as soon as she opened the box she had recalled not just the watch but the arm that wore it: a strong pale arm, ending in a somewhat elongated hand with almond-shaped nails trimmed short. Her mother's arm. In what part of her mind had this memory been locked away so completely for all these years? Everything else must be there, *everything*, but how could she get at it?

'I thought I might go outside for a while,' Dan said. 'Do you want to come with me?' She nodded, grateful to him for breaking the mood. 'Put your jacket on,' he advised her. 'It's cooler than you might think.'

It was late now and dark, for there was no moon. As she walked to the end of the house, Julia stumbled against an uneven stone, and Dan warned her to be careful. At the gable end they stopped and looked up at the points of silver light high above them. To begin with they seemed to be few, scattered and faint. Although her father was superstitious about many things he set no store by the stars, which he knew made nothing happen. Comets, eclipses of the moon, the immutable precision of the constellations: to admire their futile beauty was enough for him. As they watched the stars thickened and clustered, more and more becoming visible as their eyes became accustomed to the dark, and the night gradually revealed itself in its fullness.

Although Julia could not see Dan she could hear the sound of him fumbling in his pockets, and then there was the rasping sound of a match being struck. The little flame flared up, illuminating his profile for a few seconds as in a painting by de La Tour: the same sharp shadows, the same intensity of what could be seen in the yellow light, and then the match went out and there was only blackness again. She could smell the spent match and the smoke, see the lit point of the cigarette like a fallen star. 'May I have one of those?' From the sound of her voice he could tell where she was standing and reached out. Julia could feel his hand, warm, rough, giving her the cigarette packet and the matches. 'Thanks,' and then he saw her profile as the match flared, was extinguished.

They stood in the darkness, smoking, not talking, inhaling the smell of the earth. In the distance a bird cried, once, twice, forlorn. A breeze rustled the trees of the orchard. Even though she could see next to nothing, the atmosphere around her told her she was at home; could have been nowhere else on earth.

'Who invented the constellations?'

'The Babylonians. And it wasn't so much a case of inventing them.'

'You know what I mean,' she conceded. Cassiopeia. The Great Bear. The Little Bear. Orion's Belt. The tiny cluster of glittering lights that was the Pleiades, the Jewel Box. Its name recalled her gifts, which she could not see, but she instinctively touched her new watch, feeling the outline of the face, then reached up and stroked the brooch on her lapel.

All at once she was overcome by an intense physical longing for Roderic, a suffocating, dragging pressure that was also an emptiness, a lack. She wished then that she had been able to spend all of her birthday with him, and resented having had to come home to be with her father as usual. In the darkness Dan coughed, and she realised then that this had been his lot, this miserable aching tension, not just for a night or so but for year after year. Her mind shrank from all of this: it didn't seem decent to follow these thoughts through. Then she thought no, it should be like this. She was his child but she was a woman now, and it was right that she should understand fully the refinements of his suffering, the painful detail of all he had endured. The great bulk of the mountains was visible now against the sky. The bird in the distance cried again.

What if the people she loved were all here with her, and she simply couldn't see them in the dark? What if her mother was here with them looking at the stars, standing silently beside Dan? What if Roderic was standing between Julia herself and her father? The power of the wish made it so: suddenly she could imagine their presence so completely that they *were* there. She experienced a peace, a deep contentment such as she had rarely known before.

And when she went back into the house with Dan some time later, her eyes smarting in the bright light of the kitchen, she realised that she had just had exactly that sublime experience she had dreamed that afternoon of creating for others.

Chapter Twenty-Three

She crushed out her cigarette and looked him straight in the
eye. 'You're jealous, aren't you?' she said. They were sitting
at a café on Thomas Street on a warm June day, a couple of
weeks after her birthday. Julia had arrived some ten minutes
earlier and without any prompting had told him artlessly
about William: about how he had phoned her recently, how
he had dropped by the shop that morning and how she had
arranged to see him again towards the end of the week.
Roderic's displeasure at all of this, which he made no attempt
to conceal, was clearly something she had not expected.

'What's the problem?' she asked. 'Am I not supposed to
have friends of my own?'

'You know perfectly well that isn't the case.'

'So it's just this particular friend?'

'Just this particular person, yes.'

It was at this point that she suggested he was jealous. He
didn't respond. 'Well, you've no need to be,' she went on,
'none whatsoever He's only a friend. There's no sexual
element in it, if that's what you're thinking.'

'With men,' he said, 'there's always a sexual element.
Believe me. I know. I'm a man.' She stared straight back at
him. He couldn't fathom what she made of this. For a
moment he thought she was going to laugh, then he
wondered if she was angry. 'Anyway,' he went on, 'that's not
what I'm worried about.'

'I don't understand what you're getting at.'

How was he to explain it? Emotional seduction, which was
what he believed William to be intent upon, was, Roderic
thought, more dangerous than the usual variety. It was a
more insidious thing, more subtle, more easily denied by the

perpetrator and more difficult for the victim to identify. He understood all too well how it operated: the gradual but inexorable forcing of one's attentions upon another person, to bully them into friendship without their being able to resist, without their even being aware of what was happening. And William, who was used to getting his own way, stood a good chance of success. But how was he to explain all this to Julia? 'I just don't want you to get hurt,' he eventually said.

Julia rolled her eyes, threw him a look that silently said *Pl-ease! Give me a break!*

The waitress arrived with the coffee they had ordered when they sat down. Julia sullenly poured sugar into hers, stirred it, lit another cigarette and flung the plastic lighter down on the table with a clatter. She sat back in her chair and blew out a long stream of smoke, stared into the middle distance and did not speak. Eerily, she reminded him now of Serena, right down to the setting of the café, right down to the fact that people at neighbouring tables had noticed them, and were plainly wondering what was the reason for the tension and disagreement between the young woman and her older companion. Never before had she reminded him of his daughters, to whom she bore not the slightest resemblance, who were wholly different in their looks, their social habits and their cast of mind. Allegra excepted, they were not particularly interested in painting, and the real subtext of that interest was easy to read. He remembered how she said she would like to come to Dublin and visit him. There had been no further mention of this, but as his relationships with his daughters slowly mended it wasn't impossible or even undesirable that they might come to Ireland. Perhaps they would meet Julia. This was an idea so strange that he couldn't even begin to imagine it, for down through the years he had always found it somehow uncanny when the two halves of his life, the Irish and the Italian, met. To see Dennis and his mother-in-law sitting awkwardly side by side at dinner, or to watch Marta in the green striped drawing-room casting around desperately, trying to find some conversational common ground with Maeve, had always made him uneasy.

He drank his coffee and looked at Julia again, caught her eye. She gave a brief strange smile, as if she couldn't decide whether or not to remain cross, looked away again. Was it really possible that she was so like Serena? He remembered how his daughter's blue eyes had watched the men in the square watching her and how he had wanted to tell her things, to warn her, while knowing in his heart it was pointless. Any advice he might give Serena would be like a book written by someone late in life. Rich in moral experience and subtly expressed, to someone who came to it too young it would seem merely dull, although in the same book the same reader some twenty years later would be astonished to find the story of their whole life.

Julia seemed prepared to at least give him a chance.

'What is it exactly about William,' she said, 'that worries you?'

'To begin with, he's extremely wealthy.'

'This is true,' she agreed. 'You think that impresses me?'

'No, not at all; but it does set up a particular dynamic. He takes being rich for granted, together with everything it naturally brings with it. To put it crudely, William is somebody. Because of the social confidence his money gives him, people tend not to question this: they take him on his own terms. And they don't even realise that they're doing it. They never stop to ask: Who is this man anyway? Who is he, really? Now William himself has started of late to ask these very questions, and he's none too happy with the answers he's coming up with, but that's another day's work altogether. Just keep in mind that William is working from a position of strength. You, Julia, are not like that at all.'

As she listened to him she leaned back in her chair and stared out into the street. 'Go on.'

'Your position is a vulnerable one. You have neither money nor power. I believe you know and understand this. It isn't something you've exactly chosen, but you accept it. You want something particular out of life and you know what you have to do to get it. You've thought your situation through. That's your strength. By your own admission, what you do isn't fashionable. You're working away at your own view of the world, and you're refusing to tweak it at the edges, to blur it or falsify it in any way so as to make it more palatable to the powers that be, more commercial, more acceptable – whatever. You're determined to be absolutely true to your own vision. It's one of the things I admire most about you. It's also, if I may say so, the reason why you're living in a glorified hole in the wall, on loose change and cups of tea. But you do live in the world. Like everyone else you live in society and that's no bad thing, for the checks and balances it provides. Your vision is your own, but if it doesn't connect in any way with anyone else, perhaps you're deluding yourself. You need money of course, and you also need – what can I call it? It's something other than mere praise. It's a certain kind of endorsement. It helps reassure you on the bad days that what you're engaged upon in your work isn't simply a monumental exercise in self-deception. Which is where William comes in. He's intelligent and he's wealthy and he's powerful. He's in a position to give you that endorsement.'

'He bought my box.'

'Exactly,' Roderic said. 'Exactly.'

'Is there anything wrong with that?'

'No, but in the light of what I've just said, don't you see how it complicates things between you?'

She evidently took this to be a rhetorical question. After considering his words for a few moments she asked, 'Anything else?'

'It's also possible,' he said, 'that what William is going through at the moment is little more than a midlife crisis.'

'Meaning?'

'Meaning that when you get to his age – my age – you start to consider how your life is panning out, you start to balance the books. And the strange thing is, it never looks good. If you've failed in things, you feel it keenly. If you've been a success it seems hollow, and that's William's situation. By anyone's reckoning, he's done well. He has a marriage that has lasted, two children, beautiful home, career, money, the lot, and yet he's going about with a face like a late breakfast because he's a failure. Isn't life strange?'

'It most certainly is,' she agreed. 'You, on the other hand, really did fail in all those things, didn't you? None of them worked out.'

It struck him as a wounding and intentionally brutal remark. He didn't know how to answer her but in any case she didn't wait for a response.

'And yet,' she said, 'and yet, if all those things had gone well – your marriage and family life in particular – it still wouldn't ever have been enough for you, would it, if the painting hadn't worked out too. Am I right?'

'You know the answer to that.'

'Well, perhaps it's the same for William.'

Julia had put her finger on exactly what was, to Roderic, the most dangerous element: William was the real thing.

'I couldn't agree more,' he said. 'If painting had been only a pipe dream, then there'd be no problem. It would be enough for him to have it as a hobby. Unfortunately William really has made a huge mistake. He's done the wrong thing. It isn't just that he *thinks* he's wasted his life, he *knows* he's wasted his life. But what can he do? His situation is all but set in stone. He needs to keep his family – and himself, mark, and himself – in the style to which they're accustomed. Nor am I saying for a moment,' he added quickly, 'that I think he ought to walk out on his family. I don't consider that kind of behaviour a prerequisite for being an artist.'

231

'Do you honestly believe I would think you might?' She wasn't angry. She was sad.

He reached out and took her hand, held it tightly and she smiled at him. 'Of course not,' he said. 'Of course I don't believe that. What I mean is that it's not enough to have a gift. You have to have the courage of your gift as well. And that's where William's failing lies.'

'Danger,' Julia said. 'You keep talking about danger. What are you afraid of? What do you think is going to happen?'

'What's going to happen,' he replied, 'what *is* happening, is that William is working his way into your affections. He's on his way to becoming your friend: to your mind a sincere and trusted friend. There'll be that slight edge that there can only be in a friendship between a man and a woman, but that isn't where the harm lies; the danger isn't there. Already his wife is probably wary about what you represent, but she isn't, I think, unduly worried. She'll bide her time, because she also knows what's going to happen. You'll meet him every week to ten days, as we're meeting now, and you'll talk about things that matter to you, most particularly about your work. You'll help and encourage him in his own attempts to paint, and for a while he'll really appreciate the moral and practical support. Oh, you'll enjoy it, make no mistake. William can be good company: he's an intelligent man, with many fine qualities. It would all be perfectly valid, were it not for what's going to happen.

'Because one day, out of the blue, he'll simply drop you. There won't be a quarrel, no hostility, nothing as dramatic as that. He'll just wake up one morning and decide that he's not remotely interested in you any longer. The fact that you're an artist will have lost all its magic for him, its cachet. There are hundreds of artists out there, thousands, and you're just one of them. You're not famous or successful and show little sign of becoming so. You're a motor mechanic's daughter, for goodness' sake, and you make no secret of the fact. At the moment he finds that amusing. In time he'll consider it vulgar. You're not worth knowing so he won't want to know you.

'A week will go by and you won't hear from him, the week will run into a fortnight, if you let it go as long as that. You'll phone him up and get an answering machine. There'll be no response to the message you leave and some days later you'll ring him again. Perhaps this time you'll speak to him directly. He'll be distant, brisk and busy, far too busy to arrange to see you in the near future. He'll all but hang up on you. And you'll be puzzled and hurt by this. Because you would never behave as he's behaving, you won't be able to fathom what's happening and why, and so you may well ring him up again. This time he'll be annoyed. He'll think it can't be possible that you don't understand. He'll think you're being obtuse, that you don't know how to behave. You ought to know that this is the way the world works: that you clearly don't will only confirm in his own mind how right he is to want to have nothing more to do with you. And even you, Julia, even you, will by this stage have got the message that you're not wanted. You'll be angry and wounded that the friendship you sincerely offered to him has been thrown back in your face, like a worthless thing. And what I'm suggesting in telling you all this is that you try to spare yourself considerable pain by not getting involved with him in the first place.'

He hadn't expected to be allowed to say all this, had thought she would have interrupted him and howled him down after a couple of sentences. Instead, she heard him out thoughtfully, and remained in silence for a few moments after he had finished speaking. Then she said, 'How do you know this?'

'Because, Julia, I'm older and uglier than you are. Because, like you, I once had an open heart and life forced it shut. That's how I know. It's as simple as that.'

He was struck by how emotionally drained the conversation had left him. Signalling to the waitress for another cup of coffee, he asked Julia if she would join him. She shook her head, waited until the first set of cups had been cleared away and the fresh coffee brought to him before she spoke.

'May I tell you what I think?'

'Do, please.'

'I think the problem with William is that he reminds you of yourself. When you look at him you see the man you might have become. Say you hadn't taken to drink. Say you had instead become the person the situation seemed to require.'

'It wasn't in me. I couldn't have done it even if I'd wanted to.'

'I know, and we'll come to the reason for that in a moment. Let's just imagine that you had been able to damp it all down and lead a certain kind of life, one that went against the grain of the mental freedom that your work requires. What do you think would have been the effect?'

'I'd have stopped painting, that's for sure.'

'For sure. But don't you think that everything you'd repressed would finally have seeped out in exactly that depression and bitter anger you so dislike in William?'

'Yes, but all this is academic. I've told you, it wasn't in me to live like that.'

'And here's why,' she said. 'You told me that when you were about my age your plan was to be a schoolteacher until such time as you had established yourself as a painter. But the school rumbled you. They could see a mile off the sort of person you were – to use your own words, that it wasn't in you "to live like that". And so they said thanks, but no thanks.'

'Julia, I know all this. I'm the one who told you.'

She ignored him and pressed on. 'Now let's look at what might have happened next. What if your parents had put great pressure on you to find another job as a schoolteacher? What if, instead of being benevolently indifferent, your father

234

had been actively hostile to the idea of your being a painter? Would you still have had the courage to press on? The courage of your gift, if you want to put it that way. Perhaps you might. But what if, on top of all this, Dennis hadn't helped you? Would you still have been able to go on, or would you have got some job, as a supply teacher say, that would have worn you down until you had neither the will nor the energy for your own work? As you so rightly pointed out, we all have to live in the world.'

He couldn't believe what he was hearing. 'Whose side are you on, Julia? Just tell me that. Whose side are you on?'

'Don't be angry. It's not a question of taking sides. I'm just trying to make you see how what happened to William might have happened to you.'

'But it didn't. That's the difference. I have three daughters, and the demands of the kind of life the world implied they needed might have been enough to start me drinking, but it wasn't enough to stop me painting. If that didn't do it, nothing could.'

'Please don't be angry,' she said again. 'I want to tell you something I haven't told you before. It's about the day I met William. He asked me to sit beside him for a moment. He was on the ropes, anyone could see that. I didn't know what was wrong in his life – perhaps I still don't – but I could see the state he was in. We didn't talk at all, and then I started think of you and all that you had been through. Even before that day I often used to think of how our paths must have crossed in the city before we met. Perhaps I passed you many times on the street before I knew you. Maybe one day we even sat beside each other on a bench; maybe you were in distress like this man, but too far gone even to ask for help. I can't imagine what it's like to have to ask a complete stranger to give you some shred of comfort. It's never happened to me. What if you had asked me? If you'd been drinking heavily I'd probably just have walked away. It was too late to do anything for you, but if I helped this man, perhaps I was retrospectively helping you. So I decided I would see it through. That was why I decided to go out to his house with him, just to keep him company in whatever it was he was going through. Do you understand, Roderic? I helped William on your account. I did it for you.'

He sat in silence for some time before replying. 'You must do as you think fit,' he said eventually. 'Continue in your friendship with William, but remember, it has nothing to do with me. If our paths happen to cross I'll be civil to him, but I don't want any prearranged meetings. And I promise you this: when it all falls apart, as it's bound to do, there'll be no recriminations. I won't remind you that I told you so.'

'Thanks,' Julia said, loading the little word with as much sarcasm as she could muster, for his last remark had riled her. She changed the subject, but although they spoke of other things an underlying tension remained between them. It was only later that night, after they had parted, that they each realised this was the first serious disagreement they had had.

And William was the cause of it.

Chapter Twenty-Four

Roderic was in Julia's house one evening when a woman named Mairéad called by unexpectedly. She was a friend of Julia's from their days together at art college and had never met Roderic before. Julia brushed aside her apologies for barging in on them. 'It's no problem, we were just chatting about the exhibition that's on at the Douglas Hyde Gallery at the moment, have you seen it?' Mairéad said that she had. Gradually she became absorbed into the conversation that she had interrupted and gradually Julia withdrew.

Roderic was in an exceptionably good mood this evening, relaxed and cheerful, sitting by the empty hearth with the cat asleep at his feet. Looking at him and remembering the somewhat lonely and subdued man she'd met for the first time almost exactly a year earlier, Julia was aware of how he had changed since then. She was aware, too, and gratified to think of the part she had played in bringing about that change. Mairéad clearly found him stimulating company, exhilarating to the point of being alarming. Although they stayed on impersonal subjects – the potential of video art, the ways in which galleries influenced the very creation of the works they displayed – as Roderic warmed to his themes he emanated great waves of mental energy, seemingly unaware of the effect they might have been having – that they were having – upon her friend. *But I agree with you, Mairéad. I completely agree.* What if he had disagreed? What if, instead of being merely affable he had been actively trying to win her over?

Looking at him tonight Julia could imagine how Roderic must have been as a young man, before his powerful personality had been tempered by experience, made hesitant by self-doubt. She was aware that some people thought her relationship with him an unequal one because of the disparity in their ages, but in this they were wrong. Had they been peers, however, and met when they were both in their twenties, then there would have been a problem, Julia thought, as the sledgehammer of his enthusiasm continued to crack the nut of Mairéad's diffidence. He must have been extraordinary then, as irresistible as a force of nature. She wasn't sure that her own will would have been strong enough to resist his.

After an hour or so Mairéad departed. 'Where on earth did you find him, Julia?' she asked as she was leaving. 'He's amazing.'

Later, when Roderic had also gone home, she sat alone as the night closed in and thought about the implications of what had happened earlier. Roderic might have mellowed over the years but that powerful side of him was still real and it wasn't to be underestimated. Although Mairéad didn't realise it Julia knew full well that he had only been operating within the middle register of his personality this evening and was capable of far greater psychic force than he had chosen to employ. It was a sobering thought. In spite of herself she couldn't help thinking that he must have been a difficult proposition as a father: not a bad father, she quickly qualified, but not an easy one. To grow up in the shadow of such energy and brilliance might well make one feel outstripped and defeated right from the very start of life; might leave one like a small boat spinning in the wake of a great liner. Never once had she felt this unease in relation to Dan: dreamy, gentle, indulgent and a threat to nobody, least of all Julia. These were not comfortable thoughts, but it was necessary to face up to all that they implied.

The discussion she'd had with Roderic a month earlier just after her birthday about her friendship with William was a case in point. Even though she'd been greatly annoyed at the time, when she thought about it afterwards it forced her to ask herself some pertinent questions about William and she could see the value of that. Was he important to her? Not particularly. If he had drifted out of her life again in the weeks after he bought the box, would that have troubled her? Not in the least. But hadn't that been, at least in part, the point that Roderic had been trying to make: that it was William who actively wanted the friendship to continue and that she was merely acquiescing, thoughtlessly and passively? If she did wish to stop seeing him, even now, it would be easy enough to engineer. She could make excuses and fob him off. She could discourage him from dropping into the shop in the mornings by telling him that Hester didn't approve of her sitting chatting to her friends when she was supposed to be working (which wasn't true: so long as she gave her full attention to genuine customers when they did appear, Hester wasn't troubled by occasional visitors). She could claim to be busier than she was; she could even invoke Roderic from time to time if William wouldn't take the hint, for while he admired him greatly as a painter, she knew that he found him intimidating and would quickly back off.

And yet she liked William. To see him every so often for a drink and a chat was pleasant. Even Roderic had admitted that he was intelligent and could be agreeable company. It was true that his background and the world in which he lived were alien to hers but she didn't think that of any great significance; there was enough common ground between them to make their connection valid and real.

'What do you think, Max?' she said out loud. 'What should I do?' The cat blinked and purred, moved to jump on to her knee but she pushed him down. 'No, you're too hot with your fur, go away.' This was the nub of it: if she ended the friendship with William it would be for no other reason than to please Roderic. And that would be wrong. It was precisely because it wasn't hugely important that she had to take a stand: it was the principle of the thing. Some of the points he had made against William were valid ones. If she was determined not to be eclipsed by Roderic, well, neither was she going to allow William to dictate the terms of the friendship against her will. Even in his late forties Roderic could be a handful; but if she could cope with him as a companion surely, she thought, she could cope with William as a friend.

And so from here on out, Julia decided, she would be the one to take the initiative as far as William was concerned. The day after Mairéad's visit she rang him to suggest that they meet in town for a drink. In making such an arrangement there would be less chance of his calling round to her flat unannounced at a time that didn't suit. Determined that there should be nothing underhand about the relationship, she also made a point of ringing at a time when his wife was likely to be there, although Liz's tone, detached, neutral, as though they'd never met, *Yes, William's here, one moment please and I'll call him*, was impossible to fathom.

They met three days later in the same café where she and Roderic had all but quarrelled about William. He was there waiting for her when she arrived, and smiled when he saw her. The casual clothes he was wearing for the heat, chinos and an open-necked shirt, suited him far better than the dark business suits he had worn when she met him first. While it gratified her enormously to mark the change there had been in Roderic in the past year, it also pleased her on a much smaller scale to see how William's situation had eased in recent months. She had never expected that she would be able to follow through on her good deed of February, but to see the difference between William as he had been then and as he was now was one of the reasons she was happy to continue meeting him. If this flattered her vanity, it did so to no great degree, for she set little store by the impact she had had upon his situation.

'You look well,' she remarked as she sat down.

'I'm better than I have been,' he conceded, 'but I still have a way to go. I'm on some medication at the moment that's disturbing my sleep; it leaves me feeling very groggy and hung-over the next day.'

'I take it they're doing you some good, these tablets?'

'A bit. But I think it's my being away from the office and the fact that my time's my own that's making the real difference, to tell you the truth.'

Sun poured through the café's vast plate-glass windows and fell upon the long low yellow wooden table where they sat with their cigarettes and coffee cups. He noticed her watch and admired it.

'Thanks.'

'Is it new?'

'New to me,' and she pulled her cuff down over it, changed the subject. She asked William if he had seen the exhibition she had talked about with Roderic and Mairéad; later she took out a biography of Matisse she was reading at that time and showed it to him. He had visited the famous chapel in Vence some years earlier and described his impression of it: the scrawled violence of the stations of the cross, executed in black paint on the white walls, crudely powerful, like graffiti; the fronded aquatic pools of shifting coloured light cast by the stained-glass windows. Julia listened with interest. They talked about the concept of religious art in a secular age, then of spirituality in art, a subject on which they both held strong and opposing opinions.

Late afternoon had drifted into early evening by the time they were ready to go, and out on the pavement still they stood talking prior to say goodbye, for William was loath to leave her. If Roderic was sometimes unaware of the impact he had upon people, it was also true that Julia this evening failed to see all she might be to William, the effect that her cheerfulness, her bright youthfulness might have upon him.

'What will you do now?' he asked her.

'Don't know. Go home and make something to eat I suppose, although I don't know what. There's nothing much in the house and the kitchen looks as if a bomb hit it.'

'Let me take you to dinner, then,' William said immediately. 'Please, Julia, it would be my pleasure; no, I insist,' as she demurred. 'You can have anything you want. Do you like Indian food? I know an extremely good restaurant in town.'

But Julia wouldn't be turned even though she was sorely tempted; she'd been telling the truth about the kitchen. 'Thank you but no, really. I'll go round to Roderic's house. I want to see him in any case and he always has loads of food, he's far more organised than I am.'

But when she went round to Roderic's place and found that he wasn't at home, when she was thrown back on her own meagre resources – that fridge, that kitchen – she wondered if she were not taking all of this a little too seriously. Would it really have been such a mistake to go and have a curry with William? He was, after all, her friend.

The next time she saw Roderic she casually mentioned having met William, and his response – neutral, indifferent even – made her feel sure that she was being over-cautious. It never occurred to her that if she was making a conscious effort not to be controlled by what Roderic wanted, he too might be making a similar effort not to be controlling.

All through those hot summer months, June, July, into August when the weather finally broke, Julia was listening to a particular jazz cassette that Roderic had given to her. She listened to it all the time: as she worked in her dusty, cluttered studio and in the kitchen as she prepared her haphazard meals. She listened to it on her personal stereo as she walked through the city, past St Patrick's Cathedral, past the domes and the high curved red gables of the Iveagh Buildings, so that it was as though her life was a film and this the soundtrack to it. It was sensual music, the haunting melody of the saxophone broken by the swishing brushes on the skin of the drums, by fading cymbals and the icy sound of horns, by potent silences. She listened to it alone at night, lying on the sofa and watching the blue smoke of her cigarette spiral and drift above her. She told herself that in the autumn she would put the cassette away, and whenever she listened to it again in the future it would be as delicately evocative as the fragrances with which she was working that summer, that first full summer when she and Roderic were together. The music would give those months back to her, immutable and perfect.

What Julia did not understand was that between the joy of an experience such as she was then living and the recollection of it years later, might fall the shadow of the intervening time. She knew that each artist creates her own precursors. She knew too that a work of art was changed by being viewed through the filter of later works, but she did not understand that this was also true in life. Roderic could have told her this, so too could her father and even William.

But Julia, at this time, did not know.

Chapter Twenty-Five

The night Dennis arrived in Italy to begin his holiday Marta's parents had been invited round for dinner, an affair which turned out to be strained and uncomfortable. Half-way through the first course, Roderic rose from the table, murmured something under his breath and left the room. Dennis would have thought nothing of it and expected him back moments later, were it not for the quick tense glance he saw exchanged between Marta and her mother. They finished the risotto they were eating and when she began to serve the second course, Dennis noticed that she removed Roderic's plate but did not replace it with a clean one as she did for everyone else.

'Do you think he's feeling unwell?' Dennis asked, and Marta gave him a look as though he were being remarkably obtuse.

'He's gone to his studio,' she said shortly, and evidently none of the rest of the family expected to see him back for the rest of the evening.

It annoyed Dennis as it put a strain on the proceedings, especially for Marta. Dennis had only ever learned the most basic Italian and her parents spoke no English, so as well as cooking and serving the meal, she was obliged to keep the conversation going, never becoming too long involved in speaking one language or the other and translating when necessary. Dennis had said before dinner he was worried about not being able to communicate properly but Roderic thought it of no consequence. 'Just remember the most banal table talk from when we were growing up, those awful Saturday lunches, and you'll get the drift of things.' While they were eating dessert one of the children started to cry upstairs and Marta excused herself briefly. In her absence the atmosphere was uncomfortable. Dennis smiled weakly at her parents. Her father responded with a pained grimace, but her mother frankly glowered at him. Dennis knew he had done nothing to upset her and that it could only be a question of guilt by association. Given Roderic's rudeness, he could find it in his heart to understand her logic, even as he suffered it.

So bad did he feel about his brother's behaviour that after her parents had gone home and he was helping her to clear things away he found himself awkwardly apologising to Marta. 'But what have you done?' she said, genuinely puzzled. 'It's Roderic, not you. You've done nothing to hurt or embarrass me.' He was touched by her goodness. It would not have been right of her to blame Dennis for Roderic's faults as her mother did, but in the circumstances it would have been understandable. 'Oh, there's no point in making too big a fuss,' she went on. 'We have our good days and our bad days, Roderic and I. Marriage is like that. It could have been much worse. Leave those,' she added, waving her arms at the dishes as he moved to help wash them. 'They'll do tomorrow.'

He silently resolved to get up early and attend to them the following morning but when he came down to the kitchen he found that Roderic was already there rinsing and stacking the last of the plates. The sight of him took the sting out of his anger. It was years since he had seen Roderic tackle a sinkful of dishes, and yet in the past it had been one of his most abiding images of his brother. How often had he woken at weekends to the sound of crockery chinking, as Roderic washed up the dishes from the night before.

Roderic turned and smiled at him, 'Morning, Dennis,' and it was as if the years had not happened, as if they were back in the house in Dublin when they were living together. It had been the happiest time of Dennis's life; he wondered if Roderic now saw it in the same light.

He had meant to remonstrate harshly with his brother for his behaviour the evening before but in the more relaxed atmosphere of morning, it didn't seem right to do so. The most he could manage as the coffee was poured was: 'I felt a bit sorry for Marta last night.'

'There's no need,' came the short reply. 'She has everything she wants.'

'Does she?'

'The house, the family, you know. Why yes, everything,' Roderic said. The vague wave of his hand that he gave to encompass all this included a tiny child with startlingly blue eyes who had appeared silently at the kitchen door. She was barefoot and clad in a white nightdress. Roderic's frown vanished when he saw her and he jumped up, flinging his arms wide. 'Serena!' he cried, '*Vieni qui!*' She ran across the room and leapt up into his embrace, laughing and shrieking in delight as he tossed her up to the ceiling. She looked, Dennis thought, like a little child in a storybook who had dreamed of a jolly giant and awoke to find him there in the house. Roderic took her over to the fridge, lifted out yoghurts and peaches for her breakfast and engaged in complex negotiations with her about a bar of chocolate. Dennis sat watching and listening as his brother and niece chattered to each other in rapid Italian and wondered why it was that he had never got used to the idea of seeing Roderic speak another language with such fluency.

'You never thought to teach the children English?' he asked as Serena came to the table, but felt at once he had again said the wrong thing.

'Bilingualism isn't as easy to develop as people think,' he said. 'It's easier when it's the mother who's the foreigner in a country because the children tend to be with her more in their formative years. They get the father's language not just from him but from the society around them and it all balances out in the end. Our situation isn't like that. I always used to talk to Serena in English from the time she was born, but she was slow to start speaking in any language. So Marta's mother weighed in and said I was only confusing the child.

It was something of a bone of contention and they wore me down in time. When Allegra was born I spoke to her in Italian from the start. It's deeply regrettable, of course. In time they'll learn English, and they'll labour over tables of irregular verbs and pronouns just as I did to learn Italian. I regret it most of all in relation to our family, of course. It would make things easier, and we all might go to Ireland a bit more often.'

Dennis privately doubted this but said nothing. Serena put her hand on her father's arm, where it looked absurdly tiny. They spoke to each other briefly, at the end of which Roderic laughed. 'She asked what we were talking about and I told her we were saying what a pity it is that she can't talk to Zio Dennis in his own language. She says Zio Dennis will just have to learn Italian. What are your plans for today, by the way?'

'I'm a bit done in after the journey. I thought I'd stay local, maybe read in the garden, have lunch in that little place down the road.'

'You could do worse. I'll be in the studio and Marta'll drop the kids off with her mother on her way to work, so you'll have peace.'

This conversation with his brother over breakfast reassured Dennis. Marta's parents would not join them for dinner and that too pleased him, for with just the three of them at table it would be a more relaxed affair, he thought. But in surmising this, he was horribly wrong.

The tension between Marta and Roderic was palpable that evening, due no doubt to the fact that he had clearly been drinking heavily even before they gathered for aperitifs in the garden. She offered white wine to Dennis, who was shocked to see Roderic pour himself a large grappa, which he bolted down before immediately pouring another. He began to understand the remark Marta had made the night before: *It could have been much worse.* Certainly Roderic had been surly and rude, but he had at least been sober.

'I thought grappa was a drink for after dinner,' Dennis said.

'It is,' Marta replied.

They moved inside to the dining room and she brought out a silver platter bearing tagliatelli in a meat sauce.

'"This looks delicious, Mum." "Thank you dear. I hope you all enjoy it."' Roderic parroted, opening red wine and pouring brimming glassfuls for everyone. Dennis gently attempted to refuse, stretching out his hand when his glass was half full, but Roderic brushed his protests aside. '"The Road of Excess leads to the Palace of Wisdom."' He turned to Marta and favoured her with a rough translation of the phrase. 'Doesn't sound the same in Italian, does it?'

'It's not a particularly Italian sentiment, I'd have thought.'

'Well then it should be, because it's the truth.'

Marta ignored him. 'How was your day, Dennis? What did you do?'

Roderic pointedly did not join in the conversation but ate his food sullenly and put away three glasses of wine with it.

'Your friends I met at the time of your wedding, do you ever hear from them?' Dennis asked as Marta took away the pasta dishes and brought in another platter bearing roast meat.

'Ray went back to the States years ago,' Marta said. 'We hear from him at Christmas. He's teaching in Brooklyn now. Elsa's still living in Turin. We keep in touch and we're always intending to go up and visit but we never seem to get round to it. It's not easy making long journeys with the children.' She started to serve out the food.

'Elsa,' Roderic said softly. 'Do you remember Elsa? She used to call me Gulliver. If only she knew how right she was, how good a name it was for me. That's who I feel like. Gulliver lying on the ground, wakening up and realising that he's fastened by thousands of tiny ropes. And to Gulliver, you see, these ropes are like threads. He could snap each one like that,' and he snapped his fingers. His face was red now; he was half-way between laughter and weeping. 'But he can't do it,' he said. 'Gulliver can't break the threads because even though they're so little there are so many of them, and even though Gulliver's so big there's only one of him.'

As his brother spoke, and even as he despised him for his self-pity Dennis remembered a childhood book and how he had loathed the picture that showed exactly what Roderic spoke of: Gulliver pinned down. How it had frightened him, that suffocating image, how well he knew this fear of littleness, like the fear of insects or mice.

'It's death by a thousand cuts,' Roderic said. 'And that's me. I'm Gulliver. That's me.'

And at that point Marta's patience snapped. For the first time that evening she spoke Italian, threw some sharp remark at Roderic which Dennis was grateful not to understand as he rose to the bait and a short, ugly row developed. It ended as quickly as it had started, a sudden tense silence descending. Roderic stood up and went to the cupboard at the far side of the room where drinks were kept. He took out a bottle of whiskey and left without speaking. Marta and Dennis heard in succession the slamming of three doors: the door of the dining-room, the back door of the house, and finally, off in the distance, the door of Roderic's studio. They sat in silence for a few moments. Marta picked up the wine bottle and held it out to Dennis, a gesture he found bizarre in the circumstances. He shook his head. She topped up her own glass, but did not drink.

'For how long has this been going on?' he asked at last.

'For years,' Marta said. 'But he doesn't drink all the time. Sometimes months pass and everything is fine, and then all of a sudden he starts again. I hoped it wouldn't happen while you were here.'

'And are you afraid?'

'No,' she said immediately. 'Roderic's not a violent man. No, I'm not afraid. But I'm not happy.'

249

All this shocked and astounded Dennis. 'This is terrible,' he said.

'Yes,' Marta quietly agreed, 'it is. It's terrible. There are days when I don't know how I endure it. The children, I suppose, the baby, you know. As for the future . . .' She threw her hands wide and jutted out her chin in a gesture that expressed perfectly all her uncertainty and doubt. 'I don't expect you to be able to do anything, Dennis, but to be able to talk to you about it is already a help. I'm glad that at least you know now. I would have spared you this, but to share it helps me.'

The following day was a Friday and Dennis fled the house early, unable to face the prospect of another breakfast with his brother. He spent a gloomy morning in Siena visiting the main art gallery. It bored him immensely: so many green-faced Virgins, he thought, so many stiff, identical angels. He was particularly out of sympathy today with anything associated with painting because he was so out of sympathy with Roderic. Afterwards he had lunch in the Campo. Before leaving Ireland he had looked forward to exactly such occasions, but today no amount of veal and good wine even when served in such surroundings could prevent it from being anything other than a dismal meal. He dreaded going back to the house for another evening of strife and tension and remained in the city for as long as he decently could.

It was Roderic who answered the door to him when he finally did return. Casually dressed in jeans and a blue check shirt he was, to Dennis's great relief, sober and cheerful. In his hand he held a long two-pronged fork. 'You took a good day to yourself,' he said. 'Come through to the garden and tell me all about it.'

They walked down the hall and into the kitchen. Roderic lifted a tray of sausages and chops from the table and carried them on out into the garden, where the air was sweet with smoke from a lit barbecue, made sweeter still as he scattered herbs on the glowing charcoal. He told Dennis to help himself to wine and to take a seat, indicating a heavily padded garden sofa which swung gently as Dennis sat on it, and then more dramatically as Serena flung herself down beside him. The walled garden was verdant and lush, full of roses and vines, and he breathed in its evening fragrances. The barbecue was a stone structure, pot-bellied at the base, then tapering up into a slim, elegant chimney from which smoke drifted.

Dennis admired it and Roderic said, 'Marta's doing. If it were up to me we'd probably have one of those cheap and nasty things you buy in a DIY shop, if that. All the home improvements are her idea.'

'But you're not in favour?'

'It's not so much that I'm against it in principle, it's just that I'm too busy with other things, too busy with my work. To me, it's not what life is all about. When they were building this thing,' and he pointed at the barbecue, 'it took them ages and it was so noisy. I couldn't hear myself think in the studio. And the day after you leave we have the painters due in to do up the dining-room. No, I can't see anything wrong with it either. It's only a year since it was last done but Marta's tired of blue walls. So that'll be the whole house in upheaval again for who knows how long. Still, it's what she wants, and what Marta wants, Marta gets.'

What struck Dennis most in all of this was how resigned Roderic appeared to be. There was none of the rancour and annoyance he suspected there might have been had the subject come up the night before, and although he had a glass of red wine to hand he seemed to have forgotten about it. As he talked to Dennis he had been arranging the meat on a wire rack which he now lifted and placed carefully over the glowing coals.

'Where is Marta?' Dennis asked.

'Putting the baby to bed. This little minx,' and he nodded at Serena, who had left the sofa and gone over to see what her father was doing, 'is allowed to stay up late tonight because it's Friday. You're a minx, aren't you?' he said, pretending to chase her with the long fork, making her giggle and shriek. 'You're a villain.'

'The kids are fabulous,' Dennis said.

'Yes, aren't they? We're hoping for a third.' In the light of recent days Dennis was surprised to hear this.

'Really? That's nice,' he said sincerely. 'Would you like to have a son next time?'

'Jesus, don't you start. Do you know what Marta's mother said to me when Allegra was born? "What's wrong with you, that you can't make a boy baby?" Half in jest and whole in earnest. I want another daughter. I want to be like King Lear. I'll go and visit them when I'm old and grey and difficult. I and my hundred knights. Yes, another daughter,' he said, grabbing Serena and holding her tight, 'and then another and another and another . . .' She laughed and wriggled as he tickled her in a different place with each word, releasing her only when Marta appeared at the door which led out from the kitchen. She was wearing a cream linen dress and holding a blue glass bowl full of salad leaves, which she set down on the long tiled table where they were to eat.

'Oh, hello Dennis,' she said. 'I didn't hear you come in. Did you have a good day in Siena?'

'Excellent. And you?'

'Today was all right. I went over to see my mother at lunch time. They have an apartment in Positano, do you remember, they spoke of it the other night. I went to say goodbye to them. They're going off there tomorrow so we won't see them now for a whole month.'

Looking past Marta, who was standing with her back to her husband, Dennis saw Roderic punch the air gleefully as she said this. Marta noticed Dennis's expression and followed the line of his gaze. She turned to look at Roderic, who was now turning the chops over with an air of studied innocence. She knew he had just scored some kind of point against her but she didn't know how. Evidently it rather amused her for she shrugged her shoulders and smiled. Speaking quietly to her daughter in Italian, she asked her to bring out the cutlery and plates from the kitchen to help set the table. 'That rose,' she said to Roderic, walking over to a white rambler that grew thick against the back wall of the garden. 'The trellis has come loose and some of these branches need to be tied up. Will you help me do it tomorrow?'

'Certainly,' he said. 'We can see to it after breakfast.'

She lit citronella candles to drive away the mosquitoes. 'Are you hungry, Dennis? Where did you have lunch? Oh really? Which restaurant on the Campo?' They fell into desultory conversation about Siena. Marta dressed the salad, Serena set the table and Roderic cooked the meat. He lit a cigarette now and as he narrowed his eyes against the smoke of the barbecue, he looked exactly as he had done when cooking weekend breakfasts at the time they lived together in Dublin, jabbing at rashers and sausages in the eye-level grill of the cooker.

If lunch had fallen short of Dennis's expectations, dinner was everything he could have wished for in an Italian holiday. They ate in the warm scented garden, talking and laughing until far into the night. He enjoyed it even more than he might have done because he was relieved to be reassured about Marta and Roderic.

Dennis and Roderic were already in the kitchen the following morning when Marta came down. She was simply and lightly dressed, both for the heat of the day and for the work she was planning to do in the garden, wearing shorts and a tiny lilac vest with fine shoulder straps. The colour of the vest perfectly suited her tanned skin. It was cut low in the front and clung tightly to her, and even Dennis was struck by how alluring she looked. He also noticed how appreciatively Roderic studied her as she crossed the room, giving the lie to the idea that married people became inured

253

to each other's bodies over the years, sheer habit making them take each other for granted. They were standing side by side now and, speaking in a low voice, Roderic said something to her in Italian. Marta's eyes widened in mild shock and she blushed. Whatever the substance of the explicit compliment he had paid her, she was evidently pleased by it. She shot a quick glance over at Dennis and murmured something to Roderic, who also looked at him and then quietly replied to Marta. His reassurance that his brother would not be able to understand what he had said was actually something Dennis *could* understand, *capire*, as in *Non capisco*, being one of the few Italian verbs with which he was familiar. Marta bit her lip trying not to laugh, and Dennis felt oddly hurt at how they made of both their language and their sensuality a barrier to shut him out.

After breakfast, he happened to glance down from his bedroom window and saw them working in the garden. They were engaged in fixing the broken rose trellis that Marta had spoken of the night before and Dennis became absorbed in watching them, struck by the harmony with which they worked. Marta held a spar of wood steady while Roderic nailed it down, and then they carefully pinned up the long stray branches of the rose, debating how best to arrange them so as to give the whole a pleasing shape; warning each other against the thorns. Leaning against the window frame Dennis fell into a reverie. The absolute intimacy, the peculiarly complete togetherness that he was now witnessing unnerved him. It was like watching a single person work in the garden, so much were the two bodies of one mind. He thought of how strange a thing marriage was, and how glad he was that he had never entered into it. He knew in his heart, as he had always known, that it was not for him.

They had finished with the rose now. Roderic flopped down on the garden sofa where Dennis had sat the night before, and patted the cushions, inviting Marta to join him.

He put his arm around her shoulders as she went on talking, pointing to a wooden jardinière, painted white and containing a lemon tree. He was only pretending to listen to her, was gently pulling one of the straps of her vest off her shoulder. Protesting and laughing she pushed it back up again, pointed to a sunny, empty corner of the garden in which the lemon tree might be more advantageously situated. Roderic looked towards the place she indicated and nodded, but was again slyly pulling at the strap of her vest. Again she stopped him. He spoke. She laughed and shook her head; again he asked her something. Marta looked all around the garden as if to make sure that they were quite alone and then, to Dennis's astonishment, she simply peeled off the lilac vest and tossed it aside. As Roderic bent over her to kiss her naked breasts Dennis leapt back from the window, ashamed of spying on them and terrified of being seen.

Today was evidently one of their good days.

Chapter Twenty-Six

He spent all morning in his studio but achieved nothing; nothing that pleased him in any case. When William had last painted, many years earlier, the works he produced had been strong and assertive, making up in verve for what they lacked in technical accomplishment. On taking his canvases out of storage to look at them again he was surprised at how good he'd once been. His studies in oils of trees and rivers, his still lifes, had somehow got at the essence of the things represented, although for the life of him now he couldn't think how he had done it. This notwithstanding, his past accomplishments gave him confidence as he embarked upon his new phase of work. In the intervening years his interests and tastes had changed and what he wished to paint now were abstract works in watercolour. 'Good luck,' Julia had said to him when he told her this. 'Believe me, you're going to need it.'

To begin with his initial enthusiasm had carried him along, together with the excitement of having his own studio space and the time in which to work in it, but in the past week or so he had become bogged down and could make no progress. He found he couldn't control the colours, couldn't make them conform to the idea he had in mind and wished to express. Was that the problem – was he taking too rigid a stance, trying to impose a form upon the work rather than taking a freer and more instinctive approach? In the painting he was engaged upon this morning, executed in reddish brown tones of ochre and rust, the effect he wanted was of transparency and light, the colours seeping into each other in a feathered and delicate way. He was failing utterly in this: the more he struggled for a translucent clarity the more murky and opaque the whole thing became.

He gave up for the morning and after a short lunch alone – Liz was at work, the children off at day camp as they were on summer holidays from school – he returned to the studio. The painting looked even worse than he had thought, a heavy muddy daub, brown dominating red, the whole thing clumsy and ham fisted. There was nothing to be done but set it aside and start afresh. This time he tried to have no preconceptions but quickly found this meant he had no idea whatsoever of how or where to begin. William's mind was racing now so that he couldn't concentrate. It was precisely the worry of not being able to paint that was getting in the way and preventing him from even making a start. He stared at the blank sheet of paper, willing himself to pick up a brush as a deep sense of anxiety unfolded within him, immobilising him and putting paid to whatever last few shreds of his self-belief remained.

In mid afternoon he gave up and decided to go into the city, leaving a note for Liz to say he would probably not be back in time for dinner. As he propped it against the teapot on the kitchen table he reflected that she would be annoyed by this, but didn't consider changing his plans. Before leaving the house he went into the drawing-room to find a book to read on the train into town, and while he was there he caught sight of Roderic's painting, which depressed him even further. He saw in it exactly that combination of freedom and control that he had sought so ardently all day and that had eluded him so completely. The fields of green and blue paint complemented each other like voices singing in harmony, each depending on the other for its full resonance and power, the formal restraint serving only to accentuate a wild beauty that it barely contained. Compared to this, his own laboured efforts seemed ludicrous.

There were few people travelling into the city on this August afternoon and so he had no difficulty getting a seat on the train, but the book he had brought with him remained in his pocket. He looked out across Dublin Bay to Howth, the distant houses vague in the heat-haze. He had hoped that leaving the house would clear his head and permit him to think clearly, perhaps even to know what he might do when next he went to the studio, to break through the impasse in which he had found himself. The sea view, however, brought no enlightenment and still his mind was unfocused, was like a pack of scattered cards. The stations slipped past: Sydney Parade already, and he had given no thought to what he would do when he reached town where he often went now to wander aimlessly, to look in galleries and bookshops, to sit in pubs, wishing his life away.

William left the train at Westland Row, crossed the road and went through the back gate into Trinity College. He was aware as he emerged onto College Green that he was tracing out now a skewed version of his past life. Empty-handed and casually dressed he dawdled along the exact same route where, not so long ago, he had strode among the early morning crowds with business suit and briefcase, purposeful and directed and desperate. What had changed in his life? But *really* changed? His mind shrank from the thought. Julia. He would go to see Julia, he decided, as he proceeded up Dame Street. He knew enough now about the pattern of her day to know that there was a good chance of finding her at home at this time; and then just at that moment, he saw her on the other side of the road.

She was walking in the same direction as William; evidently she was on her way back to her house. He would have crossed over, called her name and joined her had she not been with Roderic. He trailed in their wake, hoping that her companion would leave her at some stage but that too, he knew, was unlikely. Logic said that he was also going home or, worse from William's point of view, was on his way to Julia's place. The sleeves of the blouse Julia was wearing hung down well past her knuckles, completely concealing her hands. From the depths of the left sleeve dangled a bag made of such thin white plastic that William could see through it and identify the modest haul of groceries it contained: a carton of milk, a loaf, some oranges, a tin of soup and a tin of cat food. Abruptly Roderic and Julia stopped walking and William stopped too, thereby causing a collision between himself and a woman walking immediately behind him, much to her irritation. Julia handed the plastic bag to Roderic and held on to his left forearm for balance while she stood on one leg and removed her shoe, a scuffed brown moccasin, then shook it to remove a pebble. As she did so, Roderic said something that made them both laugh, Julia so much that she wobbled and almost overbalanced. Dropping the shoe on to the pavement she shoved her foot back into it and playfully thumped him on the shoulder in response to whatever his teasing remark had been, herself said something and again they both laughed. Roderic was still holding her shopping, and by his gesture William understood that he was offering to carry it for her but Julia shook her head. He handed it back and they continued on their way. It never occurred to William how disconcerted they both would have been had they known he was observing their inconsequential but, as they thought, private stroll through the city.

Perched on a stool in a diner one lunch time not long before he had had to take leave from his job he had noticed, on glancing through the plate-glass window, a woman pass in the street. She was pretty in a rather conventional way, with blue eyes, carefully tinted blonde hair, and she wore a quilted rust-coloured jacket with gilt buttons. A silk scarf printed with Montgolfier balloons was folded around her throat. He noticed all of this, and also noticed that there was something spirited about her: the way her lips were pursed as though she were laughing at something she knew she ought not to find amusing but couldn't resist. She looked as though she was fully aware of how little her own monied elegance amounted to; conscious of how, underneath it all, she was wholly her own woman. In a fraction of a second William noticed all of this, and it was only then that he recognised his own wife.

As he walked up Dame Street now until it became Lord Edward Street, past offices and shops, past Dublin Castle, he consciously attempted to do the same thing in reverse with Roderic and Julia: to see them as though they were not people he had met, and, in Julia's case, someone he liked to consider a friend, but total strangers. How unprepossessing they looked! Ambling home in the late afternoon with their shopping and their shabby clothes – her floppy skirt, his faded cord jacket – there was nothing, but *nothing* about them, to William's mind, that suggested any kind of gift or accomplishment. No one could have guessed at their real selves, but then, wasn't that always the case? Wasn't that what was always said about murderers too, how unremarkable they seemed, and the more heinous their crime the more people insisted, marvelling upon their ordinariness? What did strike him today forcibly and surprisingly about Roderic and Julia was that they were a couple. As a complete stranger that was the only thing he could have intuited about them with any certainty. This was strange, for they weren't holding hands and apart from the moment when she had balanced on his arm there was no physical contact at all between them. And yet in their easy confidence and the relaxed way in which they talked and laughed together their intimacy could be read as easily as on the day when he had seen them in the shop, speculating on the names of the semiprecious stones. It was as though walking along the street together they were encompassed in a field of radiant light that was theirs and theirs alone.

For a moment William was overcome with jealousy, so powerful and acute it was like physical pain; it winded him and literally stopped him in his tracks. He resented Roderic so deeply that briefly he hated him. For all that he looked inconsequential he had what William wanted and yet would never, could never, have. Looking at the other man today he knew that. He was too alien, too unlike him; he would never be able to unmake himself to become what Roderic was. William had lost ground to the couple, they were still walking on and he followed them again, but half-heartedly now. Roderic threw back his head and roared with laughter at something Julia had said. It was worse than William had thought: it simply wasn't in him to be what he wanted to be. His confidence was all gone and he had no real work to set against it, nothing to prove that he had achieved something exceptional in the past and therefore might reasonably expect to produce good work again in the future. It pained him more than ever now to remember the muddy canvas over which he had laboured that morning to so little purpose. Against that he set Roderic's painting and he recalled the beauty and energy of it, the tension there was between the rich pigment and the decisive intelligence of the form; and this was, moreover, far from being his finest work. There was a playful, even foolish side to him; the side that teased Julia and sported with Max, but this silliness did not negate, indeed had no impact whatsoever upon the detached genius that made the paintings. There was no denying the reality of the other man's gift: the magnitude of it.

They had come to the top of Lord Edward Street. Christchurch was before them and as Roderic and Julia waited to cross the road William hung back. There was no point in going any further. He couldn't face either of them now and he turned away, wishing that he had never followed them in the first place.

He rang Julia a few days later to arrange a meeting. She was cheerful as ever and asked him how his work was going.

'Better not to ask.'

'Do you know what the secret is?'

'Tell me.'

'The secret is that there's no secret. You just get on with it. You just do the work.' She could hear him snort at the other

261

end of the phone. 'You think I'm joking? This is as serious as I get.' She suggested that he call by on Wednesday.

As he walked up the street to her house he smelt the smoke of a turf fire, even though it was August. He commented on it when they were on their way up to her flat and she stopped on the stairs, turned to him. 'Will you do something for me? Will you do me a favour?'

In the sitting-room, she gave him a pen and a notepad. 'I want you to write down what the turf smoke makes you think of, in as much detail as you wish to give me. Do you mind doing that?' It wasn't at all what he had expected, but he took up the pen and after a moment's thought started to write.

Turf smoke reminds me of the west of Ireland. We used to spend our family holidays there when I was a child. My mother was from Westport and we used to go there with her, my brother and I, for the whole summer. My father who was a lawyer came for occasional weekends and then for two weeks' holiday. I liked being there because my parents, especially my father, had more time for us children than was usually the case. I found him less stern, less forbidding than when we were in Dublin, to a singular degree, almost as if he were another person. We used to go to Achill. We used to go to Keem, to the sunken cove in under the headland. We were there one day, I remember, in late summer. The holidays were almost over, which I regretted, for soon we would be going back to the city and the old, rigid regimen would take over again. My mother had settled down with us children in the middle of the strand, we were paddling, playing, digging in the sand. My father had gone down to the end of the beach some little way off, was sitting in the shadow of some rocks reading. I strayed into his territory without meaning to and I thought he might tell me to go away, but he smiled when he saw me and asked me to sit beside him. We looked out to sea, to Clare Island with its mountains, where the pirate queen had lived. The atmosphere was strange that afternoon, bright and full of heat, the light before rain, the light before a

big storm. My father was staring out to sea. The sea was the
colour of pewter. To me he seemed very serious, very old,
although I realise that he can have been no older than I am now,
if that. I thought for the hundredth time of how I would never
measure up to him, neither what he was, nor his expectations of
me. I was I think about ten years old. The light was strong,
weird, making all the colours too vivid, almost painfully
intense: the green of the slopes behind us, the sand, the rocks; all
the colours drenched, saturated, like in a cheap postcard. Soon
the weather would break, and all would soften into greyness, as
the water, although riddled with light, was already grey. I could
hear the cries of my brother, my mother's voice calling to him.
My father was still looking out to sea. 'Look,' he said, 'out there,
a school of porpoises. Can you see them?' I looked to where he
was pointing out in the bay, and I saw their dark fins
shimmering in the water. It was a remarkable sight. As I write
this, I can see them again. 'Shall I tell the others?' I asked my
father, but he said no. He said that there would be other things
for all the family but this moment was for just the two of us.
We kept looking out to sea, at how the black backs dappled in
the water, shiny as black glass, the water soft metal, now dark
as lead, and it was as if my father and I were the only two
people in the world, so that there was only this moment, this
ocean, these porpoises, my father, me. It made me feel so close to
my father of whom, generally, I was afraid.

And then the light reached breaking point. The sky darkened,
and a bright fork of lightening tore down, there was thunder
and my mother called to us. It began to rain, a few heavy drops,
then more, then a torrent. I heard my brother shriek. My father
and I stood up and together we ran along the beach, seeking a
place of safety, a place of refuge.

He put the pen down.

'May I see?'

William nodded, and sat with his hands over his face, as
Julia silently read through the text he had written. She read it

slowly twice so as to give him time to compose himself. 'I had forgotten that,' he said at last when he could speak again. 'Forgotten it for all these years.' He looked up at her. Julia smiled at him and he struggled to smile back, looked away. Forlorn, he was the image of his own small son.

The task she had set him had created a strange atmosphere between them; an intimacy she did not want and was keen to dispel. 'I'm sure you're wondering why I asked you to do that,' she said, but oddly it hadn't crossed his mind. He had unthinkingly complied with her request. Julia explained the nature of the project upon which she was engaged. 'I have a list,' she said, taking it from a folder and passing it to him. 'I'm exposing people to particular scents and then asking what it evokes for them. When I have enough material, I'm going to create a work around it. These are the scents and odours I'm using.'

William looked down at the paper in his hands:

> *Hot chocolate*
> *Clean linen*
> *The ocean*
> *Hay*
> *Coconut*
> *Rotting apples*
> *Mint*
> *Bleach*
> *Tea*
> *Cut grass*
> *Turf smoke*
> *Fresh bread*
> *Roses*

'It's turning out to be a more potent idea than I had expected. People are often surprised or even shocked by what they themselves come up with,' she said as though to console him. William sat nodding at this strange young woman in her dim room whom he really didn't know, and who had unwittingly forced open a closed chamber of his heart, where his own past was hidden from himself. She took a sheaf of papers from the folder and glanced through them, told him that what had struck her so far was the discrepancy between the thing offered and the thing remembered. So far no one had simply evoked the thing itself, and strange circular links had been created. For William smoke suggested the ocean, for someone else the ocean evoked roses, and for someone else again roses were redolent of smoke. 'For they told me of being in a public garden at the end of a day when the gardeners had been cutting the heads off roses and they were burning them on a great fire, as though it were an offering, a sacrifice. From then on, the person concerned could never disassociate the smell of roses from smoke.' She took another page from the folder. She had offered someone clean linen, a sheet laundered, pressed, fresh from the line. The woman said it reminded her of betrayal.

'How will you use them? Will you transcribe them?'

'I don't think so.' She didn't like to add that that would diminish their impact by removing, say, the contrast between William's precise handwriting and the emotional force of what he expressed.

She asked then for his permission to keep the text, to use it anonymously in any project she might subsequently develop.

'Has anyone refused you yet?'

'Just one man.'

'Was it your friend?' he asked as though she had only one.

'Roderic?' she said, deliberately naming him. 'No, it wasn't Roderic. It was someone else.'

He tore the page from the notebook and looked at it as though considering whether or not to destroy it, then leaned over and handed it to her, although in doing so he had the strange feeling that he was handing over to her too much of himself, that he was giving her some kind of power over him. 'I feel,' he said deliberately, 'that I'm giving you something private. Something precious.'

265

'Yes, you are. You're doing just that,' Julia said. 'That's why I asked your permission.'

'Is this,' he asked, 'what art has become?'

'This,' she said, 'is what art has always been.'

Chapter Twenty-Seven

During their time at the Foundation Ray had a guide book, an American publication the exact title of which Roderic had forgotten over the years – something like *Europe for People with no Money*, or *Italy on Half-Nothing*. He teased Ray about it but consulted it too for his own forays around the country and it was there that he first read of the Albergo Perfetto. The name of the hotel amused him even more than the title of the book. *Cheap, clean, central, charmless*: *$*. He decided to try it on a weekend trip to Rome.

Located in a quiet street near Piazza Navona, the Albergo Perfetto advertised itself to passing trade by means of a rectangular light-up sign projecting from the wall above the front door. It bore the name of the hotel in blue letters and a single dismal star. The 'B' of 'Albergo' was missing. Behind the reception desk was a woman who, when Roderic arrived, was phlegmatically watching a quiz show on television. She regarded him with an air of grim forbearance as he signed the register and showed her his passport, as though she expected the very worst from all her guests and had yet to be disappointed. 'Room three, first floor,' she said, banging down on the counter a key attached to a tarnished and bulky brass tag. 'Breakfast at eight o'clock?' He nodded and without another word she turned back to her television.

Room three was a clean but dark place that smelt of bleach and there was an enormous bed that Roderic knew would accommodate even him. (Small beds were the bane of his life.) He had his own bathroom, something he hadn't expected given the rock-bottom price he was paying, which boasted the simplest shower he had ever seen: a shower

267

head, a tap and a drainage hole sunk in the mosaic tiled floor. There was no shower curtain. He was woken in the night by thunderous snoring, so loud that for a moment he thought an interloper must have sneaked into his room, crept into bed and fallen asleep beside him. Then he realised that he was merely a victim of the hotel's paper-thin walls. In time he would come to know that snoring was amongst the least disconcerting noises by which a guest might be disturbed. He slept again and was awoken at eight by someone hammering on his door as though the building were on fire. When he answered this summons a young woman wordlessly thrust a tray into his hands then disappeared off down the corridor. He got back into bed with his breakfast. The bread rolls were stale and he didn't like apricot jam, the only kind provided, but the coffee in the white pot was strong and hot and there was plenty of it.

He decided that whenever he was in Rome he would always stay in the Albergo Perfetto. Dirt cheap hotels were, Roderic considered, like horrendously expensive ones: you could do what you damn well pleased in them and nobody cared. It was in middle-ranking pretentious places that respectability held sway and you had to behave yourself. The Albergo Perfetto was, in its own small way, he thought as he travelled back to the Foundation by train that Sunday night, well, perfect.

Over the years the hotel never changed. The same woman was always behind the desk with her television. Sometimes for light relief she would be reading a magazine full of photographs concerning the births, deaths and marriages of the stars whose shows she impassively watched. Roderic never discovered her name, dubbed her in his mind Signora Perfetto. No matter how many times he stayed there she affected never to show the slightest flicker of recognition except for one occasion when she forgot, glancing up from her scandal sheet as he walked in and greeting him with the words, 'So, Signor Kennedy, you're back with us?' Roderic found he was vexed rather than pleased that the fiction of anonymity had been broken.

But if the hotel never changed, his own life did, and with it the hotel's function. To begin with it was a bachelor bolt-hole. In the first stages of his life with Marta and in his early marriage he would occasionally engineer reasons to go to Rome alone for a night or two. Roderic was fully aware of how pitifully limited his own vices were on these trips. A bit too much wine with his dinner was the height of it, if that, for he was not at the time a heavy drinker. But he suspected that it was the want of days such as these that many married people regretted and silently hankered for rather than lost sexual opportunities as was popularly supposed: silent, solitary days, idle and private. He guarded these sacred spaces in his life unobtrusively but fiercely, too. He was, for instance, careful not to let Marta know how important all of this was to him. Not once did he take her to the Albergo Perfetto and not only because he knew she would hate it. When they had occasion to go to Rome together they put up in a smart place where they paid for a single night rates that would have kept them in the Albergo for a week.

On his trips back to Ireland to visit his family it would sometimes happen in the early years that he needed to break his journey for the night in Rome. Then he began to arrange his flights so that this was essential on both legs of the journey, as he moved between two lives and two realities, hardly able to bear to admit to himself how unsatisfactory both had become. The few hours of blessed peace he knew at 33,000 feet, looking at the blank blue sky and drinking as many diminutive bottles of red wine as he could charm off the stewardess, was no longer enough. Over the years the glowing, shabby sign outside the little hotel became balm to his soul signalling a haven, a refuge from all that troubled and irked him in life.

His visits home took the form of a round of family calls, dinners and teas that were informal but not relaxed. Frank died. He might have been irascible with a note of threat even in his good humour, but his had been an energising presence, Roderic realised now that he was gone. Quietly depressive in a way that sapped those around her, his mother became more distant than ever, more remote. 'Poor Frank,' she said, 'we got on so well together. We were so well matched,' and she stared out of the window daring her children to deny these outlandish untruths. She was never displeased to see Roderic again, but nor was she, it had to be said, particularly interested either. Only Maeve remained at home with her in the big family house where they had grown up, where Frank had had his surgery. She worked in the same accountant's office she had been in since leaving school and looked after her mother with a rather bad grace. It pained Roderic to see what was happening to Maeve, as bitter disappointment in life hardened around her like ice on the ropes of an Arctic trawler. Like Roderic she was physically big but unlike him the formidable manner that he could just about plausibly summon up on the rare occasions he felt he needed it was her habitual temper. Her sardonic jibes – 'It must be nice having a wife who can keep you' – cut deep.

With Cliona and her husband Arthur he got on better, although sometimes he wondered what image, if any, they had of his life in Italy with Marta. He was surprised at how little curiosity they showed, how quickly and completely they forgot things he told them, and yet there was no unpleasantness, no hostility. Probably because he lived so far away and was a painter they thought they had nothing whatsoever in common with him. Even with Dennis, who couldn't have been more welcoming and with whom he always stayed, things weren't the same. And why should they be, he asked himself. His brother had his own life, solitary but busy – career and concerts, home improvements and hill walking – and Roderic no longer felt sure of his own place within it.

The brief stint of genteel socialising left him burnt out and he would crawl back to Rome, drained of all energy and worn down. It was painfully obvious to him why he had needed a few quiet hours alone to prepare himself in advance before going to Ireland. But on returning to Italy he would again check into the little hotel for a night or even two, where he now had to face up to a far harder question: why did he also need to steel himself in this way before returning to Marta and the children? In turn, he examined each element of his life but there was no one thing that he could put his finger on. It was the little details of family life, the endless decisions about minor matters, that irked him the most. All of this was somehow muddled and unclear in his mind. He knew that there had been a lie at the centre of the family that had produced him. Was it possible that there was a lie at the heart of the family of which he was now a part in Italy? Was it possible that this lie was an intrinsic and inevitable part of family life? It didn't bear thinking about. All he really understood was that he moved with increasing dread between the two houses and that, as the years passed, he needed drink to protect himself. He used to lie on his bed in the hotel room drinking his litre bottle of duty-free Jameson's from a tooth glass and thinking about it all.

At some point during the eight years since he had last been there, Signora Perfetto had departed. Her place was taken by a silent, sallow man who watched the same frantic programmes on the same television, who wordlessly registered Roderic and gave him a key. Room six. 'You don't have any other room available?' The man shook his head. Roderic went upstairs and let himself in, sat down heavily on the bed and looked around. The familiar brown lino and dingy paintwork, the chipboard wardrobe he remembered so well – that he should be here in this room of all rooms, tonight of all nights!

The day their father was buried, Dennis had driven his brother in the late afternoon from the funeral lunch to Dublin airport from where Roderic tried three times to ring Marta. He called from the check-in area but the line was engaged, then made two further attempts at the departure gate, the final one as his fellow passengers had actually started to board. On both occasions he obtained a ringing tone but no one answered. He rang again from the baggage hall in Fiumicino as soon as he landed but the response was the same. It was clear now what had happened. He was too late. He rang Marta's mother, but there was no answer there either. It was a week to Christmas, and the weather in Rome was foul. The coach journey in from the airport was interminable; the snarled traffic an inferno of accidents, flashing lights, sirens and horns. For up to ten minutes at a time the coach did not move at all. Roderic, fretting impotently and pointlessly willing the driver on, wiped the misted window with his fingers and peered out into the darkness. It was getting on for midnight by the time he arrived at the hotel and Signora Perfetto had to be summoned by means of a shrill chrome bell. He took the stairs two at a time up to room six and rang his mother-in-law again.

'*Auguri!* You're a father! *E una femmina.* Marta's well, *anche la tua figlia.*'

Your daughter. Roderic replaced the receiver, lay down on the bed and started to cry. Later, he would wonder if even Serena, at the moment of her birth, had wept with such a complete lack of restraint; would wonder that even here, in this most permissive of establishments, no one came to see what was happening to him, or at the very least to tell him to shut up. He cried with the abandon of a small child but the physical strength of a huge, healthy man in his thirties and mourned Frank as he hadn't been permitted to in Ireland. He grieved for all in his life that had been frustrated, unfulfilled and which nothing could now redeem. But he wept with relief too that he had not fathered a son. There would not be between him and his child the coldness, the lack of communication that had marred his relationship with Frank. The sound of his own howling frightened him.

Now, more than seventeen years later, he sat on the same bed in the silence of the same room and thought of how bitterly ironic it all was. For how much worse a father could he have been to sons than he had been to his three daughters?

He was awoken in the middle of that night by the sound of a woman's scream. As her long sharp cry reached its height Roderic realised that she was calling out in ecstasy, rather than fear or pain. The woman was disturbingly close to him, too, her bed evidently separated from his by nothing more than the hotel's flimsy walls. As the cry modulated into laughter then silence, a voice, voices, then silence again, the thought of this proximity astounded and aroused him. Marta had sounded exactly like this. An intense longing for her swept over him. And then, unexpected and unwanted, the thought of Gianni suddenly unmanned him.

Tomorrow he would see Marta for the first time in eight years. Eight years since . . . since what? Since he had walked out on his family, as she claimed? Or since she had thrown him out of the house, as he believed? They had quarrelled bitterly at the time about which it was and in the past year or so had resumed the discussion, this time in a more restrained and civilised fashion, but still failed to reach agreement. Marta insisted that in saying what she did she had only been firing a warning shot across his bows. She'd expected him, she claimed, to move out to an apartment in the town or in nearby Siena until such time as he came to his senses and stopped drinking, got his life back on track. That he would simply flee to Ireland had never occurred to her. He, for his part, still thought it unreasonable to have expected him to understand all of that from one simple sentence. Once committed to a reconciliation they had tried to bank down as far as possible all the hostility and resentment between them, but still he was uneasy about meeting her again.

Would she greet him coldly tomorrow? To the best of his knowledge he had only ever shaken hands with Marta once in his life and that was on the night he met her. He remembered that moment with unparalleled vividness, the rush of attraction for this lovely stranger, holding her hand for just that little bit longer than was necessary, telling her his name. He had noticed then some of the attributes he would always most admire in her, her long neck, the delicate shape of her head, the wit, the kindness in her eyes and mouth. And yet he could remember so little of the rest of that evening; could recall its general atmosphere but few specific details. He had forgotten, for example, the moment of parting with Marta at the end of the night. He had sat near her at table but had he sat beside her? It had been someone's birthday but whose he couldn't recall. Ray's? Elsa's? He remembered Enzo carrying a cake lit with many candles through the darkness of the warm summer night, down the steps and out on to the terrace where they sat at dinner. Vaguely he remembered laughter, uneven singing and how the night had fallen around them again as the candles were blown out.

Two days later, he had gone with Elsa to visit the fresco restoration project on which Marta was working. She smiled and waved down at them from high on the scaffolding. *Do you want to come up?* He pretended that he couldn't quite fathom the social codes of Italy and kissed her in greeting, feigned not to know that this was overstepping the mark with someone he barely knew. But Marta matched him by slipping a piece of paper with her telephone number into the pocket of his shirt when Elsa wasn't looking. The visit to the chapel to see the painting followed three days later so that they made love for the first time within a week of having met. The final time had been within a few days of Marta telling him to leave. That the physical side of their life had been so constant and passionate had allowed Roderic to delude himself for far too long about the state of things generally. If there was no significant problem with sex, he reasoned, then none of the other difficulties they had were such that they couldn't be overcome or simply ignored. That Marta eventually felt differently – *I think you should just go, Roderic* – had been a great shock, no matter what interpretation one chose to put upon her words.

The hotel that she had reserved for him in Siena was exactly what he would have expected from her. He checked in the following day shortly after noon and then waited for her in the lobby, with its white marble floor and its smiling concierge, with its elegant cane furniture and many green plants. She wouldn't be late: she was never late. At twelve-thirty on the dot the glass door of the hotel opened.

Marta was wearing a simple beige dress and her hair was pinned up, showing off her neck and shoulders. She didn't seem older, just more tired-looking than Roderic remembered, as well she might have done, he told himself, given her life in recent years. Her stern, somewhat defensive expression changed when she saw him and he realised that she was struggling to conceal her shock. He knew he'd gone downhill a lot in the past eight years, but surely not that much. If she thought he looked raddled now it was just as well that she hadn't seen him in the last year before he stopped drinking. 'Roderic!' The pity she felt for him and his sadness at it broke down some of their defences and made the initial moments of their meeting easier than either of them had dared to hope. She told him she had booked a table for lunch at a nearby restaurant. After the fiasco of the preceding summer, it had been decided that as much of this visit as possible would be conducted on neutral territory. Hence the hotel, hence the restaurant, on the terrace of which they took their places a short while later.

'Was this place here in my time?'

Marta shook her head. 'It's only been open a year or so, but it's become extremely popular.'

'I can see why,' Roderic said, taking in the crystal and linen, the view of the soft valley before them. A thick vine had been trained up a trellis and made a canopy above them. The sun dappled down through the leaves and Marta pointed out across the valley the three bridges that gave the restaurant its name. Ever since he arrived Italy had been conspiring to seduce him again, to make him ask how and why he had ever chosen to exile himself, to drive himself out from this Eden. They ordered melon and rabbit and steak, unfolded their napkins and helped themselves to bread from the basket on the table. The waiter brought them bottled sparkling water.

'Dennis sends you his best.'

'Give him mine when you see him.' They both knew that without him, their reconciliation would never have been possible. It was he who had brokered an uneasy peace between them in the aftermath of their separation and urged them to keep open the lines of communication in the years that followed.

'And Gianni? Where did you say he was this week, Berlin?'

'Hanover.'

He wasn't convinced that this business trip wasn't a fiction but Marta's new companion owned a factory that made luggage, so it was quite possible that he really was off at a trade fair.

'It's good to be with someone again,' she said. 'The girls like him, which is important.' She asked him then if he was seeing anyone.

'There have been a few people actually, yes,' he said, holding her gaze, 'but nobody special. You know how it is,' and he smiled.

At that moment the waiter returned to the table bringing their first courses and they fell silent until he had gone away again. Now that they had moved on to sensitive subjects, Roderic considered, it was best to keep going, to deal with the difficult things and get it over with. 'I also want,' he said rather stiffly, 'to apologise for what happened last year.'

'As well you might,' Marta said. 'I'd have skinned you alive if I'd been able to get my hands on you that day. I was livid with you. *Livid*.'

He knew this already: she had told him so at the time.

'We were all at the airport, you know. The girls were hurt, and bitterly disappointed, especially Allegra. What happened, anyway?'

Roderic sighed. 'You know how it is,' he said again, but this time he didn't smile.

A similar visit had been planned the year before, some six months after he stopped drinking. It had been Roderic's idea, but as the time approached he had viewed the prospect with increasing dread. 'I did get as far as Dublin airport that morning,' he told Marta. 'I got as far as the check-in desk, and waited in a queue for fifteen minutes. Then my turn came and the man behind the counter held out his hand for my ticket and passport. "I'm sorry about this," I said to him, not that *he* was going to lose any sleep over it, "but I'm not going." I just couldn't do it. I turned and walked away.'

'And you went straight home?'

'Yes.' This wasn't true. He'd gone and sat under the screens where the departures were listed and sat there for over an hour looking at the information on the flight to Rome. Where to check in, the boarding gate number. The information moved on up the screen as time went on and the flights ahead of it departed. Then it was being boarded, last call, and it left. He waited until the information had disappeared completely off the screen and only then did he go home. He remembered that he had started to cry in the taxi. When he got to the house he lifted the phone off the hook, took a couple of sleeping tablets and went back to bed.

Thinking of all this now he put down his knife and fork, and sat like that for several moments. For years he had longed to see his daughters and then when the moment came, he hadn't been able to face it. How would they judge him? Would they be disappointed in him? How would he cope if they disliked him? If they were angry? What if they considered him a stranger, in spite of all the letters and phone calls with which he had wooed them in recent times? 'I was afraid,' he said very slowly, 'that if I did get on that plane I would be so anxious about what was going to happen when I arrived I would start drinking again. And as the time drew nearer that feeling got worse, so that when push came to shove, I *knew* it would happen. I knew that if I got on the plane that morning in the state I was in, I would start to drink. By the time I got to Rome I would have been right back to square one. And if the only way to avoid that was by not taking the flight then that was how it had to be. I had no choice, Marta. Christ knows I didn't want to hurt you and the girls yet again but I couldn't see an alternative. I had no choice.' He sat for a few moments longer in silence.

'The last trip,' she said, 'was badly thought out. That we should meet you at the airport, that you should stay with us: it would never have worked. It's better like this. Are you nervous about meeting the girls?'

'Maybe just a bit. How do you think it will go?'

'Very differently with each of them,' Marta said decisively. 'Serena will be difficult. Extremely difficult. But don't take it personally, she's like that with everyone at the moment. Serena by name, we say in the family, but not Serena by nature.'

'Is she going through a rebellious phase, then?'

'Is she what! I don't know where she gets it from; I was never like that. Were you?'

Roderic shook his head. 'It must be a rogue gene she inherited from her Uncle Dennis. What's Serena getting up to?'

'Everything,' Marta says. 'She quarrels with me, she quarrels with Allegra, she's even had rows with my mother.' At this Roderic felt a quick surge of sympathy for Serena, which he did his best to conceal. 'She's got a horrible boyfriend, a real smart-alec. Paolo. She spends all her spare time hanging out with him. He has a motorbike.'

'You mean a Vespa?'

'No, no, a real motorbike. I think it's a Harley. They go off up into the hills,' and she tossed her chin, gesturing towards the valley before them which immediately took on a darker, more sinister air to Roderic. 'At least she's doing well at school. She's lazy, but she's smart. You won't enjoy seeing Serena, I can tell you that now,' Marta went on. 'She'll give you a hard time. She'll think she has you on a gilt pin because of all the trouble in the past, but if you want my advice you ought to stand up to her and not take any cheek.' The waiter came over to remove their plates, returned moments later bringing the meat.

Marta helped herself to more bread and turned the conversation to Allegra. 'You have nothing to worry about there,' she said. 'Allegra loves you. She adores you. You may not realise this but you've never done anything wrong in your life.'

That any member of his family could think this in the face of such firm evidence to the contrary didn't seem possible to Roderic, and he said as much to Marta.

'Oh, but if you drank it must have been my fault,' she said. 'I drove you to it, dreadful woman that I am. I must have made your life intolerable to force such a paragon as yourself to the bottle. That's the version of events you'll get from Allegra.'

'I'll try and disabuse her of that notion.'

'Will you?' she replied, and there was more than a touch of bitterness in her voice. 'Will you? If you succeed in doing so, I'll be much obliged.

'As for Oriana,' she went on, 'it's like this.' She spoke hesitantly and he knew that she was about to broach something difficult. 'I know we spoke at length before you came over about keeping everything on neutral ground, and your not coming to the house and so on.'

He nodded. That he would not visit their former family home which Marta and the girls now shared with Gianni had been very much his idea.

'You'll find that she comes across as far younger than she actually is. She's a sweet child, gentle, but anxious. She can't remember you at all and she's extremely nervous about meeting you. Given that, I thought it might be easier for her if you were to see her in surroundings that are familiar, where she feels comfortable and safe.'

'Absolutely.'

'We could go, then, straight after lunch, back to the house. She's there on her own.'

'Why not?' Roderic said, forcing a smile. Marta poured more water for herself and topped up his glass too. He was glad of this as he was not sure that he could do it now without his hands trembling.

At the end of the meal Roderic insisted on paying the bill, and reluctantly accepted Marta's promise to take him out to dinner at some stage over the coming days. Then they set off for their former home. 'The Germans left that place, do you remember them?' she said, nodding at a villa up on the hill. 'Their marriage didn't work out either. I think an American couple own it now, I don't know them.' They continued in causal talk about changes that had taken place in the area since Roderic's departure and people he had known then but they both fell silent as they drew near to the house. The trees and plants had thickened around it in the years of his absence. Marta pulled into the driveway and they got out of the car. His old home looked more imposing than he remembered it. Everything about Italy was slightly out of kilter with the image he had carried in his mind, as though he were looking at it all through some kind of filter. Marta fumbled for her keys in her handbag, then opened the door and admitted him to the hall.

He would have known it, he thought, had he been blind-folded, would have recognised immediately that cool air with its faint fragrance of furniture polish, the exact timbre of the sound the door made as she closed it behind them. They stood in the dim hall, not speaking, inches from each other, and for a split second it was as if it had all never happened: the drinking and the quarrels, the years apart. This woman was still his wife, this house was still his home. That it should be otherwise and that she was now living here with another man was unbelievable to him. They stood there on the black and white tiled floor staring at each other and he could feel between them that powerful sensuality that he always associated with Marta, that he had experienced first so many years before in the darkened chapel. He was still physically in thrall to her as he always had been, and he wanted her now, here and now. Softly he spoke her name, 'O Marta,' and she stared up at him, made no movement to resist as he lifted his hand to touch her face.

Just at that moment, a timid voice came from the top of the stairs. '*Mamma?*' Marta jerked away violently from Roderic's touch as if she had been electrocuted, and they stared at each other, shocked at what had almost happened. She was bristling with anger now. '*Mamma?*' the voice said again. '*Oriana? Si, si, sto qui.*' Struggling to compose herself she waved Roderic towards the door of the drawing room and then ascended the staircase, speaking to her daughter in Italian as she went.

The incident in the hall had completely thrown Roderic and he was further disconcerted when he went into the drawing room. It had changed almost out of all recognition. There were chairs and a sofa that had not been there in his time and the pieces of furniture he did remember – a dresser and a small table – had been moved to different positions in the room. It was dark there too because the shutters were closed, so he switched on a lamp that looked like an egg of opaque white glass and sat down on the sofa. Footsteps on the stairs, whispers. Now they were just outside the closed door of the drawing room. He could hear Marta and Oriana conferring in lowered voices, the child's voice urgent, anxious, Marta's soothing and cajoling. 'Of course I'll stay with you, at least to begin with,' he heard her whisper. 'Don't worry, darling, it'll be fine, you'll see.' But there was no one to console Roderic, who could feel his own heart beating with unnatural intensity. He was more nervous even than he had been when waiting in the hotel for her to arrive. It seemed to him in that moment that with the exception of a few paintings there was nothing in his life, but *nothing*, that he hadn't botched. Please God, let me not botch this, he thought, please let the next hour be an exception.

The door opened and Marta appeared, ushering into the room an exquisite child who was small for her eleven years. Roderic stood up and the little girl's face registered shock. 'But he's so big! So big!' she said, turning to her mother and not addressing Roderic at all. He immediately sat down again so as not to appear intimidatingly tall, and then felt foolish because he had to stand up once more to greet her properly, taking the tiny hand she held out to him and kissing her very lightly and gingerly on the cheek, so as not to startle her further. What he really wanted to do was to throw his arms around her and wail, to give himself up to the visceral love he felt for her. He wanted to carry her off in his arms, he wanted to take her back to Ireland with him to live for the rest of her life. He wanted to stop complete strangers in the streets and say to them, 'This is my daughter. My *daughter*.' She was like a child as she might have been painted by Bronzino, with her fine-boned face and her thick brown hair. He could see her in brocades and heavy green stuffs, could see her with golden chains and jewels, a small book in her hands, a classic Renaissance beauty, and yet the miracle was there was something in her that was him, in her brow, in her jaw: she *was* his daughter.

He patted the cushions on the sofa, inviting her to sit beside him, but she had already slunk into a chair opposite, safely separated from him by a low table scattered with art magazines. 'We had ever such a nice lunch,' Marta said to her. 'We went to I Tre Ponti, you know, where we went for Allegra's birthday? They had that chocolate ice cream you liked so much.' She rattled on brightly about how well Oriana was doing at school. Speaking of dance classes and piano lessons, asking questions and giving prompts, she tried to draw both father and daughter into the conversation but with limited success. Roderic wished he didn't have to talk at all. He would have liked just to look at Oriana in silence for fifteen, twenty minutes, to drink her in, to savour the full, almost Shakespearean import of the situation and think of all that had been lost, all restored. It was evidently a sentiment Oriana shared. She sat staring rapt across the table at Roderic as though he were some fabulous creature from the outer limits of imagination. She gave her mother abrupt 'yes', 'no' answers to her questions as she struggled to match this total stranger with the concept of Father.

'I don't remember you,' Oriana said all at once, still staring at him. 'I thought I might, but I don't.'

'Oh well, it can't be helped,' Roderic said, attempting to be jocular, but his disappointment was too deep to be completely hidden, and a certain awkwardness fell over them.

'We had a very nice holiday in Positano a few weeks ago, didn't we?' Marta said. She was clutching at straws by now, like a slightly desperate hostess trying to crank up the atmosphere at a party, but strangely enough this remark at last struck a chord with the child.

'We did; it was lovely,' Oriana said. 'We all had a brilliant time. Can I show him the photographs?' The little girl was already on her feet and from a drawer in the sideboard she took a brightly coloured paper wallet.

'Very well,' Marta said, 'you do that while I go and get us all something to drink.'

Roderic patted the cushions beside him again and this time Oriana accepted the invitation, settled in close by his side. 'This is Serena and me on the beach. This is Nonno and Nonna and Allegra on the balcony. This is Mamma and Allegra . . .' Four photographs in and he could understand why Marta had left the room. 'This is Mamma and Gianni in the pool,' was Oriana's caption for a photo of Marta and a man kissing in the turquoise waters of a swimming pool fringed by white oleanders. He looked at the photograph with intense curiosity and Oriana noticed this. 'You can't see Gianni very clearly there,' she said apologetically, 'but there's one later of us all at dinner where you can see him better. This is Allegra and Serena playing volleyball on the beach. . .'

By the time he got to the end of the photographs, he was grateful he had seen them. He felt vindicated, could have offered this sheaf of bland shiny images as evidence in the case for the defence. How well he could imagine this holiday! How well he could fancy the idle days, the pool and the beach, the cycling and the volleyball. Marta's mother spending the whole of the forenoon in the kitchen making hand-turned pasta for the lunch that would follow, the interminable lunch. He could see himself in the middle of all this peachy indolence, hanging around in a pair of plastic flip-flops, getting in his mother-in-law's way, bored out of his skull and wishing to Christ he was back home so that he could get on with his work.

As Oriana replaced the photographs in their wallet she said hesitantly, 'Something odd happened recently. You know that box of oil paints you sent Allegra for her birthday?

When she was showing them to me it was so strange, I just had this feeling of overwhelming happiness. I don't know why. Pure happiness. It was the smell of them, you know. It was like remembering bits of a dream I'd had long ago. There was an old chair upholstered in blue. And music. Beautiful music. And pure happiness. Nothing else.' They sat in a tense silence. He knew not to force it. Then she said, in a voice so low he could barely hear it, 'Maybe I do remember you after all. I remember Tarquinia.'

'Tarquinia!' Not for years had he thought of that summer evening, the golden light that made everything ancient and pure; the sky, the broken viaduct, the slow grasses rippling in the fields like heavy silk. It had been the last of those little islands of peace they had known together as a family. 'We had to go down into the earth but I didn't want to. Someone told me there was nothing to be afraid of, that we would see marvellous coloured pictures. He carried me down.' Yes, he'd borne her into the tomb, Pluto and Persephone as Bernini conceived them. How she'd writhed and cried in his grasp, but he'd soothed her and she did grow calm as they descended into the dark earth, where her mother and sisters had already gone. The child darted over and clung to Marta's skirt. She smiled down at her daughter and stroked her head abstractedly. A guide was talking to the assembled group about how the Etruscans had greeted death and loss with defiance, with feasting and wild music. Looking at his wife Roderic suddenly knew the truth. Their marriage was doomed. How much longer would it last, he wondered – another month? Two months, six? Whatever it might be, he set that fragment of time against the huge implacable weight of the years that had passed since the tomb had been made and sealed, since the feasting and the music. Marta's hand, so cold when he touched it afterwards. Did she find out too down there? Did she also come back up into the heat of the blinding sun with the knowledge that her marriage was dead? He could never ask her now.

285

And what were all those thousands of years of unutterable silence when the tomb was undisturbed when set against the mere eight years that Oriana struggled to get back through now to find her lost father?

'I've forgotten so many things,' she said, 'but I do remember Tarquinia.'

Chapter Twenty-Eight

MODERN PAINTERS: Roderic Kennedy, to begin with a definition: you are frequently described as an abstract painter, but I believe this is something you strongly resist. Why?

RODERIC KENNEDY: Because it isn't accurate.

MP: In what sense?

RK: Well for a start, I would resist any discussion of my work that *begins* with a definition rather than working towards one. Even then I would be wary of the ultimate importance of any label used. I can see why critics like, perhaps even need these definitions, but the problem is that they almost inevitably distract from the work. That's what it really should be about: tapping into the primary energy of the thing rather than thinking, 'I'm looking at an abstract painting or a piece of conceptual art or whatever.' It frightens people off, you see, that's the danger. It's too high falutin', makes people think that they can't, won't, be able to understand, whereas it isn't a case of understanding something but of *experiencing* it.

MP: But if in art there is to be progress . . .

RK: Progress? (*Laughs*) In art?

MP: Well yes, but . . .

RK: Go on, go on.

MP: I think I've forgotten what I was going to say.

RK: Maybe it's just as well. (*Laughs*) Look, before we go any further I'd like to clear up a few things that bother me. First, I make no apology for being a painter. There's a certain school of thought now that considers painting a waste of time: it's all been said, all been done. That for the consciousness with which we now apprehend the world, nothing adequate can be expressed through painting. I don't go along with that at all. So much of what one hears and sees nowadays is just fashion and the essence of fashion is that it passes.

MP: To approach the thing from a different angle, perhaps we could look at your life, starting with your family and childhood. Do you come from a family of painters?

RK: Oh God, no, far from it. I should qualify that, if you take art in the broadest sense of the term. My father was an opera buff, fanatically so. He used to play records all the time so there was always music in the house, Verdi, Mozart and so on. He was a doctor and his life was in most respects a straight-down-the-line middle-class existence. But that wasn't the whole story. There was this other thing, this sublime music, this . . . this parallel, radiant world in which he also lived. I mean, it wasn't just a question of his liking a bit of opera, it wasn't mere entertainment. He was passionate about it. He was in any case a passionate man, and he needed art in this way, it was essential to him. And so I think it was primarily through him that I learned, quite early on, although I couldn't have articulated it as I'm doing now, that as well as this functional, bread-and-butter world in which we all must live, there was also this . . . fabulous reality, I suppose you could call it, that is art.

MP: So how was it that you became a visual artist rather than a musician?

RK: The kind of paintings, or, to be strictly accurate, the kind of reproductions of paintings to which I was exposed while growing up was fairly conventional. Not bad, you know, but standard stuff. We had prints of Degas' dancers in the hall at home and something by Renoir, I seem to remember. My mother liked the Irish Impressionists, Walter Osbourne, that kind of thing. Now there was one particular image in the house that was the catalyst, a Malton print of the Custom House. When I was about eight the bank gave us a free calendar with photos of Dublin, which we hung in the kitchen. It had all the landmarks, the GPO, the Ha'penny Bridge and so on, and, inevitably, the Custom House. Now of course living in Dublin I was familiar with the building, and so I began to really look at and to think about these three things: the print, the photograph, and the Custom House itself. Every time I was in the city centre I used to want to go down the quays to see it, something with which my parents were soon fed up. My mother couldn't understand it, she used to say to me, 'Roderic, you saw it only last week, it hasn't changed since then, I can promise you.' But that was the point: it had. Every time I saw it, it looked different, depending on the light and weather. Sometimes it looked solid and imposing, sometimes much softer, as though it were floating there on the other side of the river, as though it were something I had imagined. Sometimes it was the dome that was the most striking thing about it, sometimes the carvings, and then another time still it would be the symmetry, the proportions of it that I noticed. I became obsessed with it. And one thing I particularly noticed was that it never *ever* looked like the photograph. There was never that odd blue sky, never that flatness.

MP: And the Malton print?

RK: The print was interesting, because the Custom House never looked exactly like that either, and yet I understood that it was somehow close to the truth of the thing, to the reality of the building, certainly much closer than the photograph. It was a sort of idealised image, it got at something essential. It was as if Malton wished to state clearly that it was impossible to represent it as it always was. And I understood that too, I had worked it out simply by looking at the Custom House. So I think that very early on I had got to grips with something significant about the idea of seeing things, and that what we take for reality isn't fixed, isn't static.

MP: Amazing. You must have been a remarkable child.

RK: Oh absolutely not, no, no, no. I can't begin to tell you how ordinary I was. And obviously I couldn't have explained it all to you then as I'm doing now.

MP: But to think a thing through like that – to make those connections. . .

RK: Oh, come on, any child could do it, they do it all the time. Perhaps not always with visual things but with sounds or words or whatever. They're capable of making those almost metaphysical connections that are outside the limits of received opinion, because their minds are free. They haven't yet been conditioned not to think for themselves. This brings us back to more or less where we came in. I mean at eight, I wasn't thinking, 'Ah yes, Malton, the Classical impulse in the art of the eighteenth century . . .' I was simply looking at things that were there under my nose and drawing my own conclusions. We're back to why I don't like definitions. If you show someone a canvas and say, 'Here's an example of Russian expressionist art, what do you think?' chances are you won't get the response you would from showing the same person the same canvas and simply saying, 'Look at this: do you like it?'

MP: But you must concede that sometimes these labels, these definitions, are necessary.

RK: Oh yes, sure. I'm all in favour of a philosophy of art, so long as it serves the work rather than trying to lead it.

MP: So to get back to your own development, what happened next?

RK: Well, I went to secondary school, and I had a wonderful teacher there, Mr Conway, Matthew Conway, and he made a huge difference as a good teacher always does. He taught me formal skills, drawing, watercolour and so on. I'd been doing this kind of thing but in an unfocused way and he gave it all more structure and direction. He introduced me to the art of the twentieth century, the modernists, Picasso, Braque and the rest.

MP: And was that the catalyst?

RK: The catalyst was late Turner. I was looking for a missing link. There was still something about getting close to the reality of a thing, the whole Custom House question you could call it, that I hadn't resolved in my mind, that I didn't understand. And then I came across a book of Turner's work from the end of his life and that was it. Problem solved. You'd see this pearly, hazy image with a bridge just visible in it, or a town that seemed to float, and that was it, it was the thing itself. Turner was a revelation to me, it was like coming home.

MP: Bringing you closer to abstraction.

RK: Bringing me closer to reality.

MP: A considerable period of your career has been spent abroad.

RK: Mmn.

MP: In Italy.

RK: In Italy, yes.

MP: Can you tell me what difference that made to your work? Do you think it was essential for you as a painter?

'What are you reading?' Julia asked. William hadn't noticed her coming into the café until she was right beside him, looking over his shoulder at his magazine. 'Oh *that*. Roderic wasn't too pleased about it,' she said as she sat down. 'They didn't tell him they were going to publish a straight transcript.'

'I'm enjoying it, there are good things in it. How is your friend these days?'

'Roderic? He's fine.'

'I half thought,' William said, 'that he might be along with you.'

'He's a busy man.'

'We're all busy.'

He could see from her face that she registered the criticism implied in this and that it displeased her but all she said was, 'Are you? Are you indeed? I'm glad to hear it. Last time I saw you, you didn't seem to be getting much done.'

'It's been going better this past week or so,' he conceded, 'but it's still very difficult.'

'I'd be more worried if you said you were finding it easy. Tea please,' she said, this last to the waitress who had come over to their table. 'Did you try doing what I suggested?'

'I did and it was a great help.'

'I thought it might be. It's important to be relaxed. If you go at the work all bottled up in yourself you won't get anywhere.'

'I brought along a few paintings today,' he said hesitantly, 'and I wondered if you might look at them for me, give me your honest opinion.'

Julia said that she would on condition that he was clear in his mind about the difference between honesty and truth. 'For I may be wrong,' she said, 'and being honest won't make me right.'

The first thing that surprised her about the work was its size, for William had chosen to work in a much smaller format that she would ever have imagined, each sheet of paper being no more than a foot square. She had also expected that the paintings would be somewhat assertive and bold but in reality they were understated, at times almost diffident experiments in colour. He had brought along two series, one executed in shades of olive green, the other in dark blue-greys that made her think of slates, of sloes, of a sky full of thunder, the colours calling up the thing as a word might. A certain area had been left unpainted on each page, its soft peach-like texture contrasting with the matt pigment that feathered or dripped into it.

As Julia silently studied each painting in turn she did her best to remain impassive and inscrutable for he was looking at her anxiously, keen to know what she thought. Again she remembered how Roderic had warned her off him and in truth it was anything but a simple or straightforward situation. Certainly William's money and status gave him a kind of power, but it was undercut by his desire for this other thing in his life: to be an artist. Being on surer ground in this area herself in turn gave her power over him and today it felt like complete power, so that William was the vulnerable one. By scorning or dismissing his work she could undermine him completely. She wasn't sure that he realised this.

Looking at the paintings she gradually became aware that her initial expectations had been utterly wrong, for these works were in fact an eloquent expression of his current insecurity. In the least accomplished paintings this became a hesitancy and an indecision that botched his technique and weakened any impact it might have had, but in the best these same qualities modulated into a delicate fragility. The colours, the form and the empty space interacted to set up a complex tension, suggesting the oriental.

'They're good,' she said at last. 'Some of them are very good indeed.' She thought the blue series better than the green, and he was glad of this for he too preferred the former. They discussed the work at length now, with Julia picking out the individual paintings she had liked and explaining why, careful always to couch any negative remarks she might make as tactfully as possible. She talked to him about control of colour and developing technique, about confidence and the need for the habit of work. William listened to her intently, drinking in every word although she reminded him again that it was only her opinion, and that she wasn't an authority on the subject. As he closed up again the leather binder in which he carried the paintings he thanked her for her help.

'My big fear,' he said, 'is that I've left it too late.'

'What, the painting? William, if you start to think like that, you're lost. Focus on what you're doing now and forget about the past. In any case, art has its own laws concerning time. It's not like other things. The years you have left may well be all you ever needed.'

The waitress brought tea and they talked about an exhibition they had both recently seen. She liked this kind of conversation with him. What she valued in her friendship with William was his intellectual companionship. Intelligent and well informed, his approach to his work interested her and his opinions on things were always worth hearing. What she didn't want to know about were his private emotional difficulties or his family life, but of late it was precisely these things that he most wished to speak of. The last time they'd met like this, he'd suddenly brought the conversation round to his wife. He told Julia his marriage had gone through a difficult patch some years earlier and had almost ended. He admitted that it had been his fault, intimating that he had been unfaithful. Only now, he said, did he realise that it had all been a way – a clumsy and badly thought-out way – of attempting to change the situation they were in.

'And perhaps it would have been better if Liz and I had separated then. We could have, you know, got on with our lives differently.'

'What about your children?' Julia said.

But he dismissed this: 'We didn't have any children then. Having them was one of the conditions of our staying together. Liz insisted on it.'

His confidences embarrassed her. 'William, I really don't think you should be telling me all these things.'

Having made the point she hoped he would be more reticent in future, but as she drank her tea today he told her that it was exactly a year since his father had died.

'From that text I wrote for you, you may have thought we were close but we weren't, not at all. He was a completely overbearing man, always finding fault with my brother and me, always banging on about achievement. My brother wanted to be a physics teacher but my father thought that showed a scandalous lack of ambition and nagged him out of it, pretty well forced him to do a doctorate. He's a research scientist now, but he went to live in Australia years ago: you can draw your own conclusions from that. I always knew that when my father died I wouldn't be grief stricken, but I don't think I ever expected to be as relieved as I was. Knowing he wasn't there made me feel free.'

It was a view with which Julia, given her own family circumstances, could neither identify nor sympathise. It struck her that the crisis into which he had plunged in the year since then was perhaps not unrelated to the loss of his father, and she wondered if this had also occurred to William. From the way he spoke, she doubted it.

She kept her own remarks limited and neutral until such time as there was a lull in the conversation, then pointed to the bookshop bag on the chair beside him and asked what was in it. He passed a huge volume on Venetian art across the table to her.

'It's only just been published,' he said. 'I bought it on something of an impulse. As soon as I saw it I thought, "Why not?" The text looks intelligent. I read something by the same man last year and it was good, lucid and to the point.'

'You're lucky to be able to buy something like this whenever the notion takes you.'

'I suppose so,' William said. 'You can borrow it in due course, if you wish.'

'Thanks. I'll take you up on that.'

He watched her as she turned the pages, more relaxed now that it was reproductions of Titian, Tiepolo and Veronese that she was examining, rather than his own work. Viewed from this angle, with her head down and her eyes lowered, she looked quite attractive, her face small and pointed against that great tangle of hair that framed it. He could see today what Roderic admired in her, something he couldn't always do.

'I'm sure you've been to Venice,' she said, without looking up.

'Many times.'

He wondered what it would be like to make love to her, a thought rooted in curiosity rather than desire, the curiosity that drove his sexual life more than any physical passion. Until you had been to bed with someone you never could tell how they would be and for William making the comparison between what he might imagine and the reality was where the interest lay. What he was imagining today was being above her, leaning over her, entering her, kissing her, brushing that great mane of hair back from that small face. . .

All of a sudden she lifted her head and stared him straight in the eye, forbidding and stern. *Stop that right now*, the look said. *Don't even think about it.* William was mortified. How could she possibly have known, he wondered. She was looking down at the book again, at a welter of angels in an updraught, golden clouds and long slender trumpets, as though a great wind were blowing through heaven. 'I always think the spirit of Tiepolo is the spirit of springtime, and of Tintoretto's as winter,' and she turned the page. Her voice was completely neutral, as if nothing unusual had passed between them a moment earlier and he began to ask himself if it had actually happened or had it all been in his mind. The sleeves of the senators' wine-dark robes dripped ermine.

He was disappointed that Roderic hadn't been along with her today, regretted that he showed so little interest in him, although he would never have had the courage to show his paintings to the other man. He would have liked to be able to count Roderic Kennedy amongst his friends. Julia was a nice girl but there was no real cachet in knowing her. She would never have admitted it but she was probably secretly thrilled to have such a successful and eminent man as her lover, even if he was old enough to be her father. Perhaps she was the kind of woman who only liked much older men.

'I suppose Roderic goes back to Italy from time to time.'

Julia didn't look up from the page she was examining and didn't reply.

'He has family there, doesn't he?' William persisted.

'He does,' she eventually agreed.

'Has he been back there recently?'

'You'd have to ask Roderic that,' Julia said.

'I would, but I never see him. Sometimes I even get the feeling that he's trying to avoid me.'

'We try not to live too much in each other's pockets,' she said. 'We each have our own lives, our own circle of friends.'

'I suppose you do. I suppose you have to. Being involved with someone so much older must present all sorts of difficulties.'

She lifted her head and closed the book. 'And what sort of difficulties might they be?'

'Well, what you've just said, for example, about not being able to have friends in common. There must be lots of things in your lives that you can't share with each other. And then of course he does have this family off abroad and that has all sorts of implications for the future.'

'Such as?'

'Obviously he won't want to have any more children. He's about my age and I can tell you this, the last thing any man wants years down the line from nappies, broken nights and the rest of it, is to start the same thing all over again.'

'I don't believe I'm hearing this,' Julia said. 'I don't believe it. Let me set you straight on a couple of points. First, you are not the golden mean against which all other men are to be measured. Just because you think or feel something doesn't mean Roderic is bound to think and feel in the same way. He's not like you; not a bit like you. He listens to people and you don't. I didn't say that we can't have friends in common, I said we each have our own life, our own circle of friends, and that's a different thing altogether. Second, there are no problems or difficulties between Roderic and me, but we're getting a bit fed up with other people trying to make out that there are, people who hardly know us. I put it down to jealousy. So there's an age difference – so what? I have everything I want in Roderic. Do you understand that? Do you hear what I'm saying? *Everything.*'

He wondered how she managed to load one small word with such a charge of erotic satisfaction. It sent a tremor through him but it wasn't pleasurable. He imagined that this was how a woman must feel, touched intimately by a man completely against her will. As she said it she passed the book back across the table to him, shoving it into his hands and releasing it as soon as it was in his grip, its great weight almost causing him to drop it. Then she nodded towards the empty cups. 'I'm paying for this.'

'Don't be ridiculous, Julia.'

'Well, I'm paying for mine.' From her pocket she took a small grubby purse and William watched her as she fished from it coins to cover the price of a cup of tea, shoved them in under the saucer.

'I'm sorry if I offended you,' he said, but the tone suggested he was the one who was put out.

'Save it,' Julia said. 'I don't need this.'

She was on her feet now, was off, and although he called after her she didn't turn back, just lifted to him the back of her hand.

Chapter Twenty-Nine

He had arranged to meet Serena in a café in the square near his hotel at three o'clock, but three o'clock came and went and did not bring her. Five past three, ten past three, a quarter past three, and Roderic's anxiety gradually changed to annoyance. He had finished his coffee and had all but given up when, at three thirty, he heard a roar in the distance. A large motorbike tore into the square and everyone stopped what they were doing to stare as it went round twice before squealing to a halt. The pillion passenger, a young woman with long dark hair – neither she nor her companion was wearing a helmet – climbed down and looked across at the café, then turned away again. She gave him a long kiss and then stepped back as he fired up the bike and roared out of the square in an explosion of noise. She stood and watched him go, listened to the racket die away in the distance and then, when there was silence again, ambled slowly over to the café and dropped herself into a chair beside Roderic.

'Hey, Daddy,' she said, as casually as if she had last seen him only that morning.

'You'll kill yourself if you fall off that thing,' he said severely. 'You should always wear a helmet.'

Serena frowned and shrugged.

'What would you like to drink?'

'I'll have a beer,' she said, adding as a gibe, 'want to have one too?'

'Maybe I will. Have you got a problem with that?'

For one brief second she believed him. Her defiance melted away and she stared at him with sheer terror, terror he recognised, terror he remembered, her face now the face of a little child, afraid of her drunken father. This was the Serena he remembered; and she, evidently, hadn't forgotten him.

The waiter appeared at their table. Completely rattled, Roderic ordered a lemonade. 'I'll have the same,' Serena mumbled.

'Would you like anything to eat?' She shook her head. Although he had won the first round he'd been too heavy handed and would have to go more gently. It was Marta who had urged him to go on the offensive as quickly and completely as possible. They sat in silence until their drinks arrived and even then he was at a loss to get a conversation going.

'You look extremely well,' he said eventually.

'Thanks.'

'You're very tall.'

'Yeah,' and for the first time she gave a glimmer of a smile. 'I must have inherited it from you.'

'You could be a fashion model.'

'Yeah, I know I could. The last time I was in Florence a woman stopped me on the street, a scout from one of the agencies in Milan. She gave me her card and told me to ring her.'

'And do you think you'll follow it up?'

Serena considered this for a moment. 'No, I probably won't bother. I thought at first it could be fun. Then I thought it would be sort of boring, just walking up and down a platform thing all day in stupid dresses.'

'Are you interested in fashion?'

'No. It's a stupid business, isn't it?'

'Still,' Roderic said, 'it was nice to have the offer.'

'Suppose so,' she said lightly, but he could tell she was secretly delighted.

Marta had made some offhand comment about Serena's looks the other day, something about how she had grown up to be 'quite fine'. By this modest understatement she had failed to convey their eldest daughter's remarkable beauty. Leaning back in her chair, Serena radiated a lazy but potent sensuality. Long-limbed, tanned, with thick glossy brown hair that fell to her waist and a fine oval face, what made her unique were her eyes. She had the same large limpid blue eyes as Roderic's mother and his sister Maeve, and combined with the Mediterranean complexion she had inherited from Marta the effect was unforgettable. As with his youngest daughter, he would have been happy simply to sit and look at her for some time without speaking, trying to square the child in his mind with the person now before him.

'So if you're not going to be a model, what would you like to do?'

'No idea.'

'What do you enjoy at school?'

'Greek,' she said, surprising him, although he knew from letters that she was doing *Classico*, the most difficult option in the Italian school syllabus. Marta had told him that in spite of Serena's laziness, her marks were consistently excellent. 'I like Greek.'

'You could study that at university when the time comes,' he said.

'Not much use, though, is it?' she replied. 'Don't know how I'd earn my living with Greek.'

He could see her weighing the next remark in her mind and deciding to risk it.

'Bit like studying painting, I suppose.'

'Oh you'd manage,' he said, refusing to rise to the bait. 'Best to do something you like and let making a living look after itself, that's what I always say.' He looked at her again out of the corner of his eye. 'You'll do all right in life,' he said, 'that's for sure.'

He intended this as a compliment and Serena took it as such. She understood exactly what he was getting at, and drank her lemonade in an attempt to conceal the smile his words provoked.

Suddenly, when he least expected it, she put her glass down hard upon the table and said, 'It was unbelievable when you didn't show up last year. *Unbelievable*. The fuss and the disappointment, I mean. Allegra cried for three days. I wasn't surprised, though. I knew you'd let us down.'

'Well, I'm here now,' Roderic said, and she threw him a look that plainly said *Big deal if you are.*

'It's good that Mamma met Gianni. I'm glad about that.'

'Yes, it's wonderful, isn't it?' he replied insincerely, marvelling at how exactly she found all his weak points, all the areas in which he was most vulnerable.

'They get on really well together,' she went on pitilessly. 'I mean really, *really* well. Know what I mean?'

'Mmn,' Roderic said. 'And what about you; do you like him?'

To his surprise, this caught her completely on the hop. 'He's all right, I suppose,' and she shrugged. 'I could live without him.'

'Oriana thinks he's nice,' he said, being at something of a loss as to what else to say.

'That's just because *she's* so nice,' Serena said, adding, 'Oriana's a great kid.' Then she said with fierceness, 'I love Oriana. I absolutely love her.'

'I know that. She told me so.'

They sat in silence for a moment. 'Your Uncle Dennis sends his love.'

'Give him mine when you see him,' Serena said. 'I like Dennis. Dennis is cool.'

Roderic drank his lemonade and considered this novel assessment of his brother.

'He still always sends us cards and stuff, remembers our birthdays. It would be nice to see *him* again.'

'For that you'll probably have to go to Ireland. He almost never goes abroad now, he hates flying.'

'We have aunts, too, don't we? Maeve and Clee – something, I can never remember.'

302

'Cliona, yes.'

'We never hear from them.'

'I don't have a great deal of contact with them either, to tell you the truth.'

Serena shifted in her chair and crossed her legs. She was wearing cut-off jeans and sandals, and there was a dark blue butterfly tattooed just above her ankle bone.

'Is that permanent?' he asked.

She shook her head. 'Do you like it?'

'It looks great.'

In the last question and answer of this brief exchange, something strange passed between them. It was as though they were simply a man and a woman rather than father and daughter. Roderic had a particular knack of being able to tune in suddenly to a sexual level in a deep, fleeting way. It was a singular trick and the ability to do it was evidently something Serena had inherited for it was there, manipulative and sly, in the way she had asked him: *Do you like it?* and the identical impulse was there in his immediate, unthinking reply: *It looks great.* Each had surprised the other and they sat in silence for a few moments afterwards. For the first time ever Roderic knew exactly, but *exactly* what it was like to be on the receiving end of his own charisma. The whole of his life seemed to flash before him. Serena, for whom this was quite a new game, wasn't shocked at all. It pleased her immensely to think she could do to other people what she had just seen done, and a glimmer of a smile crossed her face.

'It's good that it's only a temporary tattoo,' Roderic said eventually. 'It looks well but you might not always want to have it.'

Higher up her leg, on her shin, there was a faint scar. He stared at it for some moments for it reminded him of something, but he couldn't think what. Then it all came back to him. The cherry tree at Marta's parents' house. Serena lost in the branches, behind the screen of long pointed leaves, searching for the fruit she craved; then a shriek and a rush of air as she fell, a tiny female Icarus in a blue summer dress. It was Roderic who reached her first where she lay in the grass screaming, who saw the cut on her leg, 'The rake, the rake, she's fallen on the rake.' It was Roderic who carried her in his arms to the doctor's surgery, Roderic who sat beside her and held her hand as the wound was stanched and stitched. 'It'll leave a scar,' the doctor said, as he washed his hands afterwards. 'She'll have a mark there for the rest of her life.' And here was the mark; here was the proof that this was Serena.

Ever since meeting her today he had been trying to square, somewhere in the back of his mind, the sensual young woman before him with the child he remembered. Where was she now, that little girl? He hated being disturbed when he was in his studio, was unable to work with others around, but his daughters had been the exception to this and had always been welcome. Serena's footsteps as she walked over the gravel path in the back garden, then the uneven clumping noise as she scaled the four wooden steps up to the studio, the squeak of the opening door: 'Papà?' This little fugue of sounds was branded into his soul for ever. She would settle into the blue chair and chatter to him, or make pictures of her own at the low table in the corner that Roderic had set up and furnished with papers and paints for this express purpose. Sometimes she would cross to the easel and inspect his work before passing eccentric judgement on it. Lithe, mischievous, blue-eyed sprite, she was like a creature from another world where the life of the imagination was taken for granted, taken as truth. He remembered the profound companionship of those hours they spent together in the studio. Because of the strange beauty of her consciousness, his relationship with her was unlike any he had had in his life before. He found in fatherhood riches and pleasures he had never expected.

'Do you remember,' he said to her now, 'do you remember when you were a little girl?'

'You shouldn't ask me that,' she said, but he was too wrapped up in his own memories to notice the warning sign in the sullen tones of her voice. He demurred, insisted, until she turned on him with venom.

'Since you ask, I remember everything. *Everything*, do you hear me? I remember lying awake at night waiting for you to come home, with that horrible feeling in the pit of my stomach of dread, like before an exam or before going to the dentist. I remember your getting drunk at the Christmas lunch, and Mamma being disgraced before the whole family. I remember . . . no, no, you asked, and I'm not going to stop now. I remember how after you'd gone, when you went back to Ireland, you used to ring Mamma at two in the morning. The sound of the phone would wake me, and I heard her trying to reason with you, but there was no point, because you were drunk. Then at last she would hang up, and leave the phone off the hook. I would hear her crying, and I didn't have the words to tell her that she was lucky, lucky you were gone and not coming back.'

Serena was only beginning to get into her stride now. She recalled to Roderic incidents he had long since pushed to the back of his mind as being too shameful to be thought of. She reminded him too of other things he had actually forgotten, and her angry words called them up again before him in vivid and agonising detail. As she became more and more upset she started to cry and he offered her a clean handkerchief, which she accepted. She blew her nose, and then went on haranguing him through her sobs. Neither of them seemed to care that people were staring at them now, for they cut a curious figure in the quiet town square: the exquisitely beautiful teenager, furious and weeping, and the ravaged melancholy giant beside her.

Her anger, Roderic thought, was wholly reasonable. What astonished him most of all was that no one had ever called him to account in this way before. Over the years, from long before he stopped drinking, he had pointed the finger quietly at himself, had been aware of how deeply culpable he was. Marta had not reproached him in this vehement way, and Dennis's love – there was no other word for it – had been wholly unconditional. He felt a kind of gratitude to Serena for pulling him into line. He would have hated it if everyone had turned on him, unleashing ire and recrimination: it was exactly that he had feared a year ago, so much so that it had made him unable to travel. But it was right that someone did it, and Serena did it now.

'Then there was the time you went to Ireland and you stopped in Rome on the way back for two days and you never even bothered to tell us where you were. Mamma was frantic; she didn't know what had happened. You were too cowardly to ring her. I was sorry when you did come back. I'd hoped we'd never see you again. When at last you did leave for good, we were all glad, do you know that? It was a relief to be rid of you.'

Was this the truth? 'Serena,' he said gently, 'why did you come here today? You didn't have to meet me. You could have said no.'

Her response was to lower her head until it touched the table and utter a long primal howl, the meaning of which Roderic understood immediately. He was her father: that was why she had come to him.

'My darling,' and he tried to put his arm around her shoulders but she shrieked, punched him away, still howling. 'What do you want?' he asked, feeling utterly helpless.

She was so far gone she could hardly get the words out. 'I want to go home.'

Mercifully there was a taxi rank across the street from the café. He made a rough guess as to how much the fare would be, doubled it and pressed the notes into her hand as she clambered sobbing into the back seat. The taxi sped off with squealing tyres, making her departure from the square as dramatic as her arrival had been. Turning back to settle the bill for their drinks Roderic saw that everyone in the café – everyone in the square – had stopped what they were doing to stare enthralled at what had been happening. It briefly crossed his mind that he could go round with a hat, collect good money for the remarkable entertainment he had afforded them.

Back in the hotel, completely spent, he lay on his bed and looked at the ceiling. The heat in the room was stifling even though the shutters had been closed all day, and the clock in the bell tower that had kept him awake half the night struck the hour. He thought of Serena's parting shot just before she slammed the door of the taxi, half boast, half accusation: *You don't know who I am.* Did he? Well, did he? And if it came to that, did she know him? For Oriana, he was someone who shimmered at the outer limits of memory. 'You're like someone I dreamt about, long ago,' she had said, 'and now, here you are.'

When he went back to live in Ireland he had fully intended to keep in touch with his children. He rang them up, in his cups, in the middle of the night.

I want to speak to my daughters. Get Serena for me.

But it's three o'clock in the morning, Roderic.

No, it's not; it's only two.

You're forgetting the time difference; and anyway, two, three, what does it matter? They're all asleep and I'm not waking them for you. I've nothing against you talking to the girls, but not at such an ungodly hour, and not when you're drunk.

It always ended with Marta hanging up on him, and she would then leave the phone off the hook so he couldn't ring back.

He tried to write letters.

My darlings, How are you? Today I painted and then I drank.

That was all his life amounted to now. What more could he say? There were no words for the loneliness, no words to say how much he missed them. As his life sank further into failure and confusion, communication between him and his family in Italy dwindled into a series of functional and

307

increasingly sporadic exchanges. The only point in which he was constant was in meeting his financial obligations to them. A standing order was set up to transfer a fixed sum of money every month, and Roderic sometimes borrowed, got into debt or did without things he urgently needed for himself to ensure that the payment went through. Although she always thanked him politely for this when she wrote, Marta had never asked him for money, and could probably have managed quite well without his contributions. Throughout their years together she earned a good, steady salary from her job in art restoration, and she had inherited both money and property from her family. Roderic's income, from painting and occasional short-term teaching contracts, was far more erratic and brought in much less. It was Roderic himself who had instigated the standing order and insisted upon it, even though he drew scant satisfaction from it. *Mr Provider*: his own sneering put-down when he thought of himself in this context, tottering into the bank at the last minute to lodge a roll of filthy, tattered banknotes; the cave man who trails the haunch of a dead pig back to the cave and thinks that gives him the right to club his woman over the head. Still, it gave him the illusion that his daughters still needed him, and even though he saw it for what it was – just that, an illusion – it was one he did not have the strength to live without.

The clock in the bell tower bonged the half hour. Half past what? Was it possible it was already five thirty? He must have fallen asleep, in spite of everything. He was to meet Allegra in the lobby of the hotel at six. There was a kettle in the room and the wherewithal to make hot drinks, so he brewed up a coffee, lit a cigarette and washed his face in an attempt to shake himself into consciousness. As he descended in the lift, however, he still felt weary and unrefreshed, in no way ready for what was ahead.

Through the glass doors of the hotel at exactly the appointed time, he saw Marta's car pull up. Mother and daughter both got out and although he was much too far away to hear what they were saying, it was clear that a brief altercation was taking place, that Marta wanted to come in with her and that Allegra wanted to go in alone. In the end Marta threw up her hands in annoyance and got back into the car as Allegra turned and resolutely marched into the hotel.

'Papà! Papà!' she cried as soon as he stood up to greet her, and she ran across the lobby to fling herself upon him, letting the artist's folder she carried drop to the tiled floor with a loud slapping noise. It was years since anyone had launched themselves into Roderic's embrace with such enthusiasm and it startled him. This was what he had wanted, wasn't it, he thought, as he hugged her awkwardly. Surely this flood of feeling was better than Oriana's timidity and reserve, than Serena's downright hostility, and yet it unsettled him. He could feel the heat of her body through his shirt, could smell the perfume she was wearing. It was a complex, sophisticated fragrance, full of citrus and amber and endearingly unsuitable for the awkward teenager who wore it. Roderic recognised it at once: she had clearly gone into her mother's bedroom and helped herself liberally from the crystal bottle.

'I am very happy to see you, Papa,' she said in heavily accented English. 'How are you?'

'I'm fine, happy to be here, delighted to see you. I thought we might stay here, go up to my room where we can talk in private, is that all right with you?' He answered her in English, and nervousness made him speak more quickly than usual. She stared up at him, her face blank with incomprehension, so he repeated in Italian what he had just said. She smiled her agreement. He picked up her folder and carried it for her as they crossed the lobby.

Alone in the tiny lift as it creaked to the third floor, they did not speak. He was aware of Allegra staring up at him with adulation, as if he were a singer or an actor with whom she was infatuated and was meeting for the first time. Roderic was not flattered, instead he felt how unworthy he was of such regard, felt exhausted, too: an emotional rather than a physical exhaustion. The three meetings he had had so far had taken more out of him than he had realised. Roderic would somehow have to get it across to Allegra that he was not the paragon she thought. He wanted her to know the truth about him and yet not reject him, and the temptation was to tell her as much in a few blunt statements, for he doubted that he could summon up this evening the necessary tact and subtlety of approach. *I've been a complete failure as husband and father, Allegra. I treated your mother disgracefully. I know you know this and yet still I want your love and respect more than anything else in the world. Have you got that?* He looked down again at her, and she smiled up at him adoringly, her face and her heart as open as that of a baby in a pram, smiling back at a smiling stranger.

She tripped and almost fell as she stepped out of the lift. She was gauche and clumsy, as though she had not yet grown into her body, with its angular, rangy limbs.

'Your room is nice,' she said in English as he opened the door and ushered her in.

In replying this time he took care to speak slowly and clearly in short, simple sentences. 'You can see the square,' he said, opening the window to fold back the shutters. 'The church is very near. I hear the bells. The bells wake me in the night.'

Allegra nodded, delighted to be able to understand him. 'I like to speak with you like this,' she said. 'It is important for me to speak to you in your language.' The effort with which she put this sentence together and the obvious sincerity of the sentiment was touching. 'Perhaps I will go to Ireland to practise my English.'

'You speak it very well already,' he said, which was a lie but a kindly intended one. 'It's strange for me to be speaking Italian again after all these years. I'm the one who needs the practice. Would you mind if that were the language that we used today?' He had slipped out of English, even as he spoke, and was relieved when Allegra accepted his suggestion.

'I would, though, I'd love to go to Ireland,' she said. 'After all, I am half Irish, aren't I, so I'd be bound to fit in.'

Roderic was not convinced of the logic of this but said nothing.

'Uncle Dennis sent us a calendar one year and I kept it afterwards, the photos are so beautiful. I want to see the Cliffs of Moher, and I want to see bogland. That must be the strangest thing. Dublin too, I want to go there. A friend of Serena's was there last summer and she loved it.'

'Oh, it's very lively, yes, you'd have a good time.'

'Could I come and visit you?'

There was regret in her voice that she had to ask, that he hadn't immediately suggested it, and his unenthusiastic response – 'Well, yes, you could I suppose, at some time in the future' – did not redress the balance. She wasn't to know that he was wondering what she might make of his tiny redbrick terraced house with its blue painted door, in the shabby street where he dwelt like a lonely bear. How frugal and mean it would look in comparison with the splendid villa where she lived, with its bougainvillaea and vines. Would she think less of him for it?

'I bet you're really famous in Ireland,' she said. 'I bet everybody knows who you are.'

'Oh good God, no,' Roderic said, 'far from it.' His considerable eminence as a painter had not exactly turned him into a household name. The very idea of such fame made him feel ill. Life was hard enough coming to terms with his own consciousness of failure, without thinking that the entire country knew about his shortcomings.

Allegra did not share this sentiment: for a moment disappointment flickered across her features then she smiled again. 'You're only being modest. I bet you're really famous there,' and this time Roderic just smiled weakly, not having

311

the heart to disillusion her further. She was still smiling at him with that utterly uncritical devotion to which perhaps only the truly famous become habituated, thinking it their due. Roderic found it disconcerting. It was bizarre to gaze into her loving, trusting eyes, and think of how her sister had raged at him only a few hours earlier. The anger he merited was easier to bear than this undeserved adulation. Anxious to change the subject, he cast around for a suitable idea. Then he noticed the mini-bar.

'I know what,' he said in a loud, fake-jolly voice. 'Lets have a drink!'

Her face closed, she flinched as Serena had done when he threatened to join her in a beer.

'No thanks, Papà,' she said, her voice shaky.

'Are you sure?' To cover his embarrassment he knelt down and opened the tiny fridge. 'They have everything here, look, they have Coke, Sprite, orange juice, what would you like? What's this – a Toblerone, would you like that? Or peanuts, crisps: goodness, what haven't they here?'

But the thing they had in awesome quantities was the thing he could not bring himself to mention: alcohol. There were two kinds of beer; wine, both red and white; and all manner of spirits: gin, whiskey, and vodka, together with a selection of particularly Italian drinks, sambuca, amaretto and marsala. From where he knelt he looked up at his daughter, who was sitting on the end of the bed. She gazed down at Roderic crouching over his cache of drink and her look was now filled with mingled pity and terror. A great weariness swept over him. He wanted to speak, to say something to justify himself, but could find no words, and so he hauled himself up from the floor in silence and sat down beside her. She did not shrink away as he had feared she might and so he tentatively put his arm around her. Allegra responded by leaning her head against his shoulder. The texture of her hair was brittle against his cheek and again he noticed the exotic perfume he had been aware of in the lobby. The crammed fridge was still open before them. For some time they both simply sat there gazing into it, at all the bottles and cans, contemplating their past as a mystic might have contemplated his fate in a vanitas, the remarkable supply of alcohol serving the same function as the polished skull or bowl of rotting fruit. He hugged her more tightly to him, could feel her body rise and fall with each breath she drew. Eventually Allegra stretched out and gently pushed the door of the fridge shut with her foot.

'I brought some of my paintings along to show you,' she said. 'I did them using the paints you sent me for my birthday. I couldn't believe it when I opened the box; they were exactly what I wanted.'

'I'm glad you like them. They're the best you can get. You must never compromise on the quality of your materials, always use the finest you can afford. If you don't think your work merits it, you shouldn't be painting at all. Cheap pigment and canvas is a false economy in any case. I thought of buying you a good easel but it would have been too awkward to send, and in any case perhaps you already have one.'

She shook her head. 'I thought that's what Gianni was going to buy me – I sort of hinted that that was what I wanted – but he bought me a dress instead. That's typical of him, he never knows what you're getting at unless you spell it out in capital letters.'

'Do you like Gianni?'

'He's all right. He's sort of dull; I don't know how to put it. Serena really can't stand him; they're always quarrelling with each other. Oriana likes him, but then she likes everybody. Anyway, Nonno and Nonna gave me money for my birthday, and I'm going to use that to buy an easel.'

They talked around the subject and he told her the points to keep in mind when making her choice, said that he would go with her to help her. 'What I said about materials holds true for equipment too. If you don't think your birthday

313

money will be enough, let me know and I'll give you whatever you need.'

Allegra, hanging on his every word, nodded vigorously. 'I can't tell you how much I want to be a painter,' she said.

'Be careful about that idea,' he replied. 'You shouldn't be saying, "I want to be a painter," but rather, "I want to paint." It's something you do. That's how you become it, by *doing* it. Because if you become fixated on the idea of "being a painter", you end up just playing at living the artistic life rather than actually being an artist. Can you see the difference? Do you understand?'

'I think so.'

'Would you like to show me the work you have in your folder?'

They were every bit as bad as he had feared they might be. The first was a seascape in which neither the sky nor the sea had in it anything of air or water's elemental clarity and lightness. Instead, there were opaque waves of dense pigment and heavily impastoed clouds. The next painting, a portrait, and the one after that of a brown puppy were, if anything, worse.

'They're not very good, I know.'

Roderic tried to find a diplomatic way to frame his criticisms. 'I think you need to go back to first principles. You need to work on your drawing skills.'

'Will you show me how?'

From the bathroom he fetched a drinking glass, half filled it with water from a plastic bottle on the bedside table, then placed both bottle and glass on a dresser together with a second empty glass tipped on its side. There was a pencil beside the telephone and some sheets of paper printed with the crest of the hotel. 'Try to work towards something fluid and relaxed. You need to look properly at what's before you,' he said. 'Remember that drawing isn't just about making marks on a page, above all it's about how you see things. You need to learn how to look properly at what's before you, but really look, with a fresh eye and no preconceptions. Even if you're drawing something – I don't know what, a table or a vase that you've lived with and that you've seen before time without number – even if its something you've actually already drawn a hundred times, in fact particularly then, make sure that you really *see* it. Learn to trust your own eye, learn to trust the truth of the object you're looking at.'

She began to draw and as she worked, they both became wholly absorbed in the project. Roderic moved into that remote and rigorous part of his consciousness that was completely given over to art, and that had remained inviolate down through the years in spite of everything that had happened in his life. He could see his daughter's pleasure as, under his guidance, the drawing began to emerge. 'Relax your fingers more. Hold your pencil like this,' and leaning over to adjust her grip he touched her hand. Again that heady sophisticated perfume, again that physical warmth, unknown now for so many years.

Allegra sensed his sudden emotion. She released the pencil and closed her hand over his. 'Don't worry, Papà,' she said. 'We all know it can't ever be the same as it was before, but things will work out. Everything is going to be all right.'

And for the first time since his return to Italy, Roderic felt that what she said might be true.

Chapter Thirty

She came into the room carrying the cat by the scruff of its neck. With his eyes narrowed and his paws stuck straight out before him, Max looked like a small child pretending to be a ghost.

Roderic glanced up from the open book on his knee. 'This is a fine thing you've bought for yourself.'

'It was a present,' Julia said. 'William gave it to me.' She released the cat's neck and Max dropped to the carpet with a loud thud. 'It was a peace offering, as a matter of fact. We had something of a falling out a couple of weeks ago.'

'Did you indeed.' It was a comment, not a question. He turned the page. She half hoped he might ask what their quarrel had been about but instead he said, 'And now you're friends again.'

'We are, yes.'

After closing the shop one evening in early September, Hester had come up to Julia's flat. 'Someone left this for you.' The large package she handed over was so tightly wrapped and sealed that Julia had considerable difficulty in getting it open, even with the help of scissors. Inside was the book on Venetian art she'd admired some four days earlier, together with a letter from William. His apology was so complete, so finely judged and delicately phrased that she felt to refuse it would be churlish. She did, however, attempt to return the book when next she saw him but he insisted that she keep it. What he didn't realise was that because of the disagreement connected with her acquiring it, the book felt tainted to Julia. She didn't, couldn't, feel the same about it as she had when first she saw it, or as she would have done had it been a straightforward gift.

'You can borrow it if you like,' she said to Roderic.

'Sometime, perhaps, but not for the moment, thanks. I have too many other things on hand.'

'By the way, would you do something for me? Would you, when you come to see me, ring the bell twice in quick succession so that I'll know it's you?'

He looked at her shrewdly, answered her question with a question. 'So William's being a pest, is he?'

'Just a bit. Once or twice lately he's called in mid-afternoon when I'm working. I'd always let you in, but if I thought it was him I'd rather not open the door.'

Roderic pointed out that he would never drop in at a time when he knew she would be in her studio, 'But I'll ring the bell twice if that's what you want.'

'Thanks.'

He closed the book and set it aside. The cat hopped up on to the sofa beside him and he reached out absentmindedly, ruffled its fur. He looked, Julia thought, rather preoccupied.

'You're not worried about him, are you?' she said.

'Who, Max?'

'No! William.'

'Not in the least. I've told you before, he's your concern, not mine. You're a free agent. No, to be honest with you I was thinking about my old companion in misfortune, Jeannie. I saw her in town today.'

'How was she?'

'Much as she ever was.'

Wretched, in other words, tottering along unsteadily look-ing miserable and unkempt in an old brown jacket she'd had for years. She'd been wearing it, Roderic remembered, on the day she'd said to him, 'It's not as bad for you as it is for me, not being able to be with your children, because you're a man.' It was an occasion he'd never forgotten, because it was the only time in his life that he'd been sorely tempted to hit a woman.

'What did she say?'

317

'Nothing. I didn't speak to her.' *Hello, Jeannie. Piss off, Roderic.* That had been the sum total of their exchange the last time he'd seen her in the street and approached her, an experience he saw no point in repeating. 'There's nothing I can do to help her,' he said. 'It's not in my gift. It never was.'

He was always cautious in talking to Julia about his past life. While he thought it important that she knew a certain amount of all he had been through so that she might know who he was, he was wary of telling her too much to no real purpose. There was no point in simply shocking her, in imposing all his past misery for the sake of it. After he came out of hospital, his confidence all shot to pieces, he'd gone into six successive newsagents one afternoon before he could summon up the nerve in the seventh to go to the counter and actually buy a paper. Incredibly, he'd told Julia about this shortly after they got together because he thought she might find it entertaining, instead of which she'd come back on it several times in the following days. 'I hate to think of you like that. It breaks my heart.' He didn't point out that the anecdote was linked to his recovery and that it was the tales from his drinking days that were truly heartbreaking, but ever since then he had been insistent about the facts, sketched out in broad strokes, while sparing her the detail. He was mindful too of the other people who were implicated in his life and of the need to respect their privacy: Marta, Jeannie, Dennis, even.

For all that, he felt the balance was generally right and now that they were on the subject of his old life he pressed on to say, 'I'm thinking of going back to Italy again towards the end of the year.' Although he was reticent about his past, he was forthcoming about his present: ever since getting together with Julia he had talked to her freely and frequently about his daughters. He had passed on bits of news about them gleaned from letters and phone calls, sharing the minutiae of family life. Serena had done well in her exams, Oriana had got a new dog. When they sent photographs he showed them to Julia and he had recently sent to Italy a few pictures taken by a friend at a reception, in one of which Julia appeared.

'I think that the time is right for another visit. The next time I'm on the phone to them we'll try to fix up a date that would suit everyone, perhaps December or even early January.' Julia said nothing. In his turn he now thought she looked preoccupied. 'Does that sound all right to you?' he asked.

'Of course. I don't know why you're asking. It has nothing to do with me.'

In the remarks that had brought about their estrangement for a short time, William had unsettled and disturbed Julia. By speaking of the future he'd forced the issue, pushed things up the agenda long before either she or Roderic were ready for them. Although she'd always known that the complexities of his past had serious implications for their future life together, Julia hadn't yet thought them all through, much less discussed them with Roderic. She didn't believe this was an evasion; the time simply wasn't yet right. Rather than plunge straight into imponderable questions she had thought it best that they simply enjoy being together and get on with life. On the strength of that, she had always thought, they would be best equipped to deal with the difficult issues when they did arise.

But what William said had planted a doubt in her mind. Take children. The only thing she knew for sure was that she wasn't herself ready to think about having them, and wouldn't be for years yet. But what were Roderic's views on the matter? She had no idea, none whatsoever, and she had only realised this after William had so blithely predicted what Roderic must surely think. Worse, what if he were correct? What if she did ask Roderic and he stated categorically that he didn't ever want to start a second family? She didn't know how she would react to that, was nowhere near ready to deal with it. Damn William, anyway,

319

for starting all this! Even though they had re-established their friendship she realised now that she still held this simmering grudge against him. Although she knew it was irrational and unfair, she was also irritated that Roderic didn't pursue the cause of her quarrel with William so that she might broach the subject, however obliquely. Still, he knew something was up.

'Nothing in particular troubling you, Julia?' All she could do was shrug. 'Work going all right?'

'Work's going fine.'

She'd told him recently that she'd put aside the project on fragrance for the time being, as she hadn't been able to find a satisfactory form in which to present it. Instead she was collecting new material, recordings of people talking about a relationship that had been important to them. Julia would make a box for each person, incorporating an object they had chosen. These boxes would be displayed with headphones beside each one, so that while looking at each particular box the viewer could listen to the relevant recording. She got up from her chair and Max, thinking that she was going to the kitchen, lifted his head in expectation, but when she only crossed to the cassette recorder he closed his eyes and went back to sleep. 'I spoke to this woman yesterday,' she said. 'The box will have fishing flies in it, what else I don't know. I may subdivide the interior with panes of glass into a series of closed compartments, I haven't quite decided.' She put a cassette in the machine and pressed the play button. There was silence and then a woman's voice, hesitant and uncertain.

For years and years I never thought of him. There's almost nothing to remember: there never was. That's the whole point. We were both really young. It was my first job, and he was sent up from the country for a month's training. What did he look like? I have no clear image of his face. He was pale, fair-haired, I suppose he had blue eyes but I honestly don't remember. Big lad: big boned, heavily built, maybe a bit on the plump side. I'd say he had a weight problem when he got older. He had a big personality too. Not bullish or aggressive or anything, he wasn't like that, not at all. I used to hear him laughing in the next room. He used to always buy a newspaper every day, one of the tabloids, I don't know which one. The other people in the office used to say to him, 'How can you read that rubbish, that rag?' But then when he left it sitting around they'd pick it up and read it. And that drove him mad. I mean not really angry, he wasn't that kind of person, it was just he didn't like double standards. If they hadn't criticised the paper and then asked for it he'd have given it to them. There'd have been no problem. He was straight, you know? There was no side to him.

What else? His father was in the guards. I think he had a sister. He told me once that the thing he hated more than anything else was wearing brand new shoes and that if ever he was a millionaire he'd find someone with the same size feet as himself and pay them good money, just to break in his shoes. That would be their job. He told me his grandmother said she'd once seen a ghost but he thought she was making it up. I'm sure he's forgotten me. I'm sure he'd be amazed if he knew this total stranger remembered all these little things about him.

And then after a month he went away again. I don't remember his leaving, just as I don't recall the day he arrived. To be honest with you, I don't think it bothered me greatly at the time. I've probably given the impression that we were close but we weren't. We weren't at all. That's the point.

My own father was a brute; he terrorised the whole family. I left home as soon as I could and swore I'd never have anything to do with men ever again. When I was twenty I was so – well, damaged is the only word for it, I suppose – that I wasn't ready or able to learn the things this other man was teaching me without his even knowing he was doing it. That not all men were like my father. That there were decent, good men in the world too.

*One last thing: he was mad about fishing, this fellow. He
didn't like being in Dublin, couldn't wait to get back down
to the lakes again. One day when I came back after lunch he
told me he'd bought some fishing flies, and he showed them
to me. That's my clearest memory of him: of the palm of
his hand spread open, and lying on it all these little hooks
with their coloured feathers, and him naming them for
me. Claret Bumble. Sooty Olive. Black Pennell.
Jacob's Ladder.*

The effect of this was so powerful that for a few moments
Roderic didn't know what to say. 'What gave you the idea?'
he asked eventually.

'I read something a while back that spoke of "the fragility
of human relationships" and I immediately thought, No, that
isn't true. Or at least, it isn't quite that. What's extraordinary
is how fragile and yet enduring they can be at the same
time. I mean, look at my parents, what happened there
and the effect it has upon my father to this day. Then I
decided to explore the whole idea further. I'm not looking at
families – siblings, parents and children – because I was more
intrigued by the idea of people who started out as strangers
to each other. It's not just a question of how close you can
ultimately get to someone, it's also whether or not, having
been close, or even having been somehow connected at all,
you can ever really get away again.'

'That's a good way of putting it.'

'What do you think it is that makes the difference?' she
asked.

He replied without a moment's hesitation, 'Children. Once
you have children with someone you're linked to them for
the rest of your days.'

Julia was silent and then she said again that he could
borrow the book if he wished, that he could hold on to it for
as long as he pleased. Roderic looked at her, trying to work
out what was in her mind. 'I don't know what's at the back

of all this and I don't particularly want to know, but I'll tell you one thing: he's not worth it.'

'Who?' she said. 'Max?' But she did smile.

Before he left that night he offered to take her to lunch on Saturday. They clattered down the stairs together and when she opened the front door they saw at once that the moon was full. When she went back upstairs she crossed to the window and stood for some time looking out. On a night such as this it was easy to see why ancient peoples had worshipped the moon. A veil of mist gave it the quality of opal, yet still its light was considerable, enough to cast shadows. Her father would have gone outside to admire it. She imagined him standing alone at the gable of the house at the edge of the silent orchard, the compass of his world lit by this cool benevolent light. Her father! He had said he was coming to Dublin in September: he would be here this weekend. She should have remembered that when Roderic suggested lunch. Frowning, she wondered how she might square these two things but then her thoughts drifted away again and she fell into a kind of reverie.

She remembered a mysterious thing that had happened concerning the moon around the time she met Roderic, now more than a year ago. She had never spoken to him, nor indeed to anyone, about it because it had been an experience so strange that even now she found it difficult to say exactly what it was that had happened. Wandering the streets aimlessly, on that day too a kind of trance had fallen over her. Her gaze intensified until she felt she was completely entering into the life of the things she saw. She stopped outside a baker's window full of doughnuts bristling with sugar, and split crusty loaves, ordinary things in themselves but the quality of their reality was different today, as though they had always existed and could never now not be. Turning away she glanced up and noticed the moon, a little sphere of white bone in the daytime sky, insignificant and unremarkable. But it *was* the moon and to see it was to be reminded of what the world was. It was to be made aware that the earth she stood on was also a globe suspended in the darkness of space.

How busy it was in town today! She drifted to the edge of the pavement and the crowd thickened about her, waiting until the lit red figure would change to green. Then the traffic stopped and the people surged forward but still she stood there, jostled, lost, until the lights changed again. The state of heightened perception was still upon her. Once again the traffic drove past and a crowd began to gather, waiting to cross the road where she stood. She was aware of everything around her, the clear eyes of a small child carried in a papoose level with her face, the texture of an old woman's skin, the chipped paint around the button for the lights. All the noises of the city, traffic, voices, a siren and above it all the sky's blandness. And then it happened: whatever *it* was. All the noise died away, all movement abated, as if the world were slowing down on its axis, as if time itself were being held in suspension. And now, even as she stood at the heart of the city, she stood at the centre of complete stillness and silence. It was, she thought afterwards, as though she had somehow moved behind the sky. It was as if she were not just participating in the present moment – this one, here, now – but watching it from a great distance in both time and space. Everything around her no longer existed, had ended thousands of years ago. What she saw was an ancient shadow; the relentless immensity of the city was no more than a spark. Something had permitted her to glimpse behind reality. And then her consciousness broke. She was once more absorbed into the temporal world, its noise, its convincing solidity. The light changed to green but she didn't want to cross the road. She turned away and was carried off up the street, became lost in the crowd.

Chapter Thirty-One

The door of the building was ajar when he arrived so he pushed it open and went in. A small fair-haired woman in dungarees was in the poorly lit hallway, about to enter a door from which music came. Mozart: the clarinet concerto. The woman looked him over, taking in his briefcase, his shirt and his blue silk tie, his impeccably polished shoes.

'Can I help you?' she asked.

'I'm here to see Roderic Kennedy.'

She looked at his face more keenly now, and then she said, 'Of course you are. You're Dennis, aren't you?' He nodded and she knocked sharply on the door beside her own. 'Roderic! It's your brother. I'd go on in if I were you,' she said. 'I'll be in myself in a minute.'

Dennis rarely called to Roderic's studio and never without being asked. Roderic, dressed in a check shirt and a pair of jeans heavily encrusted with paint, was slumped on an old sofa, smoking a cigarette. He looked exhausted. The startling energy of the paintings that surrounded him, strong, rigorous works executed in pale colours, contrasted uneasily with the silent lassitude of the man who had made them. The smell of paint was overpowering.

'Dennis.'

'Roderic.'

He moved to make room on the sofa but Dennis was already reaching for a hard kitchen chair from beside a table covered with art materials.

'Mind you don't spoil your jacket: check there's no paint on that chair before you sit down.' He offered Dennis a cigarette which was politely refused.

'So, how's it going?'

In response Roderic waved his hand to indicate the paintings. Dennis nodded, not knowing what to say.

'Good of you to come over at such short notice,' Roderic said, staring at the ceiling.

'That's all right. I have a long lunch break today.'

'I do appreciate it, though,' and he looked at Dennis directly now, then looked away. They could still hear the Mozart from the next room.

'Does that bother you when you're working?'

'Not in the least. I like it. If I could get my act together I'd have music of my own.'

Had he been drinking? He seemed fairly lucid if somewhat depressed, but it was difficult to know. There was no evidence of bottles or glasses around, but that meant nothing.

'In fact, I'm particularly fond of music when it's on the other side of a wall. It reminds me of my childhood, when you or Dad used to play records down in the drawing room, late at night. I'd lie in bed listening until I fell asleep. Did you know that? It's one of the few things I actively like to remember from those years.'

Before Dennis could answer the door of the studio opened again, pushed by the weight of the small woman's body, for her hands were not free. She was carrying a tray with two mugs and a plate of sandwiches. Roderic looked faintly annoyed.

'Really, Maria, there's no need for this . . .'

She ignored him and set the tray on the only remaining space on the table. 'It's chicken and vegetable,' she said handing a mug to Dennis. 'You're not a vegetarian?'

He shook his head, but still demurred: he didn't really want the soup or any of the shapeless sandwiches on the plate. Maria wasn't having any of this: she stood before him holding out the mug, and gave him a look of unexpected ferocity. Suddenly Dennis made the connection. 'Thanks,' he said. 'I wouldn't get any lunch otherwise. Roderic, come on, won't you join me?'

With a slightly grudging air Roderic helped himself to a sandwich.

'There's bloody gratitude for you,' Maria said. 'Don't forget, it's your turn tomorrow. Bring the tray back when you've finished.' She refused to bring her own food in to eat with them and returned to her studio.

'Do you have lunch together every day?'

'Two, maybe three times a week, no more than that,' Roderic said. 'She's a decent skin, Maria.'

It was a couple of weeks since they had seen each other and they now fell into conversation, cautious at first but gradually more relaxed as they continued with their meal. Roderic ate hungrily, as if he needed the food. 'These sandwiches are better than they look.'

The moment came when Dennis felt he could ask, 'Have you heard from Italy recently?'

Roderic shook his head. 'Have you?'

'Mmn.'

'You have? What news is there? Are they well? Nothing's wrong, is it?'

'Everything's fine,' Dennis said. 'The girls sent me a card for my birthday, that's all. Serena's got the brace off her teeth, that's the only news.'

'And she's all right? I mean, it worked? It did straighten her teeth?'

'The card didn't say, but I expect so. Braces always work, I think.' Roderic's anxiety about this would have been funny had it not been so desperately sad. Dennis suddenly remembered his own experience on the night of Roderic's wedding and realised with a pang that this desolation had been his brother's whole life now, for years and years.

'Anyhow, to business. The painting: which one is it?'

Roderic stood up and crossed the room. He lifted a canvas that was leaning against the wall and without speaking, propped it against the table directly in front of his brother, then stood back and lit a cigarette. Dennis stared at the picture and frowned. It was all a charade, but he had to go through with it.

It had been after eleven the previous evening when Roderic rang. He engaged his brother in drunken, rambling small talk that didn't fool Dennis for an instant. Weary from a hard day at work – he had actually been half-way up the stairs on his way to bed when the phone rang – Dennis gave him short answers and did not follow up any of his conversational leads, hoping to force him to the point, until eventually Roderic blurted out: 'Would you like to buy a painting?'

Dennis closed his eyes and leaned his forehead against the jamb of the door, fighting the temptation to say, 'Look, I'm too busy to bother with this now, just tell me how much you need and I'll write you a cheque, we can sort out the details later, all right?'

'Dennis? Dennis? You're still there? Hello?'

'Yes, still here,' he said, opening his eyes, staring at his own reflection in the hall mirror. 'Certainly I'd be interested in having a look at a picture.'

'Tomorrow be all right?' Roderic said quickly. 'Could you come over to the studio around lunch time?'

Dennis closed his eyes again and kept them shut as he replied, 'I could indeed.'

'Thanks, Dennis, you're a star.'

'No you're not,' Dennis said aloud in the empty house to his own reflection after he had hung up. 'You're a complete mug.'

The painting wasn't as big as he had feared, and he hoped now that he was giving a convincing impression of assessing its artistic merits as he stared at it. In reality he was trying to guess how much he might be asked to pay. From having bought pictures from Roderic in the past, he had a very rough idea of prices, and from the size of this one he thought it unlikely that it would be more than he could afford. Out of the corner of his eye he sneaked a glance at Roderic, who was staring intently at the picture. He must be desperate for the money, or he wouldn't ask. He had only done this to Dennis a few times before.

'What have you on it?' Dennis said eventually.

Roderic named his price. It was a figure far lower than his brother had expected and Dennis was unable to conceal his surprise. Misreading his reaction, Roderic immediately protested, 'It's a reasonable price for a picture of that quality and those dimensions, believe me. You'd be getting a bargain.'

'Oh, I can believe it,' Dennis said. They fell to looking at the picture again. 'Is it a recent work?'

'I finished it about six months ago.'

'I don't know where I'll put it in the house. I'll try it out in a couple of different places, see where it fits best.' In this subtle way he gave his consent and even though he wasn't looking at Roderic as he spoke, he could actually feel his brother's relief permeate the studio.

'I'll get it over to you this weekend,' Roderic said, and waved aside Dennis's suggestion that he might collect it himself.

Now that the deal was done, Dennis could actually see the picture in itself. It was a square canvas on which bars of cream, grey and pale blue paint radiated calm. Perhaps he would hang it at the head of the stairs; there was a suitable space there. He *was* getting a bargain. Whether he wanted it or not was another question altogether. He wondered how many other paintings Roderic had sold for a song to raise some quick money.

'Are you still with the same gallery?'

Roderic's face darkened. 'We had a falling out,' he said. 'The man was a spiv. Anyway, I like to see to my own affairs.'

While they were eating lunch Dennis had covertly looked around the studio trying to guess which of the many canvases would be offered to him for purchase. He had noted a particularly small one, and he nodded towards it now as he

329

pulled his chequebook out of his jacket pocket. 'And how much are you asking for that?' he said.

Roderic looked surprised. 'I don't really know,' he said. 'I hadn't thought to sell it.' Dennis started to fill in the cheque, giving Roderic time to consider his suggestion. He could see how torn his brother was between the desire to have more money and the need to hold on to the picture.

'I'm sorry, Dennis,' he said eventually. 'I'm not ready to let that one go yet.'

'Well, keep me in mind when the time comes,' Dennis replied, completing the cheque and handing it over to him. 'I'd best be off. I'll talk to you towards the end of the week.'

When he went into the hall he noticed that the door of Maria's studio was still ajar. She was listening to Beethoven now, the late quartets. For a moment he stood there in the dim hall, that stank of paint and packet soup, listening to the sublime music. An immense grief about Roderic's life welled up in him. Cautiously he tapped on the open door.

'I wanted to thank you for lunch.'

'Pan bread and plastic ham: big deal,' she said. 'I'm sure you're used to better. Do you want to come in for a minute?'

He was struck at the difference between Roderic's studio and Maria's. Here the predominating colours were darker – bottle green, purple, claret, black. Maria was sitting at the table cutting five-pointed stars out of an Ordnance Survey map. Within ten minutes he would be back in his office at the bank, with its magnolia paint and its grey filing cabinets, its water cooler and glowing computer screen. He was still at a loss to understand how he and Roderic starting out from the same point in the same family had ended up with such different lives.

'I hope you don't mind me asking,' he said. 'How is Roderic these days?' She raised her right index finger to her pursed lips, with her other hand she pointed towards the door. They sat without speaking and listened to the sound of the door of Roderic's studio being slammed, the rattle of keys as he locked it, and then his footsteps as he walked down the hall and left the building. Maria did not speak for some moments after this, clearly trying to gauge how much Dennis already knew, and how much she ought to say. 'Had the bottle and glass been cleared away in my honour before I arrived?'

'I doubt it,' she said. 'They probably hadn't come out yet for the day. He usually doesn't start drinking until late in the afternoon. That's why I try to encourage him to have something to eat with me now and then. Get a bit of ballast before he starts hitting the bottle, you know. He'll buy us both chips tomorrow, or pizza, and I won't have to remind him. He's very proud and you have to respect that. He gets the work done too, Roderic. It annoys me sometimes when people talk as if he's completely undisciplined, for he's producing more than a lot of people who are stone cold sober every day of their lives. And that's not considering the quality of the work. He's a superb painter, your brother.'

Everything she said comforted him. 'Things obviously look worse from where I'm standing.'

Maria struggled in her mind as to how to let him down gently and decided it couldn't be done. 'Oh they're bad all right, Dennis,' she said, 'as bad as can be.'

He saw Roderic more often than she imagined, and there was little in the litany of misery she now described that was new to him. It was only the detail: he hadn't known whether Roderic drank in pubs with others or alone in the studio, and Maria told him it was almost exclusively the latter. Even though her descriptions were understated, he saw vividly the picture she described of Roderic settling down to drink at the end of the day until he was too far gone to leave the studio. He would sometimes stay the night there. 'He sleeps on the sofa. I occasionally throw a rug on him before I go home. I'll tell you this though for nothing,' she added. 'If he got that Jeannie woman out of his life he'd be doing himself a favour, for they're only dragging each other down. She's a bloody nuisance. Every time she comes round here they quarrel; I can hear them sometimes even over the music. But generally he's not at all aggressive. He's a really nice man, Roderic, when he's not on the tear.'

'Does he ever talk about his family?'

'He often talks about you,' she said. 'He sings your praises: he thinks you're the bee's knees.'

'And the others?'

She thought for a moment. 'Almost never. A few weeks back I was talking to him about families in general – well, about my family in particular, to tell you the truth – and he said he knew his parents and sisters thought that he was a complete failure.'

Only last week, Dennis had had a row with Maeve over her casual remark, 'The only consolation is that poor Mum and Dad didn't live to see Roderic's life go down the drain in this way.' Dennis had responded with more truth than charity, saying that her own life was not exactly a shining success.

'Does he ever speak of any other family members?' he asked cautiously.

'I know he has kids off in Italy, if that's what you're getting at, but no, he hardly ever talks of them. I think it's more than he can bear.'

From his briefcase Dennis took out a small leather folder. 'You have all my numbers here,' he said as he handed her his business card, 'home, office and mobile. Never hesitate to call me if the need arises, at any time of the day or night.'

She took the card, then said, 'Wait a moment.' She crossed to the table, wrote something on a square of yellow paper and passed it to him. 'If it's all getting you down too much and you need to talk to someone about it, call me. And again, don't hesitate: day or night. There are some things you shouldn't have to go through on your own.' Touched by her kindness, Dennis was for a moment at a loss to know what to say.

332

'I don't know where it'll end. Sometimes I think he's killing himself.' He was amazed to hear himself blurt out something that he had hesitated until now to admit even in his own mind.

Maria did not respond directly to this remark. Instead she said, 'Let me tell you, Dennis, someone very close to me, his father was a hell of a drinker and so I've seen at first hand the toll it takes on family members. There's only so much you can do and most times it makes no difference anyway. So you look out for yourself, d'you hear me? You look out for yourself. You'd best be off to your office, or you'll be late. And I meant what I said: call me if you need me.'

Chapter Thirty-Two

Just outside the pub, someone offered Roderic a flier for a mobile phone company which he unthinkingly took and stuffed into his pocket, wondering if the poor sap knew how ridiculous he looked. The man was actually dressed as a mobile phone, encased from ankle to head in an absurd rectangle of foam rubber from which his face stared forlornly above a console of numbers. The costume restricted his movements so that he was like a spancelled goat and could barely hobble towards the passers-by to offer them his leaflets, which in general were spurned.

He went into the pub and sat down. It was a place Julia liked, which was why he had suggested it for today. It was also a place of which Dennis was fond and it was there that the coincidental meeting of all three of them had taken place earlier in the year. Ever since then he had been more careful to arrange appointments so that there was no danger of an overlap. Holding a beermat between finger and thumb, he turned it over and over again on its edge and thought meditatively about his brother. He'd made real progress in his struggle to become less dependent on Dennis – not asking him to do little favours, to mediate between him and other family members and so forth. It had been a hard habit to break, but sometimes he thought it had been harder still for Dennis, who hadn't quite yet come to terms with no longer being needed as he once had been. Just at that Julia came into the pub in the company of a middle-aged man, rather stocky, who was carrying a plastic bag from a bookshop. Roderic couldn't imagine who he might be, foolishly so, he realised almost immediately: he should have recognised him from the photograph on her mantelpiece of the kite-flier. For when

Julia said, 'Roderic, I want you to meet my father,' he saw at once that it could be no one else.

'I didn't want to muscle in,' Dan said by way of introduction. 'Julia told me she had this arranged with you so I said I'd see her later in the day, but she wouldn't hear tell of it.'

'She did well.'

'Did you see your man outside?' he went on as they settled themselves. 'The poor fella with the leaflets? Did you ever see worse? It's not enough for him to have a rotten job, they have to dress him up like a fool to do it, make a laughing stock of him in front of the entire city. They'd have us believe that we're all on the pig's back now. And then they're always going on about choice,' he said. 'About freedom. Here's the choice your man had: sit on the dole, or take a job that makes him look like a total arse. Where's the choice in that, you tell me? Where's the freedom?'

Just at that moment a waitress came to their table. They ordered salmon salads and Dan asked for a pint of Guinness. The young woman, who was clearly not Irish, had some difficulty in understanding what was being said and hesitantly asked Julia again what she wanted to drink. She scribbled it all down, forced a smile for them, then stripped a carbon copy of their order from the notepad and wedged it between the salt and pepper. 'I wonder what part of the world she's from?' Dan said after she had gone. 'The country's full of foreigners these days, and I'd say plenty of them are having a hard time of it.'

Suddenly Dan turned to Roderic with the same frank, steady gaze that Roderic found so attractive in Julia, and so disconcerting in her father. 'I believe you lived abroad for a good few years. Julia tells me you used to live in Italy.'

'I did, yes.'

'So, will you tell me this,' he said, with his gaze still fixed on him, 'for this is something that interests me, and a thing I'd like to know. Were you ever in Pompeii?'

This was so far from what Roderic had been expecting that for a moment he was at a loss as to what to say. He simply nodded.

'And Herculaneum. What about that? Have you been there?'

Roderic said that he hadn't.

'Because people say that it's even more interesting than Pompeii, and I'd have been interested to have your opinion.'

'You're planning to go there someday, aren't you?' Julia said.

'I hope so, if I can ever get the money together and get myself organised. It would have to be a package thing, Rome and Pompeii, you know. I don't think I'd be able to manage it on my own, what with the language. The language and the money. That reminds me,' and he reached for his plastic bag, 'I'm after buying a good book, let me show it to you,' but just at that moment the waitress returned with their salads.

'Seeing as how you're so interested in history,' Roderic said as they ate, 'perhaps when you retire you might think to study history, to do a degree.'

'Me!' Dan said. 'At a university? Sure I have no education worth talking about. They'd never let me in.'

'They don't always require formal qualifications for mature students,' Julia argued 'and in any case, you know far more about history already than any student coming in with a Leaving Certificate.'

Still he wasn't convinced. 'I don't know. I'm not sure that the way they go about things there would suit me. I have my own way of seeing things.' Abruptly he put down his knife and fork. 'We know nothing,' he said. 'We like to think we know it all, but the half of it we're making up. Just imagine if in a thousand years' time, people were trying to know about us: what life was like in Dublin now. Who we were and what we were. What we believed and what we wanted. And all they had to help them work it out was Glasnevin Cemetery,

336

a few bits of jewellery, bracelets and earrings, and what they could dig up of the Naas dual carriageway. Can you imagine what'd you'd come up with? Can you *imagine*?'

Julia said it was the same with painting: that the artists of the past would be amazed if they could see what had happened to their work: altarpieces taken out of churches and broken up, the central image displayed in Washington, the right panel in Berlin, the predella in London. What would they have thought to see these religious images displayed in blank white rooms beside court portraits, beside images that to them would have been wholly profane?

'You're a painter too, aren't you?' Dan said. 'I don't understand art.' It was not a critical or defensive remark, he was simply stating a fact. 'Not just the new stuff, you know, but any of it. It doesn't speak to me, I don't know why. I've tried, haven't I?' This last was addressed to Julia, who smiled ironically at him and nodded. He returned then to the subject of the man whom he had seen handing out leaflets. 'If he's still there when we go out, I'm going to say something to him. I'm going to ask him would he not think to learn a trade. Plumber or a sparks, something like that. Something real. With a trade you can even work for yourself. No boss. Or rather, you're your own boss. Do you see what I mean? You plumb in a washing machine or you rewire a house, or, like me say, you fit a new exhaust system, and you've done something. You can point to it and you can say, I did that. Not like handing out leaflets. Handing out leaflets is no job for anybody. I'm going to tell him so.'

Roderic could see Julia was silently hoping that the human phone would have tottered off to another street by the time they had finished their lunch. He might not take kindly to Dan's impromptu career advice, no matter how well intentioned or reasonably presented.

'Did you see the moon the other night?' Dan suddenly asked.

'We did,' said Julia. 'I thought of you.'

337

'I saw it coming up low from the horizon, a big golden moon. Huge, it was, and there was silence all over the valley. There was no wind, nothing, not so much as the sound of a bird singing. Only silence, and silence and silence, and then this big golden thing, the moon. Ah, that was something,' he said, and he sat for a moment, remembering it. 'That was something worth seeing.'

Roderic was aware that in spite of all the warmth and good will of the occasion, he and Dan were not breaking through to each other on any significant level. He thought of things that Julia had told him about her father, about his bouts of headlong drinking after the death of his wife. It was something with which Roderic could identify although he knew it was not an experience about which either of them would ever wish to speak to the other.

'You must come down and visit us in Wicklow,' Dan said. 'Bring him with you some weekend when you're coming, Julia.'

Was there not in that steady gaze an element of cold assessment, or was he simply reading in the other man something that he felt he would certainly be guilty of in the same circumstances?

They finished their meal. The waitress came back to take away their plates and they ordered tea.

'I have to show you my book now,' Dan said, putting on his glasses. He took a thick volume out of the plastic bag and opened it at random. 'It's an encyclopaedia of Irish history and it's full of great stuff. Listen now; listen till you hear this. "Time,"' he read. '"In Ireland, as elsewhere, the standardisation of time was primarily a response to the exigencies of the railway timetable. Before that nearly every community had its own time. Clocks in Cork were eleven minutes behind those in Dublin, while those in Belfast were one minute and nineteen seconds ahead." Did you ever hear the like of that?' he said, looking at them over the top of his glasses. 'Doesn't that beat all?'

338

'Oh, Daddy,' Julia said, laughing.

'"It was not until Greenwich Mean Time was extended to the whole of Ireland, in 1916, that the Albert Clock stopped showing Belfast time." I think that's remarkable.' he said, leafing through the pages. 'Remarkable. Or what about this: "Haymaking was probably introduced to Ireland by the Normans." Did you know that?'

'What will you do this afternoon?' Julia said. 'Will you go to the museum?'

'Ah no. I don't go there every time I come up to Dublin.'

'You used to. Do you remember? We used to go there.' And they fell to talking of how he used to bring her as a child, in the hope that the gold torcs, the wooden canoe and the delicate fringe of Bronze Age horsehair would inspire her to share his love of history.

'And I hated it,' she said in delight, '*hated* it,' as her father chuckled.

In his mind's eye, Roderic could see them as they passed under the dome of the museum's entrance hall, Dan pausing by the glass cases as he peered at the artefacts and their printed labels, while the small, wild-haired child Julia had once been fretted and grizzled mildly beside him.

'Those axe-heads!' Julia said. 'Hundreds of them, it seemed to me. All those pots and guns! The only thing in the museum that caught my imagination was the biscuit, the prison biscuit. That's children, you see: they can't grasp the significance of a stone head, two thousand years old, but a biscuit older than your father, now that really is interesting.'

'And all you wanted,' Dan said, 'was to go around the corner to the gallery, to look at the pictures. The painting of the parrots. You liked that.'

'The parrots, yes,' she agreed. 'The Goose Girl, and Jack Yeats' horse, that looked to me as though it was made of glass.'

339

'And that one of the mountains in the west, the blue mountains. It's gone now, you know,' he added. 'The biscuit.'

'Where to?' Julia replied. 'Don't tell me they've thrown it out. They can't have done. They shouldn't have. It's a part of our heritage.'

'It probably went mouldy in the end,' Dan said. 'Nothing lasts for ever.'

His whole life, Roderic thought, had been a kind of desperate flight from the middle class into which he had been born. He had believed, especially in recent years, that he had indeed succeeded, that he had managed to escape. But if that was the case why was it that today, faced with Dan Fitzpatrick – who was quietly drinking his tea, who wanted to go to Pompeii but who had heard that Herculaneum was possibly more interesting, who thought that handing out leaflets was no kind of job for anyone, who had single-handedly brought up his daughter to be a beautiful and remarkable woman, who didn't believe that he would ever be permitted to enrol at a university, and who had, in any case, his own way of seeing things, who was simply and utterly and completely himself – why was it that, faced with Dan Fitzpatrick, Roderic had never before felt so deeply conventional?

A silence fell over them now and annealed around them, that neither man had the will to break until Julia at last said, 'Should we ask for the bill?'

Dan finally yielded to Roderic's insistent offer that he would pay, but he took out his wallet anyway, to show them something. 'A man in a pub,' he said, 'gave me this.'

He unfolded a yellowing paper, a receipt from a shop, Sweenys Haberdashery and General Merchants, and the date in perfect copperplate, *14th April 1900*.

Out in the street the weekly market is taking place. She can hear the men's voices, the sound of switches on the flanks of the animals, their lowings, the stately click of their hooves. Spring and winter struggle for the upper hand: white blossom streams from a tree at the window. She watches the mark her pen makes. The slit in the nib opens gently under the pressure of her hand; the downstroke is thick, the slanted upstroke fine as a hair. *One pair of man's boots,* she writes. *One tin of ox-blood boot polish. One pair of laces.* Then the wind blows the clouds away from the sun. Sudden light pours into the shop and the woman looks up to find her whole world translated. Brass pins; spools of black waxed thread; cards of buttons, gilt and bone and mother-of-pearl: each one of these quotidian things is now separate and distinct. It is as if she had never seen them before now; it is as if each one of them is speaking to her, pleading with her out of its own reality. It is a gift. The light races over the walls. The clouds cover the sun again and she is back in the familiar shadows, the dimness, plunged back into her element of time.

And Dan wondered aloud if the docket that the waitress now presented to them:

> Salmon salad × 3
> pt Guinness × 1
> pt Smithwicks × 1
> Ballygowan × 1
> Tea × 3
> Helena served you today
> Thank you

and the date, all printed faintly in purple ink – he wondered if eventually it might seem as poignant as the faded paper, that he folded now and replaced in his wallet, when this day too was history.

Chapter Thirty-Three

During the time that he was in hospital Roderic became fixated upon the young woman who gave the weather forecast after the news. Television was in itself a novelty for him: he hadn't had one since moving back to Ireland and much about it surprised him. In his occasional flashes of lucidity he was struck by how passive an activity it was for someone like himself who, until recently, had spent most of his waking hours in a conscious and active struggle to translate the vision in his mind on to paper or canvas. As an occupation for himself and his present companions in misfortune it was eminently suitable, but from time to time he would be amazed to think that this was how many people who had absolutely nothing wrong with them habitually passed hours of their time. He could cope only with the most anodyne of material. He watched polar bears break out of their snowy winter holts in the spring, watched a chef expertly bone a chicken and a gardener pruning fruit trees. He didn't like the news and would therefore lurk just outside the day room until he heard the music that announced the end of the bulletin, and then he would go in to see the weather report.

'Well, hello! I'm afraid I can't promise you any sunshine today; not until the end of the week in fact . . .' Roderic studied her intently, marvelling at the way she could smile and talk simultaneously. Yesterday she had been wearing a shell pink dress and a pearl necklace; today she was wearing a yellow suit and gold clip earrings. Who was she? He speculated at length on her family situation. Did she have supportive siblings? 'Over central England and East Anglia those storms will ease off as the day progresses . . .' Were her parents proud of her because she was on television or disappointed because she wasn't doing something more exciting with her life, because she wasn't an actress or a newsreader? It was hard to believe that away from her maps she actually had a life, perhaps even a chaotic and unhappy life like his own. Maybe her father was an alcoholic and she lay awake at night grieving for him, or worrying that some day the tabloids would find out and tell everyone: *Weather Girl Dad's Drunken Shame*. As though the shame was hers, rather than all his own. 'And so, then, to sum up . . .' Computerised clouds appeared and disappeared on the map behind her; neat, virtual rain fell from them. 'That's all from me for now, I'll be back after the lunch-time bulletin with an update. Until then, enjoy the rest of your day.'

She said these last six words in a husky, slightly pleading voice, as though requesting some sexual favour. Seeing that it was evidently so important to her, Roderic promised silently in his heart that he would indeed try to enjoy the rest of his day; although looking around the day room at his fellow patients, he knew he was going to have his work cut out for him.

He realised now that he was still holding the uncompleted menu card he had been given earlier.

'Mark? Have you decided what you're having for lunch?'

'Roast chicken with boiled potatoes, carrots and beans, then almond pudding and custard.'

As he listed the food Roderic surreptitiously checked off the same items on his own card. He found it impossible to make decisions these days even about something as trivial as this. He didn't like almond pudding, but it seemed simpler to order it and then not bother to eat it than to make an active decision about some other dessert. Mark had been in hospital for far longer than Roderic and was completely institutionalised, but he also had a slightly higher degree of energy than many of the other patients. Looking at his fellow sufferers, it was their listlessness rather than their sorrow that profoundly struck him. He gravitated to Mark whenever possible to try to tap into his energy, asking him now, 'What are you going to do for the rest of the day?'

'After the doctor's been round I'm going to read, then this afternoon I have an art class. It's good, that. Would you like to see my paintings?'

Roderic understood that this meant he wanted to show them to him. 'I'd love to see them,' he lied. Mark went off to fetch his folder as Roderic mentally prepared himself to praise a few clumsy watercolours of bowls of fruit, a few stiff landscapes or studies of roses.

The first picture was of a hunted-looking face staring through a mesh of heavy black bars. 'That's me,' Mark said, unnecessarily. The next page showed the same fraught, tormented face, this time against a background of arrows and spears. Slowly and wordlessly the two men looked through the batch of pictures, in which all of Mark's psychic trauma was figured forth with crude power and terrible pathos. Roderic thought of his own work and of what a disaster it would have been for him had he ever allowed his art to have this function: to become self-expressive and to serve him, rather than he serving his art. Although he had done little painting in recent months, and none at all in the past few weeks, he had at least been true to it until the end. He thought of his painting as though it were a flame, a fragile lit thing that he had guarded with his life, all his life. Entrusted to him, he had succeeded in keeping it from being extinguished in spite of the winds and storms through which he had carried it; in return, down through the years it had afforded him a subtle and complex joy. Although much of his inner life – his losses, grief and self-doubt – made its way into his work, it did so in such a manner as to be translated into something distanced and controlled, something formal and impersonal. That Mark was engaged with painting in a wholly different way was right for him, but in displaying his work he didn't realise that he was showing Roderic an abyss.

And for Roderic, to fall into this particular abyss would have been the worst thing of all.

He was at something of a loss as to know what to say to Mark, who was studying his own paintings with fierce intensity.

'Powerful work,' he murmured eventually.

'Thanks. It's good, the art class,' Mark said again. 'The teacher's nice. You should think to register for it.'

'Oh, no, no, no, no, no,' Roderic exclaimed, impressing himself as well as Mark with the force of his own refusal.

'Suit yourself. But you never know what you can do until you try. You should have a go at painting. You might surprise yourself.'

Not half as much as I'd surprise everyone else, thought Roderic, who had so far succeeded in keeping his unusual vocation a secret from his fellow patients. He would tell Dennis about this when he came in later. Perhaps it would amuse him and Roderic was grateful to have something funny, something lighthearted to share with him. Dennis was bound to come: he hadn't missed a single day so far.

'Are you expecting visitors later?'

'Don't know,' Mark replied, as he put away his work. 'Last time she was in, do you know what the missus said to me? She said, "What ever happened that you ended up in a place like this?" Ended up! *Ended up!* So I told her that if that was all she had to say she might as well stop at home.'

Roderic clicked his tongue sympathetically, although privately he thought Mark's wife's question a fair one. It was a question he had silently asked himself time without number since his admission to hospital.

He went back to the ward. On the locker beside his bed was a vase of pink carnations together with a card showing a rabbit in a straw hat. Both were from Maeve, and Roderic had been touched and surprised to receive them. If his family in Italy knew what had happened, he wondered, would they also be supportive and conciliatory? For now he absolutely didn't want them to know where he was and had made Dennis promise not to tell. He would write to them himself about it, although he suspected that it might yet be a long time before he was ready to do so. Just as he was thinking this, Dr Cullen came in. He greeted Roderic, unhooked the chart from the end of the bed and began to study it.

It was usually either Dr Sullivan who saw him or Dr Cullen. One of them was gentle and kind, the other distant and brusque, and Roderic asked himself if this was a deliberate policy on the part of the hospital: one to soften him up and the other to put the boot in when necessary. Even in his distressed state he could see that Dr Sullivan was a most remarkable person. He was an elderly man with a slightly weary air, as well he might be given the things he had heard and witnessed in the course of his working life. He knew the mind's limits and what lay beyond, he knew all the darkest corners of the human heart, but it had not made him despair. Instead he radiated compassion, grounded in deep moral experience.

When Roderic spoke about having lived in Italy, he laughed and looked at his hands. 'Let me tell you something foolish,' he said. All his life, ever since he was a child, he had wanted to go to Venice. 'And yet for one reason or another, it never happened. It didn't seem like the most obvious destination when the children were small, and the time just never seemed right. Then in due course it became somewhere to think about rather than to go, do you understand?' He laughed again and looked embarrassed. 'You know, after a particularly hard day in here' (and Roderic could picture the reality behind this euphemism) 'I'd go home and sit down and close my eyes and imagine I was there. On a balcony looking out over the lagoon, watching all the lights come on at dusk; listening to the sound of the water lapping against the building. It was enough.' And then, he said, three things that he had never expected happened. First, his children bought his wife and himself a trip to Venice to celebrate their thirtieth wedding anniversary. Second, he realised that he didn't want to go. 'But what could I do? How could I explain it to the children? I didn't want to hurt their feelings and I couldn't explain to them that it was because I knew the reality would cancel out all I'd imagined. I felt sure I was going to be disappointed but there was nothing to be done. Off we went.'

'What was the third unexpected thing?' Roderic asked.

'We arrived in winter, at twilight. There was heavy fog; we took a boat in from the airport and then the city suddenly appeared before us. It looked as if it were constructed out of water and light. The third unexpected thing,' he said 'was this: that Venice didn't in fact disappoint me, it far surpassed my expectations. And never – *not once* – had this possibility crossed my mind.'

If ever anyone, Roderic thought, deserved an experience of sublime beauty to set against all they had seen and known in life, it was Dr Sullivan, whom he was to remember always with affection and gratitude.

Dr Cullen was a different proposition altogether.

Roderic was slightly afraid of him and found his brisk perfection intimidating. Even Dennis's life, he thought, would look messy and disorganised if set against the splendid rectitude of the doctor's, although he would have had little confidence in a doctor who appeared to have made as spectacularly bad a fist of his life as Roderic himself had. In recent days, this unease had hardened into a dislike he suspected was mutual. The problem was that they understood each other just that little bit too well. He had gone to school with boys like Dr Cullen. Now they were lawyers and businessmen and auctioneers, and he had long since lost touch with them. Dennis or even Roderic might well have turned out to be like this had Frank himself not been such a wild card. It was exactly this familiarity that made them uneasy with each other. Without anything ever being said, he suspected that the doctor had little respect for

347

his life as an artist and this, coupled with his charmless bedside manner, turned Roderic sullenly against him. As a small act of rebellion, he used to try to picture Dr Cullen propositioning a woman. This morning he was actually making some headway with this baroque feat of imagination when the doctor suddenly raised his head and looked Roderic straight in the eye.

'Anything in particular on your mind today?'

'Nothing. Nothing at all.'

'There's something I've been meaning to ask you,' the doctor said, replacing the chart. 'When you get out of hospital, where will you go? What are your circumstances?'

Roderic told him that he lived alone in a small flat but he didn't like it, and that after what had happened it had bad associations. He hoped to find a new place to live as part of the fresh start he was trying to make in his life, but until such time as he had something suitable he would move in with his brother.

'How many brothers have you?'

'Just the one.'

'So you mean the man I was talking to on Tuesday?'

'Dennis, yes.'

The doctor shook his head. 'You will never live with him again. Ever. Under no circumstances.'

Roderic felt as if he was on a high wire, as if he had looked down and seen that there was no net beneath him. For a moment he couldn't speak, then said hesitantly, 'Did Dennis say that to you? That he doesn't want me?'

'Of course he didn't. If he thought it was what you needed, or even just wanted, your brother would lie on the floor and let you wipe your feet on him.'

'I know that,' he replied, unwittingly giving Dr Cullen his cue.

'And don't you think that's disgraceful? Absolutely disgraceful?'

There was nothing Roderic could say.

'You nearly went over the edge the other day, but you don't seem to appreciate that you almost took Dennis with you. If you go on like this, you will. You have a lot of changes to make in your life, and one of the most important is that you have to wean yourself off your dependence on your brother. It's bad for you and it's bad for him. Have you got that?'

'Yes.'

'Good. Right, now about your medication . . .' He talked about tranquillisers and Roderic sat listening in silence, humbled and chastened. After the doctor had left him, he sat on the edge of the bed for some time, staring at the toes of his slippers. Then he lay down and closed his eyes.

Neither of the protagonists in the drama that was Roderic's collapse had full knowledge of what had happened. This was all for the best, as each of them could just about cope with the memory of the part they had played or witnessed. Roderic afterwards remembered elements of it with pin-sharp, almost cinematic clarity, as he did many of the key moments in his life: meeting Marta, the birth of his daughters, seeing Frank in his coffin. Other aspects of the days leading up to the breakdown remained mercifully vague.

About three weeks before the end he had a row with Jeannie. There was nothing new or remarkable in this, as quarrelling was their preferred means of communication The difference was that this time when she said she never wanted to see him again, she actually meant it. When he contacted her after the usual cooling-off period of a day or two, she again told him to get lost; and then again with renewed vehemence and threatened violence when he made subsequent attempts, at which point he got the message. It came as something of a shock to be dumped by Jeannie. Even though it had never been much of a relationship it had dragged on for years and he had always told himself that Jeannie needed him more than he needed her.

Dennis called at the studio unannounced one lunch time. Roderic couldn't remember his arriving; he just seemed to suddenly be there, staring balefully at the glass and whiskey bottle.

'Want some?'

'No thanks.'

'Suit yourself.'

The place was eerily silent: there was no music from the adjoining room.

'Maria isn't around?'

'Berlin,' Roderic said. 'Academic exchange. Be gone for two months. Dead quiet, isn't it? There's a new fellow in one of the studios upstairs but he's a real stuck-up so-and-so. Say "Good morning," to him and he'll barely deign to answer you.' (It was only when thinking about this weeks later in the hospital that it dawned on Roderic: the man had been simply terrified of the massive drunk on the ground floor.)

'How's the work going?'

'It isn't. You see the thing about art is this,' Roderic said, and he drew hard on his cigarette. 'You've got to have the vision and you've got to have the technique. Vision. And technique. You've got to have the vision and –'

'All right, all right, I get the message.'

'Sometimes I think I should paint and then sometimes I think I shouldn't. I don't know.' The point he was trying to make was that although not to paint depressed him, to paint badly and then to have to countenance the end result was even worse. He struggled to find a way to explain this lucidly. 'It all comes down to vision,' he said eventually. 'Vision and technique.'

His brother put his head in his hands. His departure was as mysterious as his arrival, suddenly he wasn't there any more. Roderic, noticing this, poured himself another drink. And then he also put his head in his hands.

In the days that followed he did stop painting. To look at the poor work he was producing – sickly smears of yellow paint set in lifeless bands of grey – to look at this had easily become the worst option. But stopping painting had the curious effect of also stopping time, or at least slowing it down to a point where it appeared to have stopped. He drank more than ever now in a bid to make the hands of the clock move forward. During the final weekend before the crisis broke he didn't go home at all but stayed in his studio drinking, sleeping, crying. He'd stayed there on many other occasions when he'd been too far gone to make it back to his flat, but this time was different. 'This is what it must be like to be dead,' he thought on the Saturday. He truly felt as if he had died but that his spirit was blocked from leaving his body so that, although his physical life went on, there was nothing else left, absolutely nothing. No one needed him any longer: not his children, not even Jeannie. He was nothing but a burden to Dennis. It would be better for all concerned if he were no longer there, if he could simply disappear. And yet even as he thought and realised all these things he did not feel them. The immobilising grief he experienced numbed him, cast over him a dark reverie that provided a final fragile defence. And then at last, on the Monday morning, that too gave way. A full realisation of all he had been going through, the implications of what he had been thinking, penetrated Roderic's consciousness. Within the week he would say to Dr Sullivan, 'It was the spiritual equivalent of waking up in the middle of open-heart surgery to realise that there was no anaesthetist.'

He was overcome by a sense of horror and could no longer bear to be on his own.

Forgetting that she wasn't there he went and hammered on the door of Maria's studio, shouting her name repeatedly, then ran out into the street and tried to hail a passing taxi. The taxi driver saw him first and decided, not unreasonably, that he didn't want a huge crazed drunk in his cab. Although he managed to grab hold of the door handle the driver pressed the button to secure the locks, swerved and then accelerated away, giving him the finger and almost driving over his foot. Roderic reeled back towards the pavement and as he did so he collided with a woman, almost knocked her down. 'Oh sorry! Sorry!' The woman shrank back from him, but he registered fully her revulsion, her fear. It knocked the heart out of him and he half collapsed, half sat down on the kerb to gather his resources for the next attempt. From this low vantage point he saw the next taxi before it saw him. It was slowed down in heavy traffic and he darted out, hailed it. Not as fully alert to the possibility of drunken punters early on a Monday morning as he would have been late on a Friday night, the driver had accepted him as a fare and let him into the back of the cab before fully registering just how far gone Roderic was. Then he looked in the mirror and said: 'Right, you: out.' Roderic ignored this and gave him the address of the bank where Dennis worked. The driver turned round now and noticed how big a man he was dealing with. 'Out,' he said again, but this time with less authority, as he struggled in his mind to think which was the least worst option, to have this man in the cab or to pick a fight with him. It didn't take long to decide. He released the handbrake and they drove off.

Dennis's job was a responsible and demanding one. It was rare for him to have in the course of the day even a few moments when he was not engaged on any particular task. He had just such a hiatus now but he was not enjoying it. He stood at the high window of his office looking out and thinking about Roderic, thinking in particular about Saturday night.

One of the strange anomalies of Roderic's drinking was that it made Dennis feel he was the one with the problem. As though he had been a seeker of dark pleasures or excitement, a secret gambler, say, or a frequenter of prostitutes, his lot was now guilt, was a mania for concealment with a concomitant fear of exposure and shame. He had been trying, in the face of Roderic's visible disintegration, to cling on to his own life

352

with its regularity and measured habits, and to this end had invited one of his colleagues to supper on Saturday night, together with his wife. He was fond of Paul. They weren't intimate friends – Dennis had none – but he valued his fellowship in the office, and they shared an interest in music. He made a lamb casserole and a lemon pudding, carefully selected a few interesting wines. They hadn't even got as far as the table when it happened. They were still sitting over drinks, and Dennis had truly been relaxed and enjoying himself when the doorbell rang.

Roderic.

It could be no one else. He would be drunk. He would disgrace him. And tonight Dennis couldn't face it, so he ignored it. 'Maureen, are you all right there, can I offer you more wine?'

'I'm fine, thanks,' she said, clearly puzzled as to why he wasn't answering the door.

The bell rang again, more aggressively this time. 'So, Paul, where were we?' Dennis said, 'Wexford. Lully,' giving him his cue. The caller abandoned the bell and started to knock.

Maureen and Paul looked at each other in silence, then Maureen said, 'I, ah, I think there's someone at your door,' clearly embarrassed at having to make so foolishly obvious a statement.

'Do please excuse me,' Dennis said with elaborate politeness as he stood up. 'I shall only be a moment.'

In the hall, he checked his pockets. He had thirty pounds in cash which he would give to Roderic if he needed it, to make him go away. For Dennis had crossed the Rubicon: he wasn't going to let Roderic in. No matter what he said, no matter what his condition, Dennis would turn him away, a thing he had never done before. He would be too ashamed before his guests. Roderic, smashed and self-pitying, would deal a killer blow to his supper party and he wasn't going to put up with it. He paused for a moment, steeling himself before opening the door.

'Dennis, how are things? I'm running the Dublin marathon this year to raise money for a cancer charity. Will you sponsor me for it?' Dennis stared wildly at his neighbour. 'Sorry to make a racket, I'm doing the whole street tonight and I knew you were in, for I saw your lights on.'

His hands shook so that he could hardly fill in the form that was offered to him. His neighbour thanked him, complimented him on his fine show of roses and Dennis in turn thanked him, said goodbye. He closed the front door and stood leaning against it for some moments with his eyes shut, trying to control the emotional turmoil that threatened to defeat him. In an ideal world, he could simply go back into the drawing room and say, 'I thought it was my brother. He's an alcoholic and I'm at the end of my tether.' But it wasn't an ideal world. Paul was his colleague and he'd never met Maureen before tonight. If he talked about it with anyone, he couldn't be sure that he wouldn't start crying. 'Oh, fuck it all,' he said out loud, there in the hall. 'Fuck, fuck, fuck.' And then he realised that Maureen and Paul would have heard him. He stood there for a few minutes more struggling to compose himself, then went back into the drawing room and carried on as if nothing had happened.

He thought of all this now as he stared out over the roofs of the city, at the slates, the spires and green domes, the turning yellow cranes. Poor Roderic was out there somewhere. What was he doing at exactly this moment in his lost life? With that the phone on his desk rang.

'Mr Kennedy, there's a man in reception demanding to see you. He's very drunk. Could you get down here as quick as you possibly can?'

He could hear the fear in the receptionist's voice, could hear Roderic shouting in the background. 'DENNIS! WHERE ARE YOU, DENNIS? HELP ME!' He didn't take time to speak to the woman but simply threw the receiver back in its cradle; didn't take time to wait for the lift, but ran down the three flights of stairs to the entrance of the building.

Roderic was sitting on the floor with his back to the receptionist's desk and his forehead resting on his knees. The doorman, who was tiny, was hovering nervously over him like a Yorkshire terrier guarding a wounded wolfhound. 'He's grand now,' he said to Dennis, 'he's grand,' which was patently not true. Roderic looked disastrous. He hadn't washed or changed his clothes for days; he was paralytic with drink and he was crying, great heaving boo-hoo-hooing sobs, like a small child in distress.

'Ring for a taxi, please,' Dennis said to the receptionist, and he knelt down beside his brother. 'Don't worry, Roderic, everything's going to be all right. I'm with you now. I'll look after you.' He put his arms around him, hushed him and soothed him. From somewhere a blanket was fetched, and he tenderly placed it around Roderic's shoulders. In his place of work Dennis was famed and feared as a martinet and the receptionist and doorman both stared at him now, astounded at this unexpected side, this gentleness and compassion. 'We're going to go to my house and you can sleep there, and you'll be fine. We'll get you a doctor and you'll be looked after. Believe me, Roderic. Everything is going to be all right now.'

When they got to the house, Dennis took him straight upstairs to his own bedroom. 'Just take your shoes off and lie down under the duvet.' Bending down, Roderic struggled and fumbled with his laces but they defeated him. 'Here, let me.' Dennis knelt down in front of him and helped him out of his shoes, then settled him in the bed and pulled the quilt up around him. And then as he sat looking at his brother while waiting for the doctor to arrive, something strange happened. Under his gaze, Roderic began to change. He still looked wretched but not quite as bad as the man who had arrived in the office an hour earlier – more like the man who, to Dennis's complete stupefaction, had showed up unannounced on his doorstep late one night some years earlier. *The marriage is over. I decided to come back. Have you anything in the house I could drink?* He was definitely changing: his hair was darkening, and he had lost that bloated, raddled look. He was younger, stronger, like the troubled artist who'd lived in Italy with his wife and three daughters; like the cheerful handsome man who'd shared Dennis's house and brightened his days with his laughter, his big personality. His face in sleep looked peaceful now as he became the bearded art student, then the energetic teenager. He was shrinking before Dennis's very eyes, was becoming the curly-headed child he'd been so fond of, the toddler, the baby in the pink shawl that Sinéad had held out to him so many years ago, and whom he had loved with a deep visceral love from that moment onwards.

Will you look after him always?

Yes, I will. I'll look after him.

Chapter Thirty-Four

'Do you know someone with apple trees?'

'No.'

'So you actually bought these?' Julia took one of the apples from the wooden bowl on Roderic's kitchen table and held it up.

'I most certainly did. They were hard to find and they cost me dear.'

'How much?'

He told her and she laughed. 'They saw you coming.'

'They're organic apples,' he said, and she laughed again.

'They *definitely* saw you coming. The next time I'm down home I'll bring you some apples back, like this only better, and as many of them as you want. I'm quite serious,' she said, because now Roderic was laughing. 'My father has a great orchard, but it produces more fruit than we can ever eat – more even than we can gather.'

The apples in the bowl were local too. She knew it to look at them. No one would ever have bothered to transport such humble fruit from one end of the planet to the other. They were small apples with thick woody stalks, and some of them were slightly misshapen, swollen out more on one side than on the other. The one Julia was holding had a small grey scab on it; some of the others had leaves still attached. Their skins were blushed and flecked, green shading into a rich orange red.

'I hate those big red apples you buy in supermarkets,' he said. 'It's like eating a cricket ball. They have no taste, no fragrance.'

She inhaled the rich sweet perfume of the fruit in her hand. 'They look well against the wood of the bowl. They remind me of something,' she said, 'but I can't think what.'

'Your father's orchard?'

'Yes, but something else too. I don't know what it is.'

On returning to her own house later, Julia was amused to find that there was an apple in the pocket of her jacket that Roderic had somehow managed to put there without her noticing. She set it on the mantelpiece of the living room and for the rest of that day it was a puzzle to her, pushing her towards some lost memory to which she simply could not get back. She picked it up from time to time, studied it closely and thoughtfully, did everything she could to make it offer up its secret, but it didn't do so until the following night, which brought the first frost of that winter. She had been out visiting friends and on returning to the unheated flat near midnight she saw the apple. It was the bitter cold that made the connection. The revelation of the memory was like a trapdoor opening beneath her.

It was a morning in winter and the sky in the east was an intense deep pink. She was walking through the orchard at home, at the edge of which there was a ditch overhung with grass. This morning every blade was rimed silver and the water in the ditch was frozen. A few windfalls had been trapped beneath the ice and she stopped to look at them. Someone was with her. Someone was holding her hand; it was hot as a coal. The red of the apples was vivid through the thick glassy ice. Julia wanted to stand there and admire the trapped fruit but her companion did not wish to linger. She was chivvied along; she could remember nothing more.

Usually she cherished these fragments connected with her mother, but for some reason it was different this time. It depressed her to think that this was all she would ever have, for it wasn't enough – not nearly enough. Her sense of loss was borne in upon her with a greater force than ever before. She slept badly that night and awoke with a headache that she couldn't shake off all day. Her luck had broken, nothing went right with her. She rang Roderic in the early evening but there was no reply. He had mentioned something about going to see his brother later in the week but she couldn't recall which day. She rang her father but he wasn't there either. There was only Max to console her in her loneliness and Max was fast asleep. Then shortly after eight the doorbell rang, the two short rings that she wanted to hear more than anything else this evening.

'Oh. It's you.' William was aware of the disappointment in her voice.

'I can go away again if you wish.'

'No, please, you're welcome.'

'Is there anything in particular bothering you?' he asked when they were settled upstairs.

'Everything and nothing. You know how it is.'

'Meaning?'

She covered her eyes with her hand. 'Meaning that someone stole a silver dish when I was at work this morning and Hester went mad when she found out. That I checked my bank balance this afternoon and it was fifty pounds less than it ought to be and I have no idea why. That I had arranged to meet someone to interview them for the project I'm working on and they didn't show. I waited for ages, so that was the afternoon lost.' She lifted her hand away from her eyes and smiled at him. 'Do you really want me to go on?'

'I get the picture.'

She offered him wine from a bottle she happened to have open. 'I am glad to see you,' she said as she poured it. 'I could be doing with company after a day like that. Hope life's been treating you more kindly.'

'I don't know whether it has or not. My big news,' he said, 'is that I'm going back to work soon.'

'Well that's good, isn't it? I take it that means you're better,' but he laughed at this somewhat sardonically.

'The doctor I've been seeing said to me the other day, "Let me tell you something, William. *Cure* is a word I don't like." You can draw your own conclusions from that.'

'I know what he means,' Julia said. '*Heal* is probably more accurate. I mean, what you've been going through isn't probably something that just comes to an end. It eases off and you can get on with your life again, but it never quite goes away completely.'

This slightly disconcerted William, for the doctor had gone on to express the same idea. 'Mind you, I never thought it would last as long as this. Where are we now, October? I can hardly believe it.'

'And what exactly has changed for you during these past nine months since you left work?'

'It's been a strange time. Thinking about my life. Realising that I haven't become the person I was supposed to become. Realising that it won't ever happen now, and trying to come to terms with it.'

'And you're making some headway?'

'No,' he said bluntly. 'I should have devoted my life to painting. I won't ever be like you or like your friend. Have a reputation, critical attention, exhibitions and so on. It isn't going to happen.'

Julia laughed. '*Critical attention!* I wouldn't break my heart over missing out on that one if I were you.'

'But to have done the work, that has been a good thing, I'm glad I had that. I know nobody else cared about it but it mattered to me. It gave me a kind of spiritual freedom that I needed.'

As she refilled their glasses Julia asked why he spoke of it all in the past tense. 'You will keep painting when you go back to your job, won't you? If you want to do it so much, you should be able to work out some sort of schedule for yourself.'

'I suppose so.'

'Do you know where it comes from,' she asked, 'this compulsion to paint?'

'It was always there,' he replied, 'ever since I was a small child. I used to think it was a neutral thing but now I'm not so sure. This compulsion, as you call it. This instinct. That's how it strikes me, like an extra instinct. Not everyone has it but if you do, you ignore it at your peril. It's like the need for sex. That can also seem to be a neutral thing, but it isn't. It has a dark, blind, dangerous side.'

He told her about a man with whom he had worked when he was starting out as a lawyer, 'A real pillar of society, all rectitude and respectability. What none of us knew was that he frequented prostitutes. The police recognised him from seeing him in court. They warned him off time and again but he paid no heed. Eventually they had no option but to arrest him. It blew everything apart – his career, his marriage, the lot.'

'And you're saying art is like that?'

'I'm saying it also can destroy lives. It almost destroyed mine. I'm sure you can think of other examples closer to home.'

She knew what he was hinting at but refused to rise to the bait, only replied, 'I don't agree with you. I think sex is a good thing and I think art is a good thing.'

'You may say so; my point is that it's all a bit more complex than that.'

A silence fell over them and they sat looking at each other. Even though she was quite close to him – if he stretched out his hand he could have touched her – there was something about her that was completely remote and that didn't square with the solidity of her presence. It was like seeing a ghost and being startled to realise that there was nothing ghostly about it. Julia had removed her shoes and was sitting on the sofa with her legs folded beneath her; her long green skirt was tucked in around her feet. Her hair was pinned back from her face, which looked wan and tired. What was it about her, he wondered, that made her look so impossibly distant? Something at the core of her constantly eluded him, and the more he tried to get at her the more she seemed to recede. He had noticed this quality in her before and was

361

never sure if it was something he was projecting on to her, or if it came from her deepest self. The fits of black depression from which he suffered had this distancing effect. Often he felt as though he were experiencing the world through a sheet of plate glass, but with Julia it was something particular, something more. He didn't know her. That was the simple truth. She drank her wine and stroked the head of the cat who was asleep beside her.

'Everyone,' she said 'has trouble in life. It's a question of keeping things in perspective and trying to draw strength from the good things that one does have.'

'It's easy for you to say that. You don't know what it's like to completely fall apart. Money, family and so on; it's no consolation, it's not enough. You don't know what it's like, this kind of crisis.'

'Indeed. I've led a completely charmed life.' There was no mistaking the sarcasm.

'What I mean,' he said, 'is that you're young.'

'Age has nothing to do with it. Even little children can suffer.'

'Do you mean my son?'

'Not necessarily. No, I wasn't thinking of him.'

Again they fell silent. They were both slightly taken aback at how quickly the atmosphere between them had soured. She offered him more wine in the hope of breaking the mood.

'Thanks. What you say is true,' William went on, keen in his turn to mollify her. 'I do have good things in my life. For example, in these past months I've come to understand more about how things were between my father and myself. I value that knowledge even though getting to it has been extremely painful. Of course, your generation are far more at ease than mine when it comes to talking about psychological matters.'

Julia laughed and then she said, 'It's been ever such a long day. I'm worn out.'

She did look exhausted, William thought. She was flushed with the wine; and that distance he had noticed earlier was still there. She seemed to him like a woman in a pane of stained glass, or a figure woven into a tapestry, standing on a field of coloured flowers with a hawk at her wrist. 'You never,' he said, 'talk about your mother.'

'I don't, do I? There's nothing to say.'

'Oh, come along, I can't believe that.' She looked at him warily. He knew he ought to drop the subject but his curiosity was aroused now and he risked pressing on. 'You were very young when you lost her?'

He could see her weighing up in her mind whether or not to answer him and then she said, 'I was six when she died. Oh, I've told you,' she went on, suddenly impatient, 'there's nothing to say.'

'Meaning?'

'Meaning that I can't remember.'

'You were away from home when it happened?'

'No, I was there. I was right at the eye of the storm. It's just that I can't remember anything about it.'

'But you do know what happened?'

Again she covered her eyes with her hand. She looked weary, but she was weakening, William could see. He was wearing her down. 'It would help you to talk,' he said gently. 'It would do you good.'

'Why?'

He had no idea. He had said this only because he thought it was what she might wish to hear. 'Well, perhaps if you spoke about what you know, it might help you to remember.'

She took her hand away from her face and stared at him. 'Do you really think so?'

William shrugged. 'No harm in trying.' Still she was looking at him, clearly thinking hard. He couldn't understand what was going on in her mind and he didn't really expect what happened next.

She told him all about her mother, that her name was Eileen and that she had been killed in a road accident that Julia herself and her father had witnessed. Distracted by something or simply not looking, she'd stepped out in front of a car while out on a family shopping trip one Saturday afternoon. She'd taken the full impact of the vehicle and died there on the road moments later, with Dan's arms around her and Julia holding her hand. It upset her to speak of these things and she started to cry. William said nothing and she continued, telling him how she could remember almost nothing of her mother but fragments.

She told him about the sound of crockery in the morning, the gold watch, the apples under the ice. All her life she had kept the idea of her mother closed in her heart, like a fragile glass plate in a photographic darkroom where, under the right conditions, an image might slowly reveal itself. She had spoken explicitly of her loss to few people and never before in this flood of raw emotion that William's persistent probing had unleashed with such unexpected force. Sniffing and gulping she took a paper tissue from the sleeve of her jumper and wiped her eyes.

William sat opposite her, watching. In recent times he had found her much less attractive than when he first met her and tonight, with her face red and puffy from crying, she looked particularly unappealing. Nine months had passed since first he had sat in this room and it surprised him now to think back on it and remember how different it had all seemed at the time. Then, it had excited him to be plunged into the life of this stranger, to be sitting in this room that seemed full of a careless glamour, that bespoke freedom; but tonight it struck him as merely the shabby, dusty flat of a young woman without a proper job and with no money. Knowing her had opened no doors for him. Still she was talking, but he was no longer listening. Her confidences bored him, and he waited until she paused again then said, 'Well now, I'm sure you feel much better for that.'

Julia stared at him with incredulity.

'I should be heading for home. It's getting late.'

'Don't leave me like this,' Julia said. 'Stay a little longer. I don't want to be on my own.'

'You'll be fine.'

'I'm asking you, William, please. Just another fifteen, twenty minutes. Stay and talk to me; don't leave me like this.'

'I have a long way to go.' There was a distinct note of irritation in his voice now. 'You'll be fine,' he said again. 'Thanks for the wine. Will you see me out?'

Julia stood up. For a moment there was between them exactly that tension that he remembered between himself and Liz on the day she found out about Hannah, in the seconds before she started to hit him. When Julia moved towards him now he flinched but she walked straight past him, picked up her keys and left the room. He heard her feet descending the stairs and understood what was happening. She was waiting for him in the hall with the front door already open. He didn't want it to end like this, and he paused on the threshold. 'You mustn't think . . .' he said, but Julia gave a little growl of exasperation, put her hand under his elbow and literally pushed him out into the street. The physical contact had the same effect as on the day when she had shoved the book into his hands, a kind of sexual thrill that was wholly unpleasant. She slammed the door closed behind him and he stood there on the pavement listening to the sound of her double-locking the door and driving the bolt home.

In the weeks that followed, William's name did not come up in conversation between Roderic and Julia. Roderic noticed this but said nothing, waiting for her to bring up the subject. He was already preoccupied with his forthcoming trip to Italy at the start of the following year and was thinking of how it would be, of gifts he might bring to his daughters. He was also working hard to finish a particular cycle of paintings. Julia called to the studio one day to find him sitting at the table cataloguing slides and as it was a functional, mechanical task he was able to continue with it while chatting to her. It was a dark wet evening in November and he worked by the light of a desk lamp, glancing over from time to time to where she sat on the sofa. It eased his heart to see her there. She had stayed with him the night before and details of their lovemaking came back to him now, to flood and fill the silences that lay between them, making him feel miraculously close to her, making him feel known without anything at all ever being said.

Julia was not looking at him. She was staring at a new painting propped against the wall. It used his familiar range of colours – grey and cream, pale blue and pink – in a series of interlocked rectangles that gave the effect of a *mise en abime*. This canvas was the original of the slide that Roderic now took up between forefinger and thumb and held before the lamp. The different medium and the effect of the light appeared to make the colours stronger, more vivid, and the small scale made it curiously poignant.

'There's something I want to tell you,' she said.

Roderic made no comment and went on studying the transparent miniature that he was holding.

'It's to do with the recording about the man with the fishing flies. I was listening to it again today and I realised what it might mean to you. I can hardly believe that I didn't think of it at the time.'

He set the slide on the table and sat there for a moment. The recording *had* unsettled him. He remembered walking home in the light of the full moon and lying awake, thinking about his daughters.

'That's the whole point of the exercise, isn't it?' he said eventually. 'That everyone brings their own experience to bear upon the work. You can't be expected to second guess how everyone will react.'

'But it wasn't everyone. It was you. And it wasn't a piece of work, it was only raw material.'

'No, no, it was a good thing. It made me think,' and he picked up a pen. In minuscule script he wrote the title of the painting, its dimensions and the date along the edge of the slide, then placed it in a little transparent pocket beside the neat rows of slides he had already catalogued. 'In any case I thought you were going to say something about Mr Armstrong.'

'Oh, *him*.'

'Yes, him.' He picked up another slide and looked at it, inverted it and peered at it again. 'You haven't mentioned him in a while.'

'We had another falling out.'

He glanced over at her ironically. 'You don't say. Have you mended your fences again with him yet? And what was it about this time?'

'I'd rather not say, if you don't mind.'

Something in the tone of her voice made him turn to look at her properly. She reminded him of Max: she had that same air of sullen bristling fury as the cat did when it was in a rage.

'I will tell you this, though: there'll be no fence-mending, as you call it. This time it's for keeps.'

'What did he do, Julia?'

She didn't reply, but tears welled up in her eyes. Roderic was genuinely alarmed now; she almost never cried. He left the table and went over to where she was sitting.

'He didn't try anything on, did he, because if he did . . .'

But his suggestion only seemed to make her more angry. 'No, he bloody well didn't, but is that the only thing you can think of? It was worse than that, much worse. And I don't want to talk about it.'

Roderic was at a loss to know what William could possibly have done to upset her so much. 'When did this happen?'

'Some weeks back. I do blame myself, though. It was my fault.' He offered her a handkerchief and she took it. 'You warned me, do you remember? You told me it would end badly, but it wasn't exactly as you said it would be. I dropped him.' There was a note of almost childish triumph in the way she said this.

Roderic had promised all those weeks ago that there would be no recriminations, that he wouldn't cast her misplaced trust back at her. He struggled now to keep that promise, and wondered again what could have possibly happened. Perhaps he, Roderic, was implicated in it. William might have criticised him and they had quarrelled as a result; or perhaps Julia had somehow let him down, had been tricked into betraying some confidence which she afterwards resented and was too embarrassed to admit to. He studied her face as though he might read there the nature of their dispute, but saw only her misery.

'Whatever it was, it's over now,' he said. 'Put it from your mind and forget about it.'

Julia saw William once more after that. She noticed him in a crowd of people crossing Dame Street towards her at the end of a working day a few weeks before Christmas. Instinctively she drew back, and retreated behind a stand of postcards outside a newsagent's. As she pretended to deliberate between a view of the façade of Trinity College and a row of cattle peering over a whitewashed wall, she watched him approach. William was wearing a grey suit and over it an unbuttoned navy overcoat, with a red silk paisley scarf. He was carrying a black leather briefcase; his face was stamped with that tense and forlorn expression that she knew so well. He was close to her now on the greasy stones of the rain-slicked pavement and he stopped to inspect a rack of newspapers, folded and arranged so as to display their mastheads. She disliked watching him in this underhand way but she hoped he wouldn't notice her. Julia didn't wish to speak to him: there was nothing to say. To look at him tonight, everything about him suggested that his life and his values were alien to hers, and she wondered what had ever possessed her to think that there was common ground between them. Why had she let herself be drawn into his world? He turned away from the newspapers. For a moment just before he vanished into the crowds again, into the city night, she thought that he had indeed noticed her standing there. But if he did, he gave her no sign.

Chapter Thirty-Five

As she turns on to the narrow track, a single sheep high on the slope notices her. Bleating, it moves down the hill, and is joined by two, three others, then quickly six, ten, twenty, more, until every sheep on the slope is heading her way. 'You creatures,' she calls laughing, 'I have nothing to give you,' as they cluster by the wire that separates the track from the field. She can hardly hear her own voice over the loud humming sound of their bleating. Their backs are all stained indigo; and they run alongside the wire, tripping and tumbling, following her as she walks along until another line of wire halts their progress, penning them in. As she walks on up the valley, she can hear their sad weird cries gradually dying away.

The track stays close to the course of a river for some distance, so that she has the slope of the hill on one side and the tumbling peaty water on the other, until suddenly it rises steeply, leaving the river far below with the rowans that fringe it, with its pools and stones. The land opens out and is unfenced now. The rowans, she thinks, the rowans . . . She comes here in all seasons. She has never been out of Ireland – she never will be – but she cannot think that there is anything anywhere more vivid than the rowans when they have their berries on a clear cold day when the sky is bare – the red of the berries, the green of the leaves, the hard blue of the sky. Even the Mediterranean, she thinks, cannot offer such strong and powerful colours. But it is not like that today, for now everything is grey and dun and soft blue, muted colours of green, the old gold of faded bracken.

When human memory has been outlived, the landscape remembers. She passes potato drills from the last century, low soft shadowy ridges in the thin soil. She passes the ruins of a farmhouse, forlorn now, its windows all shattered, its front door rotted and fallen, the roof collapsed in on itself, like a fire late at night. A pert wren vanishes. The track along which she is walking is not the original route up the valley but then the track cuts into the old path, which is bounded by drystone walls. Panting from the steepness of the climb, she stops. Looking back, she can see where the old road ran straight down, the stones of its walls broken and tumbled now, but still there, resilient, because the landscape does remember. In the distance she can see other grey ruins, deserted houses, and she finds it strange how utterly and completely the human community has gone from this mountainside.

There are few trees now – a few tough hawthorns, their branches and trunks covered with lichens. She is tired but has almost reached her destination. Every time she comes here she returns to the same place, to a particular fold in the mountains. The path continues on from the point where she stops but not for much further. She settles down between the stones that form a crude seat. She is out of the wind here, and she looks back down the valley, where the slopes softly interlock. In the foreground, directly in her line of vision, there is a single thorn. The sky is a crown of light, drifting, theatrical. It is not a fine day and the sky is constantly changing. She lies back and watches huge torn grey clouds move swiftly overhead, expanding, contracting, like liquid added to another liquid, like coloured ink in water; the same fringed dissolving quality. She likes it when this happens at night, when huge wild clouds are blown swiftly over a wild moon.

Once, many years earlier, a strange and beautiful thing happened to her here. She was sitting on that day where she is sitting now, leaning back against the side of the hill with its low plants, its grasses and ferns. She had fallen into a sort of half-hypnotised, half-enchanted state, thinking of the landscape in which she was sitting but not in a willed or forced way, receptive rather than seeking to impose a thought or idea. She was aware of her own breathing, rising and falling, rising and falling; aware of the great slope of the mountain on which she sat. And then all at once she realised that the ground beneath her was alive. The earth was alive. It was as though the land against which she was leaning was the flank of a massive animal. And the sky too, the moving, shaggy clouds, the tumbling river, the thorn, the stones themselves, everything, everything, interconnected and living and complete. It was a sacred, astounding moment, and it passed as swiftly as the rushing clouds. She has never told anyone and she has certainly never forgotten it. This is why she has come to this place today, why she constantly returns. She feels she can enter here into the life of things in a way that is not possible otherwise or elsewhere. It has become a place as of which one might say, 'This is where we saw the kingfisher.' 'This is where we found the rare wild orchid.' One comes back not in the hope of finding such things again, but in gratitude for the mystery that was revealed there once.

Sitting in that same spot now, she loses track of time. Her thoughts drift. She thinks about her own life in a vague, open-ended way, wondering what will happen to her in the years to come. On her wrist she wears a gold watch and she studies it with pleasure, thinking of the man who gave it to her. At night before she goes to sleep she places it carefully in its flat leather box and then sets it open on the dressing table beside her, so that it will be the first thing she sees in the morning when she wakes. The watch has a lozenge-shaped face and a supple gold bracelet, as if fashioned from the skin of some fabulous mythical fish. As she looks at it today, she realises that all her cherished thoughts of the future are an illusion. The things she is thinking about have not yet happened and there is no guarantee they ever will happen; there is no fixed promise that anything will happen, that there is a future. Just at that moment, she hears someone approach.

A stranger. A hill walker. It is rare for her to meet anyone on this path. Once, in winter, she met a shepherd and his dog out foddering sheep, and on two or three other occasions she has met hikers like this man. He has been on up the valley beyond where the path runs out and far on into the mountains, and now he is returning. He stops and they greet each other. The man is exceptionally tall and somewhat eccentrically dressed. He is wearing heavy walking boots and thick socks, the short trousers

372

of an alpine hiker. The effect is faintly ridiculous and she tries not to laugh. On his head is a knitted woollen hat as tight as the cap of an acorn on a nut. His face is flushed and excited.

'Have you had a good day?'

'It was marvellous.'

'How far did you get?'

'Up beyond the watershed so that you could see down into the next valley, and then back down again into this one.'

'Are you out from Dublin?'

He nods. 'And you, you live locally?'

She nods in her turn.

'You're fortunate to be able to come up here,' he says, 'whenever you want.'

He thinks of the long drive back to the city, of the traffic, of the river of tail lights before him. He thinks of the suburban house to which he will return, of his family, of all the constraints of his life during the week to come. For a moment he envies this stranger so much and not just for where she lives but for her youth, her happiness. She is in her early twenties with thick curling hair, and grey eyes in an open trusting face. There is no evidence of her having already made any of those simple, fatal errors that can close a life down. She is wearing a tweed skirt and thick stockings, a dark blue jacket and a green scarf. 'It'll rain soon,' he says. 'I doubt if we'll make it back down before it breaks.'

'I don't mind. I like walking in the rain.' As he looks at her, he is overcome by an inexplicable sense of pity and compassion for this stranger. He has no idea why this should be but all at once it makes him feel close to her.

'When I was up in the mountains today something happened.'

She listens as he struggles to find words to convey the experience he has had. He evokes the physical aspect of the landscape that had triggered it – the brown velvet flanks of the mountain, the heather and thick bracken. In the silence a single bird was calling. The shifting light and the stones, the faraway pine forests, black as a winter lake: he tells her of all these things and of how, under his gaze, they had suddenly opened to afford him a remarkable insight into their

373

nature. When he has finished they remain in silence for a few moments.

And then she says, 'Exactly the same thing happened to me here once.'

The valley is now a tunnel of light. The strong blink of sun that heralds rain reaches its pitch of intensity. He suggests that she walk back down the valley with him; she thanks him and stands up, brushes a few wisps of dry grass from her skirt. They set off together and walk in companionable silence. The rain begins to fall and the sky darkens, all is greyness. She pulls her scarf up over her head. They walk through soft veils of rain under slow clouds. They pass the thorn, the broken wall that marks the abandoned road, they pass the empty farmhouse. They descend to the tree line, to where the hawthorns and the rowans grow, to where the river flows, its peaty water falling over stones. They see the sheep muster. When they reach the point where the track meets the road there is a man tending a bonfire and he greets them. They stand opposite him and all three look into the flames. The man's face, seen through the haze of the heat, gives the impression of something seen through water. They feel simultaneously the heat of the fire and the chill of the rain; there is a smell of smoke and decay. They take leave of each other standing by the bonfire to return to their lives, to fulfil their destinies.

Neither of them ever forgot the other. Neither of them ever spoke to anyone else of what had happened that day. They never met again.

Chapter Thirty-Six

As Roderic and Julia listened to the bells of Christchurch ringing in the New Year, he gave silent thanks for the year that was ending, for everything in it that had been joyful and complete. Two weeks later he returned to Italy to visit his daughters. He rang Julia at the end of every day during his time there, and although this trip was much more relaxed and enjoyable than his last visit, still he valued and needed these calls. On the rare occasions when he was briefly wrongfooted by some tension between himself and his family, to hear Julia's voice was a comfort; when all had gone well his conversation with her made it perfect, and in both cases it succeeded in bringing his daughters and lover into a single reality. In themselves they were inconsequential, these late-night chats, drowsy and rambling. From the sound of her voice he could summon up her presence, her whole world, could see her curled up on the sofa with her skirt tucked in around her feet, her book spreadeagled beside her where she had abandoned it to answer the phone. He could visualise the low-lit room, its fire, its faded rugs. Once or twice he could even hear Max purring, fast asleep beside her so far, far away.

And then at the end of the first week, something happened. He knew it as soon as she spoke, knew her so well that, even from the inflection of her voice when she said 'Roderic, hello,' he understood at once that something was wrong. 'It's nothing,' she said, 'that I feel I can talk about over the phone.' In the following days he probed gently, asked leading questions about her father, her work, about Hester and the shop, but her responses gave him no real clues.

He spent his last night in Italy in Rome and flew back to Ireland early the following day, went straight from the airport to find Julia finishing up her morning's work amongst the wardrobes and whatnots, her delight to see him again matching his at being back with her. They went up to her flat and immediately he asked what was troubling her.

Julia frowned. 'It actually happened before you left, but I only found out about it after you'd gone.'

'It's to do with William, isn't it?'

Again she nodded.

'What happened?'

'He's dead.'

For a moment neither of them spoke. Roderic was genuinely shocked by the news, and was struck by Julia's demeanour, for she looked angry, resentful even, rather than grieved.

'What happened? Tell me,' he said. 'How did you find out?'

'In the strangest, most banal way you can imagine.'

She had been feeding Max, whose bowl and dish stood in a corner of the kitchen on a sheet of newspaper that she used to change frequently. Spooning chunks of meat and jelly out of a tin, she noticed that the bowl was sitting on a page of death notices. And then all at once she recognised the name: *Armstrong*, heavily printed and then in lighter type, *William*. Max spat and hissed as she pushed him aside roughly, spilling his food as she pulled out the paper. *The wife and family of the late William Armstrong wish to thank all those who sympathised with them in their recent tragic bereavement.* Stunned, Julia sat back on her heels on the kitchen floor. There was silence but for the sound of the cat, William's old enemy, wolfing down its meat.

'He was dead a month by that stage,' Julia said. It had evidently happened shortly after she saw him outside the newsagent's in Dame Street; the thought chilled her. 'I didn't know what to do. I didn't want to simply ignore it even though we had had a falling out, as I told you.' She hadn't known what, if anything, William might have said about this to Liz and was therefore unsure how any communication might be received. 'Anyway, a few days afterwards I wrote her a letter, mainly on account of the children. I told her that I had only just heard the news. I sent her my sympathy.' By return of post, Julia received a formal printed acknowledgement, a rectangle of cream card with the text printed in sepia, 'Such a cold and impersonal thing, it seemed to me.' Standing in her sitting room with the card in her hand she felt for the first time, she told Roderic, genuine sorrow for William's death. 'For we had been friends, you know. We had good times together for all that it ended badly. I know that you always found it hard to understand why I liked him, but there was a side to him that was completely real. He had that core of artistic integrity, of genuine discrimination that you always hope to find in people but almost never do. And that made him good to know, in spite of that social mask he hid behind, that formal manner.'

She had thought that the card was the end of it and expected no more contact from William's family when a few days later Liz rang. 'She was glad that I had written to her. She said she wanted to see me.'

'And how did the meeting go?'

'It's tomorrow.'

Roderic had been studying Julia carefully throughout all of this, still struck by how angry she was. 'I feel sorry for his wife,' he said. 'How is she, do you think? How is she bearing up?'

'Still very shocked, I'd say. After a death such as that, you know . . .'

'What do you mean?'

Only then did Julia realise that she hadn't told Roderic the manner of William's passing, and yet still she was surprised that he hadn't known.

377

'What do you think I mean? What else could have happened? Didn't you guess? I knew as much as soon as I saw it in the paper, and Liz referred to it obliquely when I spoke to her on the phone. Oh, the stupid man!' she said. 'The stupid, stupid man. Now those children will have to go through everything I've gone through for the rest of their lives, only it'll be far worse because it wasn't an accident; it didn't have to happen. He didn't deserve it, Roderic.'

'His death, you mean?'

'I'm talking about his life. He didn't deserve his life: his gift, his children, none of it.'

Never had he seen her in such a fury; never had she seemed to him so young. Roderic was full of compassion now for William, whom he had never liked in life. 'It's extremely difficult,' he said, 'to come through. Not just as an artist but on a human level – to come through fully and completely. And life is very long.'

'Not always it isn't,' she said. 'Not always.'

'Months ago you said that you befriended William in the first instance because he reminded you of me. Do you remember that? At the time I wouldn't hear tell of it but you were right.' What shocked him about William's fate was that he understood it all too well and saw in it an icy version of his own destructive ways. He had always known that a certain kind of cold rectitude was every bit as deadly as more generally acknowledged ways of wrecking one's life: drink, drugs, a sex life that was completely out of control. 'Perhaps it's even worse,' he said to Julia, 'William's way, because the damage is hidden. By the time anyone realises that something is seriously wrong, it's too late.'

'But I knew. I knew right from the start. And yet there was nothing I could do.' Her anger was waning into sorrow.

'The last time I saw him,' she went on, 'he said that art could destroy lives and that it had almost destroyed his. I told him that he was wrong but now I understand.'

'He *was* wrong,' Roderic insisted. 'It isn't art that's the problem. It's when it's thwarted or denied, that's where the danger comes from.' Julia said nothing. Some fundamental point about all of this was still, he thought, eluding her. He studied her where she stood leaning against her own kitchen table with her arms tightly folded. 'Is Liz aware that you had a row with William?'

'I don't know. I don't think so. She gave no indication of it.'

'Where are you meeting her tomorrow?'

'In the Shelbourne in mid afternoon.'

Roderic was correct in thinking that the full import of William's death had still not got through to Julia, and Julia herself began to realise this when she met Liz. Julia was somewhat late in arriving at the hotel and William's widow was already there, installed on a sofa beneath the chandeliers, gazing out of the window at the bare trees of the Green, black against a colourless winter sky. The shock of what she had gone through in recent weeks had translated her and in spite of her familiar pearls, her cream wools and linens, she looked fundamentally different from the woman she had been when Julia visited her at home almost exactly a year ago. Simply seeing her today removed another layer of denial and incomprehension, and moved Julia closer to the heart of the mystery that was William's death.

'I'm sorry I didn't let you know as soon as it happened. To be honest, in the confusion of that time I simply didn't think of it. He didn't speak of you often in the last weeks; I had the impression that perhaps you had drifted out of each other's lives. Most everything connected with his painting fell by the wayside after he went back to the office. And I set no store by it. I thought it was all just a whim, something he'd got out of his system during those months he was off work, and that now life was getting back to normal. How could I not have seen the risk? That's what I still don't understand. *You* saw it, you, a stranger, the very first time you met him.' And although Julia had made exactly this point to Roderic the day

379

before, she now disclaimed it. 'But you did see the danger,' Liz persisted, 'and you took the time and trouble to warn me. I'll always remember you for that. Also you helped William with his work, you gave him moral support. He valued all of that more than you might realise. He always spoke well of you, both you and your friend. He said you were authentic. Whatever happiness and fulfilment there was in the last year of his life was in no small part due to you. I asked to see you today because I wanted to thank you,' Liz went on 'and I wanted to give you this.'

From the floor beside her she took a dark green folder tied shut with wide black ribbons. 'Open it,' she said as she handed it to Julia. Inside was one of William's paintings. It was a watercolour, one of the dark blue series that he himself had shown to her and that she had particularly admired, but on looking at it now she felt a kind of terror. It emanated bad energy of a type she had previously experienced only when looking at certain artefacts from ancient Egypt: a tremendous power that was wholly negative.

She couldn't speak the words of gratitude that Liz was doubtless expecting to hear; it took a huge effort of will not to say, 'I don't want it. Take it away from me.' Dumb, she sat there.

Liz could see that Julia was completely overwhelmed but fortunately she appeared to misunderstand the reason. 'It's as much a souvenir of William as anything,' she said. 'I don't know how good he really was – I don't know anything about painting – but he told me you thought he was gifted. And so I wanted you to have this, because of the friendship there was between you.'

A dark thought blossomed in Julia's mind: did Liz really mean all of this? Did she perhaps know that things had ended badly between her husband and his friend and was she baiting Julia, curious to see how she would react? Was she not deeply hostile to art and everything connected with it and was this gift not then as poisonous in intention as it was in effect? Julia had never been close to Liz. She looked at her closely but the other woman was inscrutable. 'Thank you,' Julia said and she closed up the folder again. 'Thank you so much.'

'He left such a lot of work. Again, it's hard for me to judge but it seems like an astonishing amount, given the length of time involved.'

'What shall you do with it?'

'I really have no idea. I've closed the room up for the moment. I have too many other things to deal with, so many practical details. No, the paintings are going to have to wait.'

Their conversation continued for some time longer. They did not speak explicitly of what William had done, but by the time they parted the enormity of it had been fully borne in to Julia. She found herself out on the cold street with the unwanted painting under her arm, thinking 'William is dead. He took his own life. William is *dead*.'

She crossed the road and went into the Green to be alone, sat down on a bench and put the folder beside her. It was late in the afternoon and the light was failing; the February sun made a vast pale watery nebula amongst the clouds. Overwhelmed by sudden grief she bent forward with her right arm coiled protectively around her head. She wanted to close out the world, wanted to be in bed, completely hidden under the blankets. The tears came and she didn't try to stop them.

'Excuse me?'

Julia unfolded herself, looked up.

'Are you feeling all right?'

His navy suit and tweed overcoat were impeccable, his leather briefcase fashionably scuffed. He had the slightly jowly look of a man who habitually ate too well and didn't take enough exercise, but his face was kindly and he was looking at her with an expression of genuine concern.

She immediately sat up straight. 'I'm fine,' she said, and she wiped her eyes. 'Never been better.'

'You don't look fine to me,' the man said. 'Do you need any help?'

'No, really, I'll be grand.'

From her pocket she took her cigarettes: a smoke would steady her nerves.

'The least I can do is give you a light,' the man said, holding out a box of matches, and she could see how bewildered he was when she said, 'Oh God no, anything but that,' and tossed the cigarette aside.

'Look, I'm going home now,' and she stood up.

'I can go part of the way with you, if you like.'

'No!' Julia said. It came out with more vehemence than she had intended. 'I mean, no thank you. You're extremely kind, but it's not necessary.'

Still he looked doubtful.

'I'd best be on my way,' but he called her back.

'You're forgetting this,' and he picked up the folder she had left sitting on the bench, handed it to her. And then he smiled. For a moment there was between them a connection that was as profound as it was brief and she was genuinely grateful for this stranger's kindness. 'Be sure,' he said 'to go straight home.'

She didn't go home: she went directly to Roderic's house and told him of all that had passed between herself and Liz, showed him the painting. 'What am I going to do with it?' she said. 'I don't want it but I can't simply burn it or throw it away. I've never in my life destroyed anyone else's art, and I'm certainly not starting with this.'

Roderic stared at her, alarmed that she could even countenance such a thing. 'It's a fine piece of work,' he said.

There was silence for a moment as they contemplated the painting. At the centre of the page was a great O like a circular cave into which the colour dripped in sharp stalactites, bristling with energy against the empty sweep of white paper. Towards the top of the page the deep blue bruised into a strong yellow that faded, faded, gradually effacing itself into the blankness of the paper itself. The colours were the colours of a storm's weird light; and the controlled passion of the work, its technical accomplishment, impressed Roderic more than he cared to admit.

'But what am I to do with it?' Julia asked petulantly.

'Look after this painting. Keep it safe. Try to see the difference between the man and the work: their separateness. I'm not saying it'll be easy, but that's what I feel you must do if you want something redemptive to come of all this – something good.'

'I do,' Julia said. 'I want that more than anything.'

They fell silent for a moment and then she said, 'In which case I'd better tell you the truth. I wasn't being straight when I told you how things ended between William and me. I told you that I dropped him but it wasn't like that at all. He dropped me. As you predicted he would. After the last time I saw him I was so angry that I resolved to cut him out of my life. When he rang, I'd hang up. When he came to the house, I wouldn't let him in. But he never contacted me again. It was all over between us from that day on.'

'And what had happened,' Roderic asked 'to upset you so much? What did William do?'

With her eyes fixed on the painting, Julia gave him a frank and detailed account of their final meeting. She spoke dispassionately, somehow managing to keep her emotions in check, but when she had finished and turned to look at Roderic she saw how shocked he was.

'You should have told me about this,' he said and his voice was full of sorrow. 'You should have told me. Oh, Julia,' and he crossed the room to where she stood. 'Close your eyes.'

He took her hand in his, brushed her hair back from her face and kissed her. In all of this there was intense physical recognition. She couldn't see him but it could have been no one else but Roderic. Then he let fall her hand and stood back, but the sense of his presence still communicated itself to her in spite of there being no physical link between them.

383

'You can't see me,' he said 'but you recognise me. You do know that it's me. Do you realise what I'm getting at? Do you understand?' When she opened her eyes again in was upon a new reality and he understood what he had just shown her even before he spoke. 'You *do* remember your mother. You do remember her.'

'May I stay here?' she said. 'May I stay here tonight?'

'Of course you may.'

She stayed with Roderic that night and when she awoke the next day she stared at where the morning light fell on the wall between the bookcase and the window. She thought of how, painted, it would appear as pure abstraction: the sharply defined oblong of lemon light on the pale surface, the two dark lines that bound the planes. It would be understood according to the titles one might give it: *Dawn Light: Window, Wall, Bookcase*, or simply a number. She wanted to point it out to Roderic, to say to him, 'Look at the wall, how the light falls there.' But he was still asleep, and by the time he awoke the sharply defined edges of the rectangle she had noted earlier had expanded, grown softer as the light became more diffuse, dissolving completely now to fill the room with the clear light of a new day.

Epilogue

In the winter she used to wake late, long after the sun had come up. She lay there drowsing under the quilt for her father's house had become a place in which to relax and dream. When finally she arose this morning she found that deep snow had fallen in the night and she came downstairs to see the kitchen bright as a studio, full of the strong flat bluish light that is reflected off snow. She had noticed before that the brighter and stronger the sun the less likely it was to penetrate the small deep windows, so that to enter the house on a hot summer's day was like finding the sanctuary of a cool dark cave. She made tea and toast, lit a cigarette and settled by the kitchen table, warming her hands around the flank of the teapot and looking out into the orchard. They had managed to gather only a certain quantity of the apples this year. The rest had been left on the trees, to fall in red rings in the long grass, to be pecked at by the birds, to hang from the topmost branches for far longer than might have been expected given the weather, the rain, the storms. There was no wind today but a crystalline stillness and each of the last few remaining apples wore an airy cap of snow. At the sound of the door opening she turned round, and her father came into the room. 'I suppose we should have gathered them all in,' she said, 'the apples.' Dan came over and stood beside her, gazed out into the orchard.

'Oh there'll be apples, Julia,' Dan said, 'when we're all of us gone.'